RUTHLESS PROTECTOR

The Institute
Book 2

A.K ROSE

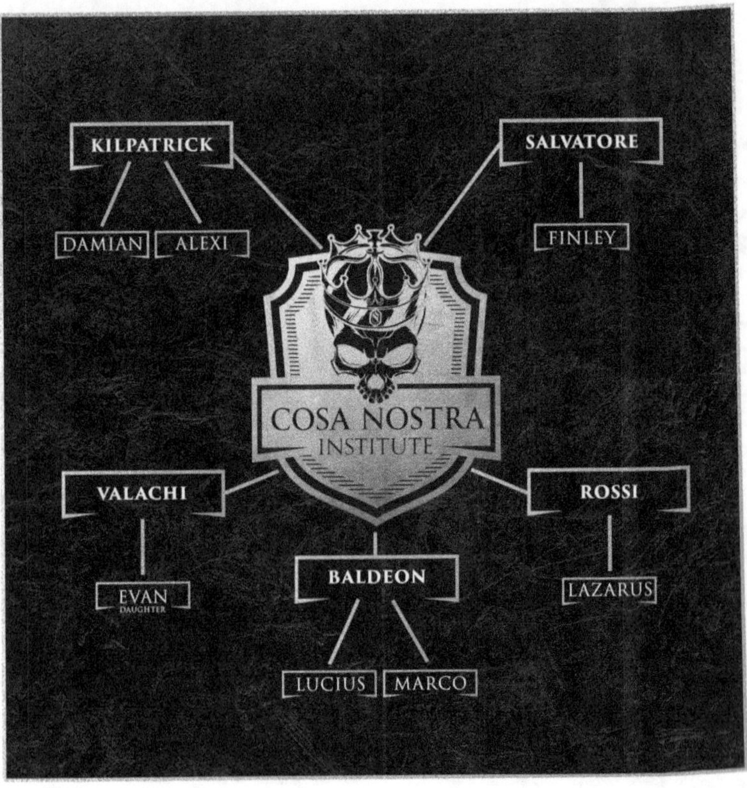
KILPATRICK
SALVATORE
DAMIAN
ALEXI
FINLEY
COSA NOSTRA
INSTITUTE
VALACHI
ROSSI
EVAN
DAUGHTER
BALDEON
LAZARUS
LUCIUS
MARCO

Acknowledgments

Thank you to a few special people, May who helped me with my very awkward French and Jess & Cassie my kickass Alpha readers. You guys are my rock.
Most of all thank you to all the readers who took a chance on this series.
This is for you...

Atlas

Please refer to my website for CW's

Kat

12 years old...

I squeezed my eyes closed. One hand rested on the door handle of my room and waited.

No...please, no. Not this again. I could run away...just like Mom did. Run away and never come back. Not for anything. But where would I go? I closed my eyes at the thought. For a second, freedom burned bright and shining in my mind. Happiness, laughter, kicking sand at the beach as I ate cotton candy and played. Freedom. That's what it looked like...until the warmth dulled and reality sank in. I had nowhere to go...and no one to come for me. *Not anymore.*

"Ms. VanHalen," the servant murmured through the door. "He's expecting you."

Still, I said nothing, just waited for that fight to die inside me... and for emptiness to take hold. Slowly, the image of freedom slipped away, taking the echoes of laugher with it. I lifted my head to the ornately carved door and twisted the handle before stepping out.

The servant's eyes widened before she took a step backwards. "There she is." She forced a smile and met my gaze. "Your father—"

But I turned and left her behind, not bothering to listen as I headed for the stairs. My heels clicked on the marble. Shimmering, polished surfaces gleamed as I reached out, placing my hand on the handrail. With each step, I left that calling behind, the call with the sound of laughter. Because that wasn't real. It was a fantasy and I was old enough to know the difference. Old enough to want for more...more than money could ever buy.

I had everything a girl could ever want. A stable of horses for me to ride. Holidays to Aspen and Italy. Pink diamonds to match my pretty white dress and knee length socks. I caught sight of myself in the looming hall mirror as I hit the last stair and made my way across the foyer. I looked perfect. Not a strand of hair out of place. Not a wrinkle in my brand new dress...a dress my father had bought for me...*for his perfect Princess.*

But as I caught my reflection, I avoided my eyes.

There was something in them I didn't like.

Something that made that ache inside me twist and moan.

Something that made the dull thud in my ears race.

As I stepped forward, that image of freedom sank further down than ever before.

I tore my gaze from the sight and kept walking, through the open doors of the foyer and into the living room. White and

"No," I growled, fighting the tears as I pushed the words away. "No, Iggy...*no*."

But he didn't get up, no matter how hard I yanked on his lead. My chin trembled when I looked at him. At the patches of gray hair that traveled along his face, and the way that fucking lump bulged out of his side, a lump the vet said there was no cure for.

"Iggy." An ache welled in the back of my throat as I sank to my knees.

Muffled roars of laughter came from underneath me, from the men who worked for my father. The same men who looked at me with sadness and pride. The same kind of sadness that lingered in Iggy's eyes as he leaned forward and licked the back of my hand.

"Don't!" I cried, and wrenched my hand away. "*Don't you do that!*"

Don't...just don't. Panic filled me, panic and the thudding in my ears. And they all laughed downstairs. Deep, booming laughter as they drank, played music, and cleaned their guns. Glinting steel filled my mind's eye now, slick with oil, hard, cruel, and merciful at the same time.

You know what happens, Lazarus, Dad's voice filled me once more. *You know our way...the Rossi way.*

Something slick slipped down my cheek. I knew the Rossi way.

The only way there was.

There was no room for weakness.

No room for the sick.

"Iggy." I smacked the lone tear from my cheek like it never existed and focused with all I had. Desperation burned inside me as I stood, gripped the lead until my knuckles turned white, and begged. "*Please*, I'm begging you. *Get. Up.*"

He just whimpered and dropped his head to the side of his bed.

"Get up. *Get up.* GET UP!"

But he didn't. My knees buckled as I sank beside him, dropping my head as pain ripped through my chest. I trembled with sadness, hands shaking, throat thick. A sound tore free, sounding sick and strange. I didn't care if I looked like a baby. I reached out with a trembling hand and brushed his long, floppy ear, lifting it at the edge and dropped it once more. It smacked the pillowed side of his bed, just like it'd done a hundred times before.

I wanted to flop it forever.

Wanted to run and play.

Wanted to still have the one good thing Dad ever let me have.

Dump dog. That's what Dad called him, trash can Iggy. We'd found him when I was five. He was so thin then, nothing more than skin and bones. We brought him home and gave him food and a bath. He was mine...*mine.*

"I hate you." I jerked my gaze to his. "I *fucking* hate you."

That pain moved higher in my throat, no matter how much I swallowed, I couldn't get it down. So I pushed up from the floor and took a step closer, still holding the lead. "You know what happens, Iggy."

He just gave a whine as I bent over and picked him up, bed and all. He was heavy in my arms, barely moving as I adjusted his weight and took a step forward. My legs moved on their own, heading toward the stairs.

Iggy gave a whine as the bitter stench of piss filled my nose. I wanted to gag and heave. But I didn't, because that's what a little kid does. A man takes care of his own. I ground my teeth and stepped, carrying him down the stairs and toward the back door. Bitter cold hit me, making me tremble in my thin shirt. The back door was already open, letting the freezing air slip in amongst the stench of their cigarettes.

But I didn't care about that now.

Laughter died as I stepped through the door carrying Iggy in his dog bed and headed for the open door.

"Laz, whatcha doin' there?" Gravel asked.

But I just kept walking, shoving the door wider with my hip until it slammed against the outside wall with a *boom!* Dad just stood amongst the others, watching me. That same cold stare never flinched as I turned and made my way down the stairs into the howling wind.

My cheeks burned as I stepped down the stairs and walked further out into the backyard.

"What the hell is he doing?" Gravel's words carried.

"What he needs to," Dad answered. "He needs to learn even in death there can be mercy."

"Take the dog to a damn vet." Gravel urged.

"No." Dad answered. "He needs to deal with it."

I lowered my gaze as Iggy's face blurred, tears fell down my cheeks as my chest throbbed and ached. "It's o-okay," I whispered. "I w-won't let you suffer anymore."

The corner of the backyard was bathed in shadows. I stepped closer and knelt, placing the dog bed on the ground. Iggy didn't make a sound as I stood, just slumped slowly to the side as I turned and strode back toward the house.

My body trembled. I wanted to blame the cold, but it was more than that. I was never going to be okay again, never going to not feel this pain. *Not ever.* I tried to swallow the lump in the back of my throat, but it wouldn't go down.

Please...

Please help me.

I clenched my eyes closed listening to the harsh rasp of his breath...and stopped my own. I stopped breathing, letting the air burn in my lungs, until with a pathetic sound the air rushed out. A stillness swept over me as I climbed the wooden stairs once more and stepped into the room. Dad was waiting for me with a gun in his hand, the muzzle pointed toward the floor. I stared at the weapon for a second, unable to meet his gaze.

"Lazarus..." he started.

It was all I needed to shock me into movement. I stepped forward, grasped the weapon from his hand, and turned, making my way back to where my best friend waited.

He was still on his side when I neared, shaking and whimpering. The rancid smell of poop was strong now as I knelt beside him. But I didn't look away and I didn't cry. Not now. Not anymore. Not when he needed me.

There was no room for the old.

No place for the sick.

Not here...not for the Rossis.

Agony burned through me as I lifted the gun with a trembling hand.

"Benj, for fuck's sake," I heard Gravel growl from the patio as I pressed the muzzle against Iggy's head.

There was no room for dying...just as there was no room for the boy in me, not anymore. Not for a Rossi...

I pulled the trigger.

Bang!

And as Iggy slumped down into his soft bed, he took part of me with him.

The part of me who'd clung to hope.

The part of me who was soft and weak.

I didn't cry, not when I placed the gun on the ground, or when I walked to the side of the house and dragged back the shovel. The ground was hard as stone. Icy winds cut through my shirt like a knives. Still, I swung and battled, screaming my rage into the earth. I punched the sole of my sneaker against the steel and dug, inch by inch...hour by hour.

The laughter didn't rise again in the house behind me. The thud of car doors rang out sometime later. Still I dug, until my palms stung and bled.

I buried Iggy in the corner of my backyard in a grave as big as I could make. When I packed the last shovel of dirt over him, I picked up the gun and turned, leaving the ruined dog bed outside.

There'd be no more trash can dogs for me.

No more weakness.

No more tears.

My palms stung as I heaved myself up the stairs, taking them one by one. My face was on fire, my body shook.

"I'm proud of you, Lazarus," Dad muttered when I stepped inside.

"Why?" I lifted my gaze to his.

He just stood there, those dark eyes finding mine.

The cold stayed with me, even after I stood under a hot shower.

And when I rose the next morning, I didn't go into the backyard.

I never would again...

For as long as I lived.

3

Kat

---

18 years old...

"Ma'am."

I opened my bedroom door, startling the maid.

She just stood there, staring at my shimmering midnight floor-length gown as she whispered, "Your father's expecting you."

Of course he was...can't forget the fucking entertainment.

But I didn't say a word, not to her. She was new anyway, not yet used to the VanHalen way. But she would be soon enough...it was either that or leave. I walked along the hallway of the east wing, My Louis Vuitton heels sinking into the plush black carpet. It was all black here now. Black halls. Black rooms. Like a rot that had slowly creeped into my world and never left.

Ruined to the core.

Just like me.

There were two people that lived in me, two I wore like a mask. My stomach clenched at the thought, but it was the truth. My entire life was lived around masks, ones others wore and ones they carved out for me. It was the mask I changed now as I walked slowly toward the west wing of our house. I could feel her leaving, like a ghost. Her warmth sliding from my soul, leaving nothing but the stony cold behind.

Heels clacked as hard marble replaced carpet. I strode through the expansive library, veering around the velvet red chesterfield sofa and past the huge black marble hearth. Open French doors called to me, urging me to stay and curl up and bathe in the warm spring sun that flooded through the windows. But didn't. I couldn't, not here...*not now.*

There was no spring for me now, not when Kat fell away, leaving the mask of Katerina in her place. *He's expecting you...* the maid's words resounded in that cold dead space inside. I left the playful sunlight of the library behind and headed toward the faint clang in the kitchen.

Sheer black fishnets peeked through the thigh-high slit of my dress. I lifted my gaze to the hallway ahead, my heart thundering. The chef turned at the sound of my heels, but he said nothing as I strode past. They never did. We...didn't speak to the help. It wasn't allowed.

I strode past the formal dining with its glinting Zenith chandelier hanging low over the twelve-seater walnut table. I couldn't remember the last time we'd sat and ate together. I couldn't remember the last time I wanted to eat. Not here in this house...*not amongst these men.*

A wave of deep raucous laughter hit me as I kept walking. My stomach tightened instantly at the sound until that cold wave of emptiness followed. The emptiness where they couldn't reach...where *nothing* could reach. That hollow touch kept me whole...and sane. I lifted my head as that sound grew louder behind the closed double doors. It was a different house, and yet the core was always the same. Secrecy. Control. *Hunger.*

My hand trembled as I reached for the doors. I froze, staring at the shaking of my thumb. It never trembled...not here. There was always nothing when I reached the doors, no feeling, no shame. Nothing but going through the motions. Nothing but the mask of Katerina. But right now...right now, my hand was shaking. My eyes followed the movement up my arm.

Something was wrong.

Something was very...very wrong.

I lifted my gaze to the gleaming black doors. There was a change in me. A *push* from that panicked beating in my heart. A whisper in my head that said, *this isn't right...this isn't right... I've got to get away from them. I've got to get away. Or die.*

I closed my eyes and felt the hallway sway. Panic flared from deep inside me, a lash of fire against the cold, stony walls I'd built inside. The flame couldn't get through, I knew that. Still, it howled and raged, shooting sparks into the darkness inside me. The darkness where Katerina roamed.

"Get it together," I whispered, and opened my eyes to stare at the doors. "They won't wait forever, and you don't want to piss them off."

I know only too well what would happen then.

Stone by stone.

That's what happened.

Each one a painful memory I'd used to build a wall. One no fire could invade, no matter how hot the flames. I inhaled hard and held it, letting the pressure build in my lungs before exhaling hard. The tremor in my hand stilled with the movement. I watched it for a second, making sure the mask was firmly in place, before I reached for the handles once more and opened the doors.

Laughter boomed along the hallway of my father's wing. I stepped inside and closed the doors behind me, that bellowing, sickening sound mingled with others before a roar of, *"You fucking cheat! Deal again!"*

I could tell them by sound now, even their laughter.

I could pick them apart in a crowd without even seeing their faces.

All of their faces.

I lowered my gaze and moved. It was automatic now, no force required. Synapses fired and muscles moved. Heels sank into the carpet as I made my way past my father's sitting room, then his kitchen and his massive study connecting with the master bedroom, until I reached the wide double doors in the middle of the wing. *His entertainment room.*

There was no shake now when I reached for the handles. I would've felt relief if I could feel at all. But I was beyond that now, beyond caring what I felt or what they thought as I pushed the double doors open and lifted my gaze.

Déjà vu.

The sensation slammed into me, over and over and *over* again.

How many times had I stood here? How many times had each monster around that table turned from the cards they held to meet my gaze? None more than the monster sitting at the head of the table, Mr. VanHalen himself.

"Katerina," my father spoke, his dark eyes glinting. The others looked at my dress...and my body. But not him. He drove into my very soul. "Where were you?"

"Getting ready," I answered, the dull sound of my own voice ringing in my head.

One simple nod was all I received. There'd be no fighting, not in front of his friends. Because that wasn't part of the game... and we all knew how much he loved to play games. I was his ace hand. His *royal flush*. I was the daughter. The heiress. Cold, closed down, *unobtainable*. My soul protected by the stony walls, ones they'd never scale.

"We're running low on Cohiba Behik. Be a good girl and get some, will you?"

I swallowed a shiver. One nod. "Of course, is there anything else you need?"

A shake of his head and my father returned to the cards in his hand. "Whose turn was it, anyway? I lost count with all you goddamn cheats."

"Haelstrom cheated," Burbank declared, still staring at me.

"Not my fault that after eighteen years you still don't know the difference between a squeeze and your asshole," Haelstrom retorted, his gaze riveted on mine.

The others laughed and chimed in.

"I'll give her a hand," Haelstrom announced, pushing his chair back.

The conversation didn't stop, barely missed a beat before someone muttered something and the laughter began once more.

"Burbank, it's your turn to deal," my father said, chuckling.

"It's always my damn turn."

"That's because you suck at it and you need the damn practice," Luge grumbled with a smile.

Six men sat around the table and not one of them said a word as Haelstrom bowed out, placing his hand on my father's shoulder as he passed. My jaw tightened at the movement. I forced my gaze away as that fire came to life inside me.

No...I growled inside. Not now.

In the deep, infernal belly of my desperation, the fire spluttered. I didn't care about the hand on my father's shoulder, or about the way they watched me as I turned and left, taking one step after another as I headed toward the room where my father kept his supplies.

The warm spring sunlight didn't reach these halls. Shadows laid claim to this part of the house. Heavy black curtains were forever drawn, the air thick and stale. Footsteps followed me, lingering long enough for the slow slide of the double doors to close and the laughter and the chiding dulled.

I lowered my gaze, my heartbeat racing.

There were no words spoken, not when I turned the handle of the room at the far end of the hallway, or when I left the door open and stepped inside. The door closed behind me a second later and the lock clicked into place.

But that fire flared to life once more. Sparks of panic leaped inside me as I stopped at the marble counter at the far end of the room. A wooden box held my father's cigars, crates of his finest whiskey stored against the wall. My hand shook as it rose. But it was far too late now...far too late as the heavy thud of his footsteps neared.

The tops of perfectly shined shoes came into view as I lowered my gaze.

"I missed you in there," he murmured against my ear.

The low timbre of the throaty sound rolled through me like a wave. I could *feel* every syllable, hitting places it shouldn't. Still, it did, drawing out the kind of heat in me that made me writhe with disgust. I shouldn't want this, shouldn't want to be controlled. Not like this...*never* like this. But this is what they called conditioning, right? This was the danger of the hunt.

He reached inside his jacket and placed something on the counter. The flash of white made me recoil.

"You always were my favorite." Haelstrom brushed strands of hair from my nape. "So cold." Warm lips pressed against my skin. "So unreachable."

His fingers skimmed the thin strap of my dress, hooking it with his finger before the slow slide. I swallowed the shudder, my insides clamping with heat.

"How much longer, Katerina?" he whispered, and dragged the strap low. "How much longer will you refuse me?"

For as long as I can.

I closed my eyes, hating the hunger as I lifted my gaze to the white mask on the counter.

The one that both taunted and terrified me, the one I'd seen my entire life.

The one I hated and craved at the same time.

Sick...I was sick.

The dark rot invaded and infected...just like his touch.

"You will be mine," Haelstrom whispered as the long slide of my zipper filled the room. "One way or another. That I promise."

4

Lazarus

---

18 years old...

I shoved open the front door to my house and stepped inside. Flurries of snow swirled up behind me, the howling wind making me shiver as I kicked the door shut with a *boom* and stepped forward, to the unmistakable ratchet of guns. I froze, my pulse driving a little harder than normal as Dad stepped into the foyer with a shotgun in his hand.

Relief spread across his face when he saw me. "Don't you answer your damn phone?"

Not when it's you nagging me, I don't. "I got busy."

"You got busy?" Anger darkened his eyes as he came toward me in three engulfing strides and grabbed my jacket, yanking me close. *"You got busy?"*

I just stared at him, then slowly muttered. "Yeah."

"You don't *get busy* when I call, Lazarus. Not now, not ever. You understand me?" he barked.

A dragging sound came across the floorboards above me, coming from the direction of my father's room. "What's going on?"

"What's going on?" Dad snapped as Gravel stepped through a doorway. Dad just turned to him and released me with a soft shove. "You hear this? *Now* he wants to know what's going on."

More was dragged across the floor, only this time the sound came from my room.

"Lazarus, go pack the rest of your stuff," Gravel directed, stepping around Dad to come between us.

He was carrying, and a lot more than usual. Black steel glinted across his chest as he moved, grabbing my shoulders. Fear lingered in his eyes as he spoke. "Something's come up. We need to get you and your father to safety."

I jerked my gaze to Dad. "What? What the hell is going on?"

Dad just shook his head and turned away. "Pack the rest of your shit, Lazarus. We leave in ten."

Leave in ten?

My gaze went toward the back door as panic moved in. We couldn't leave, this was our home...we had *Iggy,* we had Iggy. "Go where?"

But Dad just kept walking away without a goddamn explanation. "I said...*go fucking where?*"

"Underground, son," Gravel answered. "There's been talk."

I turned to him, like I always fucking did. "What kind of talk?"

He just shook his head. "The kind that makes us anxious. Now go. Get what you need, we can come back for the rest later."

Leave our home, leave our memories. The heavy thud of footsteps on the stairs drew my gaze. Taken and Harley came plodding down, both hauling heavy boxes full of our stuff.

"Kid," Taken acknowledged as he strode past.

I just watched them take our shit along the hall. Howling wind pushed in as they opened the front door behind me. A lone, sloppy leaf flew in behind them, slapping against the wall, and that's where it stayed. The house was cold in an instant. Cold and unwelcome. But Iggy...I glanced again toward the back door. "Will we come back?"

"No." Gravel gave it as real as he could. "Not while there's a damn bounty on your head."

I jerked my gaze to his as fear moved through me. "There's a bounty on *my* head?"

One nod was all he gave.

A bounty. On my fucking head. *Jesus.* No wonder Dad was in a goddamn mood.

I kept my jacket on and trudged up the stairs, making my way into the too small damn room I'd had forever. There were memories here, good memories and bad. Still, the place was all I'd known. This small, plain damn house on a street of quiet families who watched us from behind their damn curtains and hurried to cross the street when I neared. I knew what they saw when they looked at us. Thugs. Criminals.

And they were right. We *were* criminals.

The kind you didn't want to piss off...but still, this was our home.

Where the fuck were we going now? I strode to my closet and shoved the sliding door aside before grabbing my duffel bag from the floor.

"Just what you need, Lazarus," Dad ordered from the doorway.

I gave a nod and glanced his way. "Got it."

He lingered for a second before walking away. Why the fuck hadn't he told me? The thud of his footsteps echoed as I turned back, yanked my clothes from the hangers, and stuffed them into the duffel. I knew why...because of Mom.

"Anymore to go?" Taken asked as he stepped into the room.

I looked around at the posters of bare tits and souped-up cars, my crappy old TV and Playstation shoved into the corner. It was a fucking kid's room. A tired, shitty, old outdated kid's room. I just shook my head. "Nah. Just this."

"Meet you downstairs then?"

"Yeah." I shoved as much as I could into the bag, stuffing jeans and t-shirts and boxers from the dresser in at the end, until there was nothing left.

Nothing but a thin brown leather lead in the back of a drawer. Iggy's lead. The one fucking thing I'd kept of his.

"Lazarus." Dad called from the doorway. "Time to go."

I stared at that lead, remembering the pain I'd felt that night. A pain I'd never felt since and never wanted to again. I heaved the duffel's strap onto my shoulder, leaving the lead and the memories behind, and turned toward the door. "Ready."

We left in a rush, Taken and Gravel crowding each side of me as they scanned the street outside our nondescript stucco home. Gravel pulled me forward with a hand on my arm, pushing me to an idling black Explorer. "Inside, Laz."

I climbed in, throwing my bag onto the floor as Gravel slid into the driver's seat and Dad slipped into the front, literally riding shotgun. Taken climbed into the back across from me, leaving the others to make their own way. My gut clenched as I scanned the street behind us. It'd never been this bad, never been this...*careful.*

Whatever this was...it had scared them.

I turned my head as Harley closed the door to our home and met my gaze. But then we were gone, pulling away from the curb and into the street. My pulse sped as I flung my gaze around us. Taken's hand was inside his jacket in an instant, then his gun was drawn and resting beside him on the seat. In that moment, my life became all too real.

I knew who we were...and what we did. But there was one thing Dad had battered home to me. The Rossis didn't run, from *anyone.* So, as we peeled out from the front of our home, the tires squealing, I had to ask myself, *why the fuck are we running now?*

Dad said nothing from the front seat as he scanned oncoming traffic. "Gravel," he growled as a dark blue sedan shot past, then slowed with a squeal of brakes.

"I see him," Dad's second-in-command muttered, gunning the engine of the Explorer.

"Fucking bastards." Taken leaned forward, gun in hand.

"Give me a piece," I commanded, and thrust my hand out.

Taken just jerked his gaze to Dad.

"Don't look at him," I snarled. "*Give me a goddamn piece.*"

Dad gave a nod before the solider reached into his jacket once more and handed a weapon over. "Just...be fucking careful, okay?"

I shot him a look as the howl of the sedan's engine grew louder.

"How the fuck did they find us so soon?" Gravel leaned forward, cutting his gaze to the side mirror before jerking the wheel and crossing the lane of traffic.

"They were watching the goddamn house, that's how," Dad muttered, then punched the button for his window. "Over there." Dad pointed to a side street up ahead as Gravel tapped the brakes, spearing the four-wheel drive into the corner.

I slammed against the door as we shot toward the narrow opening of an alley. *Crack...crack...CRACK.* The back window of the of the Explorer shattered. I flinched a second before a meaty hand grabbed my shoulder and shoved me forward and down.

Taken was a blur, twisting to fire round after round above me. The sway of the car made me sick and the roar in my ears was deafening.

"Who the fuck are those assholes!" Taken yelled as we skidded sideways and crashed into two overflowing trashcans.

"Hood's men!" Dad barked, leaning out the window to fire.

I shoved against Taken's hand and shoved the gun to the top of the sear seat.

"Stay the fuck *down*, kid," Taken commanded, shoving me back down as I tried to rise.

Bang!

Taken gave a grunted *"Uhh!"* above me.

I looked up into his wide eyes as his hold eased. He jerked forward, spluttering. Blood flecked across the back of the leather seat as the car braked hard. There was blood...*lots of blood* pouring from a hole in the center of his throat to run down the front of him. He lunged forward and coughed, spraying warmth across my face. I froze...unable to look away from the terror in his eyes. There was a knowing, that this was it. The end. All to save me.

"Taken?" I croaked.

"Fuck!" Dad barked and crawled between the front seats to pull Taken backwards as the Explorer shot out from the side street and became airborne.

"Are you shot?" Dad cried as he flew into the air, hitting the ceiling hard.

We hit the asphalt with a huge jolt. My teeth gnashed together, tearing agony through my jaw and my head.

But I couldn't answer...I couldn't do a damn thing but stare into my Taken's eyes as the darkness dulled.

"Lazarus! Are you shot?"

"No," I muttered as warmth splattered my cheek again.

I grabbed Taken as we spun sideways.

"Fucking *bastards!*" Dad screamed and lifted his weapon.

All I could see was Taken bleeding...dying right in front of me.

"Hold on!" Gravel bellowed from the driver's seat as we skidded sideways.

From the corner of my eye, I saw a black truck hurtling toward us, headlights blinding, horn blaring. The Explorer swung hard as we shot past the front of the rig and skidded to a stop, driving me across the rear seat, colliding with Taken and Dad. Darkness was all I saw...the black of the tires...and the shimmering midnight trailer as the truck roared past.

Harsh breaths consumed me. I tried to think, tried to breathe.

"Taken?" Dad barked, heaving his friend up from the seat. "Taken!"

But there was no life in the soldier's eyes. They were glassy and unfocused, staring at the ceiling. I lifted my gaze to the blue Charger that shot out of the side street after us. My body moved before I knew it. The door was open in a heartbeat...and I was out of the car.

"*Lazarus!*" Dad roared as I rounded the front of the Explorer. My feet moved on their own as everything in my world slowed. I lifted my gun and strode across the street toward the Charger, aiming at the guy sitting in the driver's seat.

They shot one of us...

Shot and *killed.*

Boom!

The side window shattered. The guy jerked, his hands rising to shield his face.

Boom!

The Rossis didn't run.

Boom!

From anyone.

The driver slumped forward over the steering wheel. The blare of the horn shattered the vacuum inside my head and the thunder of footsteps filled my ears. I squeezed the trigger again, listening to the screams coming from the Charger. Doors were thrown open in an instant.

"Get the fuck in the car!" Gravel shoved me behind him and jerked a panicked look at the shooters. It was all to save me. I stumbled backwards, watching one of the assassins stop and turn, his dark eyes finding mine before he lifted his gun. But Gravel was there, Glock kicking back with a *boom!* Taken was dead...and it was all because of me. How many more...*how many more?*

"Lazarus!" The Explorer shot forward, Dad now behind the wheel. "Get in the car!"

The assassin screamed as Gravel's shot found its mark. I glanced over my shoulder as I lunged for the open rear door of our fourwheel drive as two oncoming cars slowed and came to a stop, watching the bloodbath play out.

"You okay?" Gravel sucked in hard breaths, charging up behind me.

"Yeah." I climbed into the car and yanked the door closed as Gravel climbed in the front.

"Go," Gravel urged Dad. "Go."

"What the *fuck* was that?" Dad barked over his shoulder as he punched the accelerator, driving me against the seat. "You could've gotten yourself killed!"

I just sat there, staring at Taken as blood slowly seeped from the wound in his throat. I said nothing as we drove toward the bunker. Cars swept past. Dad and Gravel divided their attention between oncoming traffic and their mirrors as we headed toward the city.

"Fuck me," Dad growled and combed his fingers through his hair. "I want them, Gravel. I want those bastards."

"Don't worry" Dad's second-in-command answered. "We'll get them."

"The fucking *Salvatores*," I barked, my mind going to the only ones it could be.

Dad jerked his gaze to the rear-view mirror. Fear and sadness filled his gaze.

Gravel just shook his head. "The Salvatores? No, I don't think so. They have no reason for an outright attack, besides..."

"I agree." Dad shifted gears, glancing behind the passenger seat at Taken who was on the floor, slumped against the seat. "This wasn't them. They wouldn't risk breaking the code."

"Word is it's Scion," Gravel added. "That sonofabitch has bad blood."

Dad switched lanes as the traffic grew heavier. I sank against the seat, staring at Taken's hollow gaze. Whoever it was...*I'd fucking kill them...*

Because a Rossi...*avenges their own.*

5

Kat

Two months ago...

I had to get out of here...away from these people...*or die trying.*

White masks haunted my every step as I strode through the massive glass sliding doors into the opulent foyer and kept walking, with my clutch firmly under my arm.

"Ms. VanHalen," the receptionist spluttered, and shoved to her feet. "I...*ah.*" She glanced along the counter as I strode past, searching for support. "I wasn't expecting you."

"Of course you weren't," I muttered. "Because I never fucking come here."

I strode toward the bank of gleaming elevators in the grand, expansive foyer of the VanHalen Building and pressed the button.

"Let me call up and see if your father's available."

It was almost a plea, but I didn't answer as the gleaming stainless steel doors slowly opened and I strode inside. A man stepped around the open-mouthed receptionist after me. One brow rose as he took in the panicked woman. "Are you in?" he asked casually.

I just stepped forward and punched the button, watching the doors close.

"Apparently not," he muttered.

My stomach clenched as I moved to the back wall and tried to breathe. The truth was, I hated this place. Hate those who worked here...hated the goddamn pretense of it all. They were puppets...every single one of them. *Just like me.*

"Here for an interview?"

I jerked my gaze to the guy dressed in a three-piece, dark navy Versace suit and realized he was talking to me. "An interview? No."

"Oh, reporter then?" He glanced away. "We get plenty of those here, all jostling for that insight into the famous Mr. VanHalen."

My stomach clenched with the words. An insight? I could give him the kind of insight that'd make his skin crawl...the kind of glimpse into the real life of Sebastian VanHalen that'd make him drop to his knees and throw up in the middle of this spotless elevator. Panic tried to push through the coldness inside me. But it couldn't, not anymore. Instead, a cold sweat rose, making the skin on my arms crawl.

I looked away and focused on a spot in the corner.

"No, not a damn reporter," I growled, watching the floor lights illuminate one by one as we rose higher.

"If not an interviewee or a reporter, then you must be visiting someone. A boyfriend, perhaps?" He glanced my way, only this time his stare lingered. "Or a husband?"

I have to get away...I have to get far away. Away from these people...*away from him.*

From the man who haunted my dreams...

And the white masks he wore.

"Yeah, a pretty little thing like you has to have a husband."

"You know, you ask a lot of questions for someone I haven't even met" I snapped as the elevator came to a shuddering stop on the top floor.

The doors opened and he stepped off, letting out a deep chuckle. "Haven't met, huh?"

I didn't have time to deal with this bullshit. The idiot didn't take a hint.

"I'm Garth." He shoved his hand out as I strode out of the elevator, hope burning in his eyes as the clatter of stiletto heels grew louder. "Garth Morgan."

"Ms. VanHalen." The shrill female voice made me wince. "*Ms. VanHalen!*"

I just stared at his hand, then met his gaze. "Like I said, someone I haven't met." Then I turned and walked away.

"Ms. VanHalen." The poor bitch sent to find out why the fuck I had decided to come to this...this...*glass tomb* after eight years spoke again. "We weren't expecting you."

I reached up, grabbed my black clutch from under my arm, and strode forward, ignoring the bumbling bimbo next to me. My driver was illegally parked outside the building, but right in that moment...I didn't give a damn. Not about anything...*except*...

My stomach gave a flutter. But that fear inside me pushed through, seeping through my veins, making that low part of me clench in fear. I tried to swallow the rancid tang in the back of my mouth, a remnant of the retching and heaving that had consumed me for the past two days. I swore I could still taste blood.

Fix it...fix it...fix it...

The words thrummed in my head as I strode toward my father's office.

"Ms. VanHalen." I flinched at the sound of her voice, having forgotten she was there. "I don't think he's in there."

"Oh, he's in there," I corrected, and kept walking toward the wall of windows. My father's empire was glass and steel. From all the way up here, you could see almost every inch of the city. He liked it...liked looking down...*liked thinking he was God.*

But he wasn't a god. He was a pathetic, small fucking man, riddled with desire like it was cancer. The shit was killing him...*and me with it.* Blood bloomed in my mind. Blood and terror. My stomach clenched as I stepped into the stark, soulless fucking office. Heads turned my way, shocked expressions all over their faces. *It's her...what the fuck is she doing here?*

I tore my gaze away as my father's office loomed in the background, the silver door all sparkling and shiny, spotless.

"Katerina." The woman behind the desk in front of my father's office door rose.

I winced at the sound of my name, and anger rose.

"I'm sorry, if I'd known..." the brunette started. Panic filled her eyes as she realized I wasn't stopping. She lifted her hand. "You can't go in there...*wait...Katerina, wait!*"

"It's Ms. VanHalen to you," I snapped, shooting her a glare before I shoved the handle down on Daddy's polished fucking office door and strode inside.

He jerked his gaze up from the papers lined neatly across his desk. His personal assistant sat across from him, her tweed suit godawful hideous. She jerked as though slapped, scowling as she rose.

I didn't know this one...*she must be new.*

"Who the hell do you think—" she started, turning from her seat.

But I caught the panicked shake of the idiot's head from the corner of my eye as I shifted my gaze to the man sitting behind the desk. "Hello, Father."

"Kat," he murmured without missing a beat.

"Kat?" the idiot across from him mumbled.

"Yes...*Kat,*" I barked as I swung my gaze to her. "Don't bother leaving, I'll make this short and sweet."

I leveled my gaze at the man behind the desk, letting the panic and fear coil in my stomach like a damn serpent as I reached into my clutch and pulled out a slip of paper.

Cosa Nostra Institute was written across the top of the contract.

I slid it across the desk in front of him, leaning over just enough for him to get the hint. "Sign the contract and pay the goddamn money."

Anger flashed in those dark eyes. Stony. Unfathomable. *Ruthless.* "Don't be ridiculous," he growled.

Get out...

Get out...

GET OUT!

"Pay the money" I insisted, and clenched my grip around the edge of the desk. Harsh breaths consumed me as I stared into the depths of this predator.

There was a twitch at the corner of his mouth, a tiny smirk. Arrogance raged as he leaned backwards and crossed his arms over his chest.

"Maybe I should..." Ugly Tweed Suit murmured, and took a step backwards.

"Stay," I growled, and she froze.

"You really want to do this?" my father questioned. I doubt he even saw his assistant...even when I stood in front of him. But I was the apple, wasn't I? The apple of his eye in the garden of fucking Eden, but he was no Adam. He was evil incarnate, taking bite after bite, all the way down to my core.

But life bloomed inside me.

Seeds sprouted, and desperation bloomed.

I had to get out of there. I had to find some place where they couldn't get to me, some place I couldn't be dragged away. Some place I could *think* and plan...*yeah, plan,* figure a way out of this fucking mess, one that didn't involve slicing open my fucking wrists.

"Sign the papers and pay the damn money," I demanded again. He didn't like me coming here. No doubt I'd pay for it when he came home. No doubt at all...

But right now, in front of an audience...I was forcing his hand.

"You really want to go to that...pathetic Mafia playground."

"I want to learn from the best," I argued. "You won't teach me to run a company, but they will."

But that wasn't the real reason, was it? That wasn't the reason why two weeks ago, I'd crawled from my bed at one AM, wanting to end it all. The memory rose, as I'd stood, shaking and desperate, the knife from the kitchen block in my hand, the honed edge pressed against my wrist. One slip was all it'd take and it'd all be over. One slip...and I'd be free.

But something inside me didn't let that happen.

Some tiny spark of fire. One I'd thought had been extinguished a long time ago. Still, that tiny flame waited, dancing and flickering, burning inside me, just waiting for the moment to erupt...*and burn them all to the ground.*

"You're really not letting this go, are you?"

I jerked my focus back to him. "No."

He held his ground for a second too long, then he casually picked up the pen and pulled the contract close. I'd already read it, already made sure it had everything in it I wanted. I'd already made friends and enemies with the wrong kinds of people and dragged Cosa Nostra Institute out of the dark ages and into the fucking light.

With one stroke of the pen and a sizable donation to the Commission, I was guaranteed a place in what was considered a men's club only. Now they didn't care about gender. Power was the only requirement, and right now, I felt *fucking powerful.*

"Here." My father lifted the contract and stared into my eyes. "If this is really what you want."

"It is." I took the slip of paper from his hand, folded it, and tucked it into my clutch.

I knew he'd brush me aside at home. After all, he had no one watching. But here, with his office door open and, I was guessing, half the damn floor peering into the office, watching this battle play out, he couldn't ignore me anymore.

"Thank you," I forced the words through clenched teeth, and straightened.

My chest rose with deep breaths. He didn't move his gaze from mine, those piercing blue eyes that haunted me in my dreams. Others thought the gray-flecked hair made him took distinguished, softer even. They mistook the pretense. Because when it came to Sebastian VanHalen it was all pretense, wasn't it?

Only a select few knew the danger that lurked in those icy blue eyes.

And none more than me.

Five million dollars had just been pledged to the Commission with the swipe of his hand. Five million, more than some could spend in a lifetime. But for him...that was play money. I took a step backwards and turned.

"Katerina."

I froze at the use of my name and shivers raced across my skin.

"I'll see you at home."

I tried to keep myself from running, forcing my steps to slow as I strode through my father's expansive office and into the hall. I didn't stop, didn't breathe, didn't *feel* anything until I stepped into the elevator and punched the button to close the door. A man stepped forward, taking a step into the car before I stopped him with a shake of my head. "This one's full. Take the next one."

"But..." he muttered, scowling.

My fingers shook as I stabbed the button again.

Desperation roared, screaming in my head.

Get out of here!

Get out of here!

GET OUT OF HERE!

6

Lazarus

Two months ago...

I stood in the corner of the fucking depressing room, desperate
for the shadows to consume me. The place reeked of death and
the decrepit. Faded, stained velvet sofas that were once red,
and ancient wood furnishings made up the funeral home's
wake room. It looked Mafia without even trying, like some
reject prop from the goddamn Godfather movie. Fucking
depressing. With each breath, I could feel the necrotic touch of
this place seeping deeper into my lungs.

I didn't want to be here...*none of us did.*

But here we fucking were, paying our damn respects. Respect. I
wasn't sure if the Salvatores deserved it. My gaze moved to
Dad, dressed in a suit, talking to some schmuck with beady
fucking eyes, one of Salvatore's goons, without a doubt. They
all looked the same, detached...*unemotional.* I found Finley
Salvatore standing near the doorway. The poor bastard was

goddamn gray, looking like he wanted to crawl into a hole and stay there. I knew the feeling well.

"You should be standing with your father," Gravel murmured. "You know, as a sign of solidarity."

The beady-eyed fucker talking to Dad glanced my way for the third time and met my gaze. "Looks like he's doing just fine without me," I returned.

"Fucking *Rossi*."

I caught the words drifting from across the room. Besides, if I was standing near my father, I'd miss the warm goddamn reception. I curled my lip, finding the mouthy bastard across the room. Baby-faced fucker. How old was he? Like...*twelve?* Twelve, with a man's body. I scanned his massive chest and suit jacket that fit him like a damn second skin across his arms. He stood with his boys. Just a damn punk. I gave a snigger and glanced away.

"Hey," the asshole barked across the room. "You think this is fucking funny?"

Movement came as the wannabe stepped forward, until one of his boys pushed him back with a hand on his chest. I had no idea who he was. One of Salvatore's bitches.

Muttering rose as movement came from the front door of the funeral home. And all off a sudden, the smirk on my face died. Dominic Salvatore strode in, wearing black from head to toe and an icy homicidal gaze. Jesus, the bastard looked fucking lifeless. I glanced toward Dad, standing just inside the room and out of Salvatore's line of sight.

"Shit," Gravel muttered under his breath, and took a slow step forward.

I glanced toward Finley, who just stood there nursing a glass with three fingers of Scotch. He lifted his gaze as his father entered the room. Dominic Salvatore turned his head and then looked away. But in that moment, fear and rage collided. Jesus, talk about your fucked-up relationships. It made me almost feel bad for Finley...*almost*.

"Dominic." My dad turned toward the giant of a man and held out his hand.

He was fatter than the last time I'd seen him. I lowered my gaze to his straining belt as tension coiled in my gut like a serpent.

Dominic Salvatore just stared into my father's eyes. Fuck me if Dad didn't hold his ground, his hand outstretched in a gesture of support. There was bad blood between them, bad blood that had started with the one reason we were here...*Cian Salvatore.*

Dad didn't speak much about the reason. No one did. But considering the quiet tears he'd shed two nights ago when the call came there'd been an assassination, it wasn't hard to guess that at one time my father was in love with the Irish powerhouse.

Cosa Nostra Institute. A playground for young men like Dominic and my dad. Guns, blood, hate, and loyalty were the fucking creed that place lived by. But it was more than that. It was a place for alliances, a place where an Irish Warlord offered his daughter to the most powerful, richest...*most savage of the Commission's sons.*

Then sat back and watched the fight.

Dominic Salvatore and Orlando Rossi.

One born-and-bred Cosa Nostra, the other its rival...*Stidda.*

But both went to the same institution. The same damn institution I'd attended two years ago with Finley. All in the name of putting the bad blood of the warring families behind us.

"Fucking Stidda, I can smell their stench from here."

I jerked my gaze back to the asshole who was just fucking *aching* for a beatdown. Tension tightened my muscles. I clenched my fists and took a step forward.

"Laz," Gravel murmured with a shake of his head. "This isn't the right time."

"But it's the right fucking place," I answered. "At least the wannabe gangsta won't have far to go when I kill him."

I let the words carry, giving him a smile as he curled his lips. Then I blew the fucker a kiss before chuckling under my breath, and turned. We hadn't come for a battle. Actually, it was just the opposite. Dad, Gravel, and two others hanging around outside the funeral home were all the muscle we'd come with.

It was hot in here...too goddamn hot. The stale air was choking. I reached up and yanked the top button of my white shirt open. I hated fucking suits, give me leather any day. "I need some damn air anyway," I muttered, and turned away.

"Thatta boy," Gravel muttered under his breath, never once taking his eyes off my father and Dominic Salvatore. "Go cool down."

I glanced my father's way as Dominic Salvatore took what was offered and clasped his meaty paw around Dad's hand. In a fair fight, there would be no contest. The Rossis grew up on the streets, we were leaner, tougher...*hungrier*. But the Salvatores... yeah, they were a whole other breed. Cold-blooded vipers.

They were the ones who paid to have your family taken out, the ones with bottomless pockets.

Word was they had a secret weapon when it came to money... word was they had someone called *the Ghost*. Some middle-aged schmuck who'd crawled into bed with the wrong fucking people. But no one knew for sure. If anyone came within ten fucking miles of the Salvatore house, you were pulled over, frisked...and occasionally disappeared.

Brute strength against the power of money.

It was a fucking hard choice.

I left the pissing contest behind and headed for the dust-choked air of a darkened doorway. No way was I going to step around the Salvatores like a whipped fucking dog. I reached up, unbuttoned the top of my shirt another button, and worked the damn tie loose as I strode along the hallway, searching for a way out of that fucking mausoleum that was the traditional Cosa Nostra crematory, and strode into the kitchen. There were two plates covered in plastic wrap on the counter, chunks of cheese and some kind of meat smushed together underneath. My gut tightened with the thought of someone eating that shit. White ceramic sinks and ugly green tiles. It looked like it was built in the 70s. Fuck their traditions. If I was dead I wouldn't want to be anywhere near a fucking place like this. I glanced toward the closed back door with its faded, dust-gray lace curtain and winced.

Just get the fuck out of there.

I yanked open the door and stepped out, taking in a lungful of the crisp morning air.

The place backed on to a cemetery. Winter grass was sodden and trampled. I closed the door behind me and reached into my pocket for a pack of cigarettes as movement came from the corner of the building.

Freddy and Neon lifted their gazes toward me and gave a nod.

"Boys," I muttered.

"Everything okay inside?" Freddy jerked his head toward the building.

"Just fucking peachy."

Fifteen more minutes and we'd be out of there. Twenty, and I'd be yanking off this goddamn tie and stuffing it into my pocket. Then I'd probably head to The Rock and shoot some pool, maybe work off this fucking tension with a bottle of Jack and some random piece with her head in my lap. I reached up and massaged the back of my neck.

Fifteen fucking minutes. I lifted my hand and looked at the time. I couldn't fucking wait.

"There he is...the piece of shit who laughs at a funeral. *Cian Salvatore's funeral.*"

My stomach clenched at the words as five of Salvatore's boys rounded the corner of the building and headed our way. And what did you know, the musclebound idiot led the pack.

"Shit," Neon muttered, and glanced over his shoulder.

But there was no help coming. It was three against five. I glanced at the bulge under Neon's jacket, then Freddy's. If it all went bad, then we needed to be faster. But fuck me...a shootout at a Salvatore funeral? *It'd start an all-out war,*

"Laz," Neon murmured, watching the guy come for us. "What the fuck do you want us to do?"

I ground my teeth and fought the twitch. There was only one thing we could do...*meet them head on.*

I strode forward. Fifteen minutes. They couldn't have waited just a little fucking longer?

"I think you have it all wrong." I met the muscle-bound asshole's gaze, all brawn and no brains. I'd seen guys like him crumbled. The problem was, in most cases, the heavier they were, the slower they moved. "I'm here to pay my respects."

"You *filthy* Stidda scum think you can come here on a day like this?"

"Filthy *Stidda scum?*" Freddy growled, and stepped forward. "I think you have us confused with someone else. Someone you can insult without consequences."

One of the five assholes unbuttoned his jacket. My gaze flicked to the Sig Sauer he was carrying and, for the second time in my life, the cold, empty touch of fear found me. But this wasn't like before. This wasn't shoot first and who gave a shit. This wasn't *kill or be killed*...it didn't need to be that way, anyway. Not here. *Not now.* Not when my father was standing next to Dominic Salvatore.

"Whatever happens, do not fire your fucking weapons," I commanded, and lifted my gaze to the fetus looking mother-fucker. "You're right, we are *Stidda scum.* But there's a time for war and a time to get your ass kicked, so which is it, pretty boy? You want to draw down on a Rossi, or you want to eat through a straw for the next three months?" I splayed my hand and clenched my fist.

The bastard just smiled.

"You smile like a pussy," I goaded, watching the smirk die away. "Yeah, a real nice fucking pussy. I bet you swallow cock like a pussy, too." I glanced at the assholes he needed to protect his back. "How about it, boys? He suck good? *I'm taking that as a yes.*"

The idiot broke away from the others with a roar, charging toward me like a damn bull. "Like I said, fucking pussy." I side-stepped and swung, driving my fist into a perfect uppercut.

His pack started forward, trigger-happy fucking fingers reaching for their guns. "*Uh-uh,*" I clucked my tongue and shook my head.

My boys already had their weapons out, muzzles aimed at chest centers. As pretty-big-asshole here clenched his jaw, he jerked his blistering fury my way and spluttered. "You're gonna fucking pay for that."

"What're you gonna do? You gonna shoot me at Cian Salvatore's fucking funeral?" Movement came from the corner of my eye. Finley Salvatore just stood there, not saying a goddam thing. "You want that kind of attention? Just walk away...walk away and we can forget I ever saw your pussy face."

"*Fuck you!*" he roared, reached into his jacket, and pulled his hand out.

No! Terror roared inside my head. Flashbacks followed. All I heard was the sound of shattering glass as I stared at the hole in Taken's throat. But the silver shine wasn't a gun...it was a fucking switchblade. He pressed the button and the blade jutted out, honed and gleaming.

"Now it's my turn to make a pussy out of you," the bastard snarled.

But I couldn't move, frozen by the glint of steel. All I could see was blood...and all I could feel was the cut. The asshole came for me, switching the blade from hand to hand as he smirked. "Not so chatty now?" he grinned, and swung his arm.

I tried to move, tried to duck. I'd been in fights before, school-yard bully ones, others that were more for fucking show. Not anything like the shootout that day, nor anything with a fucking knife.

Pain slashed across my middle.

"Laz!" Neon barked.

But the searing sting shocked me into moving. Only...*now I was fucking pissed.*

Blade or no blade, I didn't even see it, not anymore. I swung... and then swung again, stepping around him fast, and drove my knuckles into his kidneys. The bastard buckled, just like I knew he would. There was no stopping me now, no trigger that could be unreleased. There was a switch in me, a switch that was flicked all the way to *on.*

I drove my knee into his jaw as he dropped to his knees. The knife went flying, clattering to the ground. Shouts came from all around me as I pounced on the guy and fisted his pretty white shirt.

I was all beast.

All savage fucking Stidda beast.

And I fucking loved it.

Fear widened his eyes as I cocked my fist in the air and drove it into his face.

Thud.

Thud.

THUD.

I punched until screams started, his and others, and when they tried to drag me off him, I turned on them, roaring my rage into their shocked expressions.

"Lazarus..." my father called. *"Enough."*

I stopped, heart thundering, the heady scent of blood filling my nose...and looked down at what I'd done.

7

Kat

Two days ago...

"Ms. VanHalen?" My driver's gaze found mine in the rear-view mirror of the limousine. "Is everything okay?"

"Yes, Richard" I answered automatically, and forced a smile. "Everything's fine."

"Can I escort you inside?"

I turned my head to the shimmering black glass windows of the Hale Building standing tall like a knife right in the heart of the city. My pulse was frantic, fluttering in my veins. I tried to breathe and think.

No.

Not think.

If I started thinking...then I'd start screaming.

And I wouldn't stop.

"No, thank you. I'm ready now," I replied, staring at the front doors.

With the words, he opened his door and strode around the back of the limousine. My door was opened quietly, and a rush of warm spring air hit me as I turned. My driver said nothing as I stepped out of the car and adjusted my black wide-bottom pants suit. It was one of the many things I liked about him. Quiet, careful, formidable when he needed to be. Most of all... he didn't look at me like he wanted to tear me apart. I gave him a smile. "I won't be long."

No...not long at all.

My gold clutch was heavy in my hand, the weight unusual. The gun inside weighed heavily in my thoughts as I slipped in behind a man dressed in black and strode through the black glass doors. Cooled air washed over me as the doors closed behind me. I lifted my gaze to the row of receptionists behind the black marble counter, then glanced away as one made eye contact.

"Is there anything I can assist you with today?" she asked.

I didn't answer, just kept walking. I'd never been here before, never even wanted to think about this place. *I never wanted to even think about him.* Elevators. Just get to the elevator.

My knees trembled, but I clenched my jaw and forced myself to move. The double glass doors opened behind me and the thud of heavy steps followed.

"Is there anything I can assist you with today?" the receptionist repeated to the new arrival.

I just kept walking, my focus divided between the gun in my clutch and the howls of desperation ringing in my head. I was leaving today, climbing on our private jet and flying to Mauritius. There, the Commission would send a luxury cruiser to ferry me, and the others, to a small island far enough from the mainland to forget the rest of the world existed. Maybe there I could forget...*forget this city...forget this man.*

I stopped at the bank of elevators, pressed the button, and glanced behind me. I caught the blur of a painting high up on the opposite wall. My heart lunged at the sight, driving like a fist into the back of my throat. A portrait...*of Haelstrom Hale.*

He stood tall, powerful, his dark eyes glinting with possessiveness. A shiver coursed through my body. But it wasn't a tremor of fear...*it was rage.* I tightened my grip around my clutch, aching to feel the cold bite of the steel. In my head, I pulled the weapon free...and emptied the clip into the painting in front of me.

I wanted to hurt.

I wanted to kill.

I wanted to be free.

"Ma'am?"

I flinched as the voice intruded and jerked my gaze toward the male dressed in black as he held the elevator doors open. "Are you coming?"

Do it...do it...do it...

My stomach clenched tight, driving the bitter tang of acid into the back of my mouth. I'd never be free. Not from Haelstrom Hale, or from *the men in the white masks...*

"Ummm," the guy murmured, glancing from me to the sound of the receptionists in the foyer. "Are you okay?"

I stumbled backwards as terror rose inside me. The gun. The man. *The truth.* They raged inside me, howling for vengeance. The walls tilted as I spun. My heels clattered against the marble floor as I headed for the foyer, then stopped as I saw Richard.

My stomach rolled and I swallowed a heave. I couldn't let him see me like this, couldn't get back in that car...not yet. I looked at a group headed for the double doors of Hale Building, steaming coffee cups and brown paper bags in their hands. Richard glanced toward them, then turned, surveying the traffic. *Now...move, now.*

I rushed toward the doors as they opened and slipped around the group, then turned left. Head down...*hurrying*. I swallowed, and swallowed and *swallowed*, forcing the acid back down. Just hold on...hold on. Salvation lay in a darkened alleyway a little further ahead. I stepped into the blinding sun, looked left, then right, and hurried across the side street, to the alley smothered in darkness.

The roar of the traffic filled my head as cars swept past. *Don't look at me. Don't look at me. Don't...*

I lunged into the shadows and hurried toward the end. I didn't care if it was filthy. Didn't care about the sprouting green moss between the bricks, or the choking, rotting stench. How could I when there was rot inside me?

Foul.

Diseased.

Inescapable.

But I had to escape. I had to get away from them. I have to get away...

I shoved my hand out and braced against the bricks as hot acid shot from my mouth and splashed against the ground. I didn't think I had anything left, nothing but acid and rage. It seemed like that was a bottomless well inside me.

More came shooting from my mouth and puddled in the cracked asphalt. I gripped my clutch and heaved until there was nothing left but air. Still my stomach rolled, twisting and turning. "No more," I pleaded, and closed my eyes. "No more."

The foul air tasted almost sweet. I wiped my mouth with the back of my hand and grimaced. The sound of the traffic invaded, drawing my focus to the bright sunlight at the entrance of the alley...and the dark gray sedan parked across the opening.

My pulse sped at the sight, even before I made the connection.

Dark-tinted windows gave me little to go on.

A shadow sat behind the wheel.

But I was sure I'd seen that car before.

I racked my memory, then froze.

Yesterday. I'd seen that same car yesterday...

And last week, the same damn car passed by the house as we turned in.

I took a, step forward, the gun still in my clutch. But the moment I did, the vehicle rolled forward and pulled onto the street. I swallowed hard, panic filling me now. I knew what that warning in the pit of my stomach said...*someone was following me.*

8

Lazarus

Two days ago...

"And you're still not going?" Dad crossed his arms and leaned back on the sleek wooden counter in the kitchen. "To the island, that is."

I held his gaze, watching the old man squirm. "Why? You want me to go?"

There was a second where he paused...*and Dad never paused,* only when he wanted something.

"No. Not at all." He shoved away from the counter. His hard muscles flexed under his tight black t-shirt as he drained his coffee, leaving the cup neatly in the sink for the cleaners. "Word is the Salvatores are going."

Fuck.

Now why the hell did he have to go and say that?

Pretty boy Finley Salvatore and his broody fucking glare. I licked my lips and inhaled deep. A spark of life flared inside me. Fucking up that asshole's entire week almost sounded...*appealing*. "I asked a month ago and they said he wasn't."

Dad just gave a shrug and strode toward the door. "Looks like he changed his mind. Classes start tomorrow...it's not too late to change yours."

Sitting on a damn island in the middle of nowhere with a bunch of rich wannabes? Fuck that. Even if they had changed the rules now, letting women attend classes, I wasn't interested in the catty fucking bullshit that went with it.

Dad's boots thudded on the polished concrete floor. I looked his way, watching him stride into the hallway and out the back door. The black Bentley's engine started with a growl. Gravel was sitting behind the wheel playing chauffer, ready to take Dad into the city to '*the office*'.

We'd come a long way since our small home in the suburbs. *A helluva long way.* I drained the last of my Red Bull, yanked open the cupboard, and tossed the can into the trash. It'd taken a year to build, but the three-story house was starting to feel more like a home. Sleek, cold concrete, polished wood, and black metal. The place Dad had built all the way out here was perfect. Quiet. Calming.

I snatched my gloves off the end of the counter and strode toward the back of the massive house. Cool Spring morning air hit me as I pushed through the door. I lifted my gaze to the thick ash trees that surrounded the property. Jesus, I never got sick of it out here. My boots crunched on the pebbles as I strode toward the garage set back from the main house. A smaller building was built at the side of the towering playpen filled with bikes, cars, and four-wheel drives. Gravel lived in the rooms above the garage, and the other guys crashed here most nights when business called for it.

Business.

The Rossi name had earned a reputation in the last few years. I'd earned my own in the last few months. I yanked on my gloves, remembering my bloody knuckles from two months ago. On the day of Finley's mom's funeral...the day I'd almost beat a man to death. But pretty boy had said fucking nothing, just stood there and watched one of his men get the beatdown of his goddamn life.

I punched in the code and waited for the garage door to rise as the thought of Finley Salvatore wore at me.

Detached motherfucker.

The thought of pissing all over his goddamn parade at Cosa Nostra was sounding better every fucking second. I strode into the garage, yanked my leather jacket from the hanger, and climbed onto the Night Train. The Harley had been a gift to myself. Sleek, black...it was thunder on a clear spring day, throbbing between my legs better than anything a woman ever gave me.

I started the engine, shoved back the kickstand, and pulled forward before hitting the remote on the keyring. The garage door slid down as I eased around the side of the house and onto the driveway. Five minutes later, I was out on the open highway.

Cars whipped past me, but a few thought they'd hug my ass as I headed toward the city. One car in particular, dark gray...I divided my attention between the traffic ahead and the rear-view mirror, then swerved out and quickly back in around a slowass Jeep. Whaddaya know, the asshole behind me did the same.

Dark-tinted windows pretty well obscured the interior. It was a guy behind the wheel, that much I could tell. Just some jackass anyway. I focused on the road ahead and opened up the engine a bit. The Harley surged forward as the cars slowed for traffic lights up ahead.

Fuck that.

I gunned the engine, shooting across all four lanes, leaving the gray sedan and the asshole behind. A glance into the rear-view mirror and I was gone, turning down Hudson Avenue to take me into the city. Towering buildings rose in the distance. The heart of the city was made for stuck-up wealthy pricks, not the Rossi's. I turned the bike toward Gippsland Dark, the place where those like us worked, played...*and fucked.*

The closer I got, the darker and seedier the streets became. Trash seemed to cling to the buildings and the towering ten-foot fences that made up Gippsland. Gangs and working girls stood on every street, watching me with careful gazes as I drove past. They all knew who I was...and they wanted nothing to do with us. The Stidda ran the brothels and the clubs from this side of the Parade, stretching over three districts. No one sold anything here without us knowing...and taking a cut. Not dime bags and pussy, not guns or shakedowns. We got a cut from everything, unless they wanted to disappear.

I turned the corner and drove into the sun. But the rays weren't as bright here, dirty and clouded, like everything I saw. I down-shifted, slowed the bike, and turned into the back alley of

Empire. The back door was open. Shadows clung to the inside of the club. Neon stood outside, leaning against the open door. The amber glow of his cigarette blazed for a second before he flicked it away.

I parked the bike and climbed off, turning to look over my shoulder as a car slowly drove by. A gray sedan. My gut clenched, knowing by instinct alone it was the same guy who seemed to have followed me all the way from home. Fucker.

"Laz," Neon called.

I waited, staring at the entrance of the alley. Get back on the bike. That dangerous hunger burned in me. Hunt the fucker down.

Footsteps grew louder as Neon came toward me. "Everything okay?"

But my fucking stalker didn't return. "Yeah. Tighten the patrols on the clubs, will you?"

"Sure. Anything I need to know about?"

"Yeah, seems like I got myself a fan."

I caught the flicker of alarm as he glanced toward the alley entrance. His brows furrowed and his jaw clenched. "You got a description?"

"Beemer, gunmetal gray. Too expensive to be a Fed's. He followed me from home."

A nod and Neon grabbed his phone. "I'm on it."

"I'm going inside," I muttered, glancing toward the entrance of the alley once more.

If he was a fan, the boys would find him. It was the one thing we took as serious as a damn heart attack, especially after what happened to Taken. I left Neon behind and stepped through the open fire door and into the back of the club.

Music drifted from the front, where the girls danced and the bar was always busy. We had eight clubs just like Empire scattered through this part of the city. The Crown. The King. The Empire. All names of the rich and the powerful. But it was all a show. No one gave a fuck what the name was, as long as the girls weren't ugly and the booze was cheap.

"Laz," Freddy called, heading my way.

A nod and I kept going, striding along the hallway to the private rooms in the back. Rooms where you didn't go unless you were part of the Rossi clan, or we vouched for you. My phone gave a *beep*. I grabbed it and glanced at the message:

Gravel: Next time you ride in the car.

I grinned and texted back.

Next time you can suck my cock. A Rossi never—

Beep.

Gravel: I swear to God, if you tell me a Rossi doesn't run, Imma gonna beat your ass blue.

I just let out a chuckle, backspaced my message, and slid my phone into my pocket. There was no getting out of this now. With one fucking text about a stalker, Gravel had gone full-on protective-Momma-Bear mode.

Music came from the rooms out back, darker, slower, sexier. I turned the handle and pushed open the door to the plush Rossi rooms, revealing velvet lounges and a fully stocked bar. Two dancers twisted around poles on a raised platform. The girls here were ours, specifically picked for the guys...and there were plenty of men to keep them busy.

The Rossi clan had grown to almost forty strong, with men who patrolled the streets, men who took the money. But there was more to be made than the nickel-and-dime shit the drugs and pussy gave us. Guns were where the real cash was, stealing, selling. Those jobs were given to a select few, men who worked the nighttime raids...the core group. Men who'd take a bullet for me...and I'd take one for them.

"Lazarus." Bethany smiled as she sauntered toward me.

She was stunning, with long blonde hair and a body to die for. I just smiled. "Hey, B."

She grabbed my hand and led me toward a black lounge in the back, turning to give me a thousand-watt smile. "Can I get you a drink, honey?"

I just shook my head, my mind crawling back to the gray sedan. "No, maybe later."

She just smiled as I flopped back against the seat. But it was more than the shadow. It was something that'd been nagging me, an unsettled feeling in my soul.

"You look preoccupied," Bethany murmured, and swung her leg up, straddling me.

Perfect, perky breasts pressed against me as she murmured. "Want me to take your mind off whatever's bothering you?"

She rolled her hips, grinding against me. I waited for a reaction, waited for that aching need to thicken my cock. I waited for the memory of her throat working to consume me. But it didn't. I just lifted my head and stared into her eyes, and realized what had been eating at me...*I was fucking bored.*

Bored of this room.

Bored of this waiting.

I was bored of Bethany.

But Finley. Finley Salvatore and his poor little hurt feelings. Now that sparked a hunger inside me. I wanted to see the look on his face when I turned up on his precious little island. But it was more than that...

I wanted to know the reason he'd changed his damn mind about going.

And I wanted to ruin his fucking plans.

9

Kat

Screams cut through the air.

Guttural.

Savage.

"I'll fucking kill them!" Marco Baldeon roared.

His eyes were wide, the whites gleaming neon bright in the lights of the luxury cruiser. I tried not to look at his bloodied white shirt, or the bullet holes peppered along the wall. Glass crunched under my feet as I stumbled and caught my balance as the boat turned.

Salty spray hit me. I licked my lips. It was the taste of the salt I sought out with the swipe of my lips. The salt that told me I was alive, that I could taste as I breathed. That I was okay, even as the panicked thunder of my heart sprouted wings and fluttered like a bird trapped in my chest.

I'd felt nothing when the first cracks of the gunshots rang out... and that frightened me. I was cold, frozen, just standing there as glass shattered at my left and a shower of shards hit the cruiser's floor.

Screams followed soon after, bellows of commands before the Commission's security opened fire in return, spraying the choppy waves of the sea with bullets. I stood there, watching as Baldeon drew his own firearm and opened fire.

Any other time, this would've been horrific.

Any other time, it'd make the news.

But not when I was surrounded by the sons and daughters of the most dangerous families in the country.

Not when I was headed for an island institute that catered to *the Mafia.*

Bloodshed was a way of life for these people.

What was a little assassination attempt on the way there, if not part of the fucking atmosphere?

The boat lurched to the side and took my stomach with it. Chatter invaded my steely focus on trying not to heave. I swallowed, and swallowed again, then lifted my gaze to something in the distance, anything that'd help the queasiness. Champagne flowed and crystal clinked on a damn luxury cruiser. I smiled as the conversation gravitated my way, but inside I was panicking...

I glanced carefully around the boat, catching the brunette standing in the shadows, trying to look casual. But she was anything but. In dark blue jeans and a floral top, she looked...*normal.*

That had to be her...*Annalise Eden.* She lifted her gaze and connected with mine. I gave her a careful smile. *Easy,* I whispered in my head. *Don't spook her.*

I'd hired a private investigator without my father knowing, to give me a full brief on every person attending the island. But there was only one they couldn't find any info on, only one whose past led to a dead end and triggered a series of red flags for my PI. Whoever Annalise Eden was, she didn't want anyone probing into her private life...and if they so much as tried to, you could damn well know she'd be informed.

I shifted nervously as the boat rose on the waves. She glanced my way once more. I made sure not to look her way that time. Instead, the mask I wore in public slipped down as I smiled and made small talk with some of the others, women I already knew...and couldn't trust.

But Annalise Eden. Maybe she was someone I could depend on? Maybe she was someone who was dangerous enough to help me? *I hoped so. I really did...because I was getting desperate.*

"I'm going to fucking *kill* them," Baldeon howled again as two beefy security staff held him up from under his arms. "No one messes with a Baldeon and fucking lives!"

"Easy," a man who stood on the deck urged. "You rip your wound open any more, and I'm going to have Manny here knock you the fuck out."

Baldeon's lips curled as he fought that animal need to lash out. The engine of the cruiser roared as it cut through the choppy waves. I gripped the table as the glinting lights of the island came into view. *Thank God.*

My stomach churned and clenched. I wanted off this damn thing. *Now*.

"Building one," the older guy ordered, stabbing a bloodstained finger toward the top of the rise. "Get him to the infirmary."

Voices cut through the air. I didn't pay any attention. Not until *she* moved.

Anna was quiet, and fast, keeping her head down, not drawing attention to herself as the boat engine revved in reverse, driving us backwards toward the dock. I lifted my gaze to the towering buildings high up on the island as she stepped in behind the others. But the sight of those buildings held me. Concrete and glass, they reminded me of the Hale Building.

God, I felt sick.

"Now, careful getting off the ramp, people. I don't want you rolling a damn ankle before you even step onto the island," the guy they called the Commander growled.

I stepped forward, discreetly moving in ahead of her, not wanting to scare her off, and took my time in the damn heels. The heavier thud of steps behind me was followed by an *oof*.

Something hit the ground hard.

Laughter followed...from one asshole in particular, as I turned to see Anna sprawled out on the ground.

"Fucking hell, nice spill," he roared, and the rest of the crowd sniggered.

"Shut up, you asshole," I barked, and strode forward, driving my elbow in as I pushed him aside.

I grabbed her arm just as a low, threatening sound spilled through the air, quieting the sniggers.

"Anna."

That growl was all possessiveness. I glanced over my shoulder, to find Finley Salvatore striding through the parting crowd toward her. There was nothing I could do, nothing Finley would *let* me do, but stand aside while he took control.

"Fin?" Anna croaked, her eyes wide and filled with terror. "What the hell are you doing here?"

"Me?" He leaned over her. "I could ask you the same?"

"I got her," I declared, slipping my arm around Anna as he helped her to stand.

Then he turned on the guy who'd laughed.

I'd never seen someone react so damn fast. He grabbed the idiot who'd decided a woman tripping in front of him was funny by the shirt and dragged him up close. Threats were given and the poor asshole didn't stand a chance. Not when one of *the* family's sons had it out for you.

I just stood by Anna's side.

Watching as she turned from pale to positively gray under the island's lights.

Fin turned back, glanced my way, and came toward her. "You sure you're okay?" His thumb gently brushed her bloodied lip before she looked away.

I let them have their moment, trying not to eavesdrop, until I felt the heat of Finley's gaze. For a second, the idea floated to me. Finley Salvatore was rich, powerful, and very well connected...*and totally not into me.*

I met his gaze as he shoved out a hand. "Finley Salvatore."

"Kat VanHalen," I answered, and forced a smile.

"Do you have your building yet?" he asked, but it wasn't me he spoke to.

The brunette dragged her phone from her pocket and stared at the cracked screen. "Shit."

"It's just a phone, Anna." Finley took the broken thing from her hand. "Use mine."

"It's got all my identification," she muttered.

"You and your damn encryptions, Anna," he sighed.

"Finley," a bodyguard called from the edge of the grass. He glanced toward the brunette and gave a nod. "Anna."

"Max," she answered coldly.

Okay, so something was going on there.

"Anna...the damn password," Finley urged, his tone softening.

"Salvatoresucks," she whispered, her cheeks turning red.

"Salvatore...sucks," he muttered, punching in the letters. "No special character?"

She gave a tiny shake of her head. "No, no special character."

"Building five," he announced. "With a Miss VanHalen."

"Oh, that's me," I tried to act surprised.

"I'll make sure she gets to her building, Mr. Salvatore." A guard from the cruiser stepped forward.

A nod from Finley as he met her gaze. "Sleep, Anna. Classes start tomorrow. It's just an introduction, but you'll still need to be focused."

"Make sure she's inside before you leave," he commanded the guard. "Any problems, I want to be notified first. Do you understand?"

"Yes, Mr. Salvatore."

"And just for the record, Anna...the Salvatores not only *suck*, they lick and bite, as well."

I bit the inside of my cheek to keep from laughing as she just froze.

He left then, striding toward his bodyguard and leaving us alone.

"Come on." I slipped my hand through her arm. "Let's find building five."

I made small talk with her as the security guard led us toward our building, probing her with questions about Finley. But the evidence of her infatuation was written all over her face. Annalise Eden was head over heels in love with Finley Salvatore and, if that lion-protecting-his-mate attack before was anything to go on, Finley was a goner for her, as well.

Which made her very interesting.

I swallowed as my belly jerked and my body rocked, nauseous and still rolling with the waves. "Best friends." The words seemed to tumble from my lips amongst the lies of having the time of our lives and being the most incredible roommates ever.

Anna just smiled and laughed as the guard stopped outside one of the accommodation buildings and swiped the card to open the door.

"Your card, Miss Eden," he said as he handed Anna hers then handed me mine. "Miss VanHalen."

I took the key card and slipped it into my clutch, watching as Anna's eyes widened with wonder. It was easy to see she didn't come from money, not real money, the kind that warped your view of the real world.

The kind that created monsters...

And let them feed on the weak.

10

Kat

My mask was fixed in place the next morning, with my killer smile, too. I played the perfect best friend. Hair, makeup, clothes. Chatting to Anna like nothing was wrong in my world. And for a little while, I was lost in my own lie.

That strangling fist inside eased. I even caught myself actually laughing. *Like, really laughing.* Full belly laughter as she blushed and looked horrified, caught on the fact there were no fucking doors. I liked her...*a lot.*

She wasn't like anyone else I knew. She was easy, quiet, and careful. She was...warm. *Yeah, Anna was warm.* I chatted to her while we got ready for our first day of classes. But the desperation was always there, hovering in the back of my mind like an unseen enemy ready with a blade.

One cut, and my smile was stolen.

One stab, and my happiness was gone.

"Wow," Anna said from her bedroom doorway, eyeing my dress and heels. "You're going to class in *that?*"

I forced a smile. It's what carefree Kat would've done. "Absolutely. I'm here to make an impression."

There was a chuckle and the shake of her head. "In that, you're *definitely* going to make an impression."

I just smiled and stepped through the doorway to her room. "You better believe it. You ready?"

She fussed, checking her hair, fixing her top. She was a fidgeter, yanking, pulling, eyes downcast with the kind of demeanor that screamed *DON'T LOOK AT ME.* My smile faltered. She wouldn't last five minutes in my world.

Men like my father and Haelstrom Hale would eat her alive.

My stomach gave a howl as I snatched my clutch off the end of the bed and walked out. "Ready?"

"Ready."

We rode downstairs and stepped out of the foyer into the perfect warmth of the Mauritius sun. God, I could almost pretend the world out there didn't exist. I talked, about bullshit really, designer brands and perfume. The kinds of things someone like me would be consumed by. But Anna was distracted. I scowled as she checked her phone for the hundredth time. "You're not listening, are you?"

"Sorry," she smiled. "Distracted. Tell me again..."

I just slipped my hand free from her arm. "It's totally fine." I glanced at the buildings in the distance and checked my own phone "Catch you after class?"

Her steps stuttered. "Wait, you mean we're not together?"

"I have kidnapping and ransom analysis, although," I muttered, glancing at the other classes scheduled. "I'd much rather attend *Running your Fortune 500 Company*. You?"

"Psychology."

"Bummer." I winced. "Maybe next time. Looks like I'm over here. Catch you later, gorgeous."

"Later," Anna muttered behind me, but I was already striding toward the building in the distance, my mind drawn back to the panic that was my life. I had to come up with something. I had to find a way out of that mess.

Kill them...

Blow them all up.

Expose every dark and dirty secret.

Christ, if the media caught wind of who those people really were, it'd be everywhere...*forever*.

I'd never escape, tainted and branded for the rest of my life. No, I couldn't have that. I needed a different way to get away from them. I needed a better plan for escape.

I strode through the doors and across the foyer, my heels clicking on the tiled floor. God, I hated these shoes...and this dress. Heads turned toward me as I took one step at a time, and the chatter started. But I had a reputation, right? The redhaired heiress to a billion-dollar empire. I knew what they saw when they looked at me. It was an image I'd carefully crafted over many, *many* years.

Cold. Impenetrable...

I flicked my hair back and rose to the last stair, making my way toward the classroom.

"Hey, Kat." Some six-foot giant fell in step beside me. "It's Jake...Jake Green."

"Jake Green." I mulled the name over. "Green banks, right?"

He pushed ahead, striding toward the row of seats next to me. His teeth showed when he smiled, and he had nice teeth. "Yeah, that's me. I heard your dad made some waves to get you here."

"Sure he did," I answered.

It wasn't my father at all. If he'd had anything to do with this, I would've never even known about this place. But I did. Desperation had driven me to my laptop moments after I'd turned away from the sink in our kitchen and left the sharp blade of the knife behind. It was desperation that had driven me to do something I'd never done before.

That was to fight.

"So, you all settled in then?"

He slipped into the seat next to me. I glanced his way and smiled. "Sure. You?"

"Got a sweet view overlooking the ocean. I'm kinda pumped about the classes, and now that you're here..."

I tuned out, slid my phone free, and scrolled through Facebook and TikTok, giving a nod and a smile when it was needed. The lecturer started, and for that I was thankful. At least Jake fell silent, his eyes fixed on the front of the classroom, leaving me to scan the rest of the class.

It was easy to see who was Mafia.

Scowling glares and looming bodyguards. I scanned every gaze, catching sight of Xael in the back row. She glanced my way and gave a nod. There was a blonde next to her, someone I'd never seen before. As I stared, she glanced my way and met my gaze. There was something dangerous in her gaze, something...*not quite right.*

But then she caught Xael's seductive smile and the nod my way and gave me a smirk of her own. I wondered if she was Evan Valachi? The word was a few of the Commission's kids were here. Baldeon I'd already seen screaming and bleeding. My mind drifted to him and I wondered if he was still at the infirmary?

I passed the class in a daydream, sliding out of my seat when the others started to move.

"Want to walk to your next class together?"

I scowled and glanced up. Oh, that's right...Jake. "Sure."

"Hey, *Kat!*"

I turned at the feminine growl and caught Xael striding toward me. "Party tonight."

"Where?" I smiled, and shook my head.

Xael just gave a shrug and stopped in front of me. "I dunno, just follow the noise, I guess. This is Evan...Valachi."

I gave the blonde a critical glance. "I thought it was. Nice to meet you."

"X has told me all good things." She met my stare with her own.

She was careful, composed, tall in wide-bottom black slacks and a cream top, plunging at her breasts. She had an unwavering stare and for a second, a spike of fear coursed through my veins. The Valachis were powerful people...so that was it...*maybe*...

"I guess I'll see you tonight?" I murmured.

"Sure. Maybe. I'll see if there's no other trouble I can get into first." Xael gave me a wink and sauntered off.

"Kat." Evan nodded and followed her.

"Nice." Jake slowed his giant steps to match with mine as I shuffled my way past the desks and down the stairs. "A party."

The other students piled through the door, some going left to the stairs and another building.

"I think we're just down here," Jake said, pointing right.

I nodded and followed, letting him lead the way. He held open the door for me when we found the class, smiled and motioned me forward. He was nice...*too nice,* and I hated it. Women like me didn't get guys like him. If they did, it never lasted, and I sure as hell didn't want to see the spark in his eyes die when he realized how tainted I really was.

I sat down, catching sight of Anna striding through the door. "Ah, this seat's taken," I declared, and smiled at him.

There was a flicker of hurt before he smothered it with a smile. "Oh, sure."

"Just get *out* of my way," the snarl came from the doorway.

I glanced toward Anna as she was shoved to the side.

She stumbled as some towering broad with a resting bitchface pushed through. *Gian...something.* I tried to place her. I think her daddy owned a few casinos. Black suits and muscled chests followed her as Anna tried to right herself. My jaw clenched as I caught the flare of panic in Anna's gaze.

Anna, who was good.

Anna, who needed someone looking out for her, someone other than Finley Salvatore.

"You're just an accident waiting to happen, aren't you?" I whispered as Anna came close, carefully watching the tall bitch who'd shoved her.

"I warned you," she answered, her cheeks reddening.

Jake tried to engage me in conversion.

I had purpose now, something more than pretending to be someone I wasn't.

"Enough now." I glanced at Jake. "My friend is here."

He just stopped mid-sentence, then glanced Anna's way in confusion.

But I didn't care anymore. I was fixed on that bitch that needed an attitude adjustment.

"This place fucking terrifies me," Anna mumbled.

"Of course it does, sweetheart." I agreed, still staring daggers into that bitch as I patted her thigh. "Don't you worry about a damn thing. Kat's got your back."

"Quiet down, everyone!" the lecturer barked from the front of the room.

"You okay?" I double-checked.

She just turned her head and glanced behind us. I followed her gaze, finding Finley Salvatore holding her stare.

Goosebumps raced across my arms at the heat in his gaze. I knew that kind of look, and what it meant. Anna Eden was caught in a trap, only she didn't know yet it'd already sprung. I glanced her way, finding the dark cloud of confusion and annoyance.

"Do you know anything about some kind of initiation?" she whispered.

"Nope." I focused on the lecturer. "Why?"

"I don't know..." she glanced at Finley again. "But I think something strange is going on."

"Don't worry about it," I responded. "We have more important things to worry about."

"Yeah?" She lifted her eyes to mine.

"What the hell are we going to wear to the damn party tonight?"

"Party?" She glanced my way, her eyes widening. "What party?

"The party were going to," I answered with a grin. "Tonight."

THE PARTY WAS sexy as hell.

Thumping and dark, full of dark corners and darker deeds.

Just how I liked it.

Dark enough so that the cracks in my mask didn't show.

And for the first time, I didn't focus on the panic. I had something else to occupy my thoughts. Something dangerous...something that filled me with *purpose*.

I strode in smiling and gave a wink to a familiar face inside the doorway.

"*Hey, Jacob!*" I leaned in and kissed him on the cheek. Anna watched me cautiously as she came closer, but I gave her a special smile. She was so fucking sweet, *too goddamn sweet.* A butterfly flapping her way into a hornets' nest.

"Kat," she greeted warily from beside me.

"It's fine," I assured as I dragged her toward the kitchen.

"Isaac," I called.

Isaac Kensington, one of the golf course kids.

"Kat, you showed." His eyes widened in surprise.

He shouldn't have been surprised, this was after all, the first party of our goddamn institute year. He handed me three fingers of Grey Goose...or maybe it was a little more, who the fuck was counting?

"And who's this?" he asked, eying Anna. *No one you'll be getting close to, buddy.* "Family...who is thirsty for champagne," I hinted, searching every female face.

"Thanks," Anna said, so damn polite.

"You two don't look like family."

Tall, leggy, dead-as-fuck eyes drew my gaze. "No, we don't," I answered, catching sight of my target.

They made small talk, but I wasn't listening. I was watching the room, waiting for my chance, as the giant-ass bitch across the room unwound herself from Bernard Kissington and rose to her full height.

"Well, help yourself to anything you want," Isaac urged, and left.

"Oh, we will," I answered as the bitch rose and snapped a command to the two assholes guarding her no-tits-and-no-ass scrawny body before she made her way along the hall.

"You good for a minute?" I asked, not bothering to wait for an answer.

In my head, all I could see was the flare of pain on Anna's face and the utter contempt on the bitch's face as she'd shoved my friend aside.

"Hey, sexy!" Some guy called me.

I flashed him a smile, raked my gaze over the game of blackjack in the corner, and kept on walking, head held high, right past her bodyguards, who shifted from one foot to the other and straightened their jackets, painfully awkward like a pair of kicked balls.

But the scent was in the water...and smiles and laughter aside, I was a fucking shark.

I slowed at the cracked-open bathroom door. Black tiles and brushed stainless accessories were illuminated by the hard glare of overhead lights.

There were three stalls, two already empty. But the bitch hadn't come to take a piss. Her head was down, black dress riding high at the back of her thighs as she snorted a line of cocaine. There was a set of hair clippers on the dresser. Perfect. I grabbed them as the toilet flushed and a guy strode out of a stall, took one look at me with the clippers in my hand, and scowled. But I wasn't here for him.

"Kat," he said carefully, and left...without washing his hands.

"You see," I started, and took a careful step forward. "People know me, and I know people. Most I know by name...or the dollars in their bank account. But you..." I stared at her in the mirror as she brushed her thin fucking nostrils with her thumb. "You I know because you're a fucking cunt...and you messed with the wrong person."

The bitch didn't even have the decency to look at me.

I lashed out, spearing manicured nails through her slicked-back ash-blonde hair and fisted what I could. Her eyes flew wide, finally registering who I was here for.

"Get the fuck *off me!*" she cried, trying to stand.

But this wasn't my first catfight. I drove my knee into the back of hers, watching as she crumpled forward, throwing out her hands as she clawed for a hold of the faucets. *"Who the fuck are you?"*

Buzz...buzz. I flicked the switch on the clippers. "Katerina VanHalen."

"Who?" Her eyes were wide. So wide I could see all the way down into the festering pit of her soul. So wide, I knew she was lying. She knew who I was.

I threw my head back and laughed, then pressed the edge of the clippers against her neck. "So, you really haven't heard of me, have you?"

"N-no," she stammered, her eyes glassy with rage. "Let me go or I'll fucking hurt you."

"You'll hurt me?" I laughed, the sound maniacal and weird. "*You'll...hurt* me?"

My laughter quieted, until the silence was hollow and strange, and in its place was that unhinged part of me I usually leashed, the one I let out on special occasions...*like now.* "You hurt my friend," I snarled, my fist clenching around her hair, and lifted the humming clippers. "And that I just cannot stand."

"*Who?*" she roared.

"Anna." *Don't say her name...don't fucking say it.* "Today in the fingerprinting class."

"That auburn-haired nobody?" she wailed, her hands clawing for a hold again as she slipped. "All this for an unknown little bitch?"

"See, that's the difference between you and me," I started, and lifted the clippers closer. "You hurt my friends and you hurt me. And you know what happens when you mess with a VanHalen? The damn claws come out."

I shoved those clippers along the side of her hair, smiling as the sound of the buzz deepened with work.

Her long hair fell around her hands. She stared at it in horror... until that horror turned to utter rage. "*I'm going to get my bodyguards to fucking kill you!*" she screamed, her pale face purpling with rage.

Threats.

I'd heard them all before.

I yanked her head backwards and turned the clippers in my hand. It wasn't hair I wanted now. It wasn't hair at all.

I saw Anna. I saw innocence, the kind that had been taken from me, the kind I would've killed for, to protect...I flicked the clippers off and pressed the teeth against her neck. Stainless steel bit into the flesh above her vein.

"You d-don't even fucking know h-her. I asked around...*no one knows her*," she protested.

They didn't know her, didn't *want* to know her. I needed it to stay that way.

I eased back. "You're right, she *is* a nobody. But that doesn't give you the fucking right to do whatever you want. The next time you see her, you *will* be nice, do you hear me?"

A nod of her head and one tear slipped free.

It was a wonder she felt anything in her drug-induced haze.

"You will apologize...and you *will* stay out of my fucking way, or this," I drove the blade deeper and leaned close "will be a drop in the fucking ocean of what I'll unleash."

She shuddered, her chest heaving as tears slid down her pale-ass fucking cheeks as I pulled away, releasing her hair with a grunt of disgust. "And get some fucking sun, will you, I can see your goddamn veins. That shit went out five fucking years ago."

I gripped the clippers and stepped away, watching her fall apart, just like bitches like her always did.

Then I went to find her, my little butterfly, so perfect and strange.

The best friend I'd always wanted.

11

Lazarus

The salty air clung to my nostrils as I clenched my jaw. Desperation drove me here, all the way into the middle of fucking nowhere. I lifted my gaze to the brilliant orange sunset fading to darkness across the sky. I came because of some kind of drive inside me, some *gnawing* ache in my gut. I came because I wanted to piss Finley off...but now that I was here...I wasn't so sure.

The gray sedan wore at me like a damn thorn in my side. Neon and the others hadn't found it. I checked my phone, not yet at least. Not since the day the sedan followed me all the way from home. Dad had grown nervous...*real fucking nervous.*

The last time there'd been word of a bounty on my head, it'd resulted in one of us dying. *Shit.* I could still see Taken that day, the bullet hole in his neck, his wide stare of panic. The asshole in the gray sedan was just another fucking excuse for Dad to push me into coming here.

He was nervous.

Really nervous.

Which had resulted in increased patrols around our home and a damn tracker he'd forced me wear, as though he was afraid I'd be taken. I reached around to the knotted muscle at the back of my neck. No one in their right mind would come close to fucking trying.

Music drifted down from some asshole's apartment in the distance.

"If you're looking for Finley, word is he's up there."

I glanced toward Freddy and snarled, "Stop reading my damn mind." I took a step. "It's starting to freak me the fuck out."

"That's what you pay me for," the annoying asshole who was my eyes and ears sassed me. "Not that there's a whole lot to worry about. Although the penchant for pink *is* starting to concern me."

I jerked my gaze to his, gave him a glare, then a grin, and lunged toward him as he caught up. "What the fuck is wrong with pink?"

Freddy gave a chuckle and dodged my punch. "I didn't want to be the one to tell you this, but it makes you look sallow."

"Sallow?" I growled, striding toward the godawful fucking music. "What the *fuck* is sallow?"

"You," he answered dryly. "When you wear pink."

I reached up and massaged the muscles in the back of my neck as the laughter died away inside me. Logan just glanced at Freddy, then me, and smirked. Still that ugliness inside me reared its head as I caught sight of a group of guys heading through the glass doors. This damn place. It was full of fucking assholes with little balls and big egos. Guys like Finley, who liked to 'play' Mafia.

I slowed my steps. Maybe I could give all this a miss, just kick back and watch something on Netflix. Porn, maybe?

"You going in there or not?"

I sighed, listening to the roar of laughter.

"If you'd rather not go, we can hang out together? There's this nature documentary—"

"I'm fucking going," I muttered, and strode forward.

"Only if you want!" he called behind my back, knowing too well I'd murder him if I had to listen to him debate every goddamn thing David Attenborough said.

Everyone fucking knows Attenborough is king.

Everyone but Freddy.

I left the smirking asshole behind and strode toward the doors. Cool air-conditioned air washed over me as I strode inside and headed for the elevator.

"Lazarus."

I glanced toward the dumb schmuck who'd spoken to me. Some dipshit draped in leather. "I know you?"

"Jeremiah." He shoved out his hand. "Stone."

I just looked at the damn thing and strode toward the elevator doors as they opened. "No, I don't think I do."

I punched the button and waited for the doors to close. I wasn't here to make friends...I wasn't here for a rich-girl fuck either, no matter how loaded they were. I was here for that fucking look...

that one goddamn look on Finley's face. A look I was about to get as the elevator rose to the top floor.

I was going to find that asshole.

And...*and*...

The look on his face returned to me as he'd stood in the shadow of that fucking funeral home, watching me beat the shit out of his guy. He'd watched me...and didn't do a fucking thing to stop me.

I clenched my jaw.

Right or wrong, someone touched one of my guys like that, I'd pump them full of fucking lead.

But not Finley. Motherless, weak-ass pussy.

"Hey!" The feminine roar reached me as the elevator doors opened.

I fought a snigger and stepped out. Sounded like someone was pissed.

"You fucking asshole!" a scream followed, then the sound of shattering glass. *"How dare you talk to me like that!"*

I rounded the corner of the elevators to find...Finley fucking Salvatore with his hand around some brunette's throat. Anger flared at the sight, until I focused on his hand. There was no pressure in his grip. He was barely holding her. His splayed fingers were possessive against her neck.

Now that was interesting.

I took a step, missing his low murmur, until he warned, "You. Belong. To. *Me*. Don't you fucking get that by now?"

"No," the brunette bit back, her eyes wild. "I don't. I thought maybe we could be friends, but now I see I was wrong."

"*Just friends?*" he sneered. "Because your dad works for me?"

"He doesn't work *for* you."

"Yes...he *does*. And so do you. If you think I haven't thought about you every fucking day, then you're wrong. Two years, Anna. Two fucking years you've been there."

Two guys stepped out of the doorway behind me and glanced toward the commotion. The elevator doors opened, the blur of black drawing my gaze as Freddy and Logan stepped out. One glance from Freddy and a sigh, and I knew the fucker didn't want me here without someone having my back.

But it was Finley that seemed to be in a hell of a lot of trouble. I shifted my focus back to him.

Wow...pretty boy was all kinds of worked up.

"Look out, boys," I singsonged, drawing an audience. "What the fuck do we have here? Pretty boy has a brand new toy."

"But she still has her clothes on, Fin." I stepped closer, giving the brunette a once-over. "And I don't see the wads of cash near her snatch."

Rumor was, Salvatore's last desperate girlfriend liked him to whore her out. That said a lot more about him than it ever did about her.

Finley glanced my way, rage darkening his eyes.

"Nope." I fixed my attention on his little companion. "No money and all her clothes still on. Don't tell me you're losing your touch?"

"Fuck you, Lazarus."

I just gave a chuckle and motioned her forward. "Step aside, Finley, and let me see who's got the ice prince all worked up." But she didn't move, the quiet little thing. "Come out from there, little one. Don't be shy. I won't hurt you. Not unless you want me to. It's always the shy ones who want it fucking hard, isn't it, Fin? Always the pretty little unmarked ones who scream the loudest. Move aside, Fin...let me break her in for you."

Finley dropped his hand to his waist. His bodyguard, Max, and the dangerous-looking bastard he called Pavlov moved in an instant, drawing down. My men reacted instantly, too. Tension arced in the air like a live wire.

"*Whoa...*" I lifted my hand.

One step and I placed myself in full view. Look, I didn't fucking palm my gun. Back the fuck off, guys.

I licked my lips and glanced at the woman who had the Salvatore son in a bad fucking way. "This one's got you all riled up, hasn't she? Or is it just you, buddy? Just you with your moody fucking stare. What the hell are you doing here anyway, Salvatore? Didn't think this was your style."

"Walk, Rossi," Finley warned. "And keep on fucking walking."

Movement from the doorway jerked my attention toward the most stunning fucking redhead I'd ever seen in my life.

My heart hammered as I met her brown eyes. Something shifted inside me, something cold and aching. It couldn't have been my heart, that was for sure. Nothing made the beat in my heart boom like thunder, not unless it was a shotgun to my chest.

But that's exactly how she felt standing there, her black dress hugging her body. I licked my lips, forgetting for a second how to talk. "And who might you be, sweetheart?"

"Too expensive for you," she answered, shutting me down hard.

"Anna, stop!" Finley bellowed.

But the little brunette was fast as she scurried like a mouse away from him and tore along the hall. I saw it all in the corner of my eye, but I couldn't tear my gaze away from *her*...the stunning redhead who looked at me with a cold, savage glare. I took a step forward, keeping my voice low. "You know who I am?"

"Don't know and don't care." She sidestepped me, her focus on Finley and his fucking train wreck of a budding relationship.

I turned to watch her leave and crossed my arms over my chest. Fuck, the woman was cold. She just strode toward Freddy and Logan, who stood blocking the way, and in a careful, savage tone she commanded, "Move."

They did, glancing at me first before stepping to the side. Fuck me, she was magnificent. A stone-cold babe...and way out of my goddamn league. But Christ, that aching thing inside my chest demanded more. I licked my lips as Kilpatrick stumbled through the doorway.

"Look who it is," he slurred.

I cut him a glare and turned away. I didn't have time for his bullshit. But he followed my focus as the redhead disappeared around the corner of the hallway, heading to the elevators.

"Kat VanHalen, huh?" Kilpatrick sniggered, and stumbled, drunk, as usual. "She's too good for you, and you're too...*young* for her."

That savage part of me pushed to the surface as I jerked my gaze to his. "What the fuck are you talking about, Kilpatrick? Don't you have any more booze to drink? Just a fucking drunk... like your father."

Anger seethed in his eyes.

"Heard your dad likes to beat you," I pushed him, watching the sparks ignite in his eyes. "Heard he's a real fucking piece of work."

Kilpatrick grew still, so very fucking still, like a viper ready to strike. I let out a chuckle. A baby fucking viper, its fangs not yet fully grown and all that poison in its veins. "Go back to your party, Kilpatrick. Maybe there they'll swallow your big man fucking bullshit."

I turned to leave.

"One fucking day, Rossi," Kilpatrick warned softly.

I just laughed and kept on walking. I wasn't interested in petty fucking games, his or the fucking Commission's. The Rossis had a seat on the table, but it wasn't a seat given to us. We'd had to *earn it*. We'd had to bleed and fight and make fucking alliances with those we were sworn to hate.

Freddy and Logan fell in behind me as I strode to the elevator once more. The Cosa Nostra and the Stidda weren't friends and hadn't been for a long goddamn time. But to survive in this world...sometimes you had to make a deal with those you despised.

That fire still burned in my belly. A spark handed down from my great-grandfather to my grandfather, then to my father before burning in me. I punched the button for the elevator and waited for the doors to open. No, Stidda and Cosa Nostra weren't friends, we weren't even close. The Salvatores and the fucking Kilpatricks could huddle together like frightened little schoolgirls all they wanted.

But the Rossis...we stood alone.

Still, the redhead—the elevator doors opened and I strode inside—she was someone who could make this Rossi interested. I licked my lips. "Kat VanHalen," I murmured to Freddy. "What do you know about her?"

He just gave a snort. "I know she's rich and powerful and someone not to fucking mess with...especially for you."

"Why?" I snarled.

Freddy just met my gaze as the elevator came to a stop. "Nothing I know for sure, just rumors."

Rumors.

"What kind of rumors?" I dug, striding out.

The party from upstairs had spilled over into the foyer. Music poured from a portable speaker somewhere in the corner, laughter and the drone of conversation fought for attention. Heads turned toward me and eyes widened as I stepped out. But I didn't care about them. I cared about knowing more about the redhead.

"Nothing I want to say here." Freddy lowered his voice.

I strode through the crowd, ignoring their hushed conversations and careful gazes as I made my way out of the building. Kat VanHalen. I knew the name...Hell, *everyone* knew the fucking name. But holy shit. I didn't realize *that* was who a VanHalen was.

I left the party behind and headed for my own building, closer to the crash of the waves. Dad had wanted me to come here. Probably more because he thought here they could protect me —like they'd protected that asshole Baldeon.

The poor fucker hadn't even made it to the island without getting shot. I strode along the path and lifted my gaze to the bright lights of the buildings in the distance. Twice I'd come to this damn island and both times I'd fucking hated it. I hated their games and their goddamn alliances. I was a target more because of my name than anything else. They didn't know me, not the real me.

Not many people did.

My mind drifted to Taken...then to Iggy. Fuck me,. I still missed that dog. Missed him so much I wouldn't get another. No fucking way. I'd never be vulnerable like that again. For a damn mutt...*or for anyone.*

But as I made my way into the foyer of my own building and hit the button for the elevator, my thoughts returned to Kat VanHalen. "Freddy."

"Yeah?"

"I want to know everything you can find about her."

There was a groan and a shake of his head. "I was afraid you were going to say that."

Turned my head, I met the flare of concern in his eyes with a steely glare. "Every fucking thing, leave nothing out."

I wanted everything...where that fiery redhead was concerned.

————————————————

12

Kat

————————————————

"Goodnight," Anna muttered, and yawned. She still had that haunted look from the events of tonight.

I lifted my gaze from the bed and gave her a smile. "Night."

I need your help.

Her words still rang in my head as she shuffled away from the doorway and disappeared into her room. How many times had I been desperate to say the exact same thing? *I need your help... someone save me.* But there'd been no white knight coming to my rescue, and no dad who raged, thinking I was in trouble. But Anna did. She had what I'd pay anything for. Someone who actually cared about her.

I'd found her after she'd run from Finley tonight, found her shaking, her eyes wide. She was breathless, with a look of utter shock in her eyes. She gave me enough to go on and as Finley charged from the building after her, incensed with desperation and lust, I guessed the rest for myself.

Anna Eden wasn't just running from Finley.

She was also running from herself.

The sheets in her room rustled, and a low sigh escaped.

I waited until she was quiet and soft snores came out of her bedroom, then I slipped from my bed and strode toward my closet. The dress I had planned to wear tonight was thin...*really thin.* I slipped off my bra and pulled the sheer black material over my head before I turned. Helping Anna didn't help me. I swallowed a flare of jealousy, which was stupid coming from someone with my last name. Sometimes being rich and powerful was a danger.

No one wanted to help you when you stood out. No one wanted to keep you safe. You were watched by everyone else as they sat on the sidelines while the beast ripped you apart.

I bent, picked up my heels, and carried them as I tiptoed toward the elevator. I knew about this place they called the Cosa Nostra Institute, and it wasn't the classes that had me intrigued. It was the deals made when the sun went down, the alliances and lies earned and bargained. It was the games they played in selected buildings. The games where they didn't barter for money...but for power.

I was desperate enough to try.

I stepped into the elevator and rode down to the foyer before slipping my heels back on. Anna would be fast asleep and after the night she'd had, I doubted if she'd wake up. She'd never know I was gone. That was the plan, anyway.

I grabbed my phone and found Xael's number, typing out a message:

What building are the cards at?

Then I hit send.

I walked and waited, checking my screen before the *beep*.

Xael: Building six, top floor, ask for Bruno.

Bruno. Bruno Bernardi. It had to be.

I stepped along the footpath, lifting my gaze as one of the island's armed guards crossed my path.

"Ma'am." He gave a nod and kept on moving.

I hurried, glancing over my shoulder before turning back. Building six, it wasn't far from ours, set back further on the island and away from the dock where we'd disembarked. Lights spilled around the dark curtains on the top floor. I hurried toward the building, stepping up to the door and the guard who waited inside.

"Ma'am," he acknowledged me.

"I'm here to see Bruno?"

A nod and he strode toward the elevator, swiped his wristband across the sensor, and motioned me inside as the doors opened. I stepped in, nerves fluttering in my belly. I had no idea what to do now. No idea who to ask or what to ask for. Not for murder...*but to disappear?* Maybe.

The thought rolled around in my head as the elevator rose.

The closer I came, the more the butterflies trapped in my belly churned.

When the doors opened, a sharp bark of laughter tore free.

There was a guard standing beside the elevator. His cold, careful eyes swept over me. Okay, so that wasn't expected. I looked down and kept on walking. It was an apartment, but not one like ours. Bedrooms branched off on the left and the whole right side was set out in one sprawling room, with what looked like to be more bedrooms further along. It was bigger than ours, at least double the size.

Double the size, with an exclusive feel.

Black leather sofas sat on the left and against the glass wall looking out into the night.

There were guys there, drinking and talking, with soft, dim lights caressing the women draped over their laps.

One of them lifted his gaze and looked at me, his hand gripping a blonde's thigh.

I kept walking, past the kitchen and into what was the game room. The moment I saw the card table, my stomach clenched and a cold wash of fear gripped me. My steps hesitated and my pulse raced. I was going to be sick. *Jesus, I was going to be...*

"Hey there, would you like a glass of champagne?"

I jerked my gaze to a waiter and smiled, fighting the urge to scream. "Sure," I answered, and grabbed a glass from the tray.

Heads turned when I stepped closer, cards were splayed out on the table. The chips were ten-thousand dollars and bigger. Women were here, some I recognized, most I didn't. I was guessing they were shipped in from the mainland specifically for the party. There was another card table to the right, past the kitchen. I strode between them, catching sight of perky bare breasts of one woman with her hand buried in an open zipper, and another on her knees in the corner, naked with her legs spread.

A surge of heat washed over me.

Dark deeds and darker corners.

The place reeked of seduction and sex.

And power, we mustn't forget the power.

"Keep walking."

The low growl at my ear made me flinch. A chill washed through me as I started to turn, until a cruel grip on the back of my neck stopped me. "You want to do as you're told, Katerina."

Katerina.

My knees trembled as my name was used as a weapon.

All of a sudden, I was a kid again.

A kid helpless to fight.

A kid with no control.

"Move." The grip around the back of my neck clenched tighter, driving me forward.

"You don't have to..."

"Shut the fuck up and walk."

He drove me forward, past the poker tables and the naked women, toward the darkened bedrooms.

"At the end of the hall."

I turned with the pressure of his thumb and stumbled forward into the darkness of the bedroom before I was pushed.

My heels clattered as I tried to catch my fall. The light flared, filling the room with soft amber light.

"What the hell," I gasped as something sailed through the air and landed on the bed next to me.

Something that filled me with terror.

Something from my past.

I stared at the white mask facing up at me, my world spinning out of control.

"You think they'd just let you come without being watched?"

I jerked my gaze to the guy standing against the doorjamb. He was tall...gorgeous, with eyes that shone with malice.

"Who the fuck are you?"

He just smiled. "Your new boyfriend, didn't you know?"

Boyfriend? "No."

His killer smile sickened me. He strode forward, grabbed me around the throat, and whispered, "You will do as I say, Katerina."

"Kat," I spat through clenched teeth. "And *get your fucking hands off me.*"

"You think I don't know your every dirty little secret? You think I won't go out there and expose you to the entire penthouse filled with people? You actually came here thinking you could escape someone like Haelstrom? You really are a stupid fucking cunt."

My heart hammered, fear and rage a noxious cocktail in my veins.

"You want to hit me?" He smiled and moved closer, so close I saw the amber of his stare. "Try it and see how far you get."

He lifted a hand, moving faster than I could see as he gripped my jaw and clenched, forcing my mouth open.

"Stop it!" I roared. *"Get the fuck OFF ME!"*

The moment I opened my mouth, he dropped something inside. One lungful of air, and I swallowed and coughed.

"There," he sneered. "That should make you a little more compliant."

Fear plunged deep, cutting through me like an arctic wind. I sucked in a breath and jerked my gaze to his. "What the fuck was that?"

He just shoved me away, smiling.

"What the fuck did you just give me?" I stumbled backwards and whipped my gaze toward the bathroom.

I need to throw up.

I need to throw up.

I need—

"Whoa there." The asshole who looked like a piece-of-shit version of Shawn Mendes chuckled and lunged, barring the doorway.

I just lashed out, clawing and hitting, charging against him. "Get the fuck out of my way...*get out of my way!*"

He just grabbed me and spun, turning me around until he wound his long arms across me, holding me like a straitjacket against his chest. "Can't let you do that, Katerina."

Tears sprung to my eyes as he wrestled me. "Get out of my way." The words were thick and strange.

I tried to lift my hand, tried to shove my finger down my throat, not caring if I vomited all over him or the floor. But he grabbed my wrist in a cruel grip and forced it to my side.

"What the fuck did you give me?" I whimpered as the room started to spin.

"Just a little something to help calm you down."

"No..." I cried. "No...*no...no.*"

"I have to protect you, Katerina," he whispered in my ear. "Because you're far too precious to let go."

The amber glow of the bedroom blurred. All I saw was that white mask on the end of the bed as the fight went out of me and my arms went slack.

"That's the way," he murmured. I didn't even know who *he* was.

"Damon," he answered, as though I'd asked the question. Maybe I had? "Damon Zakharov."

I tried to focus on my breathing as the room faded, then sharpened.

"You're going to be a good girl, aren't you, Katerina?"

Breathe.

Breathe.

Breathe...

"Because if you don't, do you know what will happen? Hale will happen...and he'll be angry."

I clenched my insides. Fear was heavy in my belly.

"That's the way." He relaxed his grip, letting my hands flop to my sides. "That's much better. You're going to be my new girl-friend, aren't you, Katerina?"

You remember Mr. Hale?

My father's words resounded in my head, birthed from a life-time of nightmares. "Yes," I answered. "Whatever you need."

He chuckled, this man...Damon...*Hale.* They were all the same. Taking...taking...taking.

"Now, you'll come with me and enjoy the party...*and you'll do exactly as you're told.*"

I could only nod, only watch as he strode forward and picked up the white mask from the bed and slipped it back inside his jacket.

"Now," he ordered.

My feet moved on their own, my body no longer mine to control. It was all his now. All Hale's.

He opened the door and waited. I lowered my head and swayed as I walked.

"Easy," he growled. 'I don't want them thinking I drugged you."

I lifted my gaze to his. *But you did.*

A jerk of his head and I forced myself to focus, taking one step at a time as I walked back along the hallway and toward the card table. Faces blurred. I saw my father and his friends. I saw their greed and their...*their...their...*

"Keep walking," he growled. "I want everyone to see Katerina VanHalen is mine."

I kept my gaze fixed straight ahead, letting him lead me by the arm toward the kitchen.

"Look who it is."

I tried to focus on my breaths and the way the room seemed to roll before I lifted my gaze. Hard, cold eyes met mine from the black sofa. I knew him...I'd seen him before. Arrogant. Dangerous...*gorgeous*.

"Lazarus," Hale called. "Lazarus Rossi."

The cocky asshole tore his gaze from mine to meet Hale's. "I know you?"

"Damon...Damon Zakharov." *That's right, not Hale. Damon.*

But the sprawled-out thug just shifted his gaze to mine.

And Damon noticed.

"You know Katerina?" Damon glanced from Lazarus to me.

"Briefly."

"No," I answered at the same time.

Damon just smiled, his eyes glinting with the kind of look that made me cower. "She's beautiful, right?"

Lazarus said nothing, just watched me as Damon ran his hand down the side of my breast. "He's looking at you like you're his."

I couldn't look away from him.

His stare nailed me where I stood.

Possessive.

Carnal.

Hungry.

God, he was so hungry.

Like he would eat me alive.

"And you're shaking...like a bitch in heat. You want to fuck him, Katerina?"

But that's not what I wanted...not really. *Yes,* a small voice broke through the fog in my head. *Yes you do. Look at him. Look...at...him.*

"Go on, then," Damon growled. "Make him look at you."

He shoved me forward so that I stumbled. I caught the spark of rage in Lazarus's gaze as he curled his lips. Damon lifted his head to someone else in the room. "Turn up the music."

No one argued and the slow, throbbing beat grew louder.

"You look bored, Rossi. You also can't take your eyes off my girlfriend."

The chiffon material rubbed across my breasts as I inhaled. Here in the cool night with the dull amber glow, I was betting it was almost transparent. The material clung to my body.

"You look like a man who enjoys a good lap dance. So, give him one, Katerina."

Kat.

Not Katerina.

To Damon it was...it was always Katerina. *But not to Lazarus.*

I could see the burn in his eyes...so hot like he'd burn me alive. A tremor of cold cut through my core. I wanted to feel that heat, to dance in the flames of his hunger. I took a step forward.

"That's the way," Damon urged.

But I wasn't listening to him anymore. I wasn't hearing a thing he said. The room seemed to blur, and took my tormentor with it.

I don't know why...the song by Avion pulsed around the room. Lazarus held my gaze as I stepped closer. There was an emptiness inside me, a hollow pit I'd made into a home long ago. But in that moment, I saw the same in him. The same hurt. The same anger. The same...*need*.

Could he be the one?

All I felt was the music making me sway my hips.

All I saw was his perfect blue eyes.

Eyes I could get lost in.

I grasped the hem of my dress and lifted a knee, sliding it across his lap.

Damon spoke, but I no longer listened.

Right here and now...I wasn't the woman he knew. I was someone else, someone free...someone *whole*. I kept my gaze locked on Lazarus. He made no move to touch me. Something inside me exhaled with desire at that, and I rocked my hips, rolling and moving over his body. I lifted my hand, captured my hair, and felt my nipples pebble under the thin fabric. I didn't want him touching me. I wanted for once to be in control.

The fabric tightened as I splayed my thighs and the split moved upwards.

Lazarus lowered his gaze to my bare thigh.

It was just us.

Just him...

Me...

And the music.

As I rocked my hips lower, I felt his cock. Hard. Straining against his jeans, rubbing against me. I stared into his eyes and felt my own body come alive. Heat bloomed inside me. I was sick...sick and corrupt. Burning up from the inside. Desire swept me away as I envisioned us...*alone,* with no clothes as a barrier and no one else here. I hated myself in that moment... and loved the way he made me feel.

I reached for my breasts, fingers grazed my hard nipple. He watched everything as I trailed my hand lower, over my stomach until I pressed the thin material against my sex.

I wanted him here, *ached* to feel him inside. That need grew stronger as I curled my finger and pressed harder, finding my clit. My orgasm was brewing, seething and growling, like a beast of its own. I'd come riding him like this...come all over this pretty, blue-eyed Mafia Prince.

"Come on, Kat," Damon growled in my ear. "*Now.*"

He grabbed my arm, the grip not as cruel as it was before.

But rage flashed in Lazarus's eyes as I was dragged off him.

Darkness caught my gaze. There was a wet patch at the front of his jeans, right in the place where I'd rubbed him.

My G-string was soaked. I knew that sodden fabric wasn't him...*it was me.*

I'd never felt like that, never wanted someone like I wanted him.

That crude, savage Mafia Prince.

"Katerina," Damon barked, his dark eyes glinting with rage.

But the music and the connection to that blue-eyed mobster burned away the dull hold of the drug. I turned, shoving Damon's hand from my arm. "Don't fucking touch me!"

There was movement from the sofa as Lazarus rose.

But I was already moving, tearing away from all of them and racing for the elevator.

I didn't stop, with my heels in my hand and tears in my eyes, I raced back to our building...*alone.*

13

Lazarus

I wanted to go after her. To grab that piece of shit by the neck and hurl him from the fucking balcony. But as she ran, I realized I didn't need to. I lowered my hand to my aching cock and felt the wetness.

Not mine...*hers.*

Damon stopped in the middle of the room and turned, eying my hand as I palmed my length through my jeans.

"Your girlfriend, huh?" I growled and sneered. "We'll see about that."

He said nothing, just stared at me, thinking his height intimidated me.

I laughed. I'd taken down guys bigger than him.

And left them broken.

I strode past him and punched the button for the elevator. I'd come to learn more about her. I'd come because I didn't like what Freddy was saying, that Kat VanHalen was already spoken for by someone a lot more powerful than me.

If that was the case, then why the hell was she on the island… and why the fuck was she with a weak-ass bitch like *him?*

Something wasn't right when it came to her. Call it a sixth sense, or my throbbing cock. Call it the fact that I hadn't felt anything as strong as I felt for her in my whole goddamn life. She'd hit me like a baseball bat right between the eyes. I stepped into the elevator and stabbed the button, watching Damon whoever-the-fuck-he-was eyefuck me from across the room.

I gave him a smirk as the doors closed.

Cold night air hit me as I strode out the front doors of Bernardi's building and headed back to mine. The wet patch on the front of my jeans was icy, pressing against my dick, drawing my focus to the fact that I wore her arousal like a badge of fucking honor.

I wanted more.

A lot more.

I strode back to my building and caught the elevator, thinking about it. The TV was still on, that ugly fucker Freddy sitting on the sofa, not really watching the movie that was playing.

"Have fun?" he muttered.

"I did, actually."

One brow rose as he glanced my way. "Are you feeling okay?"

I just chuckled as his gaze slipped to the front of my jeans. "You look at my cock like that again, Freddy, and I'm gonna start to spoon you at night."

His bark of laughter tore through the space. He hit the remote and ended the movie before rising from the sofa. "Goodnight, Laz."

"Night, asshole." I responded.

He strode to his room that was right next to Logan's. Some others didn't like their bodyguards sharing the same floor, others like Finley Salvatore. But these guys weren't just my bodyguards. They were my brothers. My eyes and ears. My fucking friends. I wanted them around.

I went to my room, peeling my shirt free, and unbuttoned my jeans. *I wonder what she tasted like?*

I shook my head and shoved down my jeans as I headed to the shower. Then I stopped. *What did she taste like…I was betting she was fucking delicious.* I glanced over my shoulder at the crumpled blue denim on the floor.

My cock twitched as I let out a growl and turned back, snatching the jeans from the floor. I had to fucking know. I licked my lips. I had to find out if she tasted as good as she looked.

I lifted the material and breathed deep. The scent of her arousal clung heavy to the thick fabric. Every drop was still there. I closed my eyes and opened my mouth, sliding the denim across my lips. I could still feel her grinding on me, still see the way her fucking dress clung to her breasts.

I could still see the way she'd looked at me.

I sucked the material harder, wetting it with saliva to mix with the tang of her desire. *Fuck me.* I wanted her pussy. I wanted it more than I'd ever wanted a pussy in my fucking life. I held the jeans against my mouth and reached down, rubbing my hand across the swollen head and felt myself jerk.

No.

I wouldn't relieve the ache. I'd carry it with me. I opened my eyes and lowered my jeans, finding the wet patch wetter than it was before. I sucked her taste clean before I dropped the jeans back to the floor with a snarl and stepped into the shower.

She haunted me.

Clinging to the back of my tongue.

And to my thoughts as I washed, dried, and climbed into bed.

Sleep didn't come easy. It never did. But this time when I dreamed, this time I dreamed of her.

I WATCHED them in class the next day. I couldn't take my eyes off them. On the surface, everything looked normal. She even let him put his arm around her shoulders possessively. I wanted to rip the fucking thing off and beat him to death with it.

But I didn't.

I sat back and watched them like my life depended on it. But it wasn't my life I was playing with...it was my heart. She only smiled when others focused on them. She was frozen the rest of the time. I caught her scanning the others as she stood outside the classroom with the asshole standing at her side and laughing with a group of rich pricks. But she wasn't interested in them, she was searching for someone else.

Was she looking for me?

I stepped out of the shadows and our gazes connected. A surge of adrenaline coursed through me as I stepped closer. Her lips parted. The dumb fucking asshole next to her was oblivious as I strode toward them.

But she wasn't.

Her eyes widened as I came near, and there was a catch of her breath. Her black blouse pressed against her breasts. Breasts I wanted in my fucking mouth and I'd shoot that fucker in the face to get them. But I did none of those things. I just held her gaze while her boyfriend was fucking oblivious and strode past her into the classroom.

Don't do it.

The warning floated through my mind.

She's not yours.

But, fuck me.

I turned to see her striding through the door. The fucking idiot walking behind her was still chatting to his homies, fucking oblivious she was the one now hunting me.

I sat in the top row of some bullshit lecture. I didn't even pay the lecturer any mind. Everyone knew the Rossis were a pain in the ass. I had a reputation to live up to. She sat mid-row, closest to me.

"Okay, settle down everyone," an older guy called from the front of the room.

But she just glanced over her shoulder and met my gaze.

There was a desperation in her eyes...*a need for something I couldn't catch.*

It wasn't just sex.

The way her eyes traveled down my body and lingered on my cock told me that was part of it. But there was a dulled emptiness in her eyes that *screamed.* I shifted in my seat as the lecturer started drawing Damon's attention.

He turned his head and caught me staring at Kat, and her at me. Then the asshole put his arm around her shoulders. She stiffened at the contact, and that howl of desperation in her eyes remained.

She's not your problem.

I bit my lip and urged her.

Give me a goddamn sign and I'll change that.

But she didn't. She just sat there, looking at me with that torment.

The kind I saw in myself.

14

Kat

Help me.

I stared at the Stidda Prince before Damon shoved against my shoulder. "Eyes front, Katerina."

That brutal fist inside me clenched tighter. In the dull, sickening feeling of this morning, the events of last night came flooding back.

The mask.

The drug.

The dance.

My heart hammered as I shifted my focus back to the front of the room and tried to listen to the lecturer. But I couldn't. Not with the memory of the drug in my mind. I'd felt sick this morning. Terrified and frantic, like a cornered beast.

I couldn't let him drug me again. I'd do anything...*anything* to stop that from happening. I glanced at Damon next to me, who just turned and gave me a cover-model smile. On the outside he looked so perfect. Kind, respectful, honest even. But if there was one thing I knew with certainty, it was that monsters could hide in plain sight.

And he *was* a monster, there was no arguing that.

One of the worst kinds.

The kind who manipulates, who controls. I could still feel his hand around my throat, still feel that *ravenous need*. Desperation thrummed inside me. I fought the urge to turn and look at the blue-eyed enigma. Only, to do that would be to draw attention to us.

Attention I didn't need.

So, I focused on the lecturer in front of me, and slipped behind my mask.

I barely heard a thing he said, shaking myself out of the reverie as the rest of the class started to move.

"Come on," Damon commanded, rising to stand. "I'll walk you back to your apartment."

"No." The word came out harsh and loud.

Movement came behind me. I was aware of him, the Stidda Prince. His energy pulsed against my skin, his heat flowed through me. I waited for the disgust to settle inside me, waited for that clench in my stomach, that vile, rancid taste of my own private torture.

But there was none of that when I thought of him.

"Kat...*now*."

I jerked my gaze toward Damon as he waited at the end of the row of seats. I shuffled closer, pushing past him as I headed for the door.

He grabbed me, his fingers digging into my arm. I whipped my gaze around, desperation roaring in my veins as I met his stare. "Get your fucking hands off me."

One quick glance around us, then he leaned closer, those brown eyes shimmering. "Or what?" he pushed. "You going to claw me?"

"Hey, guys."

Damon straightened, the smile instant as one of the other women strode up. "You guys hear Baldeon is getting out of the infirmary?"

"No," Damon answered, his focus sharpening like a shark who scented blood in the water. "I didn't. Sounds like a cause for celebration if you ask me."

"Ha!" she barked, and kept on walking. "So, your place at eight then?"

My pulse quickened as he hollered, "Spread the word!"

There was a second, then the snake shifted its focus back to me. "Here that, Katerina? A party at my place. I think it'll be good for us to be seen together. For everyone to know...just how much you mean to me."

He reached for a stray strand of my hair, tucking it behind my ear.

I couldn't fight the flinch as he touched me.

But he didn't care. He didn't even seem to notice. Instead, his eyes glazed over as he smiled. "Yes, I think I like that idea very much."

"Kat?"

I jerked my gaze toward Anna's voice as she came around the corner. Relief swept through me. I used the distraction to step away.

"I was just coming to find you." I forced a smile and hurried over to her, winding my arm through hers. "I've neglected you a little today."

"Katerina," Damon called.

But I pushed Anna forward, desperately driving her along the hall and toward the stairs. "I'll catch you later!" I threw over my shoulder.

I didn't stop, didn't look. With my heart driving into the back of my throat, I hurried her down the stairs and toward the front door of the building.

"Why the rush?" She looked at me with concern.

"Need to pee," I lied.

"You do that a lot, you know. You must have a weak bladder," she mused.

"Probably." I hurried her through the doors and out into the dimming sunlight.

I'd spent all day under the controlling fist of Damon Zakharov, all day with my knees weak and my panic screaming, all day trying to work out how I couldn't get out of this without being drugged or *worse*.

"You okay?" Anna murmured. "You've got that look again."

That look.

That was the real me.

The one hidden behind the mask.

"Painful bladder," I whimpered, and hurried toward our building in the distance.

"So, I heard there's another party." She shook her head. "Is that what it's going to be, partying every night?"

"What else is there to do?" I forced a smile.

"We're going, aren't we?" she grumbled, rolling her eyes.

If I didn't...he'd come after me. If I ran, he'd hunt me down. If I stayed in plain sight like the meek little plaything he thought I was, then maybe...maybe I'd get out of this somehow.

I'd do anything.

Just not drugged.

Not again.

"We sure are," I answered. "And you're going to look like a knockout."

"No," she disagreed, and shook her head. "No more heels, not tonight. This time I'm going in jeans."

"Jesus, Anna." I groaned. "At least add a designer blouse or something."

She just laughed as we strode into the foyer. I ran for the bathroom as soon as I stepped off the elevator. But it wasn't just my bladder that was clenched tight. I used the toilet, then gripped the basin, lifting my gaze to the stranger in the mirror.

The one who'd been desperate enough to come to this place for protection.

And walked straight into the Devil's lair.

"You can do this," I whispered to my reflection. "It's not like you haven't spent your entire life with those men."

But the woman staring back at me wasn't so sure. Once she could have survived.

But everything's changed now.

My world.

My purpose.

My fear.

I pushed backwards and went into my bedroom, picking out the clothes I'd wear tonight before heading into the shower.

"You look stunning, Kat," Anna said when I reappeared, her eyes widening as she leaned against the kitchen counter.

"All part of the lie, isn't it?" I smiled, taking the sting out of the words.

More like taking the truth out of them.

But Anna stilled, and swallowed. "I don't know what you mean."

"Of course you don't." I stepped closer and grabbed the glass of champagne from beside her, taking a sip before putting it back down.

"Are you ready for this?" she asked.

No, not really.

"Sure," I answered, and glanced at the night sky through the window.

All day I'd felt this dread.

This *weight* pressing down on me.

One I was unable to get out from under.

That weight grew heavier as Anna pushed off the counter.

So heavy, my shoulders sagged.

But I forced myself forward, catching up to her at the elevators.

Waiting for partying, happy Kat to appear.

"You've got that look again."

I forced my smile wider. "Just family stuff."

She left it at that, not probing any harder, not digging any deeper.

One scratch of this glittering surface and the ruin would appear.

I stepped onto the elevator and followed her all the way out into the night. The faint sound of music grew louder as we neared. I breathed the salty air deep as my steps grew slower. Damon's building was a beacon in the distance, the lights strobing, the music thumping.

But as we came closer, I caught movement from the corner of my eye.

Lazarus Rossi leaned against Damon's building, drawing deep on a cigarette before flicking it end over end toward the grass.

"You go on ahead," I murmured to Anna. "I'll be up there soon."

She jerked a panicked gaze from Lazarus to me and scowled. "You sure you want to do this?"

"I'm sure," I answered, and waited.

Lazarus just watched me with those tempestuous blue eyes.

"Okay then." She took a step before stopping. "If you're not up in ten minutes, I'm going to come looking."

Then she left, striding toward the doorway and a small group of people who headed toward her from the opposite side. He waited until we were alone before moving, pushing his body from the wall and turning toward me.

The moment he did that, the thrumming in my veins grew stronger.

Tell him.

Tell him the truth.

"I seem to have a problem where you're concerned, redhead." Lazarus stepped closer, hard muscles rolling with his graceful stride. He lifted his hand and combed back sandy blonde hair from his face. "The kind of problem that's keeping me up at night."

He was threatening as he walked.

All malice and murder.

All vicious and violent.

Tell him!

That roaring in my head wouldn't stop.

I was rooted to the spot as he strode closer, so close I caught the blue and black in his eyes.

So close he could touch me.

So close he could hear.

He wanted me...that much I knew.

But would he want me if he knew the truth?

Would he want me...if I was pregnant?

15

Lazarus

"You're a real problem for me, redhead."

She said nothing as I stalked forward, just stood there looking like perfection and sin. Her wide brown eyes shone almost black in the wash of the building's light.

"Did you hear what I said?" I questioned, stopping right in front of her.

"I heard."

"And you're what...just going to let me suffer?"

"Why not?" she answered. "We all suffer. Why should you be any different?"

"Ouch," I murmured, and lifted my hand.

She flinched for a second before she caught herself. Still, I caught the movement. *Kat VanHalen, billionaire heiress, flinches when someone raises a hand.* Something inside me clenched. I didn't like that...didn't like it at all. I didn't like that she was with that asshole. I didn't like the look of him, didn't like that he was here.

Rich pretty-boys shouldn't come here. I licked my lips and drank in the glint of her eyes. Nor should women like Kat. She should be safe at home, not here amongst men like me.

"You want me to suffer, princess?" I repeated, and lowered my hand. "How about I keep replaying last night over in my head. But I'm thinking I'm not the only one who took enjoyment from that."

"You're wrong," she answered coldly.

I just smiled. "Wrong, huh?" There was nothing *wrong* about being turned on and we *both* knew she had been. "I don't think so, princess. I know you felt something last night. If that's the case, then why the fuck are you with that goddamn loser?"

She blanched at the words, and the spark in her eyes dulled.

"You love that fucking joker?" I growled, hating the desperate edge in my tone.

She didn't answer, which only incensed me more. I couldn't stop the need in me, couldn't douse the flames. "Tell me and I'll back the fuck off. Tell me you fucking love him...or do you just like being treated like that? Is that it, you like being used, princess?"

Fuck me, I hated the thought of that, but I hated not having her even more.

Let it be me.

Anything she needed.

However it burned.

But she didn't answer, just looked at me as the stars in her eyes died.

She turned, lowered her gaze, and strode away, the sound of her heels like the racking of a shotgun. *You fucking idiot!* The words howled in my head as she strode through the doors of the apartment building and disappeared. I licked my lips and considered another cigarette. Christ, I felt so off balance around her, like I didn't know how to behave.

Do I go after her...?

Or do I just walk away?

The thought of that...of never knowing how her lips tasted...or how she felt wrapped around my cock, made an inferno rage inside me. "Fuck it," I growled, and went after her.

"Rossi."

I jerked my gaze toward the voice as Bruno Bernardi strode toward me. "Bernardi."

He lifted his gaze to the sound of the party. "So, Marco's out," he said, his thick Irish accent making me fucking focus. "I can't wait for the asshole to start his shit."

"Just like last time," I muttered.

"Fucking A," he sighed, and pushed ahead, forcing the automatic doors to open.

I followed him inside, waiting at the elevators. The music was loud when they opened. I couldn't stop myself from looking for her, just finding her roommate, the brunette who had Finley Salvatore all worked up, lounging in the corner of a sofa all by herself.

But she was looking toward the bedrooms...and scowling. I searched the crowded room for the pretty-boy asshole, and didn't find him. There was only one fucking place they would be. Finley's target glanced toward me as I strode toward the closed doors at the other end of the apartment, feeling that savage part of me rise.

She's not your problem, that voice warned.

But I wanted to change that...and I wanted to change it *now*.

————————————————————

16

Kat

————————————————————

You like that? You like to be used?

Revulsion rolled in my stomach. I wanted to be sick. I wanted to run...but I couldn't, because I'd run here, hadn't I? I'd run, and like a stupid fucking fool, I thought I'd be able to figure this out. I thought...

What had I fucking thought?

Hoped, more like it.

I'd hoped that all men weren't cruel, cold, and manipulative. I'd hoped that I might find someone who'd help me. I dropped my hand to my stomach and strode into the elevator. Someone who'd help me decide what to do. It wasn't too late yet, I could abort the baby. But the moment the thought rose in my mind, something inside me snarled with protection.

It wasn't *Hale's...it was mine.*

My body.

My baby.

My desperate need to figure a way out of this.

The elevator doors opened and I lowered my hand to my side, fake smile on. Here was happy Kat. Here was the party girl everyone knew. Here was the mask…

"Hey, Kat!" someone called.

I just waved and kept going, scanning the room for Anna.

"Wasn't sure you'd show."

I froze at the sickening sound of his voice and fought the need to run. Fire sparked inside me. The tiny flame I clung to, even as it fought being smothered by fear. Instead, I clutched hold of that tiny spark and turned. "You seem to make it a habit of coming up behind my back, Damon."

I glared at the sonofabitch. Anyone else would see him as handsome, as the boy next door, high school quarterback, heart-melting guy. But he wasn't any of those things. He was a liar, a manipulative, cruel, drug-a girl-to-get-her-to-have-sex-with-you piece of shit. The kind I'd known my entire life.

He thought he was a Hale in the making.

But he wasn't…*he'd never be.*

Men like Haelstrom Hale didn't need to drug you to fuck you. He groomed you into thinking it was what you wanted all along. But I stared into Damon's eyes and saw that raw savagery, that need to consume and control and *break.*

"Maybe you like being taken from behind, Kat." He stepped closer and my skin crawled. He lifted his hand and brushed the hair back from my cheek. "I've waited long enough."

He moved like a serpent, lashing out to grasp my hand and drag me with him.

Fight! That voice roared inside. *Fight him. Yell. Scream. Find the nearest gun and* kill *the* MOTHERFUCKER!

I caught sight of Anna as she turned her head and saw Damon pulling me past her.

"Kat?" she murmured, frowning.

There was panic in her eyes, fear even. I thought of her, and the friendship we had. If she knew the real me, she'd change. If she knew who I was behind the pretense and the lies, our friendship would change. Agony slammed into my chest at the thought. I couldn't have that. I couldn't ruin the one good thing I had. *Because right now she was all I had.*

So I smiled, gave her a wink that made something inside me clench with disgust, and kept walking, following Damon into the bedroom before he closed the door. My heart was pounding. Tremors shook me with sickness and fear.

"I've waited long enough," Damon slurred.

I jerked my gaze to his, catching the full glass in his hand and the glassy stare in his eyes. He was drunk, *really drunk.*

I could use that. I could play my part...*a little, at least.*

"Fuck you, Damon," I growled, stoking that flame inside me a little harder. "Fuck you and your piece of shit friends. Hale..." Just his name on my lips made me want to vomit. "You're all beasts."

Damon just smiled and lifted his glass. "Beasts you fuck, little girl."

Little girl.

Piece of fucking shit. I closed my eyes as the rage inside me burned brighter. The brush of his hand on my shoulder made me want to scream like a banshee. It made me want to lash out, and hit...and keep on hitting. It made me want to find that gun hidden in my closet and empty it into his goddamn face.

It made me want to come to a damn island for protection.

The kind that didn't exist.

The hard yank on my zipper wrenched me backwards. "The beast you're going to fuck now. You don't want me to drug you again, do you? Because you know I will."

I swallowed a shudder and tried to speak.

"I'll drug you and fuck you and when I'm finished fucking you, I'll watch someone else fuck you," he growled and jerked my dress to the floor, leaving me in my underwear. "Because you are nothing but a *cunt*. Nothing but a thing to be broken, to be used in any way I want. Just like your daddy uses you and all his friends. How did that feel growing up, Katerina? To know you're nothing more than a commodity? To be used to secure the kind of deals that built your daddy's empire? You're the gift that keeps on giving, aren't you?" He reached around and grasped my breasts, kneading them with cruel hands. "You're the shining fucking star that's a whole universe. The one that I'm going to have."

"Unless Hale kills you for hurting me," I whispered.

He stopped, his fingers at my nipple. There was a second where he thought of that, where he tried to figure out just the kind of man Haelstrom Hale was. Desperation roared inside me, forcing me to turn and stare into his gaze. "You don't know him like I do. He'll be angry...*no, he'll be fucking furious.*"

The glimmer of panic in his eyes made that hope inside me soar.

He just lifted his lips.

If I could get him to change his mind...to see just how enraged Hale would be if he touched me.

"He's claimed me," I insisted. Revulsion burned through me at the words, but I had to do something. "You know how possessive he is. He'll kill any man who thinks he can use what belongs to him."

"You're lying," he growled, and lifted the glass once more.

"Am I?" I turned in his arms.

He glared down at me, but his focus was a little *off,* like he was thinking about it in his pathetic, inebriated state. I pounced on that glimmer of panic. "He's a monster," I swore. "You don't know the real man...the one behind the mask. He's ruthless and savage, and he'll tear you apart."

There was a bark of false laughter. "Fuck that, I know Hale." Still, he drained his glass before he focused that cruel gaze on me. "And I know you, Katerina. I know how you fuck because I've seen you."

He took a step and pushed me backwards toward the bed. I made the mistake of looking behind me and throwing out my hand. I hit the bed *hard.* My teeth clashed, shooting agony through my head.

"I've seen you over and over and over..." he growled, climbing onto the bed, straddling me. "You were a little younger, I must admit. But fuck me, you were spectacular. The things you let them do to you...the things you let *my father* do to you."

A mewl escaped. I tried to shake off the terror. But it was there, driving into my world. Men behind masks. Their hands touching me, pulling at my clothes, their sickening words in my ears. My mind tried to shut it out, tried to block all the disgusting things they'd done to me from my world.

My mind tried to help me survive.

But as Damon crawled higher, looming over me, he brought it all back in a rush. I looked up at him and saw those same merciless eyes as the man behind the mask, and heard the same words. "Take off your clothes, Katerina. Take them off and open your legs."

No...no. I can't...I can't...

Damon swayed and his elbow buckled before he pushed up once more.

That last glass of alcohol was hitting him harder than before.

"I'm going to make you scream," he mumbled. "Over and over...*and over again.*"

There was nothing else I could do now. Nothing that would stop this. Nothing that would *save me.*

Until something inside me took control.

The panic eased. The terror slipped away. I became *Katerina.*

The version of me that was *nothing.* That was *empty.* That was *used.*

I became a shallow version of myself. The one who reached the doorway of my family home and stepped through into the dark.

The one who obeyed my father when he asked me to fetch him cigars and whiskey. The one who listened to the heavy thud of men following behind me all the way to the bedroom.

The one who was sold, and traded, and *whored.*

It was that woman who reached for him...who took control. "You want me?" The words slipped free, but they weren't my words anymore.

They were hers.

"You want me how your father had me?"

Greed glittered in his eyes as Damon rocked back.

"Yeah," her words continued. "I can see you do. Roll over. Watch me as you take every piece of me. Stare into my eyes as you take me."

He was eager...and drunk. I prayed this would work. I prayed that he wasn't really the kind of man his father was. I prayed he had no clue how much cruelty and dominance it took to be a fucking savage.

"Is that how Hale likes it?" he sneered, desire in his eyes.

"Yes," I answered carefully. "He likes to watch me squirm."

Damon smiled and lowered his body, rolling onto his back.

"He likes to stare up into my eyes." I kept going, kept talking, kept his mind off what was really happening and I gave him something else to think about. "He likes to watch me take my clothes off, likes to watch me as I straddle him. He likes to see me ride."

Damon's breath caught as I slipped from the bed and did exactly that.

It was a fantasy come to life...a fantasy I was sure he'd played over and over in his head.

"Katerina," Damon hissed as I reached around and unhooked my bra.

Katerina VanHalen...daddy's little whore.

Revulsion rolled through me like a wave. But there was still a way I could get out of this. Still a way I could make him *believe*. Damon collapsed back against the mattress and tried to shove at his jeans. But his movements were sloppy, fumbling at the button of his jeans.

"Let me take care of that." I slipped my panties to the floor and climbed on top. "Let me take care of it all...just like I do for Hale."

"Yeah?" he slurred, getting drunker by the second.

"Yeah," I whispered, the panic inside keeping me talking, saying anything to keep his eyes off my hands. "He likes to lay back, likes it when I take control. Likes it when I treat him like a king. You want me to treat you like a king, Damon?"

He opened his eyes at the words and looked at me like I didn't exist, because in that moment, I didn't. I wasn't really there, I was in his head. I was the fantasy he was envisioning, the one where he replaced Hale. He licked his lips. "Yeah, treat me like the fucking king, Katerina."

"I will." I opened the button and pulled down the zipper.

His cock was straining, springing free as he thrust his hips off the bed, making me wobble and grip his thighs to hold on. Nothing. That's what I felt...*nothing* as I slid his jeans lower and gripped his length, stroking and twisting.

Damon groaned. My insides clenched, my stomach tightened. I drove my fisted hand down, then slipped against that slick skin all the way to the end.

"Fuck, you're good," he muttered.

I slid my body higher, splaying my legs wide so that he nestled against the crease of my pussy. And I never stopped with the movement of my hand, drawing him toward the brink of ecstasy. "Hale has it just like this," I murmured. "Close your eyes, picture me and him."

Damon did as I said, his lips parting with a groan.

"He likes it when I ride him." I lifted my hips and pushed forward, settling over him, then reached around. "Do you feel me?" I croaked, gripping his cock from behind me.

Please...please let this work.

"Yeah." Damon groaned. "Oh yeah."

"Fuck me, Hale." I closed my eyes and whispered as that empty pit of disgust opened wide. "Fuck me."

I pumped my hand harder, thrusting my hips against him in time with the motion. Until there was nothing but that nauseous revulsion. Nothing but that hollow part of me. I lost myself with the jerk of my hand, lost myself with the euphoria on Damon's face. Lost myself into the hate and the terror inside me...and didn't notice the open door.

He was there...the blue-eyed Mafia Prince.

He looked down at me, taking in the revulsion in my eyes and the cock in my hand.

"Hale's whore. You're going to be my whore too, Katerina," Damon growled. "I'm going to enjoy watching all the videos of you fucking my dad while you suck me."

There was a flinch in Lazarus's gaze. The look of disgust I saw in myself every time I looked in the mirror, and with a curl of his lips, he just turned and strode through the door.

It closed with a *thud*. But Damon didn't even notice, he was lost to the movement, tightening and trembling in my hand. With a cry of release, he came, warm and slick through the gaps of my fingers.

When he was done, he opened his eyes.

I slid off his body without him ever realizing.

He couldn't have me...

No one could.

I was beyond saving, beyond claiming.

I glanced toward the door, seeing that look of horror on Lazarus's face, and slipped from Damon's bed, swiping my hand on the sheet as I left. My chest tightened. My pulse was thunderous in my head. Tears welled in my eyes as Lazarus's stare filled me. I didn't know why it hurt as much as it did. I didn't know why I cared when there was nothing but hate inside me.

"Stay the fuck away from me, Damon," I warned as the memory of my gun returned. "I don't want to hurt you."

He lifted his head, that glazed, drunken expression on his face. "That's not going to happen, Katerina. Not when I tell Hale that I had what was supposed to be his."

17

Lazarus

Hale's whore.

A hard bark of laughter tore free from me as I left that room behind.

Hale's whore...

What the fuck had I watched in that room? What even was that? Hate and rage...*and utter fucking helplessness* filled her eyes. Her dark, empty, unfathomable eyes. Fuck. I lifted my hand, rubbing the corded muscles in the back of my neck. I'd seen eyes like that. Cold. *Dead. Empty.* The image of Taken's face filled my mind as he bled out in the back of the four-wheel drive while I sat in the back seat, unable to take my eyes from his.

That's what she was in there...*fucking empty. Dead on the inside.*

And I needed to know why.

"Laz..." someone called my name. I think it was Bernardi.

But I kept on walking. Kept on moving...because I *had to.*

I got to the elevator as the doors opened. A group strode out.

"Lazarus?" some guy called. "Lazarus Rossi, right? Fuck me...*a real fucking Mafi—*"

I reacted before I knew it, lunging to grab the poor, pathetic asshole by the shirt, and dragged him close. "Finish that and I'll ram my fucking fist down your throat."

His eyes widened, and the two others he came with just froze.

"Easy, man..." the asshole just lifted his hands in surrender. *Fucking pussy.* "I'm a fan," he murmured. "I'm a real fucking fan."

A fan? Blood, screaming...and Kat VanHalen's dead gaze slammed back at me. I shove him backwards as horror came over me, crashing down on me. I turned and stumbled for the open elevator doors as they started to close.

I had to get out of there...I had to get out.

Hale's whore.

Hale's whore.

My own reflection shone back at me, blurred and warped on the stainless steel walls of the elevator. My muscles trembled, tight and aching...*desperate.* I clenched my fist, wrenched my hand through the air, and drove it into the goddamn wall.

The blow was a *boom* inside the space as the elevator came to a stop and the doors opened. Hard breaths consumed me as I turned and stared straight into the eyes of Finley Salvatore.

He just looked at me, then his gaze shifted to the wall. *Do not speak, motherfucker.* My lips curled, that savagery burning like acid inside me. I wanted to hit something...I wanted to hit and keep on hitting, until I collapsed. The need to smash in that pretty-boy's face thundered in my veins.

He said nothing, just stood there, not moving a fucking inch as I strode out of the elevator and through the foyer.

Hale's whore.

"Fuck Hale," I growled...*whoever the fuck he is.*

I wanted to hurt that motherfucker in that moment, *really* hurt him. I wanted to tear him apart, snuff out his flame. I wanted to make it so that he never fucking existed, so I could have what was his.

Jesus...do you hear yourself?

I strode through the doors of the building and out into the night, rubbing the back of my neck once more. I didn't get riled like this, didn't get lost in the emotion...*not since...*Iggy's face filled my mind. I could still hear his whimper, still see that desperation in his eyes at the end when he didn't want to stay here with me any longer. He wanted to go...*he wanted to be free.*

I didn't get shaken, especially not by a woman.

But the moment I thought of her, that hunger came roaring back, that need to know, to feel. Fuck me...*to feel.* That throbbing music from last night found me and with it came the lightning strike of desire. In my head, her hips ground against mine, her breasts high and perfect, bouncing in front of my face to the throb of the beat as she straddled my lap and worked her body.

But that was different, wasn't it? It was different than what I'd seen tonight.

I stopped walking, standing in the middle of the walkway, and stared out at the black sea. Moonlight bounced off the surface, casting the soft silver glow as far as I could see. But it wasn't the stunning view of the ocean that consumed me. It was *her*. The redhead who'd looked at me tonight with so much disgust and loathing, so much fucking hatred, as she jerked off that piece of shit beneath her.

It was the look of a woman who was trapped, who was *nothing inside*.

Jesus Christ.

I inhaled hard, feeling that burn of torture all the way into my soul. I turned my head and looked over my shoulder to the apartment building once more. I wanted to go back there. I wanted to choke Damon out and leave him gasping and bruised and barely hanging on to life, then I wanted to turn to her, with his blood on my hands and this burning need to *fucking under-stand her*.

A scream rocked the night, sounding faint and in the distance.

It was a male's scream...a guttural scream...*a roar of despera-tion...of survival.*

I took a step, scanning the buildings and the island for the direction as the sound was silenced. *What the fuck was that?* I took a step, then another. My heart hammered, that burning heat of anger turned chilling. There was something not right...

I moved, my steps quiet and fast...*hurrying*. Two steps and I pushed into a jog as that roar came once more, loud, *savage*. Desperate, that's what it was. I caught a bead on the direction and grabbed my phone.

"Freddy," I barked. "Something's wrong."

He was alert in an instant. "Where?"

"I'm running toward the rear of the compound, toward the hangar. I think it's building six...yeah. Baldeon's...I think it's—"

"Do *not* fucking move without me, Laz. You hear me?" Freddy barked. *"Do not fucking move."*

The call was disconnected in an instant. I shoved the phone into my pocket and drove my body forward. With each thudding step, a surety found me. Baldeon's apartment...*Baldeon.* If the fucker was faking it, if the fucker was screaming because of a goddamn broken nail, I'd kill him myself.

But even as the thought filled my head I knew that was a lie.

You didn't scream like that because of a nail.

You screamed like that when you were fighting to survive.

A blur of black in the shadows moved fast, shooting from behind the building and racing toward the water. Another followed not three steps behind. *Something's wrong...something's wrong...SOMETHING IS WRONG!*

I jerked my gaze from the water as the faint sound of an engine slipped through the air as I charged toward the building. Silence surrounded me, cold, empty silence as I lunged from the grass to the hard, pebbled pavement and slammed against the door of Baldeon's building. There was a guard on the ground...dead. A gunshot to the head, eyes wide open, his face in a pool of blood.

I turned back to the sensor and fumbled for the card in my pocket, praying it got me inside. I slammed the card against the sensor, the voice in my head screaming. *WORK...WORK... WORK, YOU PIECE OF SHIT!*

The light went from red to green and the door opened.

My phone vibrated in my pocket.

But I didn't answer, I was too busy lunging into the foyer as the doors opened.

"Lazarus!"

I jerked my head up at the blur running toward me, head down, arms pistoning, his mouth contorted in desperation and rage. I glanced toward the bodyguard lying on the floor, then at Freddy. Logan was further behind him...just a dark blur in the night.

Just like the ones I saw before.

"You go in there..." Freddy panted, sucking in harsh breaths, "and I'll kick your fucking ass."

I turned as he charged through the door I held and slowed. His gun was already in his hand, muzzle lifted as he scanned the foyer, his gaze stopping at the body. "Fuck me."

I stepped into the blood and knelt beside the poor sonofabitch.

"Laz...he's..." Freddy started, then stopped.

But it wasn't a pulse I searched for as I shoved his jacket aside and jerked the master key from his belt. "I heard screams, then someone running...two someones."

Freddy jerked his gaze toward me as I lunged for the elevator and slammed the card against the sensor. *Boom!* I flinched as Logan pounded the door. The elevator opened as Freddy punched the button opening the outer door. My bodyguards surrounded me as I charged into the elevator.

Their guns were raised, and there was nothing but steely stares and the sound of hard, heavy breaths. Freddy handed me his second piece as the elevator doors opened to the top floor apartment. But he was moving before I did, pushing me aside to step into the line of fire.

Silence.

Chilling, awful, fucking silence waited for us.

We moved fast, sweeping through every room in the apartment before Freddy turned. "There's nothing here."

"No." I shook my head. "There has to be. I know that fucking sound. I know...that fucking scream."

Desperation roared inside my head as I tried to think. I knew that *terror*. The dead guard in the foyer wasn't for nothing.

Logan's phone rang. He answered it instantly. "Yeah, building five. Okay, there's one of your men dead in the foyer."

I strode toward the elevator as that panic inside me thrummed, and pressed the button. My men were beside me, like they were always beside me. We weren't just the protected. We were family...we were Rossis. As the elevator started to move, I reached out by instinct and instead of pressing the buttons for the other floors, I pressed the button for the basement.

The other floors were for security...and women we wanted to bring to the island.

But I knew in my gut that wasn't where someone like me would be taken to be hurt...*or worse.*

A chill snaked along my spine as the elevator sank lower and lower, past the bright lights to slip into the darkness. Down in the cold and emptiness was where I'd end up. I knew that.

Down in the dark where no one would hear me scream. The second the doors opened, I knew it was here, where...*he was here.*

We moved forward, striding through the gloom. A few lights flared...and in their harsh glow, I saw him. Marcus Baldeon... one of the Commission's second sons lay on the floor, his eyes wide...staring at me as I came closer.

"Jesus fucking Christ," Freddy growled.

But I barely heard him. I was moving closer, kneeling beside his body and touched his cheek. He was still warm...there was still...*hope.*

"Freddy," I growled, and reached for Baldeon's shoulder. Feeling for warmth.

Terror found me as Logan's voice bellowed in the dark.

But I wasn't listening to him.

I was seeing myself in the reflection of Baldeon's unblinking gaze.

My face. My eyes.

My death just like this...waiting for me.

But the moment I touched that cold, empty void of shock inside me, something else pushed to the surface. A face...a beautiful, haunting face and fiery red hair.

The sound of the elevator doors opening seemed loud. "Step away, now." The command came from behind me.

I lowered Baldeon's body to the floor and pushed myself upright, wobbling for a second before I caught my balance.

"Easy, brother." Freddy was beside me, grabbing me by the arm and pulling us out of the way as Matteo Ristani, the Commander of Cosa Nostra Institute, stepped forward, then stilled.

He knelt and touched Baldeon's neck, then scanned his body and the wounds, stopping at the knife embedded to the hilt into his thigh. The force it must've taken to do that was incredible. The cold, murderous rage to do any of this was alien. Who would do this? Who would come here while we were surrounded by protectors and kill one of our own?

I couldn't think of a motive, not one as sadistic as this.

"Who found him?" the Commander asked carefully.

"I did." I lifted my gaze to his.

"Did you see anything else?"

"Two men...or two others, I couldn't get a good look, running from this building toward the beach. I heard the faint sound of a motor."

"And they didn't come after you?" The dark eyes of the Commander bored into mine.

Savage eyes.

Merciless eyes.

The Albanian, they called him, The Unbreakable behind his back. He was ruthless, controlling, and staring at me. I just shook my head. "No, they didn't come after me."

"Thank Christ for that," Freddy grunted with a sigh. He glanced at the body, then looked away.

Orders were given and more lights flared overhead, brightening the basement in an instant. I took a step backwards, suddenly feeling the walls closing in.

"Rossi," the Commander stopped me. "I'm going to need a statement."

My gut clenched as I nodded and turned to leave. I had to get out of there. I had to get...*away.*

"Freddy," I whispered, the sound like a plea.

"I got you." He was right there beside me, striding forward toward the Commission's guards. "Move," he growled, and they didn't argue, stepping aside for me to stride past and into the harsh lights of the elevator.

Footsteps thundered toward us as we strode out of Baldeon's building, leaving the horror behind. Finley Salvatore ran toward us, his eyes wide, meeting mine. "Baldeon?" he growled.

I didn't have the answer. I couldn't speak.

I did the only thing I knew to do.

I left him and that night behind, making my way toward the building where she stayed, my beautiful redhead with the empty eyes. Freddy stood behind me as I stood in the shadows and lifted my gaze to the bright lights of the penthouse suite. "I need you to look into someone for me," I murmured.

"Laz, no. She's not your—" Freddy started, then stopped. "You're not going to leave that alone, are you?"

"No," I answered, staring into the shimmering lights. "No, I'm not. I want to know everything there is to know about a Hale."

"She's trouble," Freddy urged, sounding desperate. "Trouble we don't need."

But I needed her.

I needed her face in my mind.

The scent of her body on my skin.

I needed her to wash away the horror of what I'd seen tonight. Now...and forever.

Yeah, I liked the sound of that.

18

Kat

I dressed after Lazarus walked out, having seen and heard the disgusting things I'd done...*things Damon wanted me to do again.* Revulsion fueled me as I yanked on my underwear and slipped the dress over my head.

"Stay the fuck away from me, Damon," I warned, and tugged on my heels. "Just stay away from my friends and stay away from me."

He lifted his head from the bed and watched me in his drunken stupor. "You know that's never going to happen. Besides, I thought I made quite the impact with your little roommate today. I heard she's a virgin...and you know how much we like those."

We...

My pulse sped at the thought. Screams filled my head. Sickening, terrified screams. Still, I fought the panic and tugged my zipper into place, meeting his gaze. "D-don't make me hurt you."

He just smiled.

I left then, hurrying through the apartment in search of Anna, and found her sitting alone on the same damn sofa as when I'd left. "You ready to leave?" I murmured.

Relief swept across her face as she rose. "I thought you'd never ask."

We started toward the elevator, then the first message came through.

"Oh my God," came a female cried from somewhere deeper in the apartment.

"No fucking way," a guy barked.

I glanced over my shoulder as he scanned the room. "Baldeon's dead. Someone got to him."

Everyone at the party froze. A party that was meant for him, a celebration of surviving a gunshot to the shoulder. I swallowed hard as Anna whispered, "Finley..."

She swept her gaze through the room and for some reason, I followed, searching for the blue-eyed son of the Rossi family. But somehow, I knew he was gone...from this place and what he'd seen. He'd run from me now, and never look back.

"Come on," I pulled her toward the elevator. "Let's get back."

But fear filled her gaze. She swallowed hard. I could see her brain working overtime. If whoever killed Baldeon was still on the island, then they could be here. I glanced toward the others, catching the same thought sweep the room.

We had to get out of there. I jerked my gaze toward the hallway as Damon practically staggered out. He glanced at everyone frozen in place. "What's going on?"

I didn't wait for them to fill him in, just slipped my hand from around Anna's arm. "I'm going." I headed for the elevator.

Any moment they'd be leaving in droves. Any moment I'd be left alone...with Damon. I'd rather face a murderer.

"Wait." Anna hurried after me as I stabbed the button.

I left, striding through the foyer after the elevator doors opened, and hurried out into the night. We held each other's hand, scanning the darkness, our heels clacking on the pavement as we all but ran to our building.

Harsh breaths consumed me as I pressed my card to the sensor and waited for the doors to open. Then we were inside, hurrying through our own suite to watch the chaos of the night.

My phone let out a *beep*. I glanced down to find a message from an unknown number.

I heard you had a good time tonight.

My stomach clenched before I cast the phone onto the sofa. *No...no fucking way.* I didn't need to reply to know who it as from. Hale. It had to be. There was no one else who'd know. No one else who'd revel in the depravity of what I'd done tonight. No one else who'd be bold enough to torment me that way.

I hurried to the bathroom, hit the faucet on the sink and, as the rush of the water smothered the sound, I heaved and retched over the toilet. My hands shook as I braced against the wall, my eyes closed. I'd come to this island as an escape. I'd come to this island for hope. But all I'd seemed to do was make myself a target for a brand new kind of hell.

I swiped my hand across my mouth then dropped it to my belly. But no one knew the real reason I was here. No one knew the secret I held. I rose from the toilet, flushed it, and brushed my teeth before I scrubbed my hands. I wanted to wash away everything from tonight. I wanted to scrub it all away.

When I was done, I changed into my pajamas, crawled into bed, and cradled my stomach. *I needed to find a way out of this, however that came.* I closed my eyes and tried to drift off to sleep, dozing until the faint sound of Anna's voice found me later.

I roused enough to hear Finley's voice, and closed my eyes once more. Whatever connection they shared was private, and I had enough of my own drama to deal with.

I AVOIDED Damon as much as I could the next day, skipping the classes I'd been so determined to attend. There was nowhere off limits to him now, that was clear when he'd forced his way into Xael and Evan's apartment yesterday. I could still hear his threats whispered in my ear. Threats others took as seduction.

But there was nothing seductive about his grip on my arm.

Or the cruel glint in his eyes.

Anna thought he was gorgeous, smiling, her cheeks turning red as he played the part of the boy-next-door party boy. I felt sick... and it was more than the pregnancy. I *had* to find a way out of this. I had to find a way to get away from him. Only Xael saw my panic...and with a furrowed brow, she quietly sent me a text.

Xael: You okay?

What could I say? *No...no* I wasn't okay.

Damon was sitting next to me on the sofa, I quickly typed out a...*ttyl, okay?*

She nodded, watching me and Damon with interest until I took the first opportunity to leave. But I still needed help and Xael was a badass bitch, so I was hoping like hell to talk to her in person.

But right then, I kept to myself, watching Anna hurry off to class while I stayed in the apartment, until I couldn't stand being alone a second longer.

I dressed, applied mascara and a clear gloss on my lips, and went downstairs. There was a guard waiting to escort me, and another to watch the building. In the wake of Baldeon's murder, the institute had gone into overdrive. There were guards everywhere and any other time, the sight of them might've filled me with exhaustion and disgust for my name. But here and now...with Damon after me, I felt relief.

"Ms. VanHalen," the guard nodded in greeting as I strode toward him.

"I'd like to go to class."

"Certainly," he answered, and strode forward, scanning the outside of the building as we stepped out.

I followed, quiet, careful, my mind drifting as I fell into step behind him until he pushed through the door and into the foyer. "Your class is just down there, ma'am."

I gave a nod and strode away, making my way along the hallway toward the sound of voices, until I lifted my head and caught sight of Lazarus Rossi halfway down, leaning against the wall. He glanced my way and that searing gaze burned right through me.

I stopped in the middle of the hallway, my heart hammering in my chest. Heat rushed to my cheeks as he slowly pushed off the wall and turned toward me. "Figured you'd turn up eventually."

Panic filled me as he took a slow step toward me, those arctic blue eyes blazing. He licked his lips and searched my gaze. I tore my eyes to the classroom further down the hall, to the class I was supposed to attend.

"I'm guessing you thought I'd run after last night," he whispered.

I flinched at the words and jerked my gaze to his.

"Guess you figured any man would run a fucking mile after hearing the words that came out of that piece of shit's mouth." He stopped in front of me, blocking my way as he leaned close. "But there's one thing you need to understand about me, Kat. *I don't run.*"

Then in an instant, he stepped around me and walked away.

I didn't move. My heart throbbed in the back of my throat as the thud of his footsteps faded. Harsh breaths consumed me. I dropped my head, feeling a wave of giddiness sweep over me. *He didn't run...what the hell was that supposed to mean?*

I had an idea.

But I didn't like that idea.

Not one little bit.

But the more I thought of it, the more I remembered how the hunger in his eyes burned as possessive as anything else I'd ever felt, and that made me let out a long, hard exhale and whisper, "Oh fuck."

I swiveled, looking behind me to the faint sound of Lazarus's steps until there was nothing but silence. Lazarus Rossi was invested in me. A tiny surge of hope tore through me like lightning. A Rossi...I bit my lip and dared to hope just the tiniest bit. A Rossi might smuggle me out of the country. A Rossi might even know where I could hide.

If Lazarus liked me even just a little, I could use that to my advantage...as long as I didn't fuck it up.

So, just don't fuck it up.

I turned back to the sound of the class and tried to figure out how to not do that as I stepped forward. The drone of murmurs rose as I neared the door. Through the glass panel, I caught them all rising from their seats. Looked like class was over...I was winning at all levels today. I stepped aside as the door opened, and pasted a smile on my face. Carefree Kat was back.

"Hey, Kat!" one of them called.

But there were somber looks on the rest of them, brows furrowed in concern. Baldeon's death was weighing heavily on everyone, and Anna was no exception. She lifted her head, eyes widening when she saw me, and there was a smile of relief.

"You ready to skip the next one?" I murmured, and slipped my hand into hers. "I want to see Xael."

There was a flicker of nervousness in her eyes. She glanced toward the others. "You think it's a good idea to be away from the others?"

Be away from the others? Hell yeah, if it was Damon. "As long as we have security, we'll be fine. I wanted to see Xael, but I can do that later."

"Yeah, of course." Anna's brows rose as I tugged her forward, falling in behind the surge of the crowd as they gossiped and chatted. A few even glanced behind to find me. No matter where I was or who I was with, someone always wanted to pick my life apart.

I was the unknown, the secretive VanHalen who, even though I went out to parties, didn't do drugs or hook up with as many guys as I could. I was the one who went to the gala events and came home alone. Little did they know I was battling my own war within. The wall of my fortress was my battlefield. The nights my father played poker with his friends were my own personal war. They thought my life was perfect. Little did they know what it was truly like.

"I can't get that story out of my head," Anna murmured, drawing me away from the stares and the scrutiny. "The one about the creation of, you know..." She glanced around, then leaned close, *"The Commission."*

Anna had been rocked by what Xael said. The truth was, so was I.

Five controlling families tied to each other by lies, mistrust, and intimidation made a whole lot of sense. The only thing that was shocking...was that it had been created by the Salvatores.

I dragged her with me and slipped away from the crush of the crowd, heading toward the apartment buildings. I'd go anywhere on this damn island, as long as I didn't run into Damon Zakharov.

We left the towering building behind and headed for Xael and Evan's apartment, detouring around building one. There was a small army of guards standing outside. I saw the one they called The Albanian on the phone to someone. His brow was furrowed, fingers pushing back the hair from his forehead. He looked worried...*real fucking worried*. In an instant he lifted his head, and those dark eyes found me.

The Commander was a ruthless bastard. He was also the one the Commission held accountable for everything that went on from the moment we stepped onto the boats and left the same way after. Looked like he was in a world of hurt right now.

He broke our stare, then turned. The guards moved around him in a swarm as he left the main building behind. Anna glanced behind her to the thick towering palms that covered the sunny side of the buildings.

"What is it?" I asked, following her gaze.

"Nothing," she murmured. "Just thought I felt something."

A chill swept down my spine. I followed her gaze, checking the shadows, and walked faster. I wouldn't put it past Damon to stalk me...I wouldn't put anything past him, actually.

I could get away from him. First, he turned up at Xael and Evan's apartment, then he hosted the damn party for Baldeon. I would not let him control me, not let him force me to hide and tremble with fear. He would *not* force me into hiding...*no fucking way*.

———————————————

19

Laz

———————————————

The initiation. That's what this was...it had to be.

I watched Finley Salvatore from the corner of the building. The smug bastard thought he was hidden...but not from me. I smiled and crossed my arms as the asshole rubbed the back of his neck and turned away. Word was the initiation was in play. A pissy, juvenile contest for those who liked to play bad boy.

But it wasn't for me...*because I didn't play.*

I pushed off from the wall, to find Freddy behind me.

"You finished stalking?" he grumbled, looking past me to the building where Kat and Anna had disappeared.

"Stalking the stalker, it looks like," I said, motioning behind me.

Freddy pushed off the wall and peeked out, finding Finley hidden in the shadows of the towering green trees. "Huh," was all he said, then he glanced toward the building. "Anna some-one, you said her name was, right?"

"Shaw," I answered. "Anna Shaw."

The image of Finley standing over her that first night on the island came back to me in a rush. Whoever the careful little brunette was, she had Finley Salvatore in knots. I licked my lips and smiled. There was nothing I liked more than to see a Salvatore come undone.

But the smirk died on my face the moment I realized I was in the exact same fucking position. Freddy watched the realization dawn on me, and grinned. "Just caught on, huh?"

"Shut the fuck up, Freddy," I grumbled, and pushed past him.

It wasn't the same, not anywhere *near* the same.

My phone made a *beep*. I looked down and saw a message from Dad.

Looks like I'll be flying in for a Commission meeting.

My gut clenched as reality crashed in. I pressed the button, killing the screen, and slipped my phone back into my pocket. Baldeon's death would cause a big ripple through the families. They'd be worried...no, more than that...*they'd be downright terrified.*

I strode back to my own building and Freddy and I took the elevator all the way up to the apartment. Logan looked up at us from the kitchen. The counter was a damn mess of food and drinks and guns.

"How was the patrol?" I asked as I came closer.

The shake of his head told me all I needed to know. Whoever I'd seen last night running from Baldeon's building was long gone. Logan was a former SEAL, and one of the first to put his hand up for the recon mission to find those responsible.

But the fact they'd found nothing meant that whoever took the hit was more than just good...*they were exceptional.*

"Your dad text you?" Logan asked, handing me a beer.

"Yeah, looks like the party is about to be crashed."

The dangerous looking bastard just shook his head. "Don't worry. He's not staying."

"Yeah?" I popped the can and took a gulp, but I was watching him, taking in the way he avoided my gaze. "Spill..."

Logan just looked at Freddy as he came up behind me, and handed him a water.

"That silver sedan you saw..." Freddy started. "They found it burned out in one of the dump sites we use."

I just gave a shrug and lifted the beer to my lips once more.

"There was a message inside the trunk."

I froze, my hand lowering slowly.

"A mannequin that looked a lot like you," Freddy said carefully. "Complete with a gunshot to the head and a knife in the heart."

Warmth flew out of me as the image of Baldeon's face came rushing back to me. I'd tried to push it away all last night, focusing on the redheaded beauty instead. It didn't touch me... didn't involve me. It was some Cosa Nostra bullshit, not a Stidda problem...not a *me* problem.

I licked my lips. "It's not..."

"It is, Laz." Freddy placed his water bottle onto the counter, his intense fucking eyes boring into me. "This is no damn joke."

Taken's unfocused eyes came back to me as he sat slumped against the door on the day he died. Anger seethed inside me even after all these years, the kind of flame that just didn't go away. *"You think I don't know that?"*

One slow nod of his head, and the asshole pushed off the counter. But the damage was already done, wasn't it? Now it was Baldeon's fucking face I saw in my head. Baldeon's pale, pasty fucking face, and gray skin. Baldeon's throat cut so damn deep it had almost severed his head from his body. *That could be me...*

A shiver coursed through me, cutting deeper than a knife ever could.

My phone made a *beep*. I looked down and saw a message from Finley fucking Salvatore, of all people.

Watch your back. The initiation is still in play.

I curled my lips in a silent snarl as Freddy glanced at my hand. "Everything okay?"

"Nothing I can't handle," I growled, and shoved my phone back into my pocket.

Taken.

Iggy.

Marco Baldeon...

"Tell me what you found out about her..." I lifted my gaze to Freddy and watched him wince and shift his gaze. *"Freddy..."*

"Look," he started. "There isn't a whole lot to find out. She's not a party girl, if that's what you're worried about. She's fucking...*boring.*"

Boring?

I didn't think so. I lifted my gaze to his, and it was his turn to feel that desperation. "Tell me."

"She's guarded, like *heavily guarded*. But you'd expect that for someone of her worth. She's on the seat for a few of the normal boards, a children's hospital, one for battered women, and she attends the galas in their names, giving millions every year. But other than that, she's at home. Honestly...it's kinda creepy. She doesn't party like normal women her age party. She goes into that fucking mansion and she doesn't come out."

"And that sonofabitch called Hale?" I muttered, looking down at the counter.

"Now...that is where it gets...*complicated.*"

I jerked my gaze to his. "Then *un*complicate it."

He looked at Logan as though the savage bastard might save him. But he wouldn't save him, not this time.

"He's a friend of her father...and a ruthless sonofabitch. He's the founder and CEO of Hale Financial, a private equity firm that makes a living investing in struggling companies, then tearing them apart the moment they close their doors. And when I say this guy is ruthless...I mean he's one savage motherfucker. A savage motherfucker with *very deep pockets.*"

A nerve twitched at the corner of my eye. Dangerous and rich. We were rich, too...maybe not that rich, but what we lacked in that department we made up in the dangerous side of the equation.

"He's her father's friend?" I growled, feeling a little dangerous now.

Freddy just nodded. "If men like Sebastian VanHalen have any friends, then I'd consider Haelestom Hale his closest ally."

"One he allows to fuck his daughter," I muttered, hating that burn inside my chest.

But that didn't explain Zakharov.

No, that didn't explain him at all...or what I'd seen last night. "Did you find out anything about Zakharov?"

Freddy just shook his head. "Not a thing, apart from the perfect banking family. Wife, son, went to Yale of all places, and is wanting to follow in his daddy's footsteps."

The image of those empty eyes came back to me. Fuck me, she was cold inside, cold, hollow, and dead. I could still see the way she fisted her hand around that drunk asshole's cock. The way she moved her body to make it seem like she was fucking him, when all along...*she was playing him.*

There was something I wasn't seeing.

Something I wasn't understanding.

Something Freddy couldn't find out on social fucking media.

I drained the rest of my beer. "Thanks, Freddy," I growled, then crushed the can and tossed it into the recycle bin.

"You going to let that go now?" he called as I turned my back and headed for the bathroom to take a piss.

"No fucking way," I answered.

There was a snarl, then a few choice words as I stepped up to the toilet. If anything, the information Freddy had found made me even more determined to understand her. *Careful,* that small voice inside warned as I palmed my cock. Fear shifted inside me. It was an uncomfortable feeling. A *new fucking feeling.*

I didn't get involved, especially not where women were concerned.

That shit led to a whole different world of trouble.

One I'd managed to stay away from.

Until now.

20

Kat

Anna's phone gave a *beep*. She fumbled with the damn thing, jerking it from her pocket only to cover the screen and turn her body so I couldn't see her message. She was secretive...but weren't we all?

"You know what..." She stalled at the door to Xael's apartment building and slipped her phone into her pocket. "I think I'm going to head back to the apartment, okay?"

I looked behind us, at the guard at our backs, then at the one waiting inside. "You sure?"

"I just..." Anna started. There was fear in her voice, *real fear*. "I think it's just everything that's happened."

She shifted her gaze, not meeting my eyes. That warning in my stomach whispered she was lying.

"Come on." I gave her a smile. "Let's go back."

I took two steps before my phone *beeped. Xael: Looks like daddy dearest is on his way for a meeting with the Commander. They'll be tearing him a new one, I bet.*

A shiver coursed through me as I pocketed my phone. Maybe it was best to stay inside for a while anyway. God knew I didn't want to run into any of the heads of the families. *They'd know...* I couldn't stop the thought from rising inside me. *They'd know who I really am.*

But that sounded crazy.

Staying in my apartment until the coast was clear was starting to sound like a good idea. We walked back and left the guard in the foyer before we headed back up to the penthouse suite. I switched on the TV for a little noise as Anna slipped away into her room.

She didn't talk or come out of her room. So I sat on the sofa and contemplated calling Xael there and then. One glance toward Anna's room, and the idea died. The thought of Anna hearing even a little of the real me frightened the crap out of me.

I lifted my gaze to the window and the white clouds that now carried a tinge of steel gray. A black speck moved in the sky. I rose from the sofa and stepped closer to the window, watching that speck grow larger in the distance.

It was them...the five heads of the Mafia families.

I stood there, mesmerized, as another dark speck grew larger in the sky and, as I watched, one by one the helicopters touched down. *This was real...really real.* My pulse sped at the thought as Anna's phone beeped once more.

There was nothing else to do now. Nothing but wait...

All day I paced the apartment, flicking through the channels, only to finally turn the TV off. Anna didn't come out of her room, instead she talked to someone. Someone she didn't want me knowing about. When darkness claimed the night, the last helicopter landed, its bright lights glaring in the darkness.

I made myself busy and forced myself to eat something while I waited for as long as I could, then I sent Xael a message.

I need to talk to you.

Anna answered a call and talked in a hushed voice before stepping out of her room.

"Everything okay?" I asked, rising from the sofa.

"Yeah, sure, everything's fine. Just checking in," she lied.

My phone let out a *beep*. I grabbed it and checked the screen: *Xael: Dad isn't coming to see me, so the coast is clear.*

"Go." Anna nodded toward the door.

"Are you sure?" Hope flared.

"Positive. Go, have fun."

I realized then that she thought I was meeting Damon. She'd bought his lies, his sick, twisted lies. It was written all over her face.

I forced a squeal. "You're the best," I smiled, and took a step.

"You like him, right? Damon, I mean."

My steps froze, and terror found me as I forced a shrug. "He's okay."

"So, not mind blowing?"

I closed my eyes for a second and tried to stop my hands from shaking. "No, not mind blowing, Anna. That kind of romance doesn't exist, only in books and movies. I'll have my cell on me and the guard will be downstairs. Call if you need me, okay?"

I forced myself to move, bitting the inside of my cheek to stop from telling her the truth. But the truth would change how she saw me...the truth would change how I saw myself, and I wasn't ready to face that reality. Not yet...*not yet.*"

"Okay," she answered.

But I was already hurrying to the elevator, closing my eyes as I pressed the button. Revulsion tightened my stomach, driving acid into the back of my throat. *Do you like him...do you like him...do you like him?*

The elevator doors opened and I stepped inside. I couldn't get her words out of my head, couldn't burn away the look in her eyes. I braced my hand against the wall and tried to breathe.

The door opened and I pushed away, forcing the cold, stony mask into place. "I'm going to see Xael Davies."

"Yes, ma'am." One of the bodyguards nodded and prepared to accompany me.

My mind raced as we headed out into the night and along the path. In the back of my mind, Xael was my last hope and the reason I'd come here. If everything went to hell, I'd use what fragile friendship we had and ask her for the impossible...I'd ask her to kill Haelstrom Hale.

The sound of my heels rang out in the night.

Two-way chatter blared from the radio the bodyguard wore. But I focused on the darkness in front of me, slowing as we came to Xael's building. The wind was roaring, the crash of the waves carried all the way through the thick bulletproof glass as the doors closed behind me.

One command, and the guard swiped his card against the sensor and I rode all the way up to Xael's suite once more. But the moment I stepped out, I realized something was different. There was no blaring music, no drone of laughter and chatter. Xael was always partying, day, night, no matter the crisis.

But tonight, it was quiet as I stepped through the entrance and caught sight of her as she rose from the sofa and motioned her head toward the kitchen. "I was wondering when you were going to turn up."

Lazarus stood there at the end of the counter, his arms crossed in front of his powerful chest and those blue eyes burning with desire.

"What is this?" I queried, panic pushing to the surface.

"Lazarus decided to pay me a visit," Xael muttered. "Seems my place has become a drop-in center for your many suitors."

"Many suitors?" Lazarus's brow rose. "No...just the one. The only one that matters."

I froze as he pushed off the counter and stepped toward me. "I think you and I need to have a conversation, Kat...*don't you?*"

My heart was thundering in my ears as I tried to find the right words to say as Lazarus stopped in front of me and, with a chilling tone, murmured, "Unless you prefer I call on this Haelstrom Hale and take care of our little problem myself?"

21

Lazarus

She froze as she took a step into the apartment, and her brown eyes widened in fear. One panicked glance from Xael Davies to me, and I readied for her to turn and run.

But she didn't. She just stood there, looking far more fucking ravishing than she should, especially with the way I fucking wanted her.

"Well?" I took a step closer, catching her flinch before I stopped. "You want to tell me what I need to know? Do I need to take care of that Hale, or that asshole Zakharov? Or are you going to tell me you feel nothing here and break my goddamn heart? Because I *know* you felt something the other night after our little lap dance."

Davies's eyes widened as she shot a surprised look from me to the redheaded beauty.

"Hey, X," came a voice from the other room. A blond strode out from another bedroom, plucking earbuds out of her ears. Her eyes were down, focused on her damn buttons. "Is this a mark to you?"

She stopped suddenly and jerked her gaze to me.

"Maybe not the best time, Evan," Xael muttered, still staring at me.

Evan Valachi? Surprise flitted through my mind. The Mafia Princess no one saw...

"Lazarus here was asking Kat a very important question," Xael announced with a smirk. "One I'm very interested to hear the answer to."

"Lazarus..." the blond muttered, and froze.

There was a flicker of panic across her face before she took a step backwards, turned, and was gone in an instant, scurrying back to whatever room she'd come from. Another fucking fan of the Rossi name, I saw. I shift my gaze back to the real reason I was there.

I took another step toward her. "Say the word and it's done."

Just say any word...how about that? Desperation took flight inside my head. But she said nothing, not for a long time, as Xael's smirk grew wider.

Then in a small whisper she said, "Not here."

"Then where?" I asked. She lifted her gaze, her focus boring into mine. "Your place in front of little Anna? We can do this there. Hell, we can do this *anywhere,* as long as we do this, princess. I don't give a fuck."

Her lips parted. Jesus Christ, her lips. I wanted to feel them, touch them. I wanted to skim my thumb across the tender flesh before I took her mouth. That hunger burned in my veins.

"Your apartment," she answered as the color drained from her face.

There was something off about her voice. Something terrified shone back at me in her eyes and that nagging voice inside my head whispered that there was something I wasn't understanding about this woman. Some bigger picture I wasn't seeing.

"We do this there, okay?" She glanced at Xael, whose smiled died.

"You want me to leave, Kat?" Davies asked. "'Cause I totally can."

There was a shake of Kat's head. "No, no, I don't want that."

Then I stepped forward and motioned toward the elevator. "Then let me escort you."

She lowered her head and walked back the way she'd come. Silence filled the elevator as we rode down to the foyer. I didn't know what I'd expected, but it wasn't this. She didn't look at me, instead she focused on the damn elevator doors until they opened.

Logan was waiting, as was the guard assigned to her. She just took one look at the guy and commanded, "You can leave."

He just shook his head. "Can't do that, Ms. VanHa—"

"I'll make sure she get's home safe," Logan cut in, glancing my way.

There was a careful scan from the bodyguard as he looked Logan up and down, then gave a nod and left.

"We good here?" Logan met my gaze. But I wasn't the one who answered.

"Fine," Kat muttered. "Let's just get this over with."

Ouch.

Logan just gave me a careful *what the fuck* stare before he went to the doors and stepped out, scanning the darkness, then strode ahead. I said nothing, just fell in step, and for a second, I wondered what it'd be like to walk beside her...to *really* walk beside her, to share her world.

It hit me then how different we were. She was caviar and Dom, and I was Harleys and Sig Sauers. She was designer dresses that'd send me bankrupt inside a year, and I was ripped jeans and leather. She glanced toward me and those big brown eyes hit me like a fucking sledgehammer.

I didn't care in that moment, didn't care about the money or the power. I didn't give a fucking shit if she was going to ruin me... because I was pretty sure that was going to happen. In that moment, I'd gladly have laid down in front of that truck hurtling my way...the one with heartbreak written all over it.

But then she shifted her focus back to Logan as we stepped into the foyer of my building. Logan stepped into the elevator and punched the buttons for both the top floor and the one under it. I gave him a glance.

"Ah, Freddy and I are gonna take the lower floor, so we can do more patrols at night without disturbing your beauty sleep," Logan muttered without meeting my gaze.

But that *wasn't* why. I stared the steely bastard down. But he just glanced her way and stepped out as the doors opened. It didn't take me long after I stepped out to see they'd already cleared out their shit. But Kat was oblivious, scanning the suite as she stepped forward.

Crushed beer cans littered the counter. There were someone's boxers thrown over the back of the sofa. I stepped around her, snatched them, and cast them toward Logan, who caught them a second before the doors started to close.

He just gave a chuckle and shook his head. *Asshole.*

I walked around, brushing my hair from my face. "Ah, can I get you something to drink?"

She just turned on me like a damn predator. "A drink?" She took a step, her eyes glittering with something that triggered the fighter inside me. "You come to *my* friend's apartment, coerce me into coming back to your place, and ask me if want a goddamn drink?"

I frowned...was I missing something here? "Yeah. That pretty much sums it up."

Fuck me, she was fire...

She took a step, pushing me against the end of the counter. "You think just because we shared a moment that you can manipulate me into your bed?"

My jaw clenched at the words. *Manipulate?* "No. I don't," I snarled. The woman was starting to piss me off. "But look, if you want to forget this thing between us ever happened, princess, then by all means, deny it all you goddamn want. The last thing I want is for all your *'friends'* to think you're slumming it with a Rossi."

She stopped in front of me, so close we could almost touch. I lowered my head and looked down at her. Pretty rich girls like her lowered their standards for two things, sex and protection, and with a bankroll like hers, I was betting sex...well, I had been.

Now I wasn't so sure.

Her gaze shifted to my mouth, then her focus traveled over my lips. "You want to kiss me, princess?" I taunted, and fuck me, my cock came alive at the thought.

Her breasts rose with a deep breath. There was no denying the heat between us, no stomping out the fire that raged.

"Do not fucking move," she ordered. "You touch me and I walk, get it?"

Electricity tore through me as she took a small step. I gripped the edge of the counter, somehow knowing everything I wanted hinged on that moment. I was still, so fucking still, as she rose on her toes and cupped the back of my neck.

I was tall, far taller than her, but I let the woman take control, pulling me down. I closed my eyes with the kiss. It was barely a brush of her lips, barely the warmth of her breath. Still, I trembled, waiting for her. She took me again, this time kissing deeper.

Hunger moved between us. My fingers almost slipped from the end of the counter as she plunged her tongue into my mouth. A groan tore free, savage and guttural. It took my entire focus not to grab her and carry her to my bed.

But I knew somewhere deep inside, the second I did that, it'd be all over.

The spell would be broken.

The magic all gone.

Kat was unlike any other woman I'd ever known, way beyond the girls who came to the clubs and the hookups I frequently had. This was pure, and addictive. *I wanted more.* So much more. I opened my mouth for her, letting her take what she needed.

Heat moved through me at the thought.

I wanted her to use me.

To take what she needed.

My heart.

My soul.

My goddamn body.

My cock hardened in my jeans, but she never went further. Driving her fingers through my hair, she kissed me deeply, crushing my mouth with hers. The longer I didn't touch her, the more ravenous she became, as though she was free in those moments, free to do and have whatever *she* wanted. She let out a little groan that resounded through her mouth, savage and raw. Her body pressed against mine, her breasts mashed against my chest. Fuck me, she was into this, her fingers digging into the back of my neck. The more I thought about that, the more turned on I became. So was she, thrusting her hips against mine, chasing that heat between us.

I barely registered the sound of the elevator before someone cleared their throat. Kat broke away in an instant. She just looked at me, her forehead creased with a frown. Harsh breaths made her chest rise. She was rattled, *really fucking rattled.* I tried to come down from the high of her mouth. She wasn't the only one shaken here. Her gaze moved to my father as he stood in the entrance of the apartment.

He glanced her way, then met my gaze. "Hope I'm not interrupting anything," the asshole said with a smirk.

He damn well *knew* he was.

"No," Kat answered, breathing deep. "I was just leaving."

"I don't think we've met," Dad said, stepping forward, and held out his hand. "Benjamin Rossi."

She just stared at his waiting hand for a second before taking it in her own. "Kat VanHalen."

"Ah, the VanHalens." He smiled.

But Kat just flinched and swallowed hard, and that panicked look filled her eyes once more. I licked my lips, feeling the thrum of my pulse in the tender flesh as I spoke. "I'll message Logan to escort you home."

She just smiled and nodded. "Thank you."

I grabbed my phone and shot Logan a message, one I knew the bastard was expecting, as she made a move to leave.

"Kat," I stepped forward, ignoring the growing smartass fucking grin on my father's face. "I...I want to see you again."

She gave a sad smile and glanced at my father as though deep down, he terrified her. Maybe he did...*so how the fuck was I going to get past that?*

"Maybe," she murmured, and left, striding toward the elevator.

I couldn't turn away, watching as the doors opened and she stepped through.

Then she was gone, leaving me alone with my grinning asshole of a father.

"So, a VanHalen," he muttered.

"Shut the fuck up," I growled.

He just lifted his hands in mock surrender. "This is me shutting up."

I cut him a look. That *never* stops him.

"Still, she looks like a nice girl," he tried. "Even if she is *way* out of your league."

"At least I have a league," I countered.

"Seriously though, I'm glad you found someone you like." He said it as though he was actually fucking happy.

We'd never been the average father and son. We didn't toss the fucking ball or have those deep conversations. Our relationship was based on loyalty and hard fucking lessons, and the need to survive. The only way a Stidda did. Through violence.

But right then, I felt the words bubbling up inside me. I wanted to tell him about her, about the way she made me feel and the things I'd heard. I wanted to ask his—*I don't know*—his goddamn advice. I wanted to ask him about that fucking Hale and tell him about Zakharov.

But as he wandered around the apartment and looked out into the night, I did none of those things. Because it wasn't me who needed to talk.

"I don't want you going anywhere without Freddy and Logan," he declared, turning from the window to find me. "You understand me, son? Nowhere. Not classes, in fact, actually *fuck* classes. Stay here with your girlfriend. Stay here and fuck and sleep and do anything but take fucking chances."

"You're scared. I don't like it," I answered.

"Someone is making a name for themselves." Dad rubbed the back of his neck, the movement so damn familiar. "I just had to sit there and look a father in the eyes who'd just lost his damn son."

Baldeon.

"So I want you to promise me, nowhere without Freddy or Logan."

"I promise," I answered as he crossed the space between us.

He grabbed the back of my neck and pulled me close. Chest to chest. He thumped my back and the hollow sound filled my ears as I repeated, "I promise."

22

Kat

Benjamin Rossi.

He wasn't what I'd expected. I stared at the walls of the elevator as I rode down to the foyer. He wasn't what I'd expected at all. He was...*nice.* His warm smile and careful grip had made me uncomfortable. I didn't know how to process that. I licked my throbbing lips, shaken to the core.

That wasn't supposed to happen. *No, it wasn't supposed to happen at all.*

The doors opened to a bark of laughter. I stepped out to see five massive guys who looked like they belonged in a motorcycle club. They all turned, the laughter and conversation dying as I stepped closer and scanned their faces.

The big, muscled guy from before moved away from the others. Logan, Lazarus had called him. His bright eyes sparkled with amusement as he came closer. "You ready to go home?" he asked.

"Yes," I answered, scanning the others, who watched me with interest.

But every one of them was smiling as they scanned me up and down. I was used to the attention, but this felt different somehow. This didn't feel creepy or dangerous. This felt...*safe.*

"See you back home," Logan called to the others as he headed for the door.

The wind whipped my hair into a frenzy the moment I stepped out. I hurried my steps, catching up to the bodyguard. "Sorry to take you away from your friends."

He just shrugged and gave me a smile. "Gotta make sure you're safe, right?"

I wasn't used to this laid-back strength and loyalty. Even Richard, my driver back home, wasn't as...welcoming. He was paid handsomely by my father, paid not to ask questions or care outside his responsibilities.

"You care about him, don't you?" The question slipped free before I knew it.

He glanced my way. "Lazarus, you mean?"

"Yes."

There was a flare of confusion, before he answered carefully. "I'd die for him."

"Out of duty?" I pushed, trying to figure out how much a man like Logan was worth.

He slowed his steps, those careful eyes fixed on mine. "Out of loyalty and love."

Loyalty and love.

I just gave a nod and walked the rest of the way in silence. Loyalty and love. Both of them were alien to me...and terrifying. I strode into my building and glanced at the guard positioned to protect us tonight, leaving Logan in the foyer near the door as I stopped at the elevator and turned. "Logan."

He glanced over his shoulder. "Yeah?"

"Thank you."

His smile was quick. "You're welcome. Goodnight, Kat."

"Night." I gave a small smile and stepped onto the elevator.

They were nice. *Really fucking nice.* I probed my lips with my fingers, remembering the way Lazarus had felt. Hot and hard, melting under my kiss. I was swept away by him and plunged into the kind of depth I'd never felt before. There was fire in those blue eyes of his, fire and lust.

And I wanted to use him...and his father.

Don't get attached, the voice in my head warned as the doors opened into our apartment. Lights flickered in the darkness as I stepped forward into the living room, lights that rose into the night. I stepped toward the windows, watching the helicopter rise and slowly disappear.

Don't get attached? I pressed my lips together remembering how swept away I'd been in that moment, how *dangerous* he made me feel. That same heat found me again, like a beast prowling through my body, smashing through closed and chained doors into darkened rooms.

Use him, that voice whispered in my head. *Use him and we're gone.*

He wouldn't care, he wouldn't even notice when I was gone. I nodded, driving that thought home, and came back to reality. Anna's bedroom was dark and quiet. I wasn't sure if she was asleep or with Finley. So I made my way quietly into my bedroom and undressed in the bathroom before stepping into the shower.

I would use Lazarus...and anyone else I had to.

I lowered my hand to my belly and skimmed my fingers across my skin. I'd use them because I had no other choice. *Do I need to take care of that Hale, or that asshole Zakharov?* Lazarus's words filled me as I ran the sponge across my skin and over my shoulders, imagining the idea of that.

Threats.

Intimidation.

Would they work? Maybe, coming from a Rossi.

They had a reputation of being dangerous...and I had a feeling Lazarus would be every bit the bad boy I thought him to be. I dropped my head, feeling the heat of the water rush over my body as that ache of desire sparked.

Loyalty and love.

My fingers found my breasts, remembering the way he'd felt underneath me as I'd danced. I'd wanted him then...and still wanted him. But the thought of him over me sent shivers along my spine. I never wanted to be used like that. I never wanted to be hurt like that. Never again...*never again.*

Haelstrom hurt me like that. I could still feel his hand on the back of my neck, still feel how he held me down and used my body, still feel how his voice in my ear filled me with terror...the kind of terror I'd had with Damon. I hit the faucet and ended the spray. Stepping out, I wrapped a towel around my body and went into the bedroom, slipping into my pajamas before climbing into bed.

I tried to sleep, closing my eyes to the image of Lazarus.

Love and loyalty.

I wondered how much that might cost?

THE NEXT DAY WAS A BLUR. The skies darkened, leaving the clear blue skies behind for dark, broody clouds. I kept myself busy, forcing myself to attend the classes while I watched everyone else around me. The classes were slowly becoming more and more empty. Vacant seats sat visible in every row.

I didn't want to be here, yet I refused to be a prisoner, as well. So I spent the day watching for Damon, waiting for the moment he cornered me like the piece of shit he was, and held my fucking head high as I walked to the last class for the day.

That's right...fuck you, Damon.

I stepped up to the doorway and scanned those who'd already taken their seats, then exhaled with relief. The last damn class. Maybe he'd finally gotten the hint? Maybe for now he was going to leave me alone? I stepped inside and took my seat, catching a smile from one of the Mafia guys sitting five seats away...*Kilpatrick.*

"Hey." He shifted, then rose and came closer.

My pulse sped with the movement, but I kept that mask firmly fixed. "Hey yourself."

"You're Katerina, right?"

"Kat," I corrected, hating the way I squirmed at the sound of my full name.

No one used that...not unless.

"Alexi Kilpatrick." He reached out a hand.

I paused for a second, my mind racing with what all the implications of getting closer to another Mafia Prince might be and realized that it was probably worse having one as an enemy. I took his hand and forced a smile. "Nice to meet you."

He flopped down in the seat next to me and for a second, my heart fluttered in panic, until I realized he was my perfect fail-safe. I glanced at the open doors. If Damon was to walk through, there was no way he'd sit next to me now, no way he'd come near me. That turned my fake smile into something real.

"Having a good time...you know, at the institute?" he asked as he followed my gaze to the door.

"Sure," I lilted, and met his gaze.

He was wirier than Lazarus, with hard muscles under that white shirt. Long, dirty blond hair and the most intense blue-green eyes I'd ever seen made me shift uncomfortably in my seat.

"Yeah, that's good. 'Cause your daddy paid a helluva lot of money for you to be here, right? So it'd better be worth it," he muttered, leaning back in his seat.

"Yeah, sure." I said, not really knowing where the conversation was going.

"So, I've seen you with Lazarus lately," he started.

Oh, so that's where. "Yeah?"

"You know he's bad news, right?" Kilpatrick set that steely glare to mine. "Short temper, and I hear he also comes up short in the bedroom, if you know what I mean." He wiggled his pinky finger at me.

My face burned as I looked away. For some reason, anger burned inside me. "You sound jealous as fuck, Kilpatrick," I retorted, and cut him a smirk. "And for the record, seeing as how you know I've been 'spending time' with Lazarus, you'll be happy to know that hasn't been my experience at all."

I rose from my seat. Fuck him and fuck this class.

He just glared as I stepped sideways, moving along the seats, and headed for the door. Sniggers came from behind me, but I was pretty sure they were aimed at him.

"Nice one, Kilpatrick.," someone called as I hit the door.

I stepped through it, not even watching where I was going, and slammed straight into someone. I hit hard, stumbling to the side. "Shit...sorry." The words were a rush as I lifted my gaze, to the leggy fucking bitch who liked to bully my friends. *"You?"*

Anger seethed inside me as the bitch just widened her eyes and threw a panicked gaze to the open door of the classroom. "Oh shit..." she muttered. "I was just..."

I took a step toward her, unable to stop that burn.

Panic and fear crossed her face and mixed with desperation, making a dangerous combination.

"I w-was coming to find you," she stuttered.

The last time I'd seen this bitch, she was panicked in a bathroom as I pressed a pair of sharpened clippers to her neck and threatened her damn life. "Yeah?" I urged, my lips curling.

"I wanted to apologize."

The flames inside me seemed to splutter as I scowled. "You did?"

She licked her lips, shifting her weight from one foot to the other. "Yeah," she answered. "Look, I feel really bad with what happened between us."

"You mean with what happened between you and Anna, right?" I corrected.

"Yeah, that," she nodded. "I don't know what came over me. That's not how I normally am."

I doubted that...I doubted that very much.

"So I wanted to find you to let you know that." She forced a smile, fumbling with her words.

I searched her gaze, hating how that anger I had for her seemed to weaken.

"Look, I'm trying here." She winced and met my gaze. "The last thing I want is to be on a damn island with someone who doesn't like me, and I didn't know who you were."

"And now you do," I responded.

She licked her lips. "Now I do."

But I was talking about the fact that I'd have my friend's back, and she was talking about something else entirely. I saw it in the way she was acting differently around me and the sudden clarity around my name.

I took a step away, nodding.

"Can I walk with you?" she asked nervously, looking over her shoulder. "My guard has suddenly disappeared and I'm a little...scared. You know, with the *murder*."

She was scared? As much as I wanted to leave her behind, I didn't want to be *that* person. I wanted to be someone good, someone hard and tough. Someone who was...*good*. Lazarus's face filled my mind as I gave a sigh and muttered. "Sure, I was leaving anyway."

"Oh, thank God," she gushed, and fell into step, glancing once more over her shoulder as though Baldeon's killer was just one damn step away.

I just kept walking, heading down the hallway and past the darkened classrooms until we got toward the foyer.

"I hate to be a pain, seeing as you're being so fucking nice, but I'm looking for this damn teacher. He said he was in two-oh-one. I think that's just over there. Will you come with me?" She pointed to the hallway across the foyer. "It'll take like two seconds, I promise."

I glanced toward the doors and the growing gloom that was waiting for me outside. Palms swayed and bent with the brutal gusts of wind. "Sure," I muttered, and dragged my gaze from the sight. "Why the hell not."

"Thank you." She breathed a sigh of relief and took half a step ahead. "It's just up here. I promise, I'll be like a second."

I followed her, cutting across the foyer, and listened to the wind howling. It was going to storm, and I was betting Anna would stay with Finley, leaving me all alone.

"Just in here."

I nodded, not really listening, as she stepped inside a darkened classroom. My mind was drawn back to Lazarus and the kiss from last night. The kiss that had felt too good to be real—

"*Fuck!*" she howled.

I jerked my gaze up at the sound from the room.

"I've twisted my damn ankle!" the idiot called from inside.

I pushed the door open and entered, my hand fumbling for the light switch as I grumbled, "Wait a second...I'm coming."

The door closed with a *bang* behind me. I jumped at the sound as the flick of a lighter came further into the room, and Damon's face brightened in the glow.

"You really need to make better choices, Katerina." He pushed off from the wall. "You need to make better friends."

23

Kat

I stumbled backwards as Damon strode toward me from the back of the classroom.

"No," I muttered as panic filled me. I turned and lunged toward the doorway, but the deceiving bitch stepped in my way.

"I don't think so," she grinned and clucked her tongue. "I owe you for this, you rich *bitch.*" She lunged, fisted a handful of my hair, and yanked.

Agony tore through my scalp as my spine bowed with the force.

The flame of the lighter was snuffed out, but still, in the dim light coming through the small glass in the door, I caught movement as Damon came closer. "Katerina," he grinned and shook his head. "Don't you know by now you're *my* plaything?"

"Get the fuck off me!" I roared, and shoved the tall bitch away.

She just laughed and deflected my blows with her long fucking arms. One more tug of my hair, and that savage part of my nature burned right through my fear. I spun on her and lunged forward, driving *her* backwards. "You want to fucking hurt me? You have *no idea what pain is.*"

I dropped my shoulder and charged, slamming her against the wall. Her hold on my hair slipped with a cry of alarm before she stumbled. I slapped her hand away from my hair, watching as her gaze jerked to Damon's.

"You?" I whirled on him, driving my body forward, and slammed my palms against his chest. "You fucking touch me again..."

He stumbled backwards, grasping my wrists. "You'll *what?*" he barked. "You'll get your little *boyfriend* to threaten me?"

I stilled for a second before I wrenched my hands from his. My chest heaved in harsh breaths. My *boyfriend.* Lazarus, that's who he meant. Lazarus Rossi. "Yes." I watched his eyes spark with cruelty. "That's exactly what I'll do. You come near me again, Damon, and you're dead."

I took a step backwards, splitting my focus between the two predatory pieces of shit.

"I wonder what he'll think of you when he finds out the truth."

Ice plunged through my veins at the threat. Damon took a step forward as I fumbled for the door handles behind me. "I wonder what he'll think when I show him all the videos of good little Katerina." He reached into his pocket and yanked his phone free, waving it in the air. "All those *dirty* videos."

The cunt behind me sniggered as I yanked the handle and lunged through the doorway.

"Be seeing you, Katerina!" Damon called behind me as I tore along the hall and into the empty foyer.

My scalp was burning and tears stung my eyes, but in that moment, all I wanted to do was get the fuck out of there. I punched through the doors and tore out into the brutal gusts of the screaming wind. There was movement in the distance as someone else stood out from one of the buildings. I swiped the slick slide of tears with the back of my hand and strode forward.

Do not crack. I clenched my jaw. *Do not let them win.*

A tremor tore through me as I swallowed a sob. It took all my strength to hold it together, every ounce of willpower...*every burning need.* My steps blurred as the gusts stole my tears away. When I lifted my head, I stood in front of one of the apartment buildings. *But it wasn't mine...*

The darkened foyer waited in front of me, *Lazarus's* darkened foyer. Movement came from inside as the elevator doors opened...*and Logan stepped out.*

He lifted his head, and met my gaze. I took a step backwards, swallowing that thrumming sound of fear as the doors opened and he strode out.

"Kat?" Logan searched my gaze, his brow furrowing as he looked behind me. "What's wrong?"

He was in front of me in an instant, towering over me with massive strength as he reached out and gently touched my arm. "Where the fuck is your bodyguard?" He seemed to grow even more pissed as he settled those intense eyes on me. "And why the fuck have you been crying?"

Panic flared inside me as I shook my head.

"Did something happen?" He splayed his hand on my arm.

Anyone else, I'd fight and buck, hating the touch. But here and now...it was comforting. There was nothing *sick* in Logan's gaze. Nothing *wrong*. He just stepped closer, moving into a savage gust as it whipped my hair into my eyes. He was shielding me, using his own body as a buffer.

"No," I lied. "Nothing happened."

He just lowered his head, forcing my gaze to his. "You sure?"

There was something *powerful* in his focus, something commanding...and *safe*.

"Laz isn't here, if you've come to see him," he said softly.

I just shook my head. "I don't know why I'm here."

It was the truth. Why I found myself here was *scary*. But everything about Lazarus was scary. His kiss, his father, his haunting blue eyes.

"Well, I'm glad you are. You shouldn't be walking around without an escort," he growled and slid his arm around my shoulders. "Come on, let's get you home, yeah?"

I just nodded, pressing against his warmth. I shouldn't be taking comfort in this bodyguard, shouldn't be taking strength in this Stidda Mafia family. Logan just dropped his arm and motioned me forward, scanning the grounds around us as we walked.

We said nothing this time, unable to battle the roar of the wind as the sky rumbled overhead. When I stepped through the doors of my own building, my ears were muffled and strange.

"You going to be okay here?" Concern filled Logan's eyes as he stopped at the door.

"Yes." I forced a smile. "Thank you, Logan."

He just gave me a smile, a warm, friendly smile, not one filled with sick ideas and dark fantasies, just warmth, and kindness. "Stay safe, Kat. I'll have a talk with the Commander and have another guard assigned to you."

I just nodded, stepping into the elevator when it opened. I couldn't wait to be warm. I couldn't wait to be *safe*. I strode through the apartment, peering into Anna's room. But she wasn't here. A flicker of disappointment coursed through me.

My head throbbed from that bitch's hold. I lifted my hand and probed the burning spot. Panic and pain mingled inside me. I needed to move, to do *something*. So I strode into my room, took off my cream Dior top, and shrugged out of my black slacks, changing into jeans and a cashmere sweater.

Desperation crowded my mind as I tugged the hem down and made my way into the kitchen. Memories crowded in from my life and for once, they weren't dangerous. We didn't talk to the help, didn't pass so much as a command to even the servants who cleaned our bathrooms.

But when my father wasn't around, I sometimes slipped into the kitchen. Careful glances, then our chef slid a perfectly pink cup and saucer my way. The hot chocolate was rich and delectable, complete with handmade marshmallows. Comfort food in its finest form. And that's what I needed now.

I needed comfort. So I turned, gathered the supplies from the cupboard, and set to work, pouring milk into a pan and set it over a low heat. I busied myself adding ingredients and stirring, and lost myself in the movement. I caught a hum coming from my lips as the elevator doors opened and Anna stormed in.

Thunder broke overhead, crackling loudly. Anna flinched at the sound and walked past me.

"Hey, Anna?"

"Not now, Kat," she snapped.

I stilled. *Okay.* "Whoa." I lowered the spoon and came around the counter. "What's going on?"

"Nothing."

The cold bite of anger in her tone stung. Anyone else I expected it, *but not from her.* "Something's wrong," I murmured, and reached for her.

The moment I touched her, she started to tremble, shuddering and quaking.

"Hey there." I pulled her against me, desperately needing the touch as much as she did. Something was happening to me, something I didn't understand. I was changing in this place, becoming real and vulnerable. I wasn't the same woman who'd stepped off that boat onto the island, and that scared the fuck out of me. Then Anna lowered her head against my shoulder and let loose a whimper. "Hey now," I soothed.

"What's going on?" I pulled back to look into her eyes. "Talk to me."

She just pinned me with those big brown eyes. I could see she was trying. The words welled up in her shimmering eyes, but she didn't speak, she just stood there, gulping like a fish out of water.

"It's the storm, isn't it?" I said, giving her an out.

She slowly nodded, not looking toward the brooding clouds and the thundering skies even once.

"I knew it. I hate them, too. I hate that caged, restless feeling, hate how loud the wind sounds and how the windows tremble. But we're together now."

She looked at me with so much hope, hope and desperation. Her fingers dug into my arm. I couldn't stare into her eyes, not seeing the way she looked at me...*if only she knew the truth of who I was...the dirty, disgusting truth.* No. I couldn't let her see me, not the way I was.

Lie!

That anguish roared. *Lie.* "And I'm going to stay. I told Damon if he wants to see me, he can come and stay here. I can't leave my best friend alone, not anymore."

Please don't ask about him. Please don't.

She just gave a nod, relief making her shoulders sag. "Thank you," she murmured as a lone tear slipped free.

I just brushed that tear away and held her before I remembered. "Oh! I made you hot chocolate. It's perfect for days like this."

"Stormy days?" she muttered and swiped another tear away.

"Sure," I answered with a smile.

But even on days when the sun shone and blue skies commanded the sky, there were still steel gray clouds in my world, still thunder and lightning and cruel storms. I lived in my world in the brief, quiet spells between the storms, standing in the eye of the hurricanes to face down the beasts who turned my world upside down.

But that wasn't Anna's world.

Not even remotely.

I didn't know what her connection to Finley Salvatore was, but I knew who *she* was—and that was all good. She was honest and kind. She was pure, all the way through, untainted by this savage world. I poured her the hot chocolate and placed marshmallows on top, watching her eyes brighten as she swallowed her tears. See, she was good. The kind of good that something as small as a goddamn hot drink would brighten her damn world. They were store-bought marshmallows, too. But they'd have to do. It wasn't anywhere near what I wanted to give her, wasn't anywhere near the kind of comfort I wished she'd feel.

"Hot chocolate, huh? What else can you make?" she smiled.

"That's basically it. Hot chocolate. So you better like it, 'cause that's all you're gonna get, from me at least."

"Great," she muttered. "I'm gonna be as big as a whale."

"A very *awesome* whale," I countered.

Still, she drank the damn stuff, blowing gently and sipping, leaving the sticky, white foam on her lips. "It's good," she said, surprised.

"Of course, it's good," I chuffed. "I made it, didn't I?"

She just chuckled and sipped some more, giving a sigh. But the way she looked at me was strange, as sadness crept into her eyes. I drained my cup and stifled a yawn. Barely any sleep last night and after the trauma of today, I just felt *drained*.

"Come and sit, tell me about your lecture," I murmured, and made my way toward the sofa.

She followed, bringing the hot chocolate with her, and as I sat, she started talking about the lecture on money laundering. The more she talked, the more at ease I felt. She was excited about the mechanics, telling me all the things the lecturer had gotten wrong.

"You have the same look as you did when you were telling Evan how to clean five hundred thousand dollars of her money." I shook my head and smiled.

"What? No," she lied. "I just have a passing interest."

"Passing interest, my ass." I countered. "You only look like that talking about laundering dirty money and Finley Salvatore."

"Don't say that." Her face turned bright red.

"Okay," I muttered and leaned back against the sofa's cushions. "There's a whole lot going on in your eyes, Anna. Something's happened between you two, hasn't it?"

I thought for a second, she was going to pull away, maybe even rise from the sofa and tell me to go fuck myself. But she didn't, and for the first time, I realized she needed this. She needed someone to talk to. She needed someone to *confide in.*

"You could say that," she said finally.

"You want to talk about it?" I asked carefully.

She just looked away and murmured. "It's complicated."

"Complicated how?"

"Complicated that it could get me into a lot of trouble."

Silence filled the void. *Jesus.* She was in deep here, deeper than I'd realized. "You're not just talking about feelings here, are you?"

A slow shake of her head hit me hard.

Yet here she was, being honest, being *raw*. And I was still hiding two of the biggest things someone could hide. My mind turned to the life inside me. The life growing and blooming, becoming more of me than it ever could be of *him*.

"Shit, Anna., I murmured. "How deep are we talking here?"

"Are you talking about my heart?" she asked with a sad smile. "Because I'm pretty sure I saw a sold sticker on there somewhere."

"I fucking knew it," I muttered, swallowing a flare of jealousy.

She had everything she wanted and didn't want in one man, and here I had...*lies and deceit*. Haunting blue eyes filled my mind. I could still feel the kiss we'd had, still feel that hunger inside me, still feel the way he allowed me to feel when I'd taken control. "It all makes sense now. All the weirdness around him and the night of the party. You're into him and he's *totally* into you, like head over heels into you."

"Bullshit," she protested, her cheeks burning.

Oh, she knew alright. She knew what kind of effect she had on Finley Salvatore. "Like totally take a fucking bullet for you," I finished, watching her flinch.

As soon as I said the words, Lazarus burned even brighter in my mind. Christ, I didn't need to be catching feelings where he was concerned, and yet here I was...

I licked my lips and tried to pull away the moment my heart gave a twinge. "I might not be the best person to talk to about the kind of things you're feeling here, but I'm a good listener," I commented, rising from the sofa. "My door is open."

"That's because you have no door," she called as I turned.

I smiled, unable to argue with that. "True." I stifled a yawn. Pregnancy was taking more out of me than I'd realized. "But the offer is there in any case."

"You sound tired," she said, rising behind me.

"I should be," I said with a wink, swallowing the sick feeling inside me.

Just play the game a little longer, that voice said inside my head. *Just a little longer, and you'll be free.*

My phone gave a *beep.* I grabbed it and looked down.

Unknown: I'm thinking of you, Katerina.

An image followed. One of a white mask against a black satin sheet.

It could be only one person...

Hale.

24

Lazarus

Lightning erupted through the steel gray sky. I rolled over and watched the savage display, not even twitching when the *crack* of thunder came. In an instant, I was back there, in that four-wheel drive with Gravel behind the wheel and Taken rising up beside me to fire through the rear window at the car behind us.

Gunshots became thunder.

Roaring in my ears.

Making my heart race once more.

Just like it always did. Stupid fucking heart. I shoved the sheets aside and slipped from the bed. The wind was howling, tearing bits of palms free to hurtle across the Institute's grounds. Chaos. That's what it was out there, fucking chaos. I strode toward the bathroom and shrugged out of my boxers. The place was too quiet without those two assholes under my feet like my damn mother every second of the day.

I bet Logan was already up by now, drinking his acid-tinged black shit and scanning the camera log of the island for the last twenty-four hours. Overbearing sonofabitch. Fuck, I loved him.

They were my family.

My brothers.

The only ones I had and the only ones I needed. I hit the faucet and waited until the steam drifted from the water, then stepped under the spray. My muscles relaxed and my mind drifted... right to her. The redhead that was turning my life upside down.

I hadn't come here for her. I'd come to piss off Finley Salvatore, to put a fucking pin in his bright red balloon and watch him flounder all over the damn place. I came here because Dad wanted me out of the damn way. He wanted me somewhere I could be protected because it seemed like I couldn't be protected at home.

Not anymore.

I washed and scrubbed, leaning my head back under the searing spray and felt that ache in my gut. The one that told me something was coming, something dark and dangerous, something out of my control. I hit the spray and stepped out, hearing a faint *thud* in the apartment below.

We all felt it.

The storm bearing down on us.

It made us all on fucking edge.

I yanked on jeans and a t-shit before stepping into boots. My phone gave a *beep*, right on goddamn time.

Logan: Breakfast is ready. Get your ass down here.

I just chuckled and snatched my card, slipped it into my pocket, and headed downstairs. The moment the elevator doors opened, I smelled the heady scent of bacon and eggs mingled with the sharp tang of coffee. My stomach gave a growl as I strode into the apartment, meeting Freddy's gaze before he gave a jerk of his head.

A plate piled with food waited for me. That was one thing I loved about living with these guys, there was never any shortage of food. Logan lifted his gaze to me from behind the screen of the laptop. "Seems the storm hit hard last night."

I gave a nod, grabbed the fork beside the plate, and stabbed a thick slab of bacon before shoving it into my mouth.

"And there's talk of a boat off the coast again," he continued.

I stopped mid-chew, then proceeded slowly, my mind racing, taking me back to the night Baldeon was murdered, the night I saw two figures race toward the shore...and did nothing about it. Guilt welled inside me. "Did they find anyone?"

There was a shake of his head. "But we're not taking chances, not where you're concerned."

"You don't think they'd make another attack, do you?" I swallowed, suddenly not hungry any more.

"With all the increased security around the island, they'd be crazy to try. But even with unconfirmed reports of another boat off the coast, we can't take that chance. Which is why one of us will be around you twenty-four-seven."

"You mean," I stabbed a piece of egg. "One of you ugly fuckers is gonna watch me sleep?"

"Yep." Freddy just grinned. "One of our faces is gonna be the first thing you see in the morning and the last thing you see at night."

"Now that's a chilling fucking thought right there," I muttered with a mouthful of food.

Suddenly the laughter died in his eyes as he stared at me, then turned away. Was he imagining my face instead of Baldeon's? 'Cause I did, every fucking day. I glanced away, shoved the rest of the food into my mouth, and stacked the plate into the dishwasher.

Every apartment came with its own maid and chef service. But fucked if I was going to let someone clean up after me. I wasn't prissy, unlike Finley Salvatore. Speaking of...the bastard had been unnaturally quiet.

Word was pretty-boy Kilpatrick had a hard-on for me and the stupid fucking initiation was doing the rounds. But some took it way too far. Some, like Kilpatrick, used it as a way to exact justice, or revenge.

The only problem was...I hadn't done a fucking thing, *except beat a man until he lost consciousness.* But we all knew what fucking side the Kilpatricks and the Bernardis stood on. We all knew when it came to loyalty, Stidda were on their own. Which is why I'd never wanted to come to this place.

Kat's face filled my mind as I straightened and turned to the others. If I hadn't come, then I wouldn't have met someone like her. Someone who affected me far more than a woman should.

"I'm going to see Kilpatrick," I announced.

"You think that's wise?" Logan asked, his brow rising.

"Is any decision I make wise?"

"He has a point," Freddy agreed.

I just flipped the fucker the finger. "I want to put a damn end to this initiation shit once and for all. The last thing I need is to be watching my back for some idiot to play a goddamn prank."

Logan just nodded. "Let me suit up and I'll come with you."

I wanted to say, *don't bother. I'll be back before you know it.* But I knew these guys weren't playing games. Still, the thought of having them at my back day and damn night was suffocating.

"Speaking of seeing someone, Kat came around yesterday." Logan shrugged into his shoulder holster and snapped the thing tight across his massive chest.

I couldn't stop my heart from racing. "Oh, yeah?" I tried to keep the surprise from my voice. But my heart was doing some weird shit, making me feel like I wanted to palm a damn gun. "And what did she want?"

The pain in the damn ass just gave a shrug, but when he lifted his gaze to mine, the man was all serious. "I think that girl's in a whole lot of trouble, the kind she can't find a way out of."

That panicked feeling in my chest only grew tighter.

"And it looks like she's coming to you to help," Logan finished.

He took a step, but all of a sudden, I wasn't interested in seeing Kilpatrick. I wasn't interested in seeing any of them. I wanted to see *her,* to be the one who listened to whatever shit she'd got herself into and find a way out of it—the only way I knew how —*with violence.*

"What did she say exactly?" I muttered, hating the needy sound in my voice.

"Nothing," Logan answered, and clenched his jaw.

That glint was there, that dangerous glint that told me and anyone else around him to stand the hell back. Something about Kat coming here pissed him off. Something about what she *didn't* say pissed him off. I decided it was about time I paid her building a visit. Maybe this time I might even go inside, instead of standing out in the goddamn shadows like a fucking creep.

"Ready?" I muttered.

A nod, and we were walking toward the elevator, leaving Freddy behind.

The fucking wind was practically cyclonic when we stepped out. I lifted the collar on my leather jacket and tucked my head down. Logan didn't even flinch. He just scanned the buildings, seemingly fucking oblivious to the howling gusts of wind as he strode toward Kilpatrick's building on the other side of the goddamn island.

Two seconds in, and I couldn't see through the blur of tears.

Ten seconds, and I couldn't feel my goddamn face.

Thirty, and I was cursing myself for giving a damn.

Sixty, and I wanted to murder someone.

Anyone.

I didn't care.

Finley Salvatore, Alexi Kilpatrick. Hell, myself for that matter, for doing such a stupid fucking thing like this and for giving a damn. Still, I trudged between the damn buildings to come to his, and stopped. There were men inside, and I wasn't talking about the couple of schmucks the Commission assigned to each building for protection. I was talking about *half a dozen fucking men.*

"What the fuck," Logan muttered, then cut me a look. "You know about this?"

I just shook my head. No, I didn't know...and I was pretty sure if there was a secret group on the island, the Commission would know about it...*and I knew everything that went through the Commission.*

Unless Dad was holding information back from me...

I stepped up to the door and rapped my knuckles on the glass. I didn't need to draw their gazes. They already knew I was there, stepping away from their huddle as one approached the door.

"Mr. Rossi," he greeted, his gaze moving to Logan at my back.

But he didn't move out of the doorway, still barring the way.

"You going to let us in?" I barked.

A glance over his shoulder, and one of the six men gave a nod. Logan followed. One glare from the former SEAL at my back and the asshole at the door soon moved.

"Want to tell me what the hell is going on?" I challenged, narrowing in on the asshole who seemed to be giving the orders.

He said nothing, just gave me a cold, steely glare. "Just a training exercise, Mr. Rossi," he answered. But the bastard had an accent, one I'd heard before.

It was the same thick, biting accent the Commander had. *Albanian.* "Training exercise, huh?" I sneered, scanning every face before I jerked my head toward the elevator. "Then you won't mind letting me up to see Kilpatrick?"

"Alexi isn't here," the asshole in charge answered without shifting that steely gaze from mine.

Alexi, huh? Something was going on here, something I wasn't privy to. I knew there was a reason why Alexi would come back here after years of staying away. Why, all of a sudden on the eve of him taking over the family seat on the Commission, he'd just show up and make trouble.

Considering what had happened to his brother.

I suppose eating his own gun and surviving would shatter anyone, but Wraith Kilpatrick wasn't just shattered...the man was beyond saving. Word was he was still in that psych ward. Word was no one went near him...including his sweet little brother who now took his place as the head of his family.

And as I stared at this stony-faced asshole, I knew I was getting nowhere.

They wouldn't let me up there.

They wouldn't even tell me the damn truth.

I just nodded. "Sure, maybe I'll just come back."

"Yeah, maybe you should," the asshole murmured, and adjusted his jacket.

But he glanced toward Logan, waiting for him to make a move.

The only problem was...if Logan decided to act, you'd never see him coming. The best you could hope for was to wake up after the fact. My protector said nothing as I turned. He didn't move, didn't shift that brutal fucking stare from the asshole's gaze. I had to smother a smirk. The idiot just made a target of himself.

We left them behind, and I didn't have to lead the way for Logan to end up at Kat's building. We stepped inside and shook the roar from our ears.

"They upstairs?" Logan growled at the guard.

He glanced from Logan to me and slowly nodded.

"Well then, call them, for fuck's sake," Logan snapped. "I'm not going to storm into a woman's apartment unannounced."

The poor idiot just fumbled with his phone, then mumbled, "Miss VanHalen. I've got some...*men* here to see you."

"Lazarus Rossi and Logan James," my protector snapped.

I'd never seen him like this before. Never so...*careful* around a woman. Maybe I wasn't the only one holding a damn flame for Kat VanHalen? The idea of that made me feel...possessive and dangerous.

"Yes, ma'am," the guard answered, and ended the call.

He stole toward the elevator and swiped his card across the sensor. "Miss VanHalen said to go on up."

Logan stared daggers into the poor bastard. Pissed off and super wary. No one better cross Logan today...*including me.*

I stepped inside and rose with the seething bastard until the door opened and she was there, her red hair piled into a mess on top of her head. *Jesus.* She looked...

Logan swallowed hard and glanced away.

Yeah, he was interested. I knew just how he felt.

"Everything okay?" Kat asked carefully, and wrapped her arms around her waist.

Logan just took a step toward the window. She followed the movement for a second before turning to me.

"Fine," I answered, and took a step toward her. "Would you believe we were in the neighborhood?"

She smiled at that, those delicious lips curling higher at one corner. I swallowed hard, remembering how those lips had felt on mine. How, unrestrained, she was fucking ferocious. Her cheeks blushed when she met my gaze, then dropped her focus to my lips. She was remembering that heat between us, too...

Her blush deepened as she answered. "Yeah, I guess I could believe that."

"Are you safe?" Logan cut in.

She glanced over her shoulder at him and smiled. "Yes, thank you."

There was a nod of his head before he turned to the window once more. "Good.

He said it like he contemplated keeping her safe himself. I ground my teeth as that savage part of me rose to the challenge.

"Logan said you came by yesterday." I drew her focus to me.

Her blush seemed to fade in an instant, leaving a washed-out look behind. There was a flicker of fear in her eyes, a catch of her breath that anyone else might've missed. But I missed *nothing* when it came to her, not the stillness of her chest, not the way those perfect eyes seemed to flicker, tearing from my face as though she was afraid if I looked too hard I might just find something I didn't like in her.

"Sorry I wasn't there." I kept prodding. "But I'm here now...if you needed anything."

Please...please, say you need something, that desperation rose inside me. *My protection. My fucking wrath. Anything. Just ask for anything...*

But she just glanced at Logan. "I'm good now, thank you."

I glanced around the apartment, hating that I hadn't been there yesterday. "You all alone?"

"Yes," she said in a careful voice.

I flinched, my heart pounding. "I meant, your roommate's already in class? Not in a creepy way."

She just took a step closer and lowered her voice. "There's nothing about you that's creepy, Lazarus. She went to an early class."

"One of those people, huh? Early to class, a straight A student," I said, catching her smile.

"Something like that." She shifted her weight from one foot to the other.

Logan just stared out the damn window as the silence grew between us. "Well, if you need anything, you know where we are." I tried for strength and sounded like a damn sap.

"I'll see you later?" she asked.

"Yeah." I gave her a smile as hope flared. "I'll see you later."

25

Lazarus

WELL...YOU KNOW WHERE WE ARE.

Could I sound any more pitiful? Logan glanced my way as we strode into the elevator. "Don't say a fucking word," I snarled.

I tried not to see the shit-eating grin on the asshole's face, and turned away. Even the brutal wind couldn't stop the replay of my own pathetic words.

"Come on," Logan muttered. "Grab your gear and let's head to the gym, work off some of that pent-up sexual energy, huh?"

He threw a punch I saw coming a mile away. I dodged it, swatting his meaty fist away. Still, it stung as it landed in my palm. I just gave a nod, knowing that was exactly what I needed. I needed to work out how that woman affected me so damn much. I needed to work out how to handle it if she didn't feel the damn same.

We went upstairs, Logan hovering at the elevator while I grabbed my gear, then followed back to his apartment. I waited while he grabbed his gloves and a change of clothes, then we went down to the fully equipped gym and the added sparring mat.

Two minutes later, I was dressed in shorts and a t-shirt, and starting to work the coiled tension from my body with short, hard jabs into the air in front of me.

"Come on, you can do better than that," Logan jabbed, his dark eyes alight with hunger.

Freddy just grinned, watching from the sidelines since one of us had to be armed to the teeth. Logan just flanked my side, gloved hands up, protecting his face. He moved like a predator, head tucked in, muscles flexing as he lashed out with a blow toward my face.

I dodged it, barely. Moving to the side. *Always to the side.* His commands rang in my head. *Get on the outside of them, never in the middle. Do as much damage as you can.* I clenched and drove a fist out, catching him in the kidneys. He flinched and swung, his blow landing in the center of my chest.

"Good, *again*," he growled...then turned and caught me off guard with a punch to the face, catching me in the fucking nose.

Agony roared through my head. Tears came in an instant, blurring the sonofabitch. I clenched my jaw, that savagery bursting through to the surface as I blinked through the tears and went for him. My movements were ruthless this time. Gone was the tremble in my muscles, gone was the roar in my head. There was only him now, only the chance to take this fucker down.

"Good," he repeated, only this time he moved front on, exposing himself.

I swung, again and again. Two blows he deflected...but two caught their mark and in the blink of an eye, the hunter became the hunted.

I swung, jabbed, lifted my leg and kicked out, catching him in the side, making the bastard work. The harder and more focused I became, the more he enjoyed it, blocking and then coming for me...*hard*. Showing me the kind of training a former Navy SEAL had. The bastard was ruthless and consuming, and by the time he was done, I was on my hands and knees on the mat, sucking in heaving breaths.

"Good," he patted my shoulder with a heavy glove. "Very good. You're getting better."

"Better be," I forced the words through hard gasps. "Or I'll die trying, right?"

He just grinned at me, then held out his forearm.

I took it, using the leverage to heave myself up from the floor, and waited for the damn room to stop spinning.

"Better?" He stared into my eyes.

I nodded, clearer, harder, back to my old self. "Better."

There was no more panicked roar inside my head now, no more tangled mess of emotions the redhead had left behind. There was only clarity, only the darkness. Only that hunger, *kill or be killed*.

I sucked in a hard breath as I watched Freddy rise from his seat at the edge of the gym. Brother to brother, we strode out, sweaty and slick. A damn mess. But there was something about fighting and training together, something that brought us closer together.

Women came and went...but my brothers, they always had my back.

I made my away back to the apartment and left Logan in the apartment below mine. The second I was alone, I grabbed my phone and called Dad. He answered on the second ring.

"Problem?" The deep growl came through the other end.

"Many of them. I am a Rossi, after all, aren't I? But it's nothing I can't handle," I answered. "But there's a reason why I called."

"You need some fatherly advice? In over your head with a certain billionaire's daughter?"

"No," I growled as he chuckled. "The Commission meeting. I want to know what was discussed."

The laughter ended, just like I knew it would. "We discussed a lot of things, Laz."

"Anything specific to the Kilpatricks?"

"No, *why?*"

I ground my teeth, remembering the way those assholes closed ranks quick enough. "I'm not sure. But something's up."

"They assured us you were safe on the island. That with the increased security, there'd be no more attacks. The Kilpatricks are on edge...what with Wraith and everything."

"First sons are dropping all over the place, it seems," I muttered.

There was silence on the other end of the line, then quietly, "Maybe we should bring you home."

"No," I answered as Kat's face filled my mind. "Not yet."

"I don't need to remind you to be careful. Things are volatile at best."

"Another hit?" I asked.

"On the warehouse this time. The fuckers decided to have an early Fourth of July...with C-4."

I winced. The warehouse that housed the guns and a healthy stash of cocaine.

"If there's another attack, you're on the first chopper out of there." Dad warned. "I mean it."

"I hear you," I answered. The only problem was, I had no intention of leaving Kat behind. Not now...*not ever.*

We hung up, and I spent the next few hours taking a shower and switching on the TV, only to stare blankly at the screen. Everything was eating at me; Kilpatrick, Kat...Finley, the damn initiation, and the attack on the warehouse.

I had to do something. I glanced at my phone, to see it was already afternoon. One last class, then once tonight came, I'd...*what?* that asshole in my head snarled. *You gonna stand outside her fucking building again, pining for her? Christ, you're pathetic.*

I clenched my jaw. I was getting fucking sick of waiting, sick of knowing she was probably with Damon Zakharov and not with me. I was getting tired of this goddamn tug-of-war inside me. The woman was playing with my damn emotions and I was tired of waiting to make a move. I grabbed my cell and punched out a message:

Going to class and no, I don't need an escort.

My phone gave a *beep. Institute announcement: compulsory class. Building 1: Room 62.*

"Fucking great," I muttered. "Now they decide to come clean."

Freddy: Logan said it's not safe.

I'll be at building 1. You can piss and hit it from here. I'll message if there's a problem.

Freddy: Fine. But if you break a nail getting through the door, then that's on you.

I just laughed, slid my phone into my pocket, and headed for the class. The wind had died down to just gale force levels by the time I pushed through the door and headed toward building one. Compulsory class. That meant everyone had to be there, right? Even Kat.

Kat with her messy bun and hair falling down around her face. I shoved my fists into my jacket pockets, tucked my head down, and lengthened my stride. I passed building two and breathed a sigh of relief when I pushed through the main doors of building one and strode into the massive foyer.

I checked my phone again when I saw no one else. Maybe they were already inside? Room 62 was down one of the hallways. I tried to remember what kind of fucking room it was...to me they were all a damn blur. Maybe I should pay more attention in class?

I strode along the hallway, bypassing darkened rooms, and headed deeper into the underground network of armories and training rooms, until I spied an open door, the light on inside. The moment I stepped through the doorway, I caught sight of Finley.

"What bullshit class is this, Salvatore?" I growled.

He looked fucking nervous. "Don't fucking ask me," he growled. "I got the same text as you."

"Fucking compulsory classes, as if I came here to learn this bullshit."

"Am I late?" A small, feminine voice came from behind me. I glanced over my shoulder to see a small, pretty blonde stepping into to the classroom.

"Fuck no, you're not late," I snapped, feeling pissed off as I spied Alexi standing in the corner. "What the fuck is wrong with you, Kilpatrick? You look nervous..."

The asshole just flinched. "No, I'm not nervous."

"*Wait!*" A familiar voice called. But I didn't look. Alexi was watching me like a damn predator, his eyes glinting with malice, his lips curled in.

"*Anna?*" Salvatore growled.

"What's going on?"

I glanced toward the voice, finding Anna Eden. "That's what I was asking." I snapped.

Until the door closed with a *thud,* and the click of the lock sounded.

The slow hiss of the gas was barely audible, but the sharp, bitter tang in the air burned my fucking eyes. Kilpatrick turned and grabbed a mask from the counter as the stench hit me like a fist. I coughed and sucked in a lungful of acrid air. The room swayed around me. "What the fuck?"

"Anna," Finley roared as she tumbled to the side and hit the floor.

Panic roared through me as I stumbled, watching Finley's woman go down hard. Hate roared inside me as I clenched my jaw and held my breath, tearing my gaze away from the sight on the floor and focused on the door.

The guard was a blur behind it. But it wasn't my guard, was it? It was Kilpatrick's, and Logan's warning filled my head. *Fuck.* I reached for my phone, hands trembling. Kat's face was all I saw in the blur of my eyes as Alexi roared, *"Over your fucking face, Salvatore!"*

My fingers weren't working. Thick and heavy, they traced across the screen, missing the damn code to unlock it. *Get it together! Logan...call Logan.*

"It's truth serum. I rigged it," Kilpatrick barked.

In the corner of my eye, the petite blond hit the floor with a brutal *thud* and didn't move.

The room spun as fire filled my lungs. My eyes watered as the need to breathe became overwhelming. The numbers on my phone blurred more. I stabbed the screen, tried to type, and hit send. Fuck if I knew what I'd said, if anything recognizable.

Finley shouldered the door with a *boom* and screamed, *"Open this fucking door! NOW!"*

"The truth, Rossi," Kilpatrick spat at me.

My phone slipped from my hold and hit the floor with a thud. Kilpatrick was on me in an instant, grabbing my goddamn shirt, towering over me as my body expelled the builtup breath in my lungs and I sucked deep of the tainted air.

"Open this door!" Finley roared once more.

"Tell me the truth." Kilpatrick was in my face again.

Savage anger burned through me, moving deeper than any fucking drugged air. I shoved the bastard, sucking in the fire as I roared, "Get the fuck off me."

My words slurred, my hands didn't work, not like they should. Through the blinding wash of tears, I tried to clench a fist, tried to focus on the bastard in front of me...*but there were three of him.*

My knees buckled, but hands were grabbing me, driving me against the wall, and Alexi's face was right there, his eyes wild. Screaming. Yeah, the bastard was screaming. *"Tell me the truth, Rossi!"*

"No," I murmured, the pain of the last few months spilling from my lips as I tried to focus on the bastard's face. "No, we didn't order the goddamn hit. *You think we'd do that?"*

He stilled for a second, his movement a blur as something was shoved in my face. "Who ordered the hit then?"

"I don't fucking know." I tried to shove the bastard away as my stomach cramped and clenched. Jesus, I was going to be fucking sick. I was going to be...

I bit down on the insides of my cheeks. *Where the fuck was Logan?* Still those words...those fucking words spilled free. "You think we'd do something like that? We're not fucking animals."

Movement came from the corner of my eye as Finley's woman tried to push up from the floor. "Can't trust." Her slurred words reached my ears. "Can't trust the Salvatores."

I clenched my jaw and lifted my gaze to the cold-hearted bastard standing over her. One swipe of my hand, and I brushed the tears away, finding Finley's frozen face cold with fear. A hard bark of laughter roared through me as I sucked another breath. "Can't fucking trust the Salvatores."

He jerked his gaze toward mine and for the first time, I saw the real man behind the fear of his daddy...and it chilled me to the bone. He knelt and grabbed her in his arms. "Quiet now," he murmured, turning away from the rest of us, and lowered her back down to the floor.

But the woman in his arms wasn't listening...and she was starting to sing like a goddamn bird.

Laughter spilled from me in a torrent as she moaned, *"The Ghost. They'll all find out I'm the Ghost."*

The sonofabitch went fucking pale behind the goddamn mask. He looked like *he'd* seen a ghost.

The idea of that was hysterical. Still I sucked in the air, not even caring anymore as the room started to blur and swim around me. I breathed that shit deep, clutched my stomach, and roared with laughter.

All for this?

All for this?

The fucking initiation.

"No..." Finley barked. "Anna, *no!*"

"Jesus fucking Christ," Alexi muttered, sending me laughing harder. I couldn't stop, couldn't do a fucking thing. My stomach clenched, the muscles knotting like fists as I howled with laughter.

The fucking Ghost...the FUCKING GHOST!

"Alexi..." From the corner of my weeping eyes, Finley turned on Alexi. "*I told you not to do this.*"

They were going to kill each other. The idea of that made me suck in great gulps of air as I wept and howled, until the blurred room stopped spinning...and faded to black.

26

Kat

I waited for Anna all afternoon, pacing the floor of the apartment as the wind howled and the storm lashed outside. But she didn't come, leaving me hollow and empty, and feeling very much alone. My stomach gave a twinge and for the first time, I realized it was more than hunger and more than fear.

It was real...

Inside me.

Growing.

Panic set in as that twinge turned into something a little more, something with *teeth*. I clutched my belly, braced my hand against the window, and moaned. But the cramping didn't stop, making me stumble for the bedroom and hurry to the toilet. I tried not to think about the baby, tried to keep my focus firmly fixed on the future.

A future where I was far away from my father...and Hale. I shoved my jeans and panties down and looked at my panties.

There was nothing, no blood, no smear. I pressed my hand against my belly. "It's okay. Come on now...it's all going to be okay."

I was going to *make* it okay, no matter what I had to do. Whether Hale's baby inside me lived or it didn't, I'd do my damn best to make sure I gave him or her all the chances of a better life I could. Which meant making plans to get off the island.

The cramping eased as I sat there, knees pressed together, my hand against my abdomen, and Lazarus's face came roaring back to me. *Sorry I wasn't there. But I'm here now...*

My mind was caught on his words.

I'm here now. My pulse fluttered as I folded the toilet paper and wiped, checking once more for blood, then rose to flush. He was here now...there was too much hope inside me with those words, too many thoughts that raced just like my damn heartbeat. I pulled my jeans up and buttoned them, making my way out into the bedroom as my phone started to ring.

Anna?

I hurried, snatched it off the end of the sofa, and froze. But it wasn't Anna...

I closed my eyes and breathed deep before plunging back to my reality and answered the phone. "Dad."

"Katerina." My breath caught with the sound of my name like that. The cold, heartless tone. "I wanted to call and discuss some concerning reports."

"What reports?" My voice was cold, empty, devoid of the life I'd felt seconds ago.

I could hear him shift against leather and tried to picture where he was and what he was doing. I tried to plan his thoughts in my head, if only to steel my body and my mind for the onslaught. It was always a battle of wills where he was concerned, always hardening my armor and trying my best not to let him rattle my cage.

"Reports of you with some Mafia *thug*," he said coldly. "I can only assume the reports are incorrect?"

I closed my eyes, feeling the room spin. "I'm literally on an island full of them. I can hardly avoid one, now can I?"

"But are you avoiding them, Katerina? That's what I want to know. Are you *fulfilling* your obligations?"

My stomach tightened again and for a terrified second, I wondered if the baby was safe as I forced a response through clenched teeth. "If you mean, am I attending my classes, then yes, I'm attending and I'm learning a great deal."

The only thing I wasn't learning was how to cut the head off a damn snake.

"That isn't the obligation I sent you for," he growled.

Anger bled into his tone. It was subtle, cold, something others wouldn't detect. But I did...like I detected everything else about him.

"As I recall, you didn't send me."

"BUT I ALLOWED IT TO HAPPEN!"

My heart lunged, slamming against my ribs as his roar rang in my ears. A tremor coursed through me, sending shudders deep inside my belly. My voice shook and I hated that. "Then why am I here?"

The harsh sound of his breaths slowed. I was giving in, like I always gave in. Worn down, *worn away*, until I was nothing.

"Damon Zakharov," my father answered. *"He* is why you're there."

I closed my eyes and ground my teeth.

The monster came out to play now, as my father's uncontrolled anger slipped away. "You are, after all, his right of passage."

A tiny sound escaped my lips.

One I hated.

One he loved.

Silence came from the other end of the phone, until finally, "You know what you are to me, Katerina, don't you? You're my little princess. My perfect, golden child. You hold the keys to the kingdom, sweetheart. *My kingdom.* We all have a part to play here, and that is yours."

"No." The word slipped free before I knew it.

"No?"

I squeezed met eyes shut. "No," I forced through my teeth. "I'm *not* your fucking princess. I'm *not* your goddamn toy. You come near me again...you and anyone else, and I'll..."

"You'll..." he urged, baiting me. "What will you do, Katerina? Confide in a servant, like you did before you left?"

Confide?

"Did you think I wouldn't question when she started asking about your welfare? Did you think it wouldn't get back to me when she started to make demands on where you were and what 'condition' you were in? What conditions are you in, Katerina?"

Condition.

My mind raced, trying to piece it all together. The events of the last few weeks were a blur. My missed period, the panic...the terror and pain. My mind went to that night, the one when I'd pressed the knife's edge to my wrist, the night that had shattered my life and forced me to make a choice. But I hadn't spoken to any servant. I hadn't said a thing, *unless...*

"No condition," I lied, praying he swallowed it. "She must've seen how excited I was to get to go the island."

My mind narrowed in on the wrapped test at the back of my drawer, the one hidden and secret, the one no one should've found, unless they were snooping. *Oh no...*

"Don't worry," my father murmured. "She's gone. She's gone and you are alone. Damon Zakharov will be a very powerful man."

Cold plunged deep inside me. How many times had I heard those words? How many times had they ended with me locked in a room...with a stranger *wearing a white mask.* They thought they were secret, thought they could hide their depravity from the world.

My shoulders curled, that life inside me urging me to fight. *Because, what if it was a girl?*

"Damon Zakharov, Katerina. You *will* obey him. You will do whatever he wants...or I'll bring you home...*and never let you go.*"

My pulse roared in my ears as he disconnected the call.

The wind was still screaming outside the window, but I didn't hear a thing. It couldn't compete with the baying for blood inside my head. My hands trembled, gripping the phone. *Beep.*

I jerked my gaze to the screen.

Unknown: I'm thinking of you, Katerina.

I closed my eyes. Hale...it was Hale.

No matter how many times I blocked his number, he still got through. I let out a scream and threw my phone. It hit the edge of the sofa, bounced, and smashed against the floor with a *crack*. Harsh breaths consumed me. I didn't care...not about the phone, not about them.

I slammed my eyes shut as the walls closed in. I was going crazy...unraveling, out of control. Panic pushed in, slamming me with images I didn't want. *Images of my own desire.* Hungry, savage. My own cries of release resounding in my head.

Acid rose in the back of my throat. I stumbled forward, falling to my knees as I sobbed. I hated my body, hated the way it heated at their touches, hated the way I felt so out control. So used...*so dirty*.

I wanted just once to be cared for.

To be loved.

To be treated with kindness, instead of being used.

Tears slipped from my eyes as I pushed upwards. Hate slithered through my veins. They took from me, even without their touch on my skin, they still took. They robbed me of my own pleasure, stole not just my innocence, but my future as well.

There wasn't a part of me that wasn't tainted by them.,

No part of me that wasn't ruined in one way or another.

I had nothing. I *was* nothing, nothing but a possession, A *thing* to own.

I had to get out of here, had to get out of this goddamn apartment before the walls closed in on me. I strode into my room and changed into a skirt and top before yanking on thick, faux-fur-lined coat and headed for the elevator and out of the building.

"Ms. VanHalen." The guard glanced up as the elevator opened.

"Don't..." I croaked, as tears slipped from my eyes. "Just leave me the hell alone."

He said nothing, but still, he followed as I pushed out the doors. The brutal gusts of wind slammed into me, pushing me backwards. I stumbled, then caught myself. Anger burned inside me as I gritted my teeth, set my focus on the building in the distance, and pushed forward.

Dark gray clouds only grew darker as I made my way toward the building they called *Nightlife*. The building was further back on the island, and was for those who preferred to learn their lessons in chips and flesh. If I was being honest, part of me hoped Lazarus would be there again. I lowered my head, driving my body forward, and breathed with relief as I stepped out of the gusts and under the cover of the building. The guard's footsteps resounded behind me, but I tried to ignore him and slammed the card on the sensor.

The doors opened and I was inside, and in an instant, the outside world just faded away.

I stepped into the elevator and rode all the way to the penthouse floor. The blinds were drawn and dimness reigned. Up here, there was only the money and the greed and everything else just didn't exist. At the far end of the suite was a fully stocked bar, and right now I needed a drink desperately.

The baby...

The voice in the back of my mind whispered. But right now, it was either lose my sanity or quell the roar. Just one drink wouldn't hurt. Now a drink and I'll ease that ache inside me. I clutched the warm jacket around me and strode toward the glistening crystal tumblers and top shelf liquor.

"Need help?"

I turned to find a blond Irish Mafia son striding toward me. "From you? No."

"Ouch," he muttered without even a twitch in his eyes.

"Bruno, right?" I taunted, grabbed a bottle of ice-cold Grey Goose from the upright freezer, and unscrewed the cap.

"Bernardi," he acknowledged with a nod. "Ms. VanHalen."

I just chuckled and shook my head. "So you know who I am. Gonna try to hit on me now?"

"No fucking way," he answered carefully. "I quite like my head on my shoulders."

"Yeah?" I grabbed a glass and turned. "You think I'm that dangerous, huh?"

He took a step forward, stopping just before he passed me. "It's not you I'm wary of, Kat," he said with a wink.

Then he left, leaving me alone with a wide range of confusion. He made his way over to a table, a seat already waiting, five-thousand-dollar chips lined up in a row. He lifted his gaze as he sat and gave me a cheeky fucking grin and another wink.

I swallowed the vodka and relaxed as it burned its way down, watching him with interest. Another male at the table turned his head toward me, not a Mafia son, but one of their protectors. He watched me carefully, but there was nothing sexual in his gaze. If anything, he was just as careful about his scrutiny as Bruno was. Someone had warned them off me.

It didn't take a genius to figure out who that was.

Lazarus. My protector. Another swallow of the ice-cold burn and something inside me trembled with desire. My pulse raced at the thought of him warning the others away. There was something delicious about that. Something safe...and *strong.* The other male at the table tore his gaze away and didn't look at me again.

Only Bruno did, watching me carefully.

Could I relax here? In this moment, could I unfurl that fist inside myself and...*let go?*

I swallowed again, finding the glass empty. Another icy splash and I was finally getting warm.

And free...

Gone was the threatening phone call from my father. Gone were the texts from Hale. Gone were the white masks from my nightmares, until I turned and refilled my glass once more. This feeling of freedom was intoxicating. I smiled and made my way to the other table where they played poker, and past the room where music throbbed and pulsed with gyrating half-naked women and men engrossed in their perfection.

I was taken back to that night with Lazarus, to the night filled with both terror and desire. He'd made me feel alive in that moment. He'd made me feel...*wanted,* the kind of wanted I ached to feel again. The kind of wanted I could control. I lifted my glass to my lips, and saw that the glass was empty once more.

The room started to spin, taking my self-control with it.

I strode back to the bar and froze as a deep chuckle of laughter spilled out toward the front of the apartment. One that made me sick with rage...*Damon.*

I tried to swallow that burn in the back of my throat as my stomach clenched. Just when I'd thought for a second I could have a moment of peace...a second where I didn't have to battle the monsters. But I couldn't have any reprieve from the darkness. People like me didn't get that.

No. We didn't get that at all.

His laughter rebounded through the room to slam into me.

Sick...*infernal* laughter.

Mocking. Branding. Burning a hole right through me.

I dropped the glass to the counter and took a step away, feeling the room sway. Movement came from the table. Bruno Bernardi and his little hitman pals watched me. They could keep watching me. Couldn't touch me, though, could they? Not unless they wanted to find themselves on the other end of Lazarus's fist.

The idea of that entertained me, filling me with savagery as I strode forward and sought my demon out.

Demon.

Damon.

One and the same.

The alcohol burned inside me. It was all I could feel now as I rounded the hallway and caught sight of him standing with a group. Mr. Fucking Perfection. He brushed back a tangle of curls from his forehead and lifted his gaze as I barked, *"Fuck you…you lowlife piece of SHIT!"*

They all froze, all turned…and carefully took a step backward.

But I couldn't stop now. I couldn't control the inferno inside me…and the words came spilling out. "I fucking *hate* you! I hate *all* of you." Tears spilled free. I didn't know where they came from, but once they started, they didn't stop.

"Kat?" he muttered, his eyes widening in shock.

A hard bark of laughter tore free. "Oh, you sound so fucking innocent now, don't you? I wonder how your little friends might feel when they know the true you…" I fluttered my hands in their direction. But I didn't look at them…my hate was only for him. "What do you think, Damon? You think I should tell them how you really are? How you have to drug a woman for her to fuck you?"

There was a flicker of pure, cold, sickening rage in his eyes before he smothered it with a smile. "Kat," he stepped toward me. "I don't know what's gotten into you tonight, but you and I know that's a lie. I'm sorry you're having a bad night. Why I don't I take you home?"

He grabbed my arm carefully, with no hint of the real monster he was. His voice was soothing, etched with utter contempt. "Come on, Kat. Let me take care of you," he murmured, but only when he came close enough that the others couldn't see, did he smile.

I fucking hated that smile.

With a scream, I lunged, swinging my arm through the air.

He caught it so easily and dragged me against him.

I slammed into his chest and stared up into his eyes. The demon was in there, hiding behind his mask of pretense. He lowered his head, the hallway and the others blurring from view. "You are special to me, Katerina."

I tried to shake my head, tried to clear the fog from my mind, tried to hurt him, how I was hurt. "I fucking *hate* you."

He just smiled and nodded. "I know, honey. I'm sorry we argued before. I'm sorry I was a real ass. Can you forgive me?"

He rocked as he spoke, rocking and soothing. I tried to pull away but he had me around the waist, his other hand clutching mine against his chest, like we were dancing. But we weren't dancing...*were we?*

The vodka was hitting me hard, blurring the lights overhead. It wasn't until the elevator doors closed that I realized how much trouble I was in. *By then, it was too late...*

27

Lazarus

"Laz!"

I came to with a roar, only to find Freddy's face far too fucking close.

Harsh, consuming breaths plunged cold right through the burn in the middle of my chest. I lashed out, driving my fist into something hard, and screamed.

"Easy, buddy!" Freddy yanked me forward and up, pulling me to my feet.

The savage sound of my own rage rang in my ears as I stumbled forward, slapping Freddy's hold away. Still, I fucking wobbled, lightheaded and strange. *What the fuck had hit me?*

The room pulsed bright, and then blurred. I shook my head, trying to dislodge the haze and remember where I was...*and what had happened?*

Logan was a beast, grabbing someone up from the floor, ready to inflect grievous bodily harm. I blinked, dislodging the tears pouring from my damn eyes, to find Alexi's shirt bunched in Logan's fists as he lifted him.

"I'll fucking *kill you!*" the brother roared.

"Log—" my word was nothing more than a harsh hiss.

I swallowed, feeling an ache bloom in the back of my throat, and turned my head as footsteps thundered and the room was filled with suits.

"Logan," I croaked, drawing his gaze. His lips were curled in a savage sneer of violence. I glanced at Alexi, to see his eyes wide. One word, and my brother would tear the bastard apart, and Alexi knew it.

"The Code," Matteo snapped as he strode closer, tearing his gaze from Logan to me. "Forbids violence."

Still Logan didn't let go, that dangerous stare finding mine. Waiting for me to give the command.

"Lazarus," the Commander urged.

One shake of my head, and Logan let the bastard drop to the floor—*hard*. Alexi's head hit the floor with a *thud*. And as my eyes stopped fucking tearing, I saw the truth. We were in a classroom, one I couldn't quite place. A gas mask was discarded where Alexi lay, and there was another tossed near the door, separate from the tiny blond female who lay curled into a ball, moaning. I scanned the rest of the room, finding another asshole sitting slumped against a cupboard and groaning with his head in his hands. *But I was missing someone.* The thought rose, and the sharper it became the more I started to remember. *Finley...Finley Salvatore and his woman.* I sucked in the bitter-tainted air, remembering the screams and the terror, as I jerked my gaze to Alexi...*Tell me the truth, Rossi!* His howls came rushing back to me now. *Who ordered the hit on Cian Salvatore?*

The men in suits were covering their mouths. But hate flooded my veins, forcing me to stumble forward until I stood over Alexi Kilpatrick. "All this because you still can't trust a Stidda?"

He lifted his head, hate raging in his eyes as he sneered. "Never."

I saw him for the piece of shit he was. But worse than that, *I saw myself.*

"Lazarus," the Commander started as I turned and strode past him. "Wait, you need to see a doctor."

I left them behind, slamming my hand against the hallway wall as it swam. I needed to get out of there, need to get far away from these fucking Cosa Nostra assholes. Freddy's words were nothing more than a deep rumble behind me.

"Easy, brother," Logan growled, catching me as I stumbled.

He pulled my arm across his shoulders. One glance his way, and I nodded. "Shouldn't have come here."

"I know," he murmured.

"Don't fucking belong." I turned back to the hallway, carefully placing one foot in front of the other.

"We have that in common," Logan answered, then turned back to check the hallway as we stumbled into the foyer. "Right now, let's get you back to the apartment, how's that sound?"

I just nodded and tried to ignore the edge of rage in his tone. We made it out into the merciless gusts and slowly, step by agonizing step, made our way back to the building and up to my suite.

When I hit the bed, I let out a moan. My gut was cramping, my head swam. The effort to walk between the two fucking buildings had taken all I had at that moment. Logan yanked my boots off as the elevator doors opened and Freddy strode in.

"Doc's on his way," he announced. "Someone's going to have to call your dad."

"No," I growled, and rolled, forcing myself to sit up. "Not now. He's got enough on his plate."

Freddy just scowled, then nodded, finally resigned. "But soon, yeah? I don't need my ass chewed out over this."

"Fine." I flopped back down and rolled over, burying my head in the pillow.

A second later, and I was shoving frantically from the bed and stumbling into the bathroom. Acid burned my throat as I heaved and vomited, holding on for dear life.

"Now that's nasty," Freddy muttered from the doorway.

"Don't fucking look then, unless you're gonna hold my fucking hair back," I snarled.

The asshole just left. I moaned and held a hand against my belly as I retched. I don't know how long I stayed like that, clutching the damn bowl and heaving, until an unfamiliar thud of boots drew my gaze.

"Mr. Rossi." An asshole stepped into the bathroom, peered into the toilet, then settled his unflinching gaze on me. "Neale Gray, one of the island's doctors."

"I know who the fuck you are," I muttered, and peered up at him. "Am I dying? 'Cause I feel like I'm fucking dying."

He just knelt down next to me and pulled out a stethoscope. "Well, there's no blood in your vomitus, so that's a good sign. Breathe in for me...now out."

I did as he asked, wanting to shove the cold end of the fucking device up his ass. He pressed and prodded, then leaned back. "I can give you a sedative if you want?"

"What the fuck for?" I growled.

"To counter the effects of the drug in your system," he said, confused. "Or you're in for a very rough night."

"I'll take that over being fucking helpless." I moaned and turned my head as a fresh wave of nausea hit me like a fucking truck.

I heaved, groaning between breaths as the asshole just rose. "Well, if you insist. Get your man to call me if there's any change to your condition. Good luck, Mr. Rossi, you'll need it."

I wanted to flip the fucker the bird.

But I just didn't have the damn strength to do it.

Instead, I just hugged the porcelain bowl like a fucking chump and growled through the pain. I vaguely remembered Freddy coming closer and dropping a bottle of electrolytes next to me, then leaving. I sipped it when the cramping eased, and when I felt like I wasn't about to pass out when I moved, I dragged my ass out of the bathroom and climbed onto the bed, sinking into the softness of the comforter...until a voice broke through my mind.

Can't trust the Salvatores...

I opened my eyes at the voice, and that ache that coursed through my body turned into something vicious and wild. It was all because of *him*. Finley fucking Salvatore.

They'll find out...

Anna Eden's words kept coming.

They'll find out I'm The Ghost.

I closed my eyes and tried to ignore the words. But I couldn't. All this...because he wanted to keep his little fucking secret? And sprouting lies about who was behind his mother's death? Taken's blank eyes came roaring back to me, the shattering of the window still rang as clear today as it had then. I could still feel the warm splatter of his blood, still see the desperation in his gaze when he lay against the back of the seat and fucking died.

But did you see me crying and bitching about it?

Did you see me drugging those around me to exact revenge?

No. If I wanted you to pay for it...I came for *you*.

That thought grew spines and wedged in tight.

I wrestled with it, tossing and turning, moaning into the pillow until I hated the sound of my own pain. I don't know how long it was...hours, felt like days. The more I thought of it, the more pissed off I became, until I couldn't shake it and I dragged my ass to the side of the bed.

"Where the fuck do you think you're going?" Freddy growled as I pulled my boots on and downed the rest of my drink.

"Where the fuck does it look like?" I snapped.

There was a look exchanged, one of surprise and confusion.

"Back the fuck off, *both of you*," I ordered.

I wasn't messing around now. I was fucking *pissed*.

I strode into the elevator, then out of the building. *The Code. The fucking Code*...thoughts raced through my mind. I wanted to hurt some fucker and right now, Finley Salvatore was all I saw. I left the building behind as the gray sky darkened and night closed in.

"Laz!" Freddy roared behind me, but the more I thought about it, the more savage I became.

By the time I rounded the edge of building one and headed for his fucking apartment, I saw the fucker sprinting toward me.

There you are.

I clenched my fists and lunged, slamming into the fucker. "Fucking running from me, *Salvatore?*"

He stumbled backwards, his eyes wide as he shook his head. *"Get out of the goddamn way!"*

"Get the fuck out of your way? *You fucking DRUGGED ME!"* I roared. "You want me to get *out of your way?* Not until you *pay!"*

He muttered something, but I wasn't listening, not anymore. I swung, my muscles weak and rubbery. I was heavy, too goddamn heavy. But the bastard didn't fight back. Instead, he stumbled out of the arc and tried to get away. But the fucker wasn't escaping that damn easy.

"Anna..." the word was a wheeze.

"You drugged me because of a *fucking initiation?"*

"He's going to kill her!" he roared, and doubled over.

Still, I dropped my shoulder and charged, hitting him hard, lifting him off his feet, and slamming him to the ground. He hit hard, rolling, trying to shove up.

"*Fight back!*" I screamed.

But his eyes were wide with fear...only it wasn't fear of me as he screamed. "He's going to *kill* her!"

The words stopped me cold. I sucked in a savage breath. "What the fuck did you say?"

"Damon...Damon's going to kill Kat! Anna called, fucking hysterical. She's hurt...*I think he's going to do something really bad.*"

"The fuck he will," I growled as I turned and lunged.

She was all I could think of, all I could see. *Look at him looking at you,* Damon's voice flooded my mind. *You want to fuck him, don't you? Look at you, trembling like a bitch in heat.*

I knew men like Zakharov.

Knew how they used, and how they hurt.

Just like he was hurting her.

I dug deeper, driving my body forward with all I had. Still, I moved too slowly rounding the edge of a building and tore across the grass and all of a sudden, I was alone. I glanced over my shoulder, to see Finley not far behind.

"*Go!*" he roared.

I reached into my pocket, praying like hell the card was still there, and whispered a prayer to whoever was watching as my fingers hit the hard plastic edge. I dragged it free and slammed it to the sensor outside her building. But the light didn't change, still glowing red. I slammed it again. *"Come on!"*

"Move!" Finley roared, and slapped his own down, watching as the light changed from red to green and the locks disengaged.

I was charging through the foyer in an instant. Fuck waiting for the elevator. I wrenched open the stairwell door, hearing a faint scream from above echo through the hollow space.

That was Kat...THAT WAS KAT!

A bestial sound ripped from me, swallowing the muffled sound of her cries. I was lunging, driving my body two and three steps at a time up the first flight...then the next, and the next. My thighs were howling with the strain, muscles rippling and trembling, but still I gripped the railing and lunged.

Not caring about the pain.

Floor by floor.

I fought to get to her.

A scream came once more, piercing...*shrill.* I slammed through the stairwell door and into the hallway, sucking in hard breaths, my lungs on fire. "Kat," I croaked as I stumbled forward.

My body was trembling, shuddering, and jerking as another scream rang out...*but it wasn't Kat's.*

"I'm going to fucking kill you, you goddamn bitch!"

"The fuck you are," I growled, and slammed my hand against the door handle.

The door swung open and I was inside, lowering my head, charging forward. He was all I saw...*all I wanted to see.* The bastard had his hand around Kat's throat, her head hanging back, her eyes wide, *distant...just like Taken's.* I hit him hard, driving my fist into his side, forcing him to buckle sideways and release his hold.

Kat hit the floor with a *thud.* I wanted to look at her, wanted to search her tear-stained face. I *needed* to know she was okay. But I didn't. I shoved the motherfucker backwards. Only then did I see he also had hold of Anna's hair.

"Anna!" Finley roared behind me.

"What the fuck did you give her?" Anna yelled.

Ice plunged through my veins.

"He gave her something.," Anna groaned, grasping Kat and pulling her close. "Drugged her...raped her."

I jerked my gaze to hers. "What?"

Anna's eyes said all I needed to know. I found that mother-fucker and lunged, grasping him by the shirt. "What the fuck did you give her?"

"Just a little E," he screamed. *"That's ALL!"*

"You gave her fucking E?" All I could see was the pain in her eyes. "You gave her fucking E and raped her?"

"He's been doing it for days!" Anna yelled, her own rage bleeding into the room. "Leaving bruises...I saw them."

Kat just drew her legs up tight and curled into a ball. "It doesn't matter." Those words hit me harder than any fist. "It's what they all do."

"The...fuck...they...do." Hate spilled through me, hate for *any* fucking man who took what wasn't theirs to begin with. I couldn't stop myself, couldn't stop her words in my head...until I lashed out my fist and it connected with his face.

Crunch.

Then her words stopped.

For a second at least.

Thud.

Thud.

Thud. Thud. Thud.

I unleashed my fury, unleashed my pain...and this time I'd kill.

28

Kat

Blood...that's all I saw, splattered in a mask across the face of my Mafia Prince. Only this time it was a mask of rage. But he didn't stop, he didn't slow, he just held Damon by the shirt and drove his fist into his face, blow after sickening blow.

"Lazarus," I groaned, and pulled my legs in closer.

Only then did he still, his fist bloody and white-knuckled under the gore as he turned his focus toward me. Those perfect blue eyes weren't of the sky anymore...*they were arctic.*

A sickening, high-pitched wheeze came from the man in his grasp. But I didn't look at him, never turned my gaze. Lazarus was all I cared about...he was all I saw.

My protector.

My defender.

He took a step toward me as the door to our apartment was shoved open and the island's Commander strode through. He took one look at the ruin left behind from fist and fury and winced. "Jesus fucking Christ."

Then Logan was there, striding through the army of body-guards, his gaze moving to Lazarus in an instant... then it found me.

"A second son is murdered, and now this?" the Commander moaned.

"He fucking drugged her and raped her. What the fuck did you think was going to happen?"

I tried to hide the flinch of disgust, and swallowed the bitter taste of fear.

"Is that true?" the Commander demanded.

"It's okay, honey," Anna whispered beside me, and clutched my hand. "You can tell him the truth."

I didn't feel her touch, not really. I was numb, hollow and empty. Just a *thing*, right? A prize.

"I saw him rape her. I heard her tell him to stop and he didn't."

Lazarus let out a deadly snarl. "He's fucking lucky I didn't put a bullet in his brain."

The Commander just shook his head. "Fuck me. Take him to the goddamn infirmary. I want the bastard watched. *No fucking phone calls. No anything,* until I say."

Logan and Freddy moved, striding forward to stand at Lazarus's side...and right in front of me. But Lazarus wasn't done. He strode forward and I caught the tiny whimper from Damon as he cowered.

"I want to end you," Lazarus growled. "I want to beat you until I'm the last fucking thing you ever see, and then I want to dump you in the water, still alive...and watch the goddamn sharks feed."

"And I'll be right there," Finley snarled as he stepped closer. "Watching every goddamn second."

And all I saw was the men in the masks...*powerful men*. Men who'd love nothing more than to send mercenaries to kill. I couldn't have that. Not because of me. "No," I croaked, and pushed myself forward. "Let him live, Lazarus."

My protector just turned his gaze toward me. "Yeah?"

I slipped my hand from Anna's, swallowing a shudder. "Get me out of here."

In an instant, he came for me...and so did Logan, reaching for me.

"Don't fucking touch her," Lazarus commanded, and Logan's hand dropped.

I burned in the icy blue of Lazarus's stare as he came closer and knelt, sliding one arm under my knees and the other around my back before he gently lifted. "Hold on...hold on to me."

I wrapped my arms around him, lowering my head to press against his shoulder. Then we were moving, leaving the men and the mess behind and striding toward the elevator. He stared into my eyes, searching them for what I didn't know. A flicker of life...*maybe of hope?*

But he didn't realize there was no hope left.

Not where men like Damon Zakharov were concerned.

Movement came as Logan shrugged out of his jacket and wrapped it across me.

"You're safe now," Lazarus murmured as the elevator doors opened. "You're safe with me."

"I know," I answered.

He said nothing else as we strode from the building and out into the night. Even though his muscles trembled and he swallowed hard with the strain, he never once even shifted me. I lowered my head, feeling the effects of the drug move through my body.

The baby.

The words resounded. *What about the baby?* I closed my eyes as tears slipped free. I didn't know...I just didn't know. How could I protect it...when I couldn't even protect myself?

Bright lights flared as doors opened. I lifted my head, finding us in Lazarus's building. They were silent as the elevator doors opened and we strode inside.

"I'll call if there's a problem," Lazarus commanded, not shifting his gaze from mine.

But the order wasn't for me. I caught the nod from Freddy and the uncomfortable shift from Logan before the massive bodyguard murmured, "Okay, Lazarus."

"Tomorrow, I want someone over at Kat's place and all of her things brought here."

"You think that's wise?" Freddy murmured.

Lazarus broke our stare to find him. "Do I look like I give a shit?"

"That's one thing I can get on board with," Logan approved.

"Good," Lazarus declared as the elevator rose, stopping on the top floor, and he carried me out.

Then we were alone. I licked my lips, finding the cold sting of the wind had cut through the fog in my head a little. I was coming back now, slipping away from the darkness once more. I splayed my hold around his neck. "Laz."

His gaze found mine as he carried me into his bedroom, then lowered me gently to the edge of the bed. I waited for him to change now that we were alone. I waited for the monster to shine through. But he just knelt at my feet and tugged my shoes off. "Are you cold?"

His words resounded in my head for a second too long, forcing him to lift his gaze to mine. I wanted to answer him, wanted to tell him how I was always cold, *empty to the core.*

"The doc...he'll come with a rape kit," he started, looking away.

"No." I murmured.

I caught the flinch, then the flare of anger as he jerked his gaze to mine. "No?"

"He didn't..." I started. "What I mean is, he didn't fuck me."

Color bled from his face and in an instant, those blue eyes darkened. I didn't have to ask him what he was thinking, it was evident. He wanted to kill Damon, wanted to hunt him down and finish what he'd started...

"But yes, I'm cold and you're—"

He jerked, those arctic eyes growing a degree colder. "I'm what?"

I pushed up from the bed and lifted my hand to the splatter of blood across his cheeks. "A mess."

He lashed out, grasping my wrist, but not once did he squeeze, not once did he hurt me. "Give me the word, Kat." My breath caught. "Just a nod is all I need, and I'll finish it. You'll never have to see him again."

Hope flared inside me. His pure, perfect, honorable words. How many monsters would he kill for me? I didn't have to ask to know the answer. *All of them, if I let him.* "I won't see him," I answered finally. "How can I, when I'm right here?"

Surprise widened his eyes before a flicker of something moved through them. Pride, contentment. The elevator doors opened and two sets of boots resounded in the space. I lowered my hand as Logan came around the corner.

His gaze moved to me in an instant, then to my fingers touching Lazarus's face, before he swallowed hard. There was a wince at the sight, before he shifted to Lazarus. "The doc—"

"Isn't needed...apparently," Laz muttered, still staring into my eyes.

I broke his gaze, lowered my hand, and turned toward them. "There isn't anything to test," I slurred, and scowled, trying to shake off the last of the drug. "I'm fine, honestly."

Logan froze at the words, his brow furrowing, before his fists clenched at his sides. "You're not *fine,* Kat." He jerked his gaze to mine.

"How about a shot to counter the effects of the drug you ingested?" The doctor came closer, his kind eyes seeming to bore right through me.

I glanced at Lazarus, finding his brow furrowed with concern, then gave a slow nod. "Okay."

The doctor set to work, opening a backpack and pulling out a small kit. I didn't watch him, just held Lazarus's gaze. When the doc came close, Lazarus reached for my hand.

"Eyes on me, princess," my protector said forcefully.

The sting was instant in my arm, but then it was over.

"Just a check of your vitals," the doc added. He didn't even wait this time, just gently grasped my shoulder and lowered me to sit on the bed, then wrapped a cuff around my arm and pumped it tight. I barely noticed the icy touch of the stethoscope as the effects of whatever he'd given me took hold.

My thoughts became clearer, and with it, the memory of what had happened. I closed my eyes, swallowing a shudder.

"What's wrong?" Lazarus gripped my hand tighter.

I just shook my head. "Nothing. It's all okay."

Then the doc was done, tearing the cuff free. "Mr. Rossi, re-thinking that sedative?"

"No need, doc," Lazarus answered, drawing my gaze. "Rage is all the drug I need."

There was a mutter, before he and Logan left, leaving us alone once more. Goosebumps raced along my arms with a shiver. I wrapped my arms around my middle as Lazarus just stared. "He likes you."

"The doctor?" I muttered. "Hardly."

"You know who I mean." I glanced his way, but there wasn't jealousy or anger staring back at me, there was pride. "I *want* him to like you," Lazarus murmured, and stepped closer. "That way, I'll always know you're safe. You'll never have a more dangerous and loyal man at your back than Logan."

"Yes, I will," I disagreed, turning to him. "You."

I stood and crossed the small space between us. "You asked me if I was cold, and yes, I'm cold. I'm cold and my head is weird. I'm all those things when I'm around you, Lazarus. So much so, that I don't quite know how to act."

"Do you want to go back to him?"

I stiffened with the chilling tone in his words. "Who?"

"Zakharov," he answered carefully. "Do you...want to go back to him?"

Fear gripped me. "*Never.*"

A nod of his head and he exhaled hard with relief. "Good, okay. Good. I just had to make sure." He met my gaze. "I've met women who kept going back, even after their boyfriends, you know, *hurt them*. I needed to make sure that wasn't you."

Tell him...

That voice whispered.

Tell him who you really are.

That fluttering deep in my belly pushed me one step closer, but still the words wouldn't come. "You want to know who I am?"

He held my gaze. "Yeah, I do."

I swallowed the rancid taste of fear. "Then let me show you."

I strode to the bathroom, my hands working the few buttons that remained on my dress. There was an ache in my arm, and one at my side, a deep ache...*a bruising ache.*

My ruined dress hit the bathroom floor. I sensed his movement at the doorway as I reached around and unhooked my bra. For a second, I didn't want to look down...I didn't want to see what *he'd* left behind. But I did, forcing myself to confront what I'd become. Red marks wrapped around my arm, thick, angry, and raised. Purple would come soon enough, deep purple that I'd hide with highnecked tops and long sleeves, just like I'd done so many times before.

I squeezed my eyes shut at the sight as a quake tore through me, weighing down my soul. I'd thought I was strong enough to show Lazarus what kind of woman I was, a woman used, a woman *discarded.*

But as my bra fell to the tiled floor and the remnants of Damon's cruel hands shone against my pale skin, all strength left me. A sob tore free, quiet, controlled. My throat clenched around the ache, just like his fists. I clenched my jaw tight, swallowing, swallowing...*and swallowing.*

"Kat?" I sensed Laz's movement, and goosebumps raced along my arms as I reached out and switched on the shower.

But Laz didn't touch me...didn't *force himself into my world.* He just waited and in the strength of his control, I found myself opening my eyes. Slick tears carved paths down my cheeks as I clung to his gaze. "You wanted to see...so now you see."

I waited for him to flinch, waited for him to show disgust. I waited for him to turn away...

But he didn't. Lazarus gripped his shirt and tugged it over his head. My eyes were drawn to the thick, jagged line that ran down his side. A scar, raised and silver, then another, thinner one, across his shoulder.

"A knife," he murmured. "Sonofabitch caught me off guard... the first time."

I flinched, and jerked my gaze to his.

"This was a cleaver, if you can believe it." He looked down, tracing the jagged edge with his finger. "It took them a while to get me stitched up, which is why it's so damn ugly. But I didn't have Logan then."

There was a flicker of pain that danced through the glint in his eyes. But I didn't think it was ugly. My gaze drifted over his hard muscles. I stepped closer, my own aches melting away. "You were on your own?"

He just gave a slow, careful nod. "Alone and angry. It was just after I lost someone special to me, a *brother*."

I couldn't stop myself from touching him. He didn't move, just held my gaze as I traced that thick, silver edge with my finger.

"Some of us carry the marks on the outside," he said carefully, meeting my gaze. "And some carry them within."

My hand sank, falling to my side.

"You've had enough people taking from you, Kat," he continued. "But you don't need to worry about that with me. You give me what you want...however you can, and I'll be happy with that."

Something inside me fluttered, something. "What if that's nothing but this...this hollow shell of a person."

He took a step, stopping just before our bodies touched, and looked down into my eyes. "Then that's where I'll make my home."

But he made no move to kiss me, no move to do anything at all, and that burning hunger raged inside me. Instead, he waited, just like he said he would, standing there in the bathroom, the red blood splattered across his cheeks garish under the overhead lights.

He took a step forward and gently cupped my jaw, tilting my gaze to his. "I see you, Kat."

Kat.

Not Katerina.

Desire moved inside me, dark and savage, prowling that emptiness like a starved beast waiting for someone like Lazarus to come. I refused to wait any longer. I reached for him and took his hand, my thumb running across the bruised, bloody knuckles, and lifted them to my lips.

I kissed his pain, then lowered his palm to my breast.

Only then did he look from my eyes, his gaze seeking out the pale, rose-colored tips of my nipples, and he gave a deep, guttural moan.

That sound did things to me. Things I never expected.

Things I didn't think I'd ever feel.

I lifted my hands, sliding them along his shoulders to the back of his neck, and moved closer. "Do that again."

"What?" he asked huskily, and licked his lips.

"That growl, that sound. I want it again." I pressed my breasts against his chest, stealing his warmth.

I could steal it all and he'd let me.

I doubt he'd care in the slightest. He brushed his fingers down the soft curls of my hair and slid his other hand around to the small of my back. "You want me to growl for you?" he murmured, the tone husky and wild.

"Yes," I answered. "Growl for me."

He just smiled, those perfect lips arcing upwards until, in an instant, they stilled. He let out a sound that was filled with danger and desire. The rumble resounded in his chest and spilled into the back of his throat. One commanding step and he pushed me backwards until I hit the tiled wall beside the shower.

Steam poured from the torrent of water. Through the fog he came, lowering his head to mine. "You think I'm an animal, princess?" Desire bloomed inside me as he licked his lips.

"Fuck, no," I answered. "I think you're perfection."

There was a tremble at the corner of his mouth. But his smile was a glint in his eyes. My body trembled, waiting for him to take and take and *take*.

But he didn't, searching my eyes as he pulled back. "You don't like me taking control, do you?"

Taking control?

Taking my control.

"No," I whispered. "I don't."

Then he just opened his hands. "I can work with that. You set the pace. We can go as fast or as slow as you want."

"I can set the pace?" Surprise filled me.

"Yeah," he answered. "Is that okay?"

In an instant, I was back in that room with music and desire floating through me. Hunger for this man writhed and rolled under my skin like a beast of its own. I dragged my teeth across my lip and tested this man's resolve, stepping closer and reaching for the button of his blue jeans.

He just watched me and didn't move an inch as I opened the buttoned and slid the zipper down. Energy sizzled between us, arcing and crackling in the air, standing the hair at my nape on end as I pushed his jeans down low. Warmth brushed against my thigh. I didn't have to look down to know he was hard.

Hard and ready.

Still, he didn't move, didn't force himself on me.

He swallowed hard, showing total restraint, until he whispered, "I said take it slow, princess, but don't mistake me for a goddamn saint."

My breath caught as his jeans hit the bathroom floor. He tore his gaze away from mine, moving to my breasts as I slid my panties down and left them on the floor. "No one could mistake you for that, Lazarus." I reached for his face, brushing my fingers through the drying blood splatter. "Not when you're wearing another man's blood on your face."

He stepped out of the jeans and stood there, naked, *hard*, and bloody.

This was the essence of a man. One who didn't have to hide behind a mask to get what he wanted.

No, this man stood bare in front of me...and I'd never been so completely turned on in my life.

I stepped closer, took his hand, and pressed his palm against the curve of my ass. "Kiss me, Lazarus. Kiss me now."

29

Kat

"Kiss me..." I lifted my gaze to his.

He swallowed hard and leaned down. One hand gripped my hip as he lifted his other to graze his fingers along my jaw. His lips took mine, carefully, tenderly, before, with a snarl, he grabbed me around the waist and lifted. Heat pummeled my back, splattering my hair against my shoulders as he walked me under the spray.

He kissed me, hard, his mouth claiming mine as I hit the coolness of the tiled wall.

But I didn't care.

In that moment, I was all his.

All heat.

All fire.

Burning like an inferno.

His hands slid around to cup my ass, pulling me against him. My desire echoed deep in his mouth, making him thrust between my thighs. Heat radiated from my pussy. It throbbed with a mind of its own, forcing me to tilt my hips, meeting his soft push between my thighs.

*Fuck, I wanted him...*like I'd never wanted anything else in my life.

I wanted this...this raw, beautiful thing.

He pulled back, his eyes shining brightly. "You okay?"

I sucked in a deep breath, confusion rising for a second because he actually *cared.* "Yes." I glanced toward the running shower. "But shouldn't we wash?"

Laughter glinted in his eyes, before he chuckled. "Sure, we can do that."

Slowly, he lowered me to the floor. I brushed my wet hair back. I must look a mess. But he didn't seem to notice, or care. He just grabbed a thick sponge, squeezed soap onto the surface, and reached for my hand.

With perfect care, he ran the soap up my forearm, then my shoulder, and across. I wanted him to touch me, to caress me. *To look at me.* And as though he'd read my mind, he lowered his gaze.

There was no room for the sponge, not anymore. It dropped from his hand to hit the shower floor with a *splat* as he cupped my breast, running his thumb across my nipple. "I dreamed of doing this, and more."

"How much more?" I slid my hands over his chest and moved closer.

"A lot fucking more."

There was no room for the past here, nothing could touch me. "Show me."

He moved closer, leaving the water to run down his cheek. One tiny tilt of his head, and he opened his mouth. The rivulet of water rushed in, then he angled my head up, his thumb skimming my lower lip. I opened my mouth on instinct as he lowered his head.

Water cascaded from his mouth to mine. I swallowed, feeling the warmth sliding down the back of my throat as he groaned. His fingers slid down my neck, his thumb following the valley of my throat, coming to rest at my collarbone.

He moved faster than I could track, hitting the faucet and ending the spray before grabbing the soft, white robe and wrapping it around me. "Just for now," he murmured. "I don't plan on letting you get cold."

He lifted me once more. I wrapped my legs around his hips, and pressed my chest against his. Droplets of water slipped from the tips of his sandy blond hair. I brushed them away, leaning down to kiss him. But the moment he lowered me to the bed, my body just froze.

Fear gripped me, sending tremors along my spine. Lazarus just rose above me, his gaze locked with mine. "What's wrong, Kat?" I couldn't answer, couldn't speak. "Talk to me."

My spine was pressed against the mattress. I knew I was safe, but still, unseen hands gripped my neck, driving the back of my head against the pillow as the brutality of their actions assaulted me. I slammed eyes closed, forcing the past back into that black hole where it belonged.

Until Lazarus stepped away.

Sensing the movement, I opened my eyes.

"You don't like to be on your back," he murmured, but it wasn't a question. "You don't like to be grabbed from behind, you don't like to be...*handled.*"

He turned away from me, and for a second, I felt agony plunge deep. I'd ruined it. We'd had something special, something real, and I'd ruined it. The black tie in his hand draped toward the floor as he strode back toward the bed. He tied one end of it around his wrist with awkward movements, then wound it around the center post of the headboard. "You'll need to tie my other wrist, Kat."

"What are you doing?" I rose from the bed as he sat, moving into the middle.

"I can't tie it on my own." He stared into my eyes. My heart thundered watching him, trying to restrain himself. "You need to do it."

I just shook my head. "No, you don't want this..."

"Don't I?" he growled as his hard cock bounced against his thigh.

I licked my lips and moved closer, turning to straddle him on hands and knees. The movement felt powerful, *claiming my own hunger.* I grabbed his wrist, my fingers barely closing around the girth before I lifted his arm and pressed his wrist against the wall. I was back in that moment with him underneath me, with the searing hunger roaring inside me. I had the power here. *I had the control.*

He stared up into my eyes "Use me, any way you need."

His cock twitched with the words. I reached down and grasped him tightly, listening to that moan slip from his lips once more. So much power. *Brutal* power, barely restrained.

I'd seen him beat a man almost to death.

He'd do more if I let him.

He'd kill, and hurt, and maim, and he'd do it all for me.

All for me.

But right now, with my fingers wrapped around his thick, hard length, he was nothing more than putty in my hands. "You want me to *use* you?" I murmured.

"I want to fuck you," he snarled, his eyes alight with savage hunger. "Ride my cock, my face, I don't fucking care, just as long as you do it."

I clenched my jaw with a savage need and worked my way down to the hilt of his cock before sliding all the way to the head. A tiny, glistening bead welled at the tip. One perfect tear. He dragged his teeth across his lip and groaned, his untied hand sliding from around the bedpost. I wanted that bead, wanted it in my mouth. I pulled back, letting his hand drop to the pillow beside him. But he didn't reach for me, didn't twist his fingers in my hair and ram his weapon into my throat.

Instead, he fisted the sheets, holding on as I slid lower...and licked the tip.

"Fuck me, I'm gonna come," he warned.

"No, you won't," I urged, lowering again, taking more into my mouth.

Slick skin slipped across my tongue as I slowly pumped my hand, working that tight skin to the end and back again. The thick vein pulsed against my thumb. He was so hard...so very hard. But I wasn't anywhere near done.

I rose, giving him one last lick, and ordered, "Move down the bed, Lazarus."

He did as I instructed, his hands sliding along my thighs until I spread them wider for his chest. His gaze moved between my thighs.

"Is that okay?" I asked.

"Okay?" His eyes widened. "Fuck me, I'm about to explode just looking at you. Can I touch you?"

One nod, and he slid his thumb down the top of my slit, finding that tiny nub. Warmth moved through me, making me close my eyes.

"No, Kat," he urged. "I want you to look at me."

I did, meeting those perfect blue eyes. Blue eyes that didn't remind me of anyone else. Blue eyes that were only Lazarus, and as he stroked me, I came alive.

"That's it," he encouraged as I lifted to meet his touch.

His fingers slipped along my crease before he curled one finger and slipped it just inside. He fucked me like that, teasing, torturing, his finger barely inside, before he slid it free. He gripped my hips, fingers digging into my ass as he pulled me upward, shifting my weight. Panicked, I lashed out, grasping his wrist as he settled me higher....so I straddled his head.

He lifted his head, his eyes not shifting from mine as he licked me gently.

"Oh shit." I shuddered, my grip around his wrist easing.

"Let go, princess," he moaned, moving lower.

His hands slid around my thighs, holding me against his mouth as he pushed his tongue inside me.

My hand moved to his head, my fingers sliding through his damp hair as I thrust against his mouth. "God, that feels so good."

He licked and sucked, drawing on tender flesh until that hunger turned urgent. I wanted him...*needed him*. I needed more. I needed *harder*. Needed that place inside me stroked and licked, a place his tongue couldn't reach.

"I need..." I moaned, looking down at him. "I need more."

"Condom?" he murmured.

Did it matter? "You don't need to...if you don't want."

"Fuck, I want to come inside you," he groaned.

I lowered my body, kissing his mouth. He tasted salty and slick. He tasted of me, slipping his tongue inside as he worked my body lower.

He broke the kiss as I hovered over him. "Kat," he started.

But I was lowering my weight, grasping him, guiding him inside me. He was big, stretching me until he slid all the way in. His gaze burned like the blue belly of a flame, flickering and dancing, never moving from mine as I raised up and rolled my hips, riding him in deep, languid movements.

Nirvana waited at the edge.

The edge where his cock rubbed.

The edge where I lost myself.

I dropped my head as a tremor coursed through my body.

"Kat," he moaned, and closed his eyes. "*Jesus...*"

I thrust against his body...*using him* over and over again. And in the act, I found that secret burn, the one which came to me in the quiet of the night, the one starved and desperate, making me rub between my thighs until I climaxed. But here, with Lazarus deep and thick inside me—here, that aching desperation came alive. I cried out, slamming my hips down in brutal, merciless thrusts...and came apart, crying out his name. "*Lazarus.*"

Warmth spilled inside me. His fingers dug against the muscles of my thighs as I arched my back. Hard breaths sawed in and out, leaving me floating up there, until I crashed back down. I dropped my torso, and he caught me, pulling me down beside him.

"Jesus Christ," he gasped, his arm flopping limply across my belly. "That...that was..."

"Mind-blowing," I finished with a smile.

He turned his hand, his fingers splaying across my abdomen.

And deep inside me, a feeling fluttered.

Like a butterfly trapped.

No, not trapped...*reaching.*

For him.

We lay like that, his hand claiming something he didn't even know. I tried not to think of it, tried not to feel the spark of hope as it detonated like an atomic blast.

"Talk to me," he said after a while. "Tell me what you're thinking."

What I was thinking?

If I told him that, he'd run from me...and he'd keep on running. "I'm thinking that I'm starving."

And at that moment, a growl tore from my belly, making him chuckle. "Lucky you told me that, otherwise I'd never know."

I ached with the loss, reaching out to clutch his hand as it slid from my belly. But then he turned, rolled to press against my side, and kissed me deeply before breaking away. "Let me feed you."

I let him pull away, watching his muscles tense as he rose from the bed. Fuck me, I'd never seen anything so spectacular. One comb of his fingers through his hair, and he strode toward the kitchen, naked and goddamn perfect.

I waited for a second, checking between my thighs, then rolled.

"There's clean sweats just in the closet," he called from the kitchen. "Help yourself to whatever you need."

I slid from the bed and padded into the closet. A small wall safe was open, and a pile of cash and a gun sat on top of some folders. The money I didn't care about, but the gun...my mind slipped to mine, tucked away in my own closet. A gun I wanted to use. I would, if there was no other way out.

The clatter of a frying pan tore me out of the thoughts. I grabbed a pair of soft sweat shorts and pulled them on before grabbing a white tee.

The smell of frying butter drifted through the air as I pulled it over my head.

And the soft rumble of...*singing?*

That panicked quiver came from my belly once more at the sound.

I pressed my palm against my abdomen, whispered a prayer to whoever was listening, and stepped out.

30

Lazarus

She stepped into the kitchen and my heart stuttered. Her red hair was damp and curling around her shoulders, shoulders covered with my damn tee. The sight of her dressed in my clothes made me fucking hard...*again.* But I focused on the pan in front of me, pouring the pancake mixture into nice even rounds.

"That smells delicious," she declared.

Her belly gave another rumble, which made me smile. "Sounds like he agrees with you."

"He?" she whispered quietly, drawing my attention.

I glanced her way, finding a look of shock before a flicker of panic cut through.

Her fear only made me chuckle louder. "The ravenous beast in your stomach," I explained, and shook my head. *What else did she think I meant?*

"Oh," she murmured, and slid up onto a stool on the other side of the kitchen island.

I flipped each pancake, making sure to rotate the pan and get them cooking evenly, just how Taken had taught me, before sliding the first one onto the waiting plate, then poured another.

I grabbed butter and maple syrup from the refrigerator and turned with the plate in one hand, fork, butter, and syrup in the other. "Now, you're not one of those women who says they're starving and eats like a mouthful and that's all, are you?" She just grabbed the plate and the fork, then the butter and syrup, spreading and pouring generous amounts onto the soft fluffy morsels, then stabbed the things with single-minded ferocity. "Obviously not," I answered myself.

She smiled and ate, chewing carefully before taking another bite. Before I knew it, or was even ready, she wanted more. I focused, my damn heart pulsing in the back of my throat, and worked the damn pan before sliding another onto her plate.

She ate that one too.

I'd made pancakes for the guys a hundred fucking times...and not one of those times had I felt like this. *Proud. Powerful.* She closed her eyes as she chewed and swallowed, and I was captured by the movement of her throat. My cock twitched, reminding me the fucking hard-on wasn't going away anytime soon.

Even though I'd just had her...*I wanted her again.*

I was torn between wanting to see her dressed in my clothes and tearing the damn things off to find that delicious heat underneath. I wanted her, my wrists tied, or untied. Her pussy rubbing all over my damn face, any way she fucking wanted, I didn't care. I was all fucking in...

And as always, a single thought broke through to ruin it all.

A memory of Kat curled against that fucking sofa, her knees drawn tight together. I wasn't stupid. I knew the haunted look of someone who'd seen shit. I knew what that fucking distant stare of someone hurting looked like. And this woman in front of me, this woman stabbing and chewing the damn packaged pancake mix and loving it like it was some five-star masterpiece, had fucking suffered.

Hell, she was still suffering.

The only thing I didn't know was what to do about it.

I lowered my gaze to the faint bruises across my knuckles starting to darken.

Or maybe I did...

Kat made a low, satisfied moan and lowered the fork, the second pancake mostly eaten. "I can't do it," she complained with a shake of her head.

I just leaned across the island, plucked the last piece from her plate, and popped it into my mouth. "You did damn well. Not even Logan carb-stacks like that on loading day." I gave her a smirk.

She widened her eyes. "Hey!" And gave me a playful jab to the stomach.

One I easily caught in my hand and pulled her close, that mischievous flicker in me turning into something a little more *starved*. And she saw it. Gone was that detached stare. She was all here in this moment. All real...all *mine*.

"You want this?" I asked her, pressing her hand against my stomach.

I was laying it all on the line here. My heart, my goddamn emotions, handing it all over on a damn platter for her to have... or discard. I'd never wanted anyone like I wanted her, never *needed* anything so fucking much in my life, not even Iggy...not even Taken.

This woman...with a single glance, she brought me to the edge of that yawning fucking pit and I was ready to hurl myself into the darkness, ready to do whatever it took to have her, *and keep her*.

"Yes," she answered softly, turning her body toward mine. "I want this."

Why? The question resounded in my head. *Why him? Why not me from the first goddamn second I saw you?*

Why not me...

I clamped my jaw tight shut, thankful the desperate damn words hadn't reached my lips, and moved closer, so close our bodies touched. So fucking close, I could smell the syrup on her breath. Fuck, that sounded good. I leaned down and brushed my lips across hers. "Good, princess," I murmured against her mouth. "'Cause you're not going anywhere."

Her answer was to kiss me, to open that delicious fucking mouth for me.

My cock wanted in...*again.*

It wanted so far in...her mouth, her slick pussy. I wanted her stretching around me. I wanted her damn moans of pleasure.

But I had to do it right. Her on top, right? Her unrestrained, unburdened.

She lowered her hand, sliding it down my stomach to cup my length. Jesus fucking Christ.

She pulled away just enough to murmur, "You're hard."

"Princess," I moaned. "I'm always fucking hard when you're near me."

"Like that night I danced for you."

I swallowed a shudder, remembering how fucking wet she'd been when we were through. "Yeah, just like that…"

"I want to dance like that again for you. Will you let me?"

She had to fucking ask? "Baby, you can dance like that for me anytime the mood fucking strikes you. Hell, even if that's all you do, I'll die a happy man."

She stiffened in my arms, her voice growing cold. "But you're not dying, Lazarus."

I pulled away, catching that glint of fear in her eyes again. She searched my gaze. I could see her desperation. Is that what she was so scared of? That I was going to die…that I was going to leave her? "No, I'm not going to die."

Before her, I wouldn't have given those words a second thought.

Before her, I wouldn't have cared, apart from loyalty to my damn family.

But here and now, with that panic in her lingering so close to the surface, I cared a whole fucking lot.

"Men like you fight," she whispered. "Men like you kill. Men like you do whatever it takes."

Whatever it takes. Maybe she did know me. I lowered my body to stare right into her eyes, that cold edge of hunger roaring to life inside me. "You're fucking right we do."

She lifted her hand, her fingers sliding through my hair. "You protect what's yours." A tremor coursed through me with her words.

"Is that what you are?" Hope fucking flared as I licked my lips. "Are you mine, princess?"

"Yes," she answered without hesitation. "Yes, I am."

My lips curled. *Mine.* Mine to protect. Mine to defend. I grabbed my phone and opened Spotify, finding a song with a heavy beat, choosing Bleedin' Out by edIT and sent it softly through the surround sound. Even without much volume, the beat pulsed through me, slow and seductive.

I grabbed her hand and led her toward the living room, where I dropped to the sofa. Cold leather hit my bare ass. I didn't give a fuck if I was still naked, and one look from her said she fucking liked watching me move. Soft lights spilled through the space as I sat back.

"I'm not really dressed seductively," she grumbled, stepping toward me in the baggy sweats and tee.

I reached down, gripped my fucking length, and murmured, "I don't know about that."

Dusky pink nipples peaked the white tee as she stopped in front of me, swaying with the music. I was lost to her, to the way she raked her fingers through her damp hair, and the way her hips swayed.

"Come here." I reached for her hand, pulling her to me.

She climbed onto the sofa, straddling me. Fuck me if my cock didn't hit her just right, pressing between her thighs. Desire sizzled between us as she braced her arms on either side of my head. I lowered my hands to her hips, feeling her grinding, until I had to bite my fucking lip to stop from coming.

I lowered my gaze. Her breasts were skimming the shirt, but it was too fucking big...too much room. I grabbed the bottom of my shirt on her and lifted. She ducked her head, letting the garment slide from her body. Then she was bare to me, bare, with the baggy sweats hanging around those gorgeous fucking hips.

I cupped her breasts, feeling the weight in my palms.

She rose, taking her weight from my cock, and her nipples filled my mouth. Christ, they were perfect, soft and smooth, the most delicious thing I'd ever tasted. I licked the peaks, feeling them tighten before the warmth of my mouth turned them soft once more.

Her moan mingled with the beat as she dropped her head back. Her fingers tangled in my hair, her urgency pressing me against her, desperate for more. I slid one hand between her thighs, stroking her through the soft material of my sweats.

She was going to come all over my damn clothes and I couldn't be fucking prouder. I was lost to the feel of her, lost to the heat of her body and the tremble that coursed through her as I rubbed.

"Fuck me," she moaned, and lowered her gaze, connecting with mine. "If you fuck me, I'm going to scream."

I shoved the sweats down, forcing them over her ass, and gripped her hips, lifting her until she pulled one leg up, then the other, dislodging the pants in a fucking heartbeat. Still, it was too long, too long to feel the cool air across my cock, too long until her slick warmed my fingers. I lowered my gaze, catching the dark, rusty red strip of her hair at her slit, and I sank my fingers inside.

She whimpered and rose, arching her back, forcing her nipples against me. But I wanted her slower this time. I wanted to take my goddamn time and watch her. I slipped a finger along her crease, feeling her quiver with my touch.

"You like this, princess?" I teased. "Like my fingers inside you?"

"I like your cock more," she moaned, and rolled her head forward. "Thick and hard, sliding inside me."

I clenched my jaw at the words and reached for my shaft, aiming the head against her precious little slit. "Like this, you mean?"

She dropped her weight, and her warmth closed around the head as I pushed inside. Her gaze was fire as she met mine. "Just like that." Up and down, she rode, her thighs trembling with the strain.

I couldn't bear it, lifted my hips on her downward slide, and plunged deep inside. She stilled, a look of utter bliss on her face. I could fuck this woman all night and all day to chase that look of ecstasy. I would devote my entire existence to making her come.

My fingers went to her clit. I watched her slit widen, watched her tilt her hips toward my touch, watched my cock sliding inside. With a savage growl, I gripped her and slammed her body against me. She let out a sudden, panicked sound. But the slow smile across her lips said it all. The woman was torturing me, driving me insane with desire.

"I want this," she whispered, and for a second, I didn't understand what she meant.

Want this, as in...my cock ramming inside her? Want this, as in her on top?

But the intensity in her stare said it was more than that...it was more than *this*.

It was *us*.

All of us.

Together.

"Fuck yes," I growled, and slid my arms around her body, twisting her without thinking.

She landed on her back on the sofa and for a second, she froze. *Oh shit...oh shit. Oh. Shit.* Then, with her eyes wide, she pulled me down against her. Her legs wrapped around my hips, and her heels pulled against my ass, wanting me inside her.

I kept my weight on my arms, braced on either side of her head, and rammed my hips forward, gaining inch after sweet, goddamn inch, until her eyelids fluttered.

Mine.

That word resounded as all feeling but her left me. My balls tightened as her pussy clenched. I was lost in oblivion...utterly fucking lost. Nails gouged my side as she jerked her hips up, but I barely felt the sting as she stilled and released the most delicious sound I'd ever heard.

I came with a roar, the guttural sound rumbling in the back of my throat as I arched, sinking deep, and spasmed inside her. *For the second time.*

No condom. The words floated through my mind before they were gone. But I didn't care, not with her. She had me completely and as I came back to reality, I realized the music was still going, though the beat had morphed into something else. Still, all I heard was the frantic sound of her heart as I lowered myself and pressed my lips against hers.

She sucked in deep breaths and gave me a small smile, until my damn phone rang. "Goddamnit," I muttered and slid out of her. No call this time of the fucking night could be good.

"Finley Salvatore is here screaming and yelling, demanding to come up," Freddy reported.

I could hear the asshole ranting in the background. "What the fuck does he want?"

"He thinks Anna is up there."

"Here?" I muttered. "Why the fuck would Anna be here?'

"Fuck knows, but he's adamant."

I know she's up there! Finley roared in the background.

"Anna?" Kat pushed up, concern filling her eyes. "What's happened?"

"What do you want me to do?" Freddy questioned.

I rose from the sofa, leaving Kat behind, and headed for the bedroom. "Give me a second, I'm coming down."

I hung up the phone and glanced over my shoulder as I pulled my jeans back on. Trust a goddamn Salvatore to ruin the fucking mood.

This better be fucking worth it...or there'd be hell to pay.

31

Lazarus

"Everything okay?" Kat called, drawing my focus.

"I don't know. I'm going down to see what the fucking problem is." I glanced toward her, my gaze lingering on those soft peaks of her prefect breasts. "You'd better get dressed, but stay here where you're safe. I won't be long."

I yanked up my jeans and tugged a t-shirt down low as I strode toward the elevator. I had no idea what I was walking into, for all I knew there could be a bullet downstairs with my damn name on it. I thought of that as I stabbed the button and the elevator doors closed. For the first time, a tremor of fear coursed through me. Coming after me was one thing, but not Kat.

She was off limits.

I knew fear in that moment, knew how men like Dominic Salvatore lived, constantly afraid someone would come for those he loved. It made me realize why Dad never remarried after my mom, made me realize how fucking brutal this life actually was. I lifted my gaze and clenched my jaw as the elevator came to a stop and the doors opened.

Finley Salvatore was waiting for me.

But so was Logan. He just stood there like a damn brick wall, one side to me...and the other to everyone else.

"Easy now," he warned, and lifted his hand.

The move only seemed to piss Finley off. He tore his gaze from me as I stepped out and snarled at my bodyguard. "Get the *fuck* out of my way."

Logan didn't budge, not for a second. But Finley wasn't after retribution. The male was *wild*. Desperation made him frantic, whatever was eating him...had its fangs in deep.

"Is she up there?" he barked.

I swallowed a flicker of rage. "If you're talking about Kat, then you know that's none of your damn business."

It always came down to that. That axe they had to grind, Like *every* woman was too good for a Stidda.

"Not Kat...*Anna,*" he answered.

A chuff slipped from my lips as I combed my hair back from my face. "Why the fuck would Anna be in my apartment?" His seething rage said it all. I couldn't stop the smirk. "Oh, you had a little lovers' quarrel and she left your scrawny ass? Maybe she's not as stupid as I thought."

Finley strode forward. "Let me up there...*now.*"

Now I was getting pissed off. I took a step, blocking his way to the elevator. "Back the fuck off, Salvatore. She's not up there."

"The *hell* she isn't," he raged. "Let me up there now...*or...*"

I stilled, that burn of anger turning ice cold. "Or what?" I warned, and took a step closer. "You going to declare war for this fucking woman?"

"If I have to."

He was deadly serious. I'd never seen Finley so fucking serious. It shook me, enough to put the poor bastard out of his misery. "She's not up there."

"I don't fucking believe you," he snapped.

I was getting nowhere, not when he looked like *that*. "You want to see for yourself, *fine*."

Logan scowled at the words. He didn't like Finley coming upstairs. Hell, he probably didn't like *any* male coming upstairs where Kat was concerned, *including me*.

But this wasn't his fucking decision, was it? I pressed the button and stepped back inside. "Kat's upstairs and she'd had a hell night...*so be fucking respectful*."

"I just need Anna," he sputtered, and raked his fingers through his hair. "I think something's wrong...like *really* wrong."

Yeah, no shit.

The bastard couldn't keep still, jumpy and breathing heavy, even running his hands through his hair over and over again. Frantic. That's what the brother was...*pure fucking frantic*. The sight scared me. I'd never seen him like this...hell, I'd never seen anyone like this.

"You think she's running?" I murmured.

He jerked those brown eyes to mine, fear dancing so close to the surface it balanced on a knife's edge. Then the elevator stopped, the doors opened, and Finley was striding through the apartment, heading straight for the bedroom, where Kat was...*like hell he was.*

I strode ahead, outmatching his strides, and gave him a savage glare.

The bastard seemed to remember where he was and stopped in the middle of the living room.

"Lazarus?" Kat called my name, and the sound of that made my damn heart race.

"Yeah, it's me," I answered.

"What's going on?" She stepped out of the bedroom, concern filling her eyes.

"It's Fin," I muttered. "He's worried about Anna."

She came closer, looking from me to Fin. "What about Anna?"

I hated that tremor in her voice, hated the panic in her eyes, hated the way she wrapped her arms around her body defensively. I wanted to protect her from that kind of feeling. I wanted to be the one to end her fear. "It seems she's gone missing."

She just looked to Finley as her fear turned savage. "What happened?" But he didn't answer, just stood there, pale and shaking. She strode toward him, her tone turning icy. "*What happened?*"

"She left," he answered slowly.

"Just like that?"

He swallowed hard. "Yeah."

"Did you...hurt her?" There was a warning in her voice, one that was far too fucking telling.

I waited for him to answer *'fuck no, I didn't hurt her'*, but he didn't. He didn't say the words, and my disdain for the fucking Salvatores just went a little deeper. *You pieces of sh—*

"I think she's in trouble." Finley's words jerked me from the growing hate. "And she's about to do something fucking stupid. Something I won't be able to fix."

"What the fuck?" I muttered. There was only one reason why he'd be rattled like this, only one reason why someone like Anna would run. "You think she's going to talk? How much does she even fucking know about you, anyway?"

Finley just turned and met my eyes. I saw why the panic now, saw why all the fear. I didn't need to hear the words, they were written all over his face, but still, he said them. "She knows it all."

Jesus...

Jesus *Christ.*

I knew what would happen if she did talk. I could see it all, Kat fucking broken when they found the body of her friend washed up on the beach. There was no way she'd make it off the island alive. "Then you'd better hope you find her, Fin." The warning tore free. "Before it's too late."

He flinched at the words, the bastard paling in front of us, before he swallowed hard, gave a nod to Kat, and left. When the elevator doors closed with a *thud,* Kat turned to me. "What's going to happen?"

What's going to happen? Nothing good. "He's going to find her," I answered, giving her the kind of hope I wish I had. "That's what he's going to do."

Her brows furrowed. "And if he doesn't, what then?"

A pang tore through my chest as I took a step closer. "Then we'll figure it out together."

Unspoken words filled her eyes, darkening the brown until they shone almost black. "All because she wanted to escape."

"No, princess," I murmured, and brushed the back of a curled finger along her jaw. "If she disappears, it'll be because she spoke about things not meant to be spoken about."

The color left her face then, turning her perfect skin to ashen gray under my touch. "Once you're in, there's no getting out, right?"

I didn't understand why those words made such an impact. Surely, she understood the kind of men we were? And the kind of families we belonged to. She was on an island owned by the Mafia, for Christ's sake.

"Would you do that to me?" She met my gaze. "Would you hunt me down and kill me because I said something I shouldn't?"

"Hunt you down?" I repeated, the words hurting more than they should. "Princess, I'd tear the vast reaches of Hell apart to find you...*if that's what you wanted.* But I'd never hurt you, not in a million fucking years."

Her breaths deepened and her pupils dilated. She seemed to draw in my words and carve them into her fucking soul. "You'd never let anyone else come for me, right?"

"Not unless you wanted them to," I answered, lowering my head. I wanted to kiss her, wanted to breathe life into those pale lips, lips that just seconds ago had been pink and lush, filled with life.

"And if I didn't?"

A twitch came at the corner of my mouth at the thought. "Then you'd never have to worry about them ever again."

Damon Zakharov.

That's who she was talking about. It didn't take a fucking genius to figure it out. I cupped her jaw, tilting her mouth up to mine, and kissed her. She was trembling, her arms still wrapped tight around her chest defensively. But the deeper the kiss grew, the more she warmed to me, lowering her hands and sliding her arms around my waist. This was how I wanted it to be between us. *Always protected...always safe.* Her fingers splayed against my shoulder, pressing me harder against her.

She moved against me, rubbing and moaning. That tiny, dangerous, little sound vibrated through my mouth before she pulled away. I wanted to stay with her, wanted to lift her feet from the floor and take her to our bed. I wanted to fuck her until the shadows in her eyes brightened, and the only man that lingered in her head was me. I wanted to taste every fucking inch of her...claim her over and over again so that *any* man who came near her knew who'd come for him if he dared fucking touch her again.

Because the woman was mine.

Not to own, or to control. And not to fucking *use.*

But to protect, to cherish, to pull out of the darkness and into the bloody, dangerous light that was my world...and my family. My thoughts drifted to Logan. A man like him would fucking destroy anyone who dared touch her...if I wasn't around. I needed that, someone I could depend on. *But what if it became something more between them? Could I live with that?*

I broke the kiss and stared into her eyes. I wasn't sure if I could. But there was one thing I did know...*I wasn't done with Damon Zakharov.* "I need to go out for a little while," I whispered. "You think you'll be okay here?"

"Now?" she scowled. "It must be like one or two in the morning."

I knew she wanted an explanation but I just couldn't give it. Instead, I captured the perfect point of her chin and kissed her lower lip. "Shower, take your time, rifle through my damn things for all I care. I'm an open book where you're concerned. Just don't..." a tremor tore through me. "Just don't leave. I'll have Freddy at the door in case you need anything."

"You're going after her, aren't you? You're going after Anna."

"Is that what you're worried about? That I'm going to hurt her?" I asked.

The truth raged in her eyes. I had a reputation, even amongst my own kind. The Rossis had come from street thugs. We were the brutal and merciless underdogs, always fighting to retain our seat on the Commission...but there were certain things we didn't do, and hunting down the best friend of the woman I care for was one of those things. "That's not who I am," I answered. "But don't worry, you'll figure that out the more time we're together."

"That confident, huh?" she said carefully.

"Yeah, when it comes to you, I am."

I dropped my hand and stepped away, hating leaving her. But if I didn't, then I'd take her to bed...and make her stay there. As much as that thought appealed to me...seeing Damon Zakharov appealed to me more. "I'll call Freddy," I murmured. "He'll keep you safe until I get back."

She said nothing as I grabbed my phone and punched out a message. There was one thing the Rossis weren't...and that was fucking weak when it came to defending those we cared for. Once you were family...we'd take a fucking bullet for you, or in Kat's case, deliver a message, one I wanted to be loud and goddamn clear.

I stepped into the elevator as I hit send, so by the time I reached their apartment, Freddy was waiting for me with his arms crossed over his chest and a look of concern. I strode out and into their apartment, looking for Logan.

"You sure you want to do this?" Freddy asked without moving.

I just glared at him over my shoulder. "Am I sure?"

"Hey." He raised his hands in surrender. "I'm just asking here, making sure you're prepared to go to war for this woman."

"What he means is, once you declare your intentions, there's no going back," Logan added, striding from the bedroom as he snapped on his shoulder holster.

"I'm pretty sure I made my intentions clear when I broke his damn cheek, but look, if it takes knifing the bastard in the throat to make it a little clearer, then that's what I'll do."

Both of them just stared at me, until Logan smothered a twitch of a smirk and looked away. "Okay then," the brother added. "Let's go make some enemies."

"I'll be back as soon as I can." I glanced toward Freddy. "Keep her safe, whatever it takes."

He just gave a nod and watched us step into the elevator.

Logan said nothing as we dropped to the foyer and strode out. The island's guard stood near the door, watching the darkness through the window.

"All quiet?" Logan asked, drawing his gaze.

"Yes, sir," the guard answered, his gaze moving from the guns strapped to Logan's chest to me.

Only then did he flinch.

I must look threatening.

Good.

I strode out with Logan at my side. "Finley Salvatore thinks Anna is running."

"If that's the case, then she better run hard and fast. Dominic Salvatore is no man to mess with...and Finley has all the makings of a ruthless bastard to have as an enemy."

I glanced his way as my hair lashed my face. "Is that a warning?"

He just glanced my way. "Call it a recommendation."

A recommendation to be allies with Finley Salvatore. Now that, I hadn't seen coming. But Logan wasn't one to push a point, so he just walked the rest of the way in silence. I shoved his words away as we cut across the Institute's grounds, until the faint *crack* of gunfire carried on the wind.

Logan stopped walking, shifting his gaze to scan the dark. "Get to the infirmary, Laz," he instructed without looking my way.

Urgency filled me. It was far too late to turn around, even if I wanted to...*and I didn't want to.*

This night was filled with danger, and I felt dangerous in it.

Hollow with hate.

With my bruised fists clenched at my sides.

I shifted my gaze to the main building in the distance and gritted my teeth. I was coming for Zakharov...ready or not.

32

Lazarus

The sound of gunfire grew louder as we stepped up to the main building. Movement came from inside, a blur of men dressed to kill. Logan palmed his gun and drew it from the holster. But the movement didn't head our way. No, they disappeared toward the rear of the building and were gone in a heartbeat.

I waited, fists clenched, pissed that I hadn't brought my own gun. *But I knew why I hadn't.*

No gun...then no temptation to use it, *right?*

But fuck, I wanted to use it.

"Clear," Logan muttered, and stepped up to the scanner.

We didn't give a shit who saw us go in...I just didn't want to be stopped before I was done, and when it came to protecting Kat, I was never *done.* The electric doors opened and we strode inside, making our way along the familiar halls.

It was only days ago that my father was here, meeting with the Commission in the wake of Baldeon's death. I jerked my gaze

toward the walls of the building and thought of the gunshots...
Finley...*and Anna.* Was it happening again? Were they coming
for another of the Commission's sons?

My pulse sped at the thought. Maybe it was a good idea I was
away from Kat...for the moment at least. "Message Freddy and
make sure he's on high alert. No one gets into that apartment,
not unless it's you, me, or the fucking Commander himself."

"Sure." Logan strode out, grabbing his phone with one hand,
the other still holding his Sig Sauer, relaxed at his side.

Glass and steel blurred around me. Even the roar of the wind
still battering the windows faded as I focused on the darkened
hallways up ahead. All I cared about was her, that redheaded
woman who'd somehow nicked my skin and crawled inside,
working her way toward my heart.

The marks Damon had left behind on her body really got
to me.

I'd seen bruises on women before.

Seen worse, too.

But not on someone I felt like this about.

Not someone I'd kill for.

And I will kill for her if I need to.

The faint light of Logan's phone disappeared as I strode
forward, leaving him to fall behind. The brother knew instantly
where he was needed...and this was all me. I shoved through
the closed double doors of the infirmary and lifted my gaze to
the row of rooms up ahead. The bright lights of the nurses'
station cast a glow across the floor, almost reaching the rooms
on the opposite side.

But only one of them had a closed door, and that was where I headed. One glance over my shoulder, and I slowed, watched for movement, and eased the handle down before slipping inside.

Harsh wheezes filled the room. A broken nose for sure, maybe even a shattered eye socket. A few months of healing and he'd be good as new, ready to drug and rape the next woman. The beast inside me writhed with the thought. The image of him standing over her was burned into my mind.

I wanted this one burned into his.

I stepped around the curtain and neared the bed. The faint glow of moonlight cut through the massive windows, illuminating the swollen face of Damon Zakharov, asleep in the bed.

"Seeing you standing over her like that," I murmured, listening to the change in his breathing as his eyes opened. "I wanted to kill you."

He flinched as he came fully awake. One panicked gaze behind me to the closed door of his room, and he swallowed *hard*.

"Don't worry," I said, my voice strangely calm. "No one knows I'm here. You see, they're all busy protecting those on the island. Just another one of the perks of living by a code, a code that stands between me, and the chance of you making it through this night alive."

"You...c-can't," the piece of shit stuttered. "You can't kill me."

I just smiled and nodded. "You're right. The repercussions of that wouldn't be good, even for a Rossi." I gripped the bars of the bedrails and leaned over him. "But don't mistake that for you surviving a second longer after you get off this fucking island."

He just froze, those wide eyes fixed on mine.

"I'm coming for you," I promised. "And you'll fucking scream before I'm through. I'll bury a knife into your chest...and I'll do it slow, inch by inch. You'll watch that blade go in, Zakharov. You'll look into my eyes as you die and know what you've done."

"Because of *Kat?*" he protested. "Sh-she's nothing. A fucking whore. You want her? Then just go ahead and fuck her, for Christ's sake. She's not mine."

"She's nothing?" I growled as the words slammed inside me.

"I don't own her," he sputtered frantically. "She's Hale's, but he'll let you have her, at least until they're married."

"Married?" That savagery rose inside me. *Married?*

"Until then, she's fair game. He said so himself." Zakharov licked his lips. "He said I could use her as entertainment, he wants her *used*. Serves her right for coming here."

"Use her." An icy touch snaked its way along my spine. "Like she's nothing."

"She *is* nothing, man. She's a whore...a fucking cunt. My Dad's had her, and his friends have all had her. I only had her the once, but she's all yours if you want her."

A twitch came at the corner of my mouth.

"You don't have to threaten me to do it," he urged, totally fucking oblivious at how close to death he was right then.

"Laz," Logan warned as I clenched my fist.

My body shook uncontrollably as Damon glanced at Logan standing against the wall. He hadn't seen him until now, hadn't realized that we weren't alone. But now he knew. His brows furrowed, and the sonofabitch licked his lips and turned back to me. "Lazarus, man. You don't have to threaten me to take her. I admit I shouldn't have done that in front of Salvatore's woman. But you beat me good for it. I learned my fucking lesson there."

I expelled a pent-up breath and tried to remember how to breathe. "You see, that's a problem for me." I closed my eyes and strangled the fucking railing. "It's a problem because she *isn't yours to give away*. She isn't mine...and she isn't that fucking Hale's. And I didn't *beat* you for raping her in front of *anyone*. I beat you for *raping* her, full fucking stop."

The stupid motherfucker just looked at me like I'd grown two heads, and started talking again. "She's not like anyone else," he started. "She's not a woman you love."

I opened my eyes and dropped in nice and close so he could see the truth in them. "You see, that's where you're wrong...and I'm going to make it my life's fucking mission to change that. The moment you step off this fucking island, you're mine Zakharov, you and your filthy fucking father. I'll assassinate your entire goddamn family because I can't fucking stand the thought of you drawing breath in the same world as hers."

"Don't be fucking ridiculous, Rossi."

He didn't get it...*he really didn't get it.* "How the fuck do you sleep at night?" I searched his eyes for the answer.

His busted lip curled as the glint in his eyes sparkled. "Well fucking spent after riding the fuck out of her."

I lashed out in an instant, still seeing the thick fucking marks from his fingers around her arm, marks I wanted to leave around his throat. But Logan was there, grasping my forearm.

"Not now," he cautioned, his voice deep with the promise of violence. "Not here and not now."

I tore my grip from around the bastard's throat and listened to him cough and splutter as he inhaled hard. "You come after me like this for a piece of *pussy?* You're fucking *MAFIA!* " He screeched.

"You take something perfect..." I tried to keep it together, tried to remember the fucking code we lived by. A code that right now I'd strangle as well. "Something...*priceless*. Something no one should take. Me? I'll just take your fucking life. There's nothing worthy about that, and when I do...*I'll be sending you straight to Hell.*"

"Then I'll be waiting for you," the bastard sneered through broken front teeth. "I'll be waiting for you to come after me. You and everyone else I fucking know."

"You better." Rage quaked in my voice. "Because I'll tear you apart there, as well...you and every other man who took from her."

Cruelty glittered like stars in his eyes as he smiled. "That's going to be a long list, Lazarus."

*A long list...*the words hit me like a shotgun blast to the chest. *A long goddamn list...*

That chill inside me grew colder.

"Not for long," I said as I turned away. "Not when I'm done."

33

Kat

I paced the floor of the apartment, glancing out the window as the storm still raged. Tall palms whipped and swayed back and forth with the violent gusts of wind, and far in the night, the pitch black ocean crashed against the shore.

But it wasn't the view of the water I wanted right now. I wanted to face the green rolling grounds, desperate to watch for Lazarus to return. But as the seconds grew into minutes, I became afraid he wouldn't come back.

"You're going to wear a track in the floor, you know that, right?"

I bit my lip and jerked my gaze toward Freddy, who stood near the door, his presence alone making me fearful. Was he here to protect me...or *to keep me confined?* I was naive if I thought I could trust him. His loyalty was to Lazarus...and Lazarus had left me. So that left me uncertain and afraid. I hugged my body and paced, trying to think of a way out if this all went wrong. *Run and hide.* That's all that filled me.

But run where?

My phone gave a *beep,* drawing my gaze. Through the cracked screen, I caught the message.

Unknown: I'm starting to lose my patience, Katerina. Call me immediately and stop blocking my fucking calls.

My heart leaped at the sight. I snatched my phone free, punched in my code, and pressed *block number.* Panic made my fingers tremble before I cast the phone onto the sofa once more. I needed to do something soon...*First, I needed my gun.*

My hand dropped to my belly and the splayed fingers caught the flutter deep inside, low, tiny. My thoughts became frantic as I tried to plan this all out.

"My Connie touched her belly like that."

I froze, having forgotten for a second he was even there, and dropped my hand. "Sorry?" I forced a smile and glanced his way.

But the tall, brooding male just watched me as he leaned against the wall. Those careful eyes missed nothing, falling to my belly before finding my gaze once more. My pulse thundered as I held his gaze. *Oh shit...oh shit...oh shit.*

"Her belly," he repeated with a slow nod. "She used to touch it just like that when she was pregnant, said she felt a *quickening.*"

I forced a laugh. "Pregnant? God, no." I shook my head.

But there was no resistance in his eyes, he didn't swallow my lie, and when the sound of the elevator opening came, he glanced at my belly once more. Then Lazarus was striding into the apartment, glancing at Freddy before shifted his attention to me. Something had happened in the short while since he'd left. Something that honed that harder edge in him. I felt it now as Logan followed, watching Lazarus like a damn hawk.

Dangerous...that's what they were in this moment.

But were they dangerous for me?

"Everything okay?" I asked, desperate to gauge his emotions.

There was a second when he scowled before answering. "Yeah."

Still he just stared at me like he wanted to say more...*a lot more.* I glanced toward Freddy, who'd kept his gaze fixed on me, and all of a sudden, the walls closed in.

"We're downstairs," Logan muttered. "In case you need anything."

Lazarus just glanced at the bodyguard over his shoulder. "You going out there?"

"Yeah. I'll keep you updated."

A nod and the two guards left, and we were alone once more with the sound of the elevator doors closing.

"Laz?" I whispered. "What's going on?"

He just dragged his hand through his hair. I caught the tremble, and the careful look in his eyes as he took a step closer. "I could ask you the same," he answered. "You seem a little jumpy."

I tried to slow my sawing breaths. "The storm, and you leaving, and I was attacked tonight. So yeah, I feel a little jumpy. Especially when you up and left."

"The attack." He came closer, but that hardness in him didn't soften. "I wanted to ask you about that."

A tremor coursed through me as he lifted his hand. I fought the urge to flinch, fought that whisper in my head to *leave now...*

"Is there anything you want me to know?" he asked, his focus boring into me.

I met that cold, steely hunger with my own. "Yes," I answered through gritted teeth. "There is...I was stupid tonight. I was stupid, and angry, and drunk." He said nothing, just waited, and the silence grew hostile. "I couldn't get our kiss out of my head. I kept thinking about it. I'd already warned him to stay away from me. But then I saw him at that party, laughing and joking...and...*and...*"

"And," Lazarus urged. "You what?"

I flinched, dragging my gaze back to his. "I reacted, okay? I hit him and kept on hitting him. I wanted to claw his goddamn eyes out. I wanted to...*I wanted to make it so he never touched me again.*"

"And you don't feel the same way about us?" he growled. That edge of danger turned to hunger as he reached out and grasped the back of my neck. "Because I need you to tell me here, Kat. I *need* to understand where the line is for me when it comes to you."

"The line?" I repeated, my mind racing.

I didn't understand what he was saying here, couldn't work out what that meant. But deep down, I realized it was important... everything hinged on this moment. One wrong word, and he'd pull away and I'd ruin any chance of escape. *Not just escape... I'd ruin any chance with him.*

A tremor coursed through my chest, fluttering and flapping. "What are you asking me?"

His lips curled from his teeth. He was so savage in that moment, unhinged...*desperate.* "I want all of you...or none."

All of me or none...

His hold around my neck tightened, and something inside me howled with burning need. I wanted that savagery...I wanted him violent and *unhinged.* I wanted him so far removed from the cold, stony exterior of Hale and all the other demons of my past. I wanted him to have me like no one else had ever had me before. I lifted the bottom of my shirt, forcing him to break his hold as I pulled it over my head.

He said nothing, just stared into my eyes as I pushed the sweats down low. "You want all of me, Lazarus?" I whispered. "Then it's yours to take."

A bestial snarl tore from his lips as he took a step forward, grasped me around the waist, and lifted. I wrapped my legs around his waist as he walked toward the bedroom and threw me onto the bed.

There was no stopping him this time.

No holding back.

No tying up his own goddamn wrists to make himself less of a threat to me. There was a beast inside him, one that wanted to mark and claim and *control.* And I wanted that, more than I'd ever wanted anything else before. "Yes," I groaned as he grabbed me and flipped me over.

"Say stop, Kat." His voice was guttural and strange. "Say stop right now, and I'll stop."

"No," I whispered, and lowered my head. "Never with you."

The slow slide of his zipper made me fist the sheets. I arched my back as his fingers pushed between my thighs and he growled. "Fuck me, I want you."

I lowered my head and parted my thighs, heat coursing through me as he slipped his fingers inside. "Jesus." I slammed my eyes closed.

The soft *thump* of his jeans sounded as they hit the floor. His fingers never stopped, stroking and sliding, slipping along my crease before parting my cheeks. Slick warmth dribbled down to hit my ass. I clenched, tightening, feeling that wetness find its way down to my pussy.

"Have you ever...have you ever had this?" He circled the tight band of muscle.

I swallowed a shudder and shook my head, my body puckering against his touch.

"So, this is...*mine?*" His finger pressed against my hole.

Flames licked inside me with the words, but he didn't stop, pushing in slowly only to slide back out. "All this, *is mine?*

I opened my eyes. "Yes," I gasped as he nudged against that tight ring, sliding all the way in. "It's yours."

"Don't you fucking come, Princess," he warned and knelt. His thumbs dug into the flesh of my ass as he pressed his face into the crease. "Don't you dare fucking come, not until I tell you to."

"Oh God," I whimpered at the slow slide of his tongue.

That inferno inside me reached higher and higher...*and higher,* until I trembled with desire.

His thumb pressed against my back opening as his tongue probed my pussy, both working in tandem, making me arch my back and widen my thighs.

"That's the way," Lazarus growled against my cunt. "Open for me, Princess. I'm going to take it slow, okay? You trust me, right?"

I gave a frantic nod as he rose up behind me. Warmth pressed against my ass. The slow slide of smooth skin made me bite my lip. But it wasn't his fingers, not anymore. Panicked fluttering of my pulse filled my head. I readied myself as he pressed harder.

"Open for me, Kat," he urged.

I tried to concentrate, tried not to let my fear get the better of me. But the moment he pushed in, I bucked under his body.

"Easy now," he groaned.

But he didn't stop.

In and out...in and out...*in and out.*

The thick head of his cock pushed inside, then slid free, working me wider with each gentle thrust. The friction grew between us. I pushed against the fisted sheets, driving my body against his.

I couldn't think, couldn't focus, breathtakingly aware of every inch of his cock inside me, driving deeper...*harder.*

"Oh, Jesus...Kat," he groaned.

The sound of my name did things to me I never expected. With a whimper, I shoved against him, forcing his cock deeper until it was all I felt, thick and hard, stretching me until I cried out.

He stilled for a second, before I whispered, "Don't...*stop.*"

"Mine" he murmured against my ear. "You understand me? This...*is now mine.*"

His weight drove me against the bed. He was a beast in that moment, breaching my defenses with a hard, determined frenzy. And with every brutal thrust, I came apart further. I wanted more, wanted harder. I wanted to be used by him...to be totally used. "More," I cried.

"I can't stop," he growled. "Fuck, you feel so good. I want *it all.*"

I arched my back as he bucked, slamming his cock deep inside.

And with a whimper, I came, writhing under him. "Use me," I cried. "I want you to use me."

His fingers were cruel against my hips, driving into my flesh as he slammed home. My pussy clenched and clenched, desperate to hold onto what wasn't there.

Because he was hilt deep in my ass.

With a savage sound, he buried himself deep and stilled. Warmth filled me. Delicious uncontrollable warmth as my senses fired, over and over until I collapsed flat on the bed. Heaving breaths consumed me. I was spent, thoroughly...undeniably spent.

He had it all...every part of me.

My pussy, my ass...my damn heart.

I closed my eyes as a tremor carved a line through me. Lazarus collapsed onto the bed beside me with a tortured moan and grabbed me, pulling me close.

"Princess," my Mafia Prince gasped as he tried to catch his breath. "You're not going anywhere now, I hope you realize that. You're staying right here."

"Beside you on the bed?" I teased as I shifted my weight, turning so I pressed my spine against his side.

His strong arm was like a band around my waist as he held me against him. "Exactly." That hardness was gone now. He was back to the Lazarus that had left this apartment, not the one filled with rage and torture.

"What happened out there?"

His chest stilled, his breath caught before it rose and sank once more. "Nothing you need to worry about."

I pushed up on trembling arms, twisting until I found his gaze. "What if I want to worry?"

His brow furrowed for a second. A battle raged inside his mind, one that played out in the crystal blue of his eyes. "I went to see Damon Zakharov."

I froze at the words, my heart throbbing hard in my chest. "You went to see him...why?"

"Why wouldn't I?" he searched my gaze.

It wasn't to check on his welfare, that was for sure.

"You went to threaten him," I whispered, the heat of desire cooling instantly. "But he said something. He said something you didn't like. Something that made you come back here...and..."

The corner of his mouth twitched. He didn't need to say the words.

I knew.

Disgust bloomed inside me, cold and infernal, stealing away the traces of his love. I pushed away, and he didn't fight me, letting me slide away from him on the bed and clutch the sheet to my chest.

"You're with me now," he said. "Not just in this apartment, but in the world outside when we leave this island."

I flinched and found the truth burning in his stare. "You don't know me," I answered. "You don't know my life. You don't know my father. He won't like it."

"See, there's one thing you need to learn about me, Princess." That hardness was back again, sharp and cutting as he pushed up on strong arms. "I don't give a fuck what anyone else thinks. I care about me...and it looks like I care about you. So, what do *you* think? You want to slum it with a Stidda?"

Slum it with a Stidda.

The savage street thugs that had earned a reputation for being blood-thirsty and deadly. This was my one chance to get away from Haelstrom Hale and my father. This was the one chance I had to protect me...*and my baby.*

Tell him...

The voice urged inside my head.

Tell him now...

I opened my mouth, the words welling in the back of my throat, desperate to escape...as his phone rang.

"Fuck," Lazarus snapped, and shoved up from the bed. He rounded the foot and bent, grasping his jeans from the floor and tore his phone free before answering. "What is it? There was a fucking attack? Finley and Anna...shit, okay, I'll be right there. Yeah..." he glanced my way. "I'll tell her. *I said I'll fucking tell her,*" he snarled, and ended the call.

"What is it?" Panic filled me. "What the hell happened?"

34

Kat

"There was an attack." Lazarus lowered the phone and met my gaze. "Looks like Fin and Anna were caught in the middle. But they're okay."

"Oh, Jesus..." I whispered. "Are they hurt? I mean, Anna...*is she hurt?*" My mind raced, creating the kind of images my heart couldn't handle.

"She's alive, they're both alive." His voice softened, easing the blow of his words. "But Fin's bodyguards...they're gone."

*Oh, Jesus...oh, Jesus...*The air rushed from me in an instant, leaving the room to sway.

"Whoa, there." Lazarus grabbed hold of my arm, and pulled me against him. "It's okay, Kat."

His strong arms wrapped around me. I lowered my head to his chest as my phone made a *beep*, the sound barely audible. Still, I knew who it was...who it *always* was. He wouldn't leave me alone...*he'd never leave me alone.*

"You're okay," Lazarus repeated, his hand splayed against my back, pressing my chest against his. "They're alive, and you're safe."

"I want to see her." The words slipped free. I lifted my head, finding his gaze. "I need to make sure she's okay."

There was a shake of his head. "Not a good idea, Princess."

But the bloody images in my head were relentless, the deafening sound of gunshots so loud, I flinched in his arms.

"Okay," he muttered. "Okay, Kat. You won't rest until you see for yourself that Anna is safe, will you?"

Relief swept through me as I closed my eyes. "Yes. I need to see her. I need to know..."

"Morning will be here in a few hours, daylight is better."

"I want to go now, Lazarus." I opened my eyes. "You don't have to come...I can ask Logan."

The bulging vein at his temple pulsed. "No," he said with a shake of his head. "Get dressed. I'll take you."

I slipped my arms from around his body and stepped away, hurrying before he changed his mind. I had no clothes, none that were mine, at least, so I turned to the bathroom, found my panties and bra in a heap on the floor, and made my way into his closet.

There was something eerily familiar about rifling through his clothes. Something I couldn't quite put my finger on as I bypassed the open safe with the gun sitting on the stack of bills.

Because I'd never felt like this before.

Never felt so...*comfortable,* not even in my own skin. I yanked a pair of black jeans from the hanger and slipped them on over my panties. A long-sleeved black shirt was next. I buttoned it, tied the ends into a knot, and stepped into the bedroom.

Lazarus was waiting with a leather jacket in his hands. He froze when he saw me. His eyes widened like I'd hit him in the chest. I took a step closer as his gaze drifted upwards.

"I hope it was okay I helped myself to your clothes?" I whispered, unsure.

He just swallowed hard and took a step closer, dropping the jacket in his hand against the edge of the bed. One hand cupped the back of my neck as the fingers of the other plunged through my hair. "Princess, you can help yourself to anything and everything I own. I have nothing...*want* for nothing, except for you."

He lowered his head and I closed my eyes.

My body still hummed from his touch. But it warmed once more, welling in the pit of my belly and blooming outwards. He was saying something here, something that real words failed. I lifted my head and stared into his eyes. "Good, then I guess it's time we discussed brands., I whispered, catching his smile in the corner of my eye.

He pulled away with a chuckle. "How about I just hand you my credit card and you get whatever you want?"

"What kind of limit are we talking here?" I joked, looking at the well-worn leather jacket waiting for me. A shiver raced through me as he picked it up from the end of the bed and held it out for me.

"Sky's the limit for you, Princess."

I just chuckled. Poor bastard, I'd send him broke within a month. Still, as he slipped his jacket over my arms, I inhaled the rich scent of leather and *him*. There wasn't a piece of clothing in the world that would smell like this.

And I didn't want there to be.

He waited while I stepped into my flats, and held out his hand. It was the most natural feeling in the world to take it in mine, like we were made for that simple act. And as his fingers slipped between mine, that flutter deep inside my belly grew bolder.

We made our way downstairs. Both Logan and Freddy were waiting in the foyer, armed to the teeth. Freddy glanced at my hand in Lazarus's, then met my gaze. He knew...he knew the truth and he was waiting for me to tell Lazarus. I swallowed the panic and looked away.

My pulse sped with the thought. The more I felt about Lazarus, the more that was on the line.

What would happen if he reacted badly?

If he was sickened by the thought of another man's baby in my belly?

What would happen if he cast me aside?

I clenched my hand around his as we walked out into the night, heading toward the main building. Logan was at my side, his weapon in his hand. I felt a strange comfort in his presence, the kind of protection I'd never experienced before. Could I really put my trust in them? Trust them with my heart...and my life?

I thought about that as Lazarus led me forward. I lowered my head as the wind whipped strands of my unbrushed hair against my cheek. The cold wind seemed to cut through me, making me shiver.

As though Lazarus knew, he pulled me close and wrapped an arm around my shoulders. Heat filled my cheeks with the movement. He just met my gaze and smiled, the curl of his lips knowing. As though I was finally catching up with the way things were going to be for us.

My focus slipped to Freddy, but this time he just looked forward and lengthened his stride to surge ahead, leaving us behind. The movement wasn't lost on Lazarus as he scowled and fixed his gaze on the back of his bodyguard's head. His lips parted, the words right there, as movement came from our left.

Logan's hand was up in an instant. I hadn't even seen him move, but he had the gun trained on one of the Commission's security guards as he stepped into sight. The guy just lifted his empty hands, his gaze shifting from Logan to Lazarus. "They're expecting you, Mr. Rossi."

Lazarus just nodded and slid his arm from around my shoulders, taking my hand once more. He was in charge here. The one the others turned to...the one I turned to.

Our steps echoed in the space as we stepped through the electric doors and headed along the hall.

"Kat?" Anna cried, standing in the middle of the hall.

My heart leaped. "Anna!"

"*Kat!*" she sobbed, and lunged forward.

I left Lazarus behind, tearing my hand from his as I raced to her.

She was a mess, with wind-swept hair and wide, shell-shocked eyes. But I'd never felt so much relief as we collided. Her arms were around me in an instant, her head buried against my neck as she sobbed and shook.

"Hey, there," I murmured, holding her tight. "Hey...it's all okay. You're safe now...*you're safe.*"

"Salvatore," Lazarus said, drawing my attention to Finley as he stepped out of the shadows.

Anna's grip tightened around me. For that, I was grateful. I stiffened as I caught sight of the blood. Finley's face was splattered. His shirt was a mess. The blood looked almost black, stuck hard against his chest in the moonlight. His gaze never moved from Anna in my arms. The cold, possessive stare sent a flare of panic through me, making me pull away.

"What happened?" I asked her, wiping away the shine of tears on her cheeks.

She just stared at me. But there were no words, just fear echoing deep in her eyes.

"We were attacked," Finley answered for her, his voice stony and strange. "But everything is okay now, isn't it, Anna?"

She stiffened, her gaze pleading before it crumbled, and she gave a nod.

Something had happened tonight. Something that irrevocably changed both of them in the space of a few hours. I saw it in the way Lazarus was focused on Finley. A flicker of...*fear* crossed my Prince's eyes as Finley met his gaze.

"Max and Pavlov?" Logan murmured.

"Dead," Finley answered. "Both of them. Taken out as the hangar was stormed."

"What the hell were you doing in the hangar?" Lazarus asked.

But there was no answer as the heavy thud of footsteps grew louder. The Commander neared, his gaze missing nothing. "I've assigned a temporary security detail...until you leave."

"Leave?" I murmured and jerked my gaze to Anna's. "You're leaving?"

Stars shimmered in her eyes before she slowly nodded.

"Anna will be returning home with me," Finley answered.

"How about you let her speak for herself?" I snarled, and took a step forward, my hand sliding into hers.

Lazarus watched me like a hawk as Finley just glanced at Anna and gave a shrug. "Tell them."

"I'm going back," she whispered. "I shouldn't have come in the first place. This place just doesn't feel right."

"The hell it doesn't," I croaked as a pang of agony plunged deep. "What about me?"

She just gave me a sad smile and took my hands in hers. "There's nowhere you could go that I won't find you," she answered. "You're stuck with me, Kat. Like a red wine stain on your favorite dress, you'll never get rid of me."

Tears blurred her face. "But I don't want you to go," I whispered, hating how needy I sounded.

I'd never had a friend like Anna, never had anyone who wasn't out to get a piece of my name or my money. But not with Anna. She never even cared how much I was worth. The memory of her hiding on that boat came roaring back to me as I wrapped my arms around her and pulled her close. "I love you," I whispered.

"Not as much as I love you," she murmured against my ear. "But I have to go."

I swallowed hard and pulled away.

"Promise me we'll catch up when you're back home?" Anna said hopefully.

"I promise," I lied.

The truth was, there'd be no catching up with anyone if this all went wrong. Just like everything I had in my life, my friendship with Anna would be tainted. If I ran, they'd pick apart the last moments of my time here and I was sure they'd pick apart Anna's, too.

They'd watch her, haunt her. I glanced at Finley, who just watched us with the chilling gaze of a killer. Maybe it was good she was with someone like Fin? Maybe my father and Haelstrom Hale would leave her alone.

The more that thought took hold, the more painful it became.

No friends.

No protection.

Just me...and my unborn child.

"Okay," Finley murmured, taking a tentative step toward Anna, his voice careful. "I better get you back now. You must be exhausted."

From running for her life, right? I hadn't forgotten how frantic Fin was only hours ago...and how strangely calm he was now, even with two of his closest advisors dead in some mysterious attack. One squeeze of my hand, and she stepped away.

She glanced at me over her shoulder as she left, heading deeper along the halls before she disappeared.

"Is the island safe?" Lazarus looked toward the Commander. "Do not fucking lie to me."

He glanced my way before the Commander answered, and I knew he was thinking about more than his own safety here.

"I don't know." Traces of his Albanian accent edged into the Commander's words. "I assumed it was, but after tonight... I can't be certain."

Lazarus jerked his attention back to the older man. "Was this an attack on the Commission?"

Something in the way the Commander fell silent told him more than words ever could. Lazarus just gave a nod. "Kat will be staying with me until the Commission decides to close down the Institute."

There was a flinch, but the Commander just nodded.

"Kat," Lazarus held out his hand. "Let's get you some rest."

I took his hand, letting him lead me back to the apartment once more, my heart filled with desperation and pain. If they closed down the island, then I was done...I'd be forced to go back home.

35

Lazarus

She was quiet and withdrawn in the wake of taking her to see Anna, letting me lead her back to the apartment without saying a damn word.

"Kat," Freddy spoke her name as the elevator doors opened. She flinched before meeting his gaze. Something passed between them. Something that made my brother slowly nod and murmur, "Sorry this didn't turn out better, but you're safe with Laz...you're safe with us."

She just stared at him...then swallowed hard. Her voice was husky as she whispered, "Thank you, Freddy. That means a lot."

Then I took her inside and slipped my leather jacket from her small shoulders that sagged under the weight of her worries. Silence was a beast that stalked us, watching us with ravenous eyes. I felt it's stare, was aware of its movement. Hell, I was aware of any movement when it came to her. I moved into the kitchen, poured her a glass of water while she slipped off her shoes and stepped out of my damn jeans.

They were too big for her, but seeing her dressed like that, my black shirt tied around her small waist and her red hair in a tumble of curls around her shoulders, had brought me undone. I'd been hit by a blow I'd never seen coming, one that had hit me square in the center of my chest.

"Here." I held out the glass of water.

She took it with trembling hands. I drew my shirt free and stepped out of my boots before taking the glass from her hands to set it beside her on the nightstand next to her side of the bed.

Her side.

Just like that, my bed was divided...one side mine, the other hers. I strode around and climbed in, pulling her down beside me. The whisper of sheets was the only sound. Her tears came slowly, welling in that tiny space against her nose before they spilled free.

I just held her, unable to figure out what to say.

Words failed me.

But there was no way I'd fail her.

This was a night filled with betrayal and brutality, and I'd caused more than my fair share. But it could've been far different. I could've been too late. Too late to save her...too late to do what needed to be done.

"Sleep, Kat," I whispered. "I'll watch over you."

She closed her eyes and the slick trail of tears eased. It didn't take long in my arms for her breaths to deepen. I watched her chest rise and fall and even though exhaustion consumed me...I lay awake.

———

I CAUGHT snatches of sleep while she lay pressed against me, just enough to make my eyes gritty, when I felt her breathing change. She opened her eyes and just lay there, until slowly her hand slipped over mine across her belly.

"Morning," I murmured, my voice husky.

She shifted in the bed, rolling over to face me, her perfect brown eyes dark with pain. "I have something I want to tell you. But I need to prepare myself first. I want...your undivided attention. So how about dinner tonight, just the two of us?"

Fear danced in the back of her eyes. She held my gaze, clung to it like it was the only thing keeping her afloat. "Okay," I murmured, giving myself over to this woman.

Still, my heart raced with her trepidation. I forced a smile and kissed her softly, taking the corners of her lips.

Whatever she had to tell me, I'd listen...and I'd try my best not to lose my shit.

She's Hale's but he'll let you have her, at least until they're married...

Zakharov's words resounded in my head as I pulled away. Whatever relationship she had with that Hale bastard, it wasn't like this. It couldn't be...but I'd wait and ready myself for whatever choice she made.

"So, dinner," she said, sliding her hand along my arm. "Just you and me."

"Just you and me," I repeated as her stomach gave a growl.

She stiffened at the sound, then smiled.

Fuck, I loved it when she smiled, hating as she rolled out of my arms and slipped from the bed.

My elbow ached and the muscles of my shoulder were rock hard from holding her. But it was a good ache, a *contented ache.*

A *beep* cut through the apartment, forcing me from the bed. I padded out into the kitchen, grabbed my cell from the end of the counter, and pressed the button. But the screen was blank. No messages waited for me.

Another *beep* from the corner of the sofa drew my gaze. Kat's phone sat on the armrest. I strode over, grabbed it, and fought the desire to brighten her screen to see who was trying to force their way into our world.

Because it *was* ours now. The sound of the shower drew my gaze, tearing me from that hunger to know every secret of her world. I strode toward the counter and slid it next to mine, knowing deep down she was going to tell me she'd been arranged to marry that fucking Hale.

But she wouldn't be for long.

I didn't care what it took.

She wasn't leaving me.

I turned to the refrigerator as the sweet scent of my bodywash drifted through the air. I'd need to get the woman her own stuff soon before she used up all mine. A glance at the clock and I realized it was well past lunch. It figured, after crawling into bed around three or four in the morning. So I grabbed what I could, finding bacon, lettuce, and tomato. Teamed with a loaf of crusty white bread, I set to work making her food, igniting the frying pan and dropping in a dollop of butter and some bacon.

By the time she switched off the water and stepped out, her hair wrapped in one towel and her body in another, I was buttering the thick slices of bread and layering them with a couple of perfect leaves of lettuce and thick slices of tomato.

"That looks delicious," she said, sliding onto a stool. "I'm starved."

"See, we don't need a chef." I slid a perfect sandwich her way. "I cook, I clean...I beat the shit out of anyone who fucking touches you."

She flinched at the last part and I kicked myself. *Fucking idiot.* I shifted focus, grabbing half of my sandwich and taking a mammoth bite. She ate with careful bites, chewing and swallowing, making her way through half of it before she waited.

I turned, opened the fridge, and grabbed a can of Pepsi before handing it her way.

"So, what will happen now?" she asked...then added. "With the island, I mean."

I gave a shrug. "I guess it depends what the Commission decides, either we're exposed here, or they want us to sit tight."

"What does your dad say?"

I just gave a shrug, giving her my undivided attention. "I don't think it really matters, here, there...I seem to have a target on my head. The only difference is, here we *should* be able to see them coming."

She popped open the can and took a swallow before placing it back down. "So, if we're at risk even at home, then we should stay."

"Unfortunately, Princess, it's not up to us," I explained. "The island is run by the Commission. They decide what happens." She said nothing, just pushed her plate away slowly. "You don't want to go back, do you?"

Careful…

That voice warned in my head.

"No, I don't," she answered. "And I won't be…"

I widened my eyes at the words. "You got somewhere else to be, Princess?"

She swallowed, her gaze fixed on mine. "Yeah, I think I do."

Fuck me, if my heart didn't leap at the words. My phone gave a *beep* this time. I reached over, grabbed it from the counter, and illuminated the message.

Dad: We need to talk.

I winced, then lifted my gaze to hers. "I gotta take this, Princess."

She just gave a nod, watching me as I strode from the kitchen and into the living room, pressing dad's contact. But it didn't matter what I was doing, I was still aware of how she slipped from the stool and strode into the bedroom again.

"Laz," Dad answered. "What's the situation there?"

The situation?

"The situation is fucked," I answered the only way I could. "Another attack. This time they came after Finley."

"Jesus," he groaned, and his audible exhale was a roar in my ear. "We know for sure he was the target?"

The frantic gaze of Finley Salvatore filled my mind. Was I sure he was the target? Something inside me said *no*. "I don't...no."

"No?" A creak echoed behind him, as though in this moment I had his undivided attention. "So, who do you think the target was?"

I think she's in trouble. Finley's words echoed in my head. *And she's about to do something fucking stupid. Something I won't be able to fix.* "To be honest, I'm not sure there was a target. Something went on last night, something no one wants us finding out" *That Anna Shaw isn't just any rich brat...that she's the Ghost, the most cunning money launderer the dark Mafia world has ever known.* If Finley Salvatore thought I'd forgotten what I'd heard in that classroom, then he was very much mistaken. I remembered alright...and I knew exactly what was at stake here for the Salvatores. "I can't be certain."

"Well, then I'm going to need you to be certain here, Laz. Especially as you're my proxy at today's meeting."

"Meeting?" I snapped back to attention. "What damn meeting?"

"Satellite linkup. I can't be there, so I'm giving you a chance here," he explained.

The full weight of his words hit me. *His proxy*...my chance to step up and become the new leader of the Rossi line. I licked my lips as a shiver coursed along my spine. "You sure about this?"

"I'm sure. The question is, are you?"

I caught my breath. Purpose. Power. I glanced toward the bedroom, listening to Kat moving around as she dressed. "Yeah...yeah, I'm sure."

"Good, 'cause I'm putting a lot of trust in you. We don't need a hothead at the table, son. We need someone controlled, someone who can make solid, informed decisions, someone who can step into my shoes, when I'm not there. And by step into them...I'm talking in the next hour."

And why can't you be there? The question bloomed for a second before it was snatched away like a leaf in the wind. "I can do it," I answered, that hunger moving deep. "I won't let you down."

"See you don't, son," Dad murmured, "I'm proud of you, Laz," he said, and ended the call.

Jesus...

A Commission meeting and I was included. I ran my fingers through my hair.

"Everything okay?" Kat asked, stepping into the doorway.

"Yeah," I smiled, meeting her gaze. "Yeah, everything's fucking golden."

She smiled, and even though there was a trace of sadness in her eyes, I still took it. I crossed the space between us, gripped the back of her neck, and looked deep into her eyes. "You going to be okay here for a little while? I got a thing on."

"A thing," she repeated.

I was mesmerized by the movement of her mouth as she spoke. I licked my lips and lowered my head until my lips brushed hers. "And when I'm done, Kat, I'm taking you to bed, and I'm not letting you go...not until our dinner tonight, where you tell me about every fucking demon hunting you..."

Her breath stilled. Under the pressure of my thumb, her pulse jumped.

Yeah, every fucking demon.

I wanted them all...wanted to look every one of them in the eyes before I took them down.

And Haelstrom Hale was at the top of that fucking list.

"O-okay" she stuttered, and rolled her head backwards under my grasp.

I took her mouth like a fucking animal, high on power, dangerous with need. Kat VanHalen was mine and so was the Rossi seat at the Commission. I'd take it, too...before Finley took his.

My cock hardened, both with the feel of Kat yielding under my mouth and the thought of staring that fucker in the eyes knowing I had what he wanted. She unleashed a soft, mewling sound that only incited my desire even more.

I wanted to fuck her now, hard and fast, to yank her panties to the side and bury my fucking cock deep. I wanted to be all kinds of savage with her, mark her...*fill her with my seed.* Hell, I wanted her big and round, carrying my child.

"Laz," she moaned.

I dropped my hand and broke the kiss. "I have time," I whispered, and cupped her breast.

Those brown eyes widened, then fluttered closed as I skimmed her puckered nipple under her shirt and reached for the bottom. Her arms rose into the air. Her shirt was gone in an instant. Perfect dusky pink tightened as I lowered my head and licked her.

One shove and my sweats were gone from her body. I sank my fingers between her legs, finding that sweet fucking heat.

"Oh, fuck." She wound her arms around my neck. "More, Lazarus."

Fire burned inside me at the sound of my name. "Say that again." I pushed in deep, hearing the tiny catch of her breath. "Say my fucking name, Kat."

"Lazarus," she groaned.

My cock twitched, punching against my zipper. She was warm, and slick, growing wetter as I danced around her clit and slid back inside. "I'm going to fill this pussy," I promised, dragging my teeth across the peak of her nipple.

Her arms tightened, shoving her breast deeper into my mouth as she lifted her leg, and rocked her hips. Underneath the pain and the fear, my little Princess was a wildcat. She just didn't know it.

And I had all the fucking time in the world to draw that feral little tiger into the open. I slipped my fingers from her drenched pussy and opened the button of my jeans. A quick slide of my zipper, and I gripped her hips, lifted her, and slammed my cock inside.

"Oh," she whimpered, and arched her back.

I braced her weight, pulling out far enough, then rammed home. Her eyes fluttered as her lips parted. I rode her hard and fast, slamming deep with every brutal fucking thrust. *"Mine,"* I whispered, staring at her in a haze of ecstasy. *"You're mine, Kat. All fucking mine."*

She opened her eyes and held my gaze. Her legs wrapped around my waist. "Fuck me harder." I had no choice but to carry her to the bedroom and lower her to the bed.

Bracing my hands over her head, I arched my spine, caging her underneath me. She stared into my eyes, her body jolting with every thrust. There was nowhere she could go...*even if she'd wanted to.*

The thought made me fuck her harder. My heart was thundering, my hips pistoning, and that tiny *ugh...ugh...ugh...*sound at the back of her throat turned into a long, guttural moan.

She clenched her pussy, gripping my cock until my balls drew tight, and I came. I slammed my eyes closed, and drove deep inside her. I wanted every inch of her full of me, every fucking inch of her skin licked and catalogued. On instinct, I dropped my head to the side of her neck.

My words were punctuated with harsh breaths. "Nowhere left to run now, Kat." I grazed the line of her neck with my lips, then nipped her hard enough to make her flinch.

But she liked it.

Her pussy did, at least.

Clamping tight around the base of my cock, she milked me.

I lowered my head and let out a moan before I pulled free.

My phone gave a beep, drawing me away from the consuming trance I was in around her and slamming me back into reality. "I've got to go," I groaned, and pushed off her. "You going to be okay here?"

"Yeah," she smiled, her chest still rising and falling rapidly. "I think...I think I'm gonna need a minute anyway."

I just grinned, straightening at the foot of the bed. Her legs were splayed, that creamy slick shining against the lips of her pussy. Fuck me, if the sight of that didn't make me want to fuck her again. She was a damn temptress, a fucking witch. One I'd gladly sell my soul to for one more goddamn taste.

"Do not fucking move," I growled, tearing my gaze from her cunt. "You hear me? Lie right there, just like that. I'll be as fast as I can."

My fucking phone *beeped* once more, making me curse under my breath. I tore my gaze from her, snatched my jeans and shirt from the floor, and hurried for my phone.

36

Lazarus

"You ready for this?" Freddy asked as I stepped into their apartment.

I combed my hair back and worked the tension from my shoulders. Fuck, I still smelled like her. *Good.* "Yeah," I muttered, meeting my brother's gaze. "I am."

"I've got two guards coming to watch the building while we're gone." Logan was heading toward me, strapping his holster around his shoulders, and met my gaze. "She's going to be fine, Laz."

Still, the thought of her alone...

"No one's going to attack in the daylight," he urged. "No one's that fucking dumb, anyway."

I nodded, needing to shift my fear. A meeting with the damn Commission was not a place to be distracted.

My phone gave a *beep.* I glanced down.

Mateo: Meeting in 5.

"Ready, brothers?" I asked, and met their gazes. "Looks like we're on."

Logan's lips curled in a look of savage pride as Freddy growled, "Let's fucking do this."

We made our way into the elevator, then out of the building. I glanced at the two guards heading our way, the bulges under their jackets somewhat comforting. But they weren't me...or Logan. I tore my gaze from them to the building in the distance, the sooner I was done there, the better.

But something made me glance over my shoulder, finding the two guards as they headed toward the building. Fear raced across my skin, sending a shiver along my spine.

"We're going to be late," Freddy urged, glancing my way.

As though the brother knew what I was thinking.

They weren't me...

They weren't Freddy...

They weren't Logan.

The sooner this meeting was over, the better. All of a sudden, the seat at the Commission's table wasn't as inviting as Kat was. "Let's just get this over with," I grumbled.

Logan glanced my way as we stepped up to the electric doors. "Thirty minutes," he murmured. "Thirty minutes and I'll have you back to her."

I nodded.

Thirty minutes and she was mine...*again.*

37

Kat

I rolled and pushed myself up on the edge of the bed, grabbing Lazarus's sweats and t-shirt from the floor as I went. They were crumbled, smelled of my own desire, and not my clothes. I glanced toward the bathroom and contemplated a second shower, then decided against it.

My body ached, but it was a good ache. The kind of throb that made me smile as I headed for the bathroom. But staying here full-time wasn't an option...not unless I had my things. So, I used the toilet, wiped and flushed, then pulled on Laz's clothes once more, sliding my arms through the sleeves of his leather jacket, and slipped my flats on.

By the time I stepped into the elevator, I was grinning.

Laz wasn't going to buckle...and he wasn't going to run.

For the first time in forever, I felt hope dance inside me.

I lowered my hand, remembering Freddy's words. He wasn't going to tell Laz, not until I did, at least...and that was happening tonight. Tonight. I splayed my hand wide against my belly, feeling that flutter. A *quickening,* Freddy had called it.

"A quickening," I murmured as the elevator came to a stop and the doors opened.

Two guards were waiting for me, dressed in gray suits.

They turned as I stepped out, their hard gazes fixed on me.

"I need to go to my apartment," I stated. "I'll be a while."

One of them stepped toward me. "No, we wait here."

I flinched at the bite in his tone and felt the cold, arrogant side of my nature push to the surface. It was a nasty side of me, destructive and detrimental, and much needed when I dealt with vultures, both at home and in the media. And it was a side of my personality that rose to the surface now as I took a step forward. "I don't remember that being a question. I *am* going to my apartment. You can either escort me or I can call the Commander."

I pulled my phone free and pressed against the cracked screen, punching his name from my contacts.

The asshole guard just looked at his buddy. I didn't care about their disapproval. I didn't give a fuck one way or the other. No one was going to ruin this day for me. Not two pissy bodyguards or Freddy's careful looks. I was getting my clothes from the apartment and making sure everything was perfect when I told Laz what I had to tell him.

"Fine," the asshole guard muttered.

I fought the twitch of a smile. "Fine," I repeated, and strode toward the doors.

CCTV cameras blinked above me as I made my way out of Laz's building and turned right. But the guard's attitude was wearing at me. Being silent, broody, and dangerous was one thing. But being fucking rude to those he was paid to protect was another.

Heavy footsteps resounded behind me, *right behind me.* "You're too close," I snapped. "Back off."

But they didn't fall back, and the thunderous sound of heavy boots smacking the concrete grew louder, until it was all I could hear. I ground my teeth and drew Laz's leather jacket tight around me as the wind whipped strands of my hair free.

"I bet you're missing your boyfriend right about now." The low snarl came from behind me, far too close to my ear.

I flinched at the closeness and jerked my gaze to his.

Dark brown eyes bored into mine.

Forbidding and foul.

Pitiless...right to his soul.

"Get the fuck *back, now,*" I commanded, and hurried my steps, trying to put distance between us.

Without quickening his, he bore down on me, hunting me like a predator.

My heart hammered as I lifted my gaze to the front doors of my building.

"Yeah, I bet you're wishing he was here, right about now," the guard growled at my back as I stepped around the towering palms in the garden outside my building. "We came for him... but fuck, we'll just take you instead."

A hand clamped over my mouth, rough fingers smashing my lips against my teeth.

For a second, I didn't understand what was happening.

For a heartbeat, I lost all thought.

Until something inside me screamed *FIGHT!*

I sucked in a hard breath, drawing in the fetid scent of his hand. But under that...was a tang that made my blood run cold. *Bitter and suffocating,* a scent I'd tasted in the back of my throat before.

When I was younger.

When I'd started to fight.

I bucked my body, howling with rage as my feet were lifted.

"Get her!" the guard barked.

Cruel hands grasped my legs and fingers dug into my calves as I howled and screamed...*and the world started to blur.*

"Huuuurrrrryeee!" The word slurred in my mind.

That panicked feeling in my belly moved deeper. It was all I held onto, all I grasped.

Until the face of my protector roared to the surface.

Blue eyes blazing with hate.

Lazarus! I screamed in my mind. *LAZARUS!*

38

Lazarus

"So let me get this straight." Adrian Bernardi leaned forward on his desk and stared down the camera. "You can't track down these bastards who've attacked us, nor can you put the damn island on lockdown?"

Mateo Ristani, the island's Commander and protector, answered carefully. "At this time, no. In the wake of last night's attack, and other circumstances outside our control, we've suffered extensive casualties. So, until our personnel levels are replenished, we just don't have enough guards."

"Then *get them*," Bernardi snarled.

The hairs on the back of my neck rose. Now I saw were Bruno got it from. His father was a fucking savage. Thick Irish accent, that brooding, unflinching stare. He was more dangerous than the IRA, more sinister than any high-level corrupt cop, more formidable than even Dominic Salvatore...when he was pissed, at least.

"Adrian," Michele Valachi murmured. "I understand you're furious. But let's hear what Mateo is proposing."

The Commander just swallowed hard, shifted his gaze to me, then back to the camera. "We condense the buildings. Have three buildings with each floor occupied. The remaining guards will be divided evenly, utilizing the private security for the heirs of the Commission, of course."

There was a twitch on Adrian Bernardi's lips. "So, your idea is a backpacker-hostel type scenario?"

Jesus.

The Commander shifted in his seat. "Until we get rein-forcements."

"And when will that be?" Michele cut in.

"Three days, four at the most. I've sent a request for a team of mercenaries to hunt them on the shore. They'll be sending their first lot of reports in three hours."

"Three hours until even the most basic of protection is watching our blood," Adrian growled.

Three hours.

Three hours, then Kat would be safer. I glanced toward the closed door, picturing Freddy and Logan waiting just outside. This meeting was taking too fucking long...*far too long.* "There's no sense in bitching about what *should be done.*" The words slipped from my lips.

The Commander flinched and mumbled, "Here, here."

I hadn't realized I'd spoken out loud. But now all eyes were fixed on the screen in front of me. I swallowed hard and cleared my throat. "What I mean to say is, we're not fucking useless here. Bruno," I glanced toward Adrian Bernardi, then to Michele Valachi. "And Evan, Alexi, Ms. Ivanov, and I." I glanced at the decrepit old geezer sitting in a pitch black study and continued. "Are trained to protect ourselves. So we're better served combining forces. It's why we're here after all, isn't it? Make alliances...be allies. What better time to do that than right now?"

There was silence.

Uncomfortable silence.

"We're under attack here," I urged, feeling that Stidda savagery rise to the surface. "And we *need* to counterattack. The best way to do that is to protect ourselves, gather our forces, and plan our attack. The Commander here is the best man for the job."

There was a twinkle in the Commander's eyes. I shot him a hard look, *don't get turned on.*

"You're right," Adrian muttered with a nod.

Was there a hint of pride in his eyes? Fuck. He leaned back. "Get it done, Commander. I expect a full briefing as soon as your men are in Mauritius."

"Will do," Mateo gave a nod and leaned forward, "Gentlemen," before hitting the button and ending the call. "Fuck," he said, and exhaled hard, then shot me a hard-to-read look. "Thanks for having my back there."

"I didn't," I growled, and pushed from my seat. "It was the only logical step. But be warned, Commander, one more fuck-up... one more attack, and I'll come for your fucking job."

It wasn't a threat.

It was a promise.

I grabbed the door handle and yanked it open. Freddy and Logan glanced my way as I strode out and headed for the door.

"Everything okay?" Freddy prodded, falling into step.

"If you mean, are we going to be bunking with a heap of rich kids and Mafia heirs, then yeah, sure."

"Jesus, that sounds like fun."

"Sounds like a fucking disaster.," Logan muttered. "A bunch of rich, opinionated pains in the ass."

"Hey." I cut him a glare. "I'm one of those *pains in the ass.*"

"Exactly," he muttered, and stared straight ahead as we strode through the doors and out into the howling wind once more.

I lengthened my stride, desperate to be back with Kat once more. A sense of urgency hummed inside me, deeper than my pulse, hungrier than hate.

"Laz," Freddy called. "Brother, slow down."

My phone *beeped* in my pocket. No doubt it was Dad calling to either ridicule or congratulate me. Both I didn't give a shit about, not in this moment. I lifted my gaze to my building in front of me as that eerie, threatening feeling inside me grew.

"Logan," I murmured, calling for the brother, even though I had no idea what I ask asking him for.

Still, he strode ahead and moved in front of me, placing himself directly in the line of any oncoming fire, and scanned the island's grounds for movement.

His gun was in his hand in an instant. He moved faster, stepping around the giant palms to stride toward the building doors. One scan of the keycard and they opened. My fucking heart was booming in my ears as the two guards turned, took one look at Logan and his gun, and froze.

"What is it?" one of them asked, reaching for his own piece under his jacket.

"Who the fuck are you?" Logan growled, looking from one to the other.

The asshole just scowled, glanced toward his partner, and answered. "The protection for Ms. VanHalen."

"No, you're not," I snarled, and strode closer. "You're not the ones who were here before."

"Before?" The idiot looked confused. "We were held up for a second, but we've been here the entire time."

I jerked my gaze toward the elevator. "And you've seen her? You've seen Kat?"

The scowl only grew deeper as the asshole just shook his head. "No, I assumed—"

I didn't stop to hear the rest, striding toward the elevator as that pressure built inside me. It was getting hard to breathe, getting hard to hear anything over the pulsing of my heart. Logan stepped in behind me as the doors opened.

"She's fine," Logan urged. "She's fine."

But the brother didn't sound convinced as the elevator came to a stop and the doors opened. He was into the apartment first, scanning the living room, letting me go ahead to check the bedroom.

"Kat," I called, listening to the silence. *"Kat, are you here?"*

She wasn't in the bedroom. I glanced at the rumpled sheets and made for the bathroom. She wasn't there either. "She's not here, Logan." I jerked my gaze to his. "She's not here."

He grabbed his phone and punched in the number. "Freddy, she's not here."

There was an audible *"Fuck!"* from the other side.

That panic had a name now...

Emptiness.

"I want those guards found, Logan," I growled as my fists clenched by my sides. "I want them hunted down and I want her back in this goddamn apartment *now.*"

A nod of his head and my brother clenched his grip around the phone. "I'll get the Commander on the line."

39

Kat

I felt weightless for a moment, before my side slammed against something hard and cold. Salty water splashed my face, jerking me awake. I surfaced from the darkness, driving to the light. I blinked and opened my eyes.

There was a man sitting above me, perched on the side of a dinghy as we became airborne again. I let out a cry as the impact with the water smashed me against the hard bottom again, drawing his gaze.

"Easy," his voice cut through the roar of the motor. "We flip, and you're dead."

He looked at me like I was nothing. I tried to remember what the fuck happened, and focused on my hands. A plastic strip bound them together. Panic punched me hard as I looked at my feet. One shoe was missing...but my ankles were bound, too.

Hands and ankles.

We came for him...but fuck, we'll just take you instead.

The words came back to me in a roar, carving through the remnants of the drug. But the bitter taste still lingered in my mouth under the briny spray. "What the fuck are you doing?" I growled and shoved against the bottom of the boat.

My elbows locked, then buckled as we hit the surface once more. They were taking me somewhere...somewhere far from the island. *Lazarus.* "Stop..." I cried. "Stop right now. I can pay you..." my stomach tightened with fear. "I can pay."

That stony, bottomless stare found me as the bodyguard glanced my way. "Oh, you'll pay, Ms. VanHalen. I have no doubt about that."

I just held his gaze as the words sank in. My head smashed against the hard rubber as we drove far away from any hope of saving me. *Lazarus*...my gaze blurred with his name. My throat tightened, choking down on a sob.

I don't know how long we were on the water for, minutes... hours, as I jolted and slammed against the bottom of the boat. I curled my knees tighter, forcing my hips to take the impact. I tried to remember what they'd told us in class when they talked about kidnapping, tried to remember to stay calm as the cold ocean spray hit me, smacking against Lazarus's leather jacket.

My teeth gnashed, slamming home with every jarring jolt.

Until finally the boat suddenly slowed.

The motor roared, fighting through the muffled sound in my ears and I slid against the boat's bottom as we turned. "You don't have to do this," I whimpered. "You can just tell me what you want." I licked the salt from my lips and tasted warm tears. "Right here and now. Whatever you want, it's yours."

The guard didn't answer, just stared straight ahead as the other one steered the board. I caught a glimpse of trees hanging overhead and the familiar sound of cicadas before we stopped. The faint sweet scent of sugarcane danced through the humidity and heat. Were we back on Mauritius? The guard just leaned down, his mouth a menacing sneer. "Now, you're gonna be good, aren't you, Ms. VanHalen? You don't want me to drug you again, do you?"

A chill cut through me. *No...no, anything but that.* Tears slipped from the corners of my eyes as shook my head. "I'll be good. I'll be good."

I nodded, then the boat turned sideways and hit hard against a wooden dock. *Stall them.* "He'll find you, you know that, right? When he does..."

That merciless stare fixed on mine as, without answering, he just reached forward and grabbed my arm.

"No...*no!*" I kicked and bucked, unable to control that roar inside me. The other guard grabbed my feet as I fought their hold.

"I fucking told you," he snapped at my other abductor before grabbing a gun from his side, then took aim in the center of my chest, and fired.

Thwack! I screamed until a hand clamped across my mouth. Screamed because death was coming for me. Screamed because this had all happened so fast. Screamed because—

"*Easy!*" he growled in my ear. "It's just a damn tranq."

I punched out, desperately trying to wrench my hands free as the effects of the drug swam in my system once more.

"I warned you," the cruel bastard in front of me growled. "Night night, Ms. VanHalen."

▭

DARKNESS...THAT'S all that waited for me. A blur... something loud clattering in my ears, the sound brutal and grating. But the emptiness waited down below.

Waited with open arms and pulled me back under once more.

"Wake up."

I tried to open my eyes. Tried to fight against the consuming hold over me. Something was wrong. My mind swam, unable to fit the jumbled pieces together. *Something was really wrong.*

"You gave her too fucking much."

I tried to push up, toward the grating sound as it clattered in my ears. *Help me...help me...somebody...help...me.* A *click* sounded. Light flooded my eyes. Blinding, even with my eyes closed. My head rolled and I tried to lift my hand to shield the glare. My body refused to move like it should.

There was a nasty taste in my mouth, and a coldness that wrapped tightly around me.

"This is how it's going to be, Katerina."

The sound of *that* name kicked inside me, and adrenaline punched through my veins, driving me to the surface. I blinked and tried to focus, finding the dark blur moving behind the spotlight.

"Now, look into the camera," he growled, and grabbed my arm. "And plead for your life."

My lips curled, the hate blazing inside me now, tearing me from that haze. "Fuck you," I snarled. "*Fuck you!*"

His grip was cruel. But I had a lifetime of rage burning through me.

And I wasn't anywhere near done.

$$\rule{4cm}{0.4pt}$$

40

Lazarus

$$\rule{4cm}{0.4pt}$$

"What the fuck do you mean, they weren't your men?" I took a step, my gaze boring a hole through the Commander as he stared at the screen on his phone.

I watched two men escort her from the building...two men not more than a step away from her, and they didn't come back.

"They aren't mine," Mateo repeated, lifting his gaze to mine. "I know every man in my employ and these men...they're not mine."

*They're not his...not his...*I tore my gaze from his and stumbled toward the doors of the building.

"Laz!" Freddy called, but I was already running...already driving my boots into the pavement, already charging toward the only place she'd go to...*her apartment.*

Nothing else mattered in this moment.

Not the breath in my lungs.

Or the agony that cut like a knife.

Nothing.

I rounded the edge of the garden, my boots skidding on the concrete before I lunged again, driving my body toward the doorway...until I caught the glint of something under a palm.

Thunder roared not more than two steps behind me as I stopped, sucking in harsh breaths.

"Laz," Logan called my name.

But I couldn't move, frozen by the dark outline as the palm leaves moved, revealing her phone.

Logan followed my gaze and sucked in a deep breath. "Jesus," he murmured and stepped closer.

Footsteps moved in, and the world seemed to blur. Logan lifted his head and barked orders, but all I could see was that cracked screen as her phone illuminated...*ten missed calls...now eleven.*

Movement came all around me as the Commander skidded to a stop at my side. Orders were given, panic whipped like a savage gust around me. I knelt, grabbed her phone from the soft, rich dirt, and pressed the screen. Something white caught my eye in the distance, closer to the doors. I left them behind, strode closer, and picked it up. "It's her keycard," I muttered, my words strange and detached.

The Commander jerked his gaze toward one of the other men. "Search the building." They rushed in, leaving me behind, Freddy and Logan at my side.

"We'll find her," Logan reassured.

I met the brother's eyes, that hard glint shining with malice. "If she's dead…"

His jaw bulged under the strain as he closed the distance in a heartbeat and grabbed my shoulders. "She's *not* dead, Lazarus. We'll find her…*you hear me? We…will…find…her.*"

I nodded as the *slam* of the stairwell door echoed through the space. I'll find you…*you hear me, Kat? I'll find you.*

41

Kat

"Say the goddamn words." My abductor loomed over me, his eyes nothing more than menacing pools in the faded light.

"Fuck you." I lifted my head from the floor and spat.

He strode closer and I fought the urge to flinch. But there was no fighting my whimper as he grabbed my arm and wrenched me from the floor. "You will do as *I* say, Katerina," he commanded.

But he had no idea who he was dealing with.

He had no idea that every fucking time he called me that name, something dangerous in me reared its head. "Go to fucking *Hell*, you *pathetic* piece of shit!"

There was a low chuckle as he stilled, his fingers digging into the flesh of my arm. "You see...now that's just uncalled for."

He moved in a blur, driving his fist through the air and into my side.

Agony roared through me as the air rushed from my lungs. The blinding light was gone, leaving me reeling in the dark. I doubled over and my knees buckled, dropping me back to the floor. I blinked and gasped as stars detonated behind my eyes.

Through the bright flashes, thick-soled boots neared. He crouched down, the shine of his gun all I could see. "Now, I'm only going to ask this one more time, then I'm going to get angry. Say the words, Katerina...say the words for good old dad."

I drew my knees closer as that agony moved through my side and curled around the baby. I tried to keep it together, tried to keep the tears from welling in my eyes, tried not to suck in the filth and the stench of this place.

This place where they held me.

Far away from the perfect shimmering island...

Far away from Lazarus.

The blinding lights shone in my eyes once more, blurring his face behind the camera. He waited...waited for me to say the words he wanted me to say...waited for me to fight and scream, to force his hand and to use the gun he carried.

But would he do that?

Would he shoot me and leave me in this hovel to die?

Flashes of memories came in.

The look on everyone's faces the night Baldeon disappeared.

The way Anna gripped my hand and wept, whispering the gory details of what had happened.

Details Finley had told her.

Details of how Baldeon had died.

Hands tied behind his back.

His throat cut so deep it severed his spine.

"Say the words, Katerina." My abductor urged.

That radiant glare made my eyes widen and my breath catch. I licked dry, arid lips and started, shifting my gaze to the camera. "Dad, it's me. I'm alive, but I don't know where I am...give them the money, okay? Give them whatever they ask for."

42

Lazarus

Her building was empty. We searched every floor and every room, tearing through the empty space until there was nowhere left to turn. I called Finley Salvatore and spoke to Anna, but between her frantic cries I got the information I was dreading. She hadn't heard from Kat at all.

No one had heard from her.

I stared at her phone in my hand and swallowed the tremble of fear.

"We're turning around," Finley growled. "We're coming back."

I didn't like the sense of relief that washed over me at the words, didn't like this *vulnerability* as I muttered, "Yeah, thanks."

"I've got a team working on the CCTV cameras," the Commander said as I hung up. "Don't worry, we're going to find her. In the meantime, I have every man available combing the island."

Every man available.

Didn't we just have a meeting addressing his lack of personnel? "Logan," I growled, and glanced his way.

The brother was on the phone, talking to a former commander of his about a team of mercenaries. There would be no expense spared, nothing we wouldn't do. When he hung up the phone, he turned to the Commander. "I'll conduct a sweep of the buildings myself. Have your men fan out and check the perimeter, especially those ruins on the west side of the island."

"The cabins are boarded up." The Commander shook his head. "I don't think—"

"That's right," I snarled, meeting his gaze. "You don't *think*... you just *do*."

There was a flicker of anger in Mateo's eyes, a moment where I expected him to push the boundaries of my anger...and right now, that wouldn't be a good move. But then he just gave a nod. "Fine. I'll have a team of men work through the cabins and report back."

I turned to Freddy. "Take buildings one through five, I'll take six through eleven."

"Laz, no. This could be a fucking setup." Freddy shook his head. "You can't go on your own."

"He won't be on his own." The husky feminine murmur came from behind me.

Through the open glass doors came Xael Davies, striding in wearing black jeans, heavy boots, a black leather vest, and a set of Berettas. Behind her came Bruno Bernardi, and behind him, his own personal security.

"We search together." Bruno glanced at Freddy, then Logan. "That okay with you?"

"Yeah," Logan muttered, looking at the weapons Davies was packing. The savage bastard's eyes glittered, don't tell me he was turned on seeing a woman armed to the teeth?

Now was not the time for a fucking romance.

"Okay then," Xael muttered, and gave a nod. "When you're ready, sweetheart." She cut those dark eyes my way and, with a nod, I was striding toward the doors, leaving my team behind, praying like hell we found her alive.

The memory of Baldeon's face haunted me as we headed toward the sixth building with guns drawn. I took strange comfort in the bite of the patterned steel grip of my piece as Bruno slammed his card against the reader and the doors opened.

"I'll take the stairs." I cut a glance toward the elevator. "You take the elevator."

I didn't wait for them to move, just strode toward the stairwell door and yanked it open. But there was no movement for the elevator, no stabbing of the button, just footsteps behind me.

I glanced over my shoulder, cutting Davies, then Bernardi, a glare. "I told you—"

"Let's get one thing straight, Rossi." Xael scowled. "Be worried all you want, but don't be a dick, 'kay? We're not Freddy or Logan. We don't take orders from you."

Then she pushed past me, strode through the stairwell door, and started climbing, the slam of her boots resounding as she took them two at a time.

Bernardi stared after her with brows his raised, then did the same, stepping past me and starting upwards. I followed, because getting furious was all there was left for me. Angry was one thing...but stagnant was another, and there was no way in hell I was letting *anyone* else get to Kat before me.

That hunger raced in my veins.

Running and humming...

Like a wolf in full flight.

Paws pounded against the earth. Claws digging in, driving me harder...*faster.*

I charged after them, gripped the cold steel railing, and heaved myself up flight after flight until we reached the top.

"*Kat!*" Xael roared.

The sound of her name only made my pulse boom in my head. Her name welled in the back of my throat, like a wad I could neither swallow nor release. So it stayed there, wedged tight, sharp edges digging in as I tried to breathe around it, tried to let that runaway panic drive me from room to room and floor after floor, until on the lowest floor, we checked the elevator and strode out emptyhanded.

We moved from building to building, stairwell to stairwell, until the Commander called. The decrepit cabins on the fair side of the island were empty, and his men were doing a sweep through the thickets and the blackberry brush on their way back to the Institute's grounds.

I hung up the phone as the weight of that hit me. I didn't know whether to be relieved with the news or not. Something inside told me this wasn't like Baldeon's murder...this was different. If it was, we'd find a body, somewhere obvious—a shudder tore through me—somewhere close enough to do what they needed to do...and be done.

My phone rang and I snatched it up before the second ring. *Commander* splayed across the screen as I barked. "Yeah?"

"Surveillance has picked up something," he barked, the pounding of his footsteps audible in the background. "I'm heading to the control room now."

"I'm on my way," I replied, drawing Bernardi's focus, then Davies's.

I hung up the phone. "They think they found something."

"Oh, thank fucking God," Xael groaned with relief.

"I'm heading to the control room." I headed toward the doors, punching in the number for Logan.

I relayed the information to my bodyguard, listening to a door slam against a wall in the background as he carved through building after building searching for her.

"I'm on my way," Logan responded, and hung up.

I raced out of the foyer and across the Institute's grounds, heading for building one. By the time I charged through the doorway, Logan and Freddy were waiting for me. Bruno and Xael were right behind me, puffing and panting as we slowed.

I sucked in harsh breaths, my thighs heavy and hard as I strode toward the CCTV control room. The Commander was waiting, standing outside the door as I neared. "I wanted to wait for you," he stated.

But I didn't care about words, I cared about action. I cared about knowing what they'd found. I shoved the door open as soon as he'd placed his finger in the scanner and strode in, making my way toward the bank of monitors against the wall.

The control room guard shoved up from his seat as I charged in, Logan and the others at my back.

"What is it?" I growled, my gaze shifting to the monitor in front of him, the one with a dark blur in the middle of the screen.

"I think it's a boat," he answered, making the image bigger.

But the more it grew, the more blurred it became. "Pan out," I snapped.

My gaze was riveted on that fucking blur, my pulse pounding in my ears. I needed it to be a boat...needed to see her alive. But the more he scrolled out and the smaller those pixels became, I saw it wasn't her at all.

"Two men by the looks of it," Logan observed beside me. "That's a special forces dinghy, fast and quiet, used for covert operations. Where was this taken?" He asked the guard.

"Off the east coast at one-fifteen today," he answered.

One-fifteen.

Logan just looked at me. I knew without him speaking...knew in that fucking look. My gut clenched. *No...don't you dare fucking say it...don't you dare fucking say it.*

I tore my gaze from his and fixed on that blur on the screen, the image of two men sitting on the sides of the dinghy as it raced from the beach of the island and toward Mauritius. But there was no Kat...

I clenched my fist...until my knuckles popped with the strain. I wanted to punch something...*no, I needed to punch something*.

A phone rang as I ground my teeth and breathed through my nose.

"Sebastian VanHalen" the Commander murmured.

I wrenched my gaze to Mateo as a flare of panic crossed his face. "I see, there's been a ransom. Please, send me the recording..."

The air seemed to leave my lungs.

And for a second, none replaced it.

I existed in nothing.

No time.

No space.

Not alive.

Not dead.

Suspended in fear.

43

Kat

Darkness replaced darkness. In the moments after the blinding spotlight and the camera, they left me lying on my side as the faint shadows on the cabin floor grew darker. Hard breaths were all I had. Air and thought. Panicked thoughts. After a few moments, I tried to work feeling into my hands.

The binding wasn't as tight now, leaving me room to stretch and curl my fingers. But my shoulders ached, my muscles hard and cramping. Every time I lifted my head, I felt the strain tearing along my shoulders and into the sides of my neck. "Please...please help me up."

Movement came from the corner. Heavy steps rang out. It was some kind of cabin or hut. Under the heavy thudding of my heart, I could still hear the faint chirping of cicadas. We were on Mauritius, somewhere away from the heavily populated areas, somewhere where they could bring a woman, bound and terrified, and hold her captive without being seen.

My abductor came closer, reached down, grasped my arm, and wrenched me up to a sit. "You going to cause a scene?" he asked, staring down at me.

I didn't meet his gaze, just shook my head meekly. "No."

He knelt and reached behind me. Steel slid along my skin, the edge sharp, making my stomach clench with fear before *snap*. The bonds around my wrists snapped free, leaving my hands to fall to the sides under their own weight. Agony tore along my arms, making me moan and drop my head forward. I couldn't even lift them, couldn't do anything but hang my head and close my eyes.

"Here," he muttered.

Something hit my lap and rolled.

Water.

I reached out on instinct, grabbing the bottle even as pain roared through my shoulders. My lips were dry and hard, remnants of salt lingering at the edges of my mouth. I managed to unscrew the plastic cap and lifted the bottle to my lips, taking big gulps. Water slid down the back of my throat and sloshed in my belly. I gulped, taking as much as I dared, then stopped.

The sandwich Lazarus had for me kept hunger at bay, but my throat had been dry. Shallow, fast breaths and the battering of the wind on the boat ride here had stolen the moisture from the back of my throat, moisture that clung now as I swiped my mouth with the back of my hand and finally lifted my gaze to him.

He watched me with a cold detachment, as though I weren't a person at all, just a means to an end, a means they wanted. "He'll send it," I murmured. "He'll send you the money."

He just knelt in front of me once more, the gun shining in the holster at his waist. "But will he send me the Stidda prick, that's what I want to know."

My breath caught as I stared into those flat, dead eyes.

His lips curled into a smirk.

"Money, and the cocky Rossi bastard's head on a spike," he sneered. "That's what we want..." he dragged his teeth across his lower lip and lowered his gaze, taking in the oversized leather jacket and sodden white t-shirt still clinging to my skin.

He reached out, parted the jacket with a swipe of his hand, and stared.

I knew what he looked at...*knew that kind of hunger.*

Knew it all too well.

The soft cotton shirt clung to my breasts. The lacy outline of my bra was something that excited him. Would he rape me? I fought the need to clamp my legs closed. My core clenched tight, drawing my focus to that tiny life in my belly. A life I'd tried so hard to protect.

We'll take you instead...

Their words resounded in my head and kept echoing. They'd come for him, for Lazarus. I stared into his eyes now, as his gaze took in my body. A shiver quaked through me, drawing a smile from his lips. He thought his leering gaze was responsible, thought that one lick of those lips, and I'd crumple.

But the tremor inside me wasn't from fear...

Oh no.

It was rage.

I clenched my jaw tight as his eyes flicked to mine. He stilled, brow furrowing for a second, when I didn't look away. He didn't expect that...and it concerned him. He pushed to stand, never once taking his focus from mine.

He left me then, stepping back into the shadows.

I clutched the bottle of water, drew my legs tight, and clung to that taste of venom as I watched him. Silence stretched between us in the dark, silence and hate, as I rubbed my shoulders and lowered my body to the floor once more. Pain throbbed in my side from his fist. I curled my knees close and slid my hands under my head. Silence and darkness stretched out to me. In the emptiness, I heard them murmuring words I couldn't catch, and after a while, I stopped caring. It'd been hours...hours since 'd been taken.

Hours since I'd been brought here.

My mind drifted to Lazarus, and I closed my eyes.

Tears welled in the corners. He'd be frantic, enraged. He'd do things...things I was grateful for. If there was anyone who'd find me—it was him. That knowing lingered inside me like a fever. He'd find me...he'd find me...*he'd find me.*

44

Lazarus

"Take a good fucking look!" I shoved the picture into the ugly motherfucker's face. *"Who the fuck are they?"*

One hand gripped his open, grimy, floral shirt. The other was a fist, the knuckles split and bloody, throbbing with pain and need. Just like the rest of me.

Hard breaths were consuming as I shoved the asshole against the worn corrugated sheeting, and the walls bowed under the force. It was just a hovel. A foul, diseased fucking hole in the ground that served homemade rum in filthy glasses from wooden drums out back. Just a shanty. One of many I'd torn through tonight like a goddamn hurricane. So many I'd lost count.

"Laz," Logan growled, drawing my attention.

The brother just looked at the poor bastard in my grip, then met my gaze and shook his head. He gripped the semi-automatic assault rifle across his vest. The rest of his vest was laden with spare clips, knives, a pack of supplies. But it was his gaze that held me. A gaze filled with retribution and rage.

That I'd cling to.

That I'd unleash like a weapon of my own.

I'd use Logan, like he used his gun. Use him to find her...use him to hunt those goddamn bastards down. *Whoever they were.* But they weren't here. Not here...

I shoved the bastard away, letting him stumble with his eyes-wide, his hands palm up in front of him as he stuttered. "Don't know...don't know...*don't know.*" That's all he kept saying, over and over...*and over again.*

Forty-nine.

That's what I held onto as I turned and strode after my brother, shoving aside the ruined blue tarpaulin. Forty-nine islands in Mauritius. Forty-nine islands just like this one, filled with seedy fuckers that'd only be too willing to abduct a woman like Kat.

Only too willing to do things to her.

The kinds of things that made my gut roll.

I stumbled, slinging my arm out to brace myself.

"Whoa there," Logan muttered, grabbing my arm. "Laz?" His voice was etched with concern.

"I'm fine," I snarled, meeting his gaze.

I shoved away from him, stumbled along the dirty street, and sloshed through a puddle. I didn't feel the water seep into my boots, didn't feel anything. "Find the next one, Logan," I commanded.

His stare was heavy on the back of my neck. But he didn't argue. He knew that was pointless, almost as pointless as chasing after a ghost. I lowered my gaze and, in the silver spill of moonlight, stared at the image in my hand.

The image of two men hurtling away from the Institute's island in a special forces dinghy. Men we didn't even know had Kat. But we had nothing else to go on. So this is what we clung to. This is what we could use. I stepped closer to the Jeep and climbed into the open back. Logan and Freddy climbed in, one in the driver's side, the other in the passenger's.

A shadow neared from the opposite side before the bastard gripped the roll bar and heaved himself into the seat next to me. I turned my gaze, finding the hard, unflinching stare of Finley Salvatore, and gave a nod.

The bastard hadn't even changed clothes.

The bottoms of his black pants were ruined with mud. His perfect white shirt was splattered and smeared with blood. He looked fucking ridiculous. I swallowed a flare of gratitude as the engine of the four-wheel drive started and we pulled away from the grungy bar with a screech of tires.

Wind buffeted my eyes and flicked my hair.

I glanced away from Finley, remembering the force he'd been when their Sikorsky touched back down and they raced out from under the rotor blades. Anna had been quiet, too fucking quiet. But instead of standing around wringing her hands and crying like the others, she demanded to be shown to the control room...and to be sent a copy of the ransom video.

Finley seemed to think she could somehow find Kat. That she was some genius with hacking and code. I swallowed the heavy feeling of desperation. I didn't know anything about that. I knew violence. I knew fists. I knew the glint of fear in a piece of shit's eyes when I knew he was lying.

"Yeah," Logan muttered into his mic as he handled the Jeep around decrepit buildings and along filthy streets. "He's fine."

I glanced out into the night, knowing exactly who he spoke to. My dad had stopped calling my cell, finally getting the hint after I ignored his calls for the last three hours. Hell, I ignored all their fucking calls, except the Commander's. His I took, but only because I was desperate for news...*any news*, good or bad. I closed my eyes for a second, feeling the weight of exhaustion. *But, please, for the love of God, let there be good news.*

Logan's voice drifted as we hit bump after bump and turned, making our way to another fucking hovel where the seedy bastards who stabbed you in the back while they snatched your wallet hung out. Fuck, I felt tainted just touching them, but when the Jeep skidded to a stop outside yet another fucking dive, I was the first one out of the vehicle, hauling myself out until my boots hit the ground, and charging toward the blaring lights and the sound of raucous laughter.

They were nothing to me.

A means to get to her.

A way to take back what was mine.

I tore through the place, my gaze searching, finding the biggest, baddest motherfucker and strode toward him with the image of those men in the boat in my hand while the rest of my team fanned out, finding anyone who might have information. If bribery didn't work, then there was always fury.

Dive after dive.

Man after man.

Threats after questioning.

Still, no one knew the two men in the boat.

And when the sun rose in the distance, I slumped forward, resting my forehead on the back of the driver's seat in front of me. Thirty-two hours until Logan's special forces team got here. Thirty-two until there were more of us. "Take me to the next one, Logan."

"I can't," he replied, steering the Jeep toward the faint sparkling lights in the distance. "There's nothing open, not anymore, Laz. Not for a few hours."

I just nodded. Spent. Exhausted. Filled with grief.

He drove us somewhere. I neither knew where we were heading, or cared. When we pulled up at a gleaming apartment building that reminded me of the Park Hyatt Hotel, he killed the engine.

"Where the fuck are we?" I growled as he climbed out.

"Some place where we can rest, now get the fuck out, Laz, or I'll throw you over my damn shoulder."

I just glared at the savage bastard as he climbed out and rounded the rear of the four-wheel drive, snatched a pack from the back, and headed toward the massive automatic doors. I had no choice but to follow when the others did.

The concierge just nodded, then looked away as we passed and headed to the massive elevator. He tried to keep himself busy, sneaking a glance as we strode inside before the doors closed. In the reflection of the doors, I saw what we looked like.

Wraiths.

Bloodied.

Merciless.

Haunted.

The doors opened at the penthouse suite. Logan strode toward the massive black double doors and punched a code into the keypad, watching as the light blinked from red to green.

We were inside in an instant, striding through the luxurious home filled with black and silver. "Whose place is this?"

"The Commander's," Logan answered, tossing his pack through the air until it hit the white leather sofa. "Shower and sleep, Laz. In a few hours, we're back up and at it, then we're back at the island by night tomorrow and the new team will take over."

A new team. Ten guys in total. Ten of Logan. I just held his gaze, then nodded.

"I'll take the couch," Freddy volunteered, and strode toward the kitchen.

"I'm showering and sleeping. Wake me when you're up," Finley muttered, his boots tracking mud along the shining marble tiles as he headed for a bedroom and closed the door behind him.

Then, resigned...I followed, headed toward the main bedroom and closed the doors.

THE SPEEDBOAT CARRIED us toward the bright lights of the Institute, swerving side to side, whipping my hair one way, then another. I stared at the lights until my eyes stung and blurred with tears. My hands were shaking...my body numb.

We'd said nothing as the boat pulled up against the dock and waited as we climbed in.

There was nothing left to say.

We'd covered barely two islands in the last eighteen hours of smashing down walls, then people.

Eighteen hours of nothing more than blank stares and the shaking of heads. Eighteen motherfucking hours while we waited for Logan's team to hit Mauritian shores, until the Commander called and summoned us back for a full briefing. And it looked like I was about to have a meeting with Sebastian VanHalen, Kat's father.

I tried to feel something other than detachment. Tried to remember this was a man's daughter we were dealing with. He'd be distraught. He'd be sick with rage and fear. I tried to think how my father might react and came up with *terrified*.

I'd need to make a good impression there. I looked down at the creased, bloodied shirt that the hot shower twelve hours ago had tried to fix. But no matter how much scrubbing I did, it didn't help. I looked how I was; nothing more than a barbarian, nothing more than a thug, not worthy of his daughter's presence, let alone her goddamn heart.

It didn't matter...*she had mine.*

I looked away as the boat's motor eased, idling hard as we rode the waves, turning sideways until we bounced hard against the dock. There was a man waiting, ready with the rope. But I was already rising from the leather seat at the rear.

"We've got time for a shower," Freddy suggested.

I just nodded, followed him up onto the pontoon, and looked over to where the luxury cruiser was docked. The same cruiser that had ferried her here just days ago. Days, fuck it felt like a lifetime. Maybe that was hope speaking? I wasn't sure anymore.

I made my way toward my building, my steps slow and heavy, my head hanging low.

"I'll have a shower, fill Anna in, and meet you there," Finley said, his words slurred with exhaustion.

I just looked up, then nodded.

My enemy was now my ally.

Go fucking figure.

I followed Logan and Freddy into the elevator at the building, then was hit by something hard and heavy, something that took the wind out of me. I slammed my eyes closed, remembering the last time we rode this elevator, desperately searching for her.

And the thought of going up there, seeing the mess of our sheets, and the scent of her lingering in the air was almost too much to bear. "You won't have time to go to both apartments," Freddy muttered. "Best you just shower in ours and I'll grab your things from upstairs, yeah?"

A tear slipped from the corner of my eye as I nodded, slow, thick, barely a tear, more viscous like blood.

Maybe it was blood.

Tears of blood.

A heavy weight settled around my shoulders as the elevator came to a stop and Logan walked me inside.

"You fucking reek, brother," the low growl came from beside me. "I was praying for us to go faster on the trip over here so I didn't need to smell you. But now we're here, double shampoo, yeah?"

I gave a hollow bark of laughter as he shoved me toward the main bedroom Freddy had called shotgun on, and kicked off my boots. It was a different decor, white tiles on the floor, where upstairs had been black. Subtle touches, still it made all the difference—to my heart at least, as I peeled off my grimy shirt and dropped it to the floor. Jeans were next, the bottoms covered in thick mud.

I hit the shower and stepped in, letting the hot water hit my back and slide down my shoulders. Then I scrubbed, hard, shampooing my hair until it squeaked, and by the time I shut off the water and stepped out, my things were waiting on the edge of the bed and there was food on the counter.

My stomach clenched at the sight as Freddy shoved half a sandwich into his mouth and started undressing heading toward me. "I'll be quick," he promised.

I dressed, grabbing clean black jeans, a black tee, and my vest...*but not my jacket.*

Because she had that.

Christ, I hoped she still had it. The thought of her having something of mine with her was strangely comforting. I shrugged into the vest, strapped it tight, and slid my gun under my shirt at the small of my back before tugging on clean military boots and zipping them tight.

By the time I was ready, Logan was showered, shaved, and helping himself to a platter of sandwiches and food on the counter.

"You should eat something," he urged around a mouthful of food.

I looked at the stuff, and saw the sandwich I'd made for Kat, then just shook my head. Instead, I grabbed a Red Bull and chugged the contents. Minutes, that's all it took us, before we were in the elevator once more, but fuck, it felt like forever.

I swallowed a tremor as the doors opened and we were striding across the Institute's grounds all lit up by spotlights. Movement came from the side as Finley jogged toward us, looking refreshed. *Fucking asshole.*

"Anna said she's making headway on the code of the ransom. Said she's isolated everything she can from the recording. Said that Kat looks scared, but okay and that's what we need to hold onto. She's a fighter, we know that, right?"

I just stared straight ahead. "Yeah, she's a fighter."

The automatic doors opened to building one as we stepped close. I expected men to be gathering in the foyer, but there was no one. Just silence, until the faint drone of voices filtered through. I headed toward the sound, knowing instinctively they were sitting in the same conference room I'd sat in hours ago...right around the time Kat was being abducted.

I pushed through the doors and stepped in, my gaze moving to the group of men on the other side of the room. Suits everywhere, but one stood out in particular. Steel gray, the edges sharp.

"Lazarus," the Commander called my name. His dark eyes glinted, moving from me to Finley, then Logan and Freddy at my back. "I'm glad you made it."

"Why wouldn't I?" I muttered as the man in the gray suit turned.

Dark, beady eyes glared at me from behind him. Damon Zakharov stood there, his face swollen and misshapen. His broken front tooth showed as he sneered. I swallowed that flare of hate and tore my gaze away. What the fuck was he doing here anyway?

"Sebastian, this is—" the Commander started.

"Lazarus Rossi," The voice that came from Kat's father was devoid of any kind of emotion.

Not hate.

Not rage.

Not any trace of fear.

It was just...*nothing*.

"Mr. VanHalen." I nodded.

"Lazarus and his team have been searching the mainland, trying to locate anyone with information on Kat's whereabouts." Mateo caught him up to speed.

"Katerina," Kat's dad corrected as he turned back to Mateo. "It's Katerina."

I fought the flinch. She didn't like that name...didn't like it at all.

"Thank you, in any case," came a deep, resounding murmur at Sebastian VanHalen's side.

I jerked my gaze to the male at his side. Deep brown eyes, perfect fucking skin. The man looked like a damn model, flecks of gray hair at his temples, dressed in an immaculate black suit that I was pretty fucking sure cost more than my damn Harley.

He reached up, adjusted the cuffs of his suit, and dismissed me with a curl of his lip. "But we'll take it from here."

The hair on the nape of my neck rose instantly. *Who the fuck did this guy think—*

"Mr. Hale," Mateo murmured, clearing his throat. "I don't think you should be too hasty..."

"Mr. Ristani, with all due respect, you have no authority where the safety and well-being of my future wife is concerned."

"Your future fucking wife?" I snapped.

Gone was the heaviness of exhaustion. Gone was that loss of control. I was laser fucking focused now as I took a step closer, closing the distance between me and this cunt in a three-piece suit. Sebastian VanHalen just looked at me like I wasn't worthy enough to tread on as Haelstrom Hale crossed the space between us, stopping at my side. "That's right. Make no mistake, *boy,* when this is over, she won't belong to you."

I turned my head and stared into the eyes of my enemy.

Something savage carved its way through me, slithering out of the darkness of my soul.

And bared its goddamn fangs.

45

Kat

"Get up."

I opened my eyes, jerking my gaze up at my abductor, and blinked. "What?"

He lashed out. The toe of his boot drove against my thigh with a *thud*. "Move."

Sleep was snatched from me as I shoved upwards, drawing away from his blows. "Did he pay?" My voice was hoarse and croaking.

He said nothing, just stared at me. I licked my lips and felt that deep flare of agony move through my side, a reminder of his cruel fists. The leather jacket slid from my body, falling to the floor. I reached out, snatching it against me, and pushed to stand. "He paid you, right? He paid you the money?"

"No," he answered. "He didn't."

Fear moved through me. "That can't be right. He wouldn't..."

"No more talking...*move.*"

I'd waited all day, too scared to sleep. All day curled in that one spot in the corner of the cabin, desperate for them to tell me I was free to go. But that never happened. Not last night as the wind howled through the cracks in the wooden floorboards, nor all day as the gloomy shadows still clung to the cabin. An ache throbbed in my chest and radiated outwards. Desperation was all I had now as hope slowly started to fade away.

"Bathroom," he snarled, shoving me forward.

I crossed the floor, scanning the empty rooms. It was the second time I'd been allowed to pee since they'd handed me an apple, a green banana, and another bottle of water. When I'd asked for a blanket to stave off the night coolness, he stared at me until I slowly made my way back to the corner of the room and draped Lazarus's leather jacket over my body.

I glanced behind me to where he followed, then stepped into the small, filthy bathroom. I closed the door behind me, until he shoved his boot in the way, stopping it. "Make it quick."

My pulse sped at the words. Maybe they were moving me somewhere else, somewhere the Institute's guards were to collect me? Panicked thoughts shoved the last traces of exhaustion away. Dad had to have paid. There was no way he wouldn't...*no way...*

I watched the open crack of the door while I slid the sweats and my panties down. I was grimy and stank, still wearing yesterday's clothes. Clothes that held traces of the scent of sex. I gripped the soft cotton shirt and pulled it against my nose as my bladder released.

The ache in my side pinched, making me draw the shirt a little higher. A bruise bloomed across my side, dark and throbbing. I pulled my shirt down and hurried to wipe before washing my hands and bending low.

My abductor said nothing as I splashed water onto my face and washed my eyes. One small shove of the door and he watched me like a hawk watched a field mouse from high above.

I swallowed a shudder and looked away from his reflection.

I tried to think, tried to fight the lingering exhaustion from my mind. He would've paid in an instant. He would've had a team of people around him, and the best negotiator money could buy. The memory of that day in his office came roaring back to me. I gripped the cracked, filthy sink and stared at my reflection. He was angry, furious I was defying him. Out of control with rage.

I allowed it to happen!

His scream came back to me as movement came from my right. "Out." My abductor gave a jerk of his head.

But he didn't move from the doorway, crowding the space, giving me no room to get past...not without—

I licked my lips, curled my shoulders, and, with my pulse thundering in my ears, I turned my body, scraping my spine along the doorframe before he moved, pushing in, trapping me between the frame and his body.

"Turn around."

I closed my eyes for a second, frozen with fear.

Turn around, Katerina...take off the dress. My father's voice echoed from my past. *I want them to see what a beautiful young woman you are.*

Take it off.

Lay on the table.

Let them do whatever they want.

My core clenched tight with the memories as they slammed into me. "No." The word was a hoarse whisper. I opened my eyes and met his gaze. "No, I won't turn around. I won't walk when you tell me to walk. I won't sit where you tell me to sit. I won't do a *fucking* thing you want me to."

He smiled then, and that cruel glint shone like a midnight star in his eyes as he lowered his head and whispered, "I was hoping you'd say that."

He moved fast, grabbing a fistful of my hair, and dragged me from the doorway. Fire lashed my scalp, stinging instantly. I screamed, grasped his hand around my hair, and kicked, driving out with my bare foot. I fought him, throwing my weight as I twisted and stumbled. The agony tearing across my scalp the whole time, filling my eyes with tears.

There was nothing else to do now, nothing else but to fight and keep on fighting.

Until the end.

Because he hadn't paid the money...*he hadn't paid the fucking money!*

A scream ripped from me, sounding like a savage animal as he drove me back against the wall. The back of my head impacted with a *THUD!* Stars detonated behind my eyes, blinding me for a second. Stunned, I tried to gasp as tears streamed down my cheeks.

"He paid the money..." I whimpered, grasping my abductor's hand in my hair, and stared into those soulless eyes. "He had to have."

But that merciless bastard in front of me just sucked in a hard breath and leaned in close. "Daddy doesn't care about you, Princess, no one does...*now turn around before I break your fucking arm.*"

His fist tightened in my hair before jerking my head backwards. Every twitch, every movement, was like an inferno ripping across my head. Agony consumed me, tearing across my scalp and down my neck.

He shoved my head backwards, driving it against the wall once more.

I dropped my hands from his. Defeated, I stared into the black pools of his stare and whispered, "Okay...okay, I'll turn around."

His hold eased and my head throbbed with its own pulse as I turned, lifting my hands meekly to splay my palms along the walls. Memories shattered, driving into the present.

You're mine, Katerina, Hale's words resounded as the man at my back grasped my wrist and pulled it from the wall. *You're mine and no one will ever take you from me, do you understand? No one will ever take you away.*

Hale's words echoed as my wrist was grasped and he yanked me around again.

If it was between going back to him...and death, then I'd choose death.

Lazarus's face burned in my mind as the realization hit home.

I'd choose death rather than spend another second with a man like Hale.

But for Lazarus...I'd fight until my last breath.

Cuffs snapped around my wrists once more, only this time they were cuffed to the front. "Walk," my abductor snarled. "Make a fucking move again and I'll knock you the fuck out."

But I didn't fight him, not anymore. I stumbled forward with one bare foot, and the other still in my flat. I don't know why I still kept it on...I didn't know why of all things I'd held onto it. I lifted my heel, stepping out of the shoe, as he drove me toward the doorway by my bound hands.

The other man was waiting, opening the door as I stepped out of the cabin and into the night.

"Get in." A gleaming, steel gray four-wheel drive waited in front of me. The rear door was open, the interior light like a beacon.

I wanted to move...*I tried to move.* But fear froze me, forcing me to meet my captor's gaze. "Are you going to kill me?"

"Now why would we kill twenty million dollars?" he muttered, then jerked his head toward the waiting vehicle. "Get in."

They're not going to kill me...they're not going to kill me.

That was all I needed to shatter that hold fear had on me, so I stepped down the old wooden stairs and crossed the dirt in front of the cabin to the brand new Explorer and started to climb inside.

The rich scent of leather hit me as I grabbed the handle. My knees trembled as I stepped up, buckling before I hit the seat. A hard shove from behind me, and I sprawled across the back seat before the door was closed behind me with a *slam!*

Doors opened and closed, and the deep growl of the engine filled the cabin. How many times had I sat in the back seat of a vehicle being chauffeured around in gowns and glamor. And never once did I think it would be any other way, never once did I think my life would take such a sudden turn.

Never once did I think I'd be fighting for my life.

Headlights cut through the weeping willows that surrounded the cabin. The murky water shone in the distance. Pitch black was all around us, not even a twinkle of lights pierced the gloom. I realized how isolated we were out here, how the cover of darkness was just one more barrier from anyone finding me.

We pulled away, turning in a tight circle. I hadn't seen the car when they brought me here, forced to walk after they'd beached the boat and covered it with a dark tarp, then large branches. I'd known then the kind of men who'd taken me, knew that these weren't just someone willing to snatch and release for a few hundred thousand dollars.

No, these men were professionals.

Trained, skilled, and now, as we drove away in the brand new four-wheel drive, I realized they were connected and had money. I gripped the leather seat and shoved, scanning the road ahead. "Where are you taking me?"

They said nothing as they glanced along the empty road and gunned the engine. The force pushed me back against the seat. I shivered, my head aching and pulsing, burning from his hold on my hair. I gently probed the ache, massaging as I stared through the window, desperate to find a house...a set of head-lights. *Anything.*

Even when the faint twinkle of lights cut through the trees, it was too late. We were flying down a dirt road, until they slowed at an intersection, turned right, then we were on the asphalt.

We drove for an hour. I watched the minutes on the dashboard clock tick by and tried to find some kind of marker in the night of where we were as my hands slipped to the door handle. I knew it was hopeless, but still I pulled quietly, testing the lock. But it held as my captors focused ahead, as though they knew I'd try to escape.

I stared straight ahead, watching minutes turn into an hour on the clock, until faint lights grew brighter in the distance. Red flashes drew my focus, and further along there were green. I scanned the road behind us, then fixed on that brightening glow as fear grew heavy in my belly. It was some kind of ware-house, one hidden behind a towering fence topped with razor wire.

A hangar.

A hangar with a plane. "No," I whimpered, and turned to the door once more.

"It's pointless," my captor muttered as I yanked on the handle and punched the buttons.

Then I twisted, glanced at the rear door, and knew in my heart it was hopeless. "No," I cried, shaking my head. "Please...*no.*"

My head was in agony, my wrists stung from the plastic cuffs as they cut. Still, I clasped my hands together and lifted them. "I'll send another recording. *I'll send another, and he'll pay.*"

The four-wheel drive just pulled up hard at the airport hangar and the gate started to open. I jerked my gaze toward the movement, catching the tail end of what looked like a small cargo carrier. My heart lurched, battering the inside of my chest as I twisted in my seat. My voice was shrill and piercing. *"Please don't put me in there. Please...I'll do anything,"* I sobbed, tears sliding down my cheeks. *"I'll be good. I promise you, I'll be good. I'll be good...I'll be..."*

Under the glare of the headlights, a door opened to the hangar and a man stepped out. The bright glare died in an instant, leaving me staring into darkness once more. "Please..." I begged. "Please don't do this."

My captors climbed out of the car. The one in the passenger's seat stepped toward the rear door. I grabbed the arm rest and pulled with all I had as he yanked the handle and tried to open the door. But I fought, muscles straining until agony tore along my forearms. He just stared at me through the tinted windows and yanked once more, making me cry and hold on, until I couldn't anymore.

Then it was over. The door yanked open and he snarled, "Don't make me hurt you, Katerina." He reached for me. It was instinct that drove me backwards. That innate fight for survival that made me kick off, driving my heel into the center of his chest.

He stumbled backwards and that was all I needed. I scurried forward, driving my body through the gap of the front seats until I was behind the wheel. Panic fueled me as I stabbed the start button of the car and was rewarded with the throaty growl of the engine.

YES!

With cuffed hands, I grasped the gears and yanked as the engine died. *"No!"* I screamed.

My captor growled behind me, the sound savage and terrifying. Desperately, I stabbed the button once more. But this time there was nothing, nothing but silence.

"It's called a kill switch," he snarled behind me. *"You stupid little bitch."*

I screamed, slamming both hands down on the horn. The sound was instant and *deafening*, blaring through the darkness like a scream.

"Fucking *cunt!*" he roared, reaching across me as the driver's door was yanked open...and my pitiless attacker grasped me by the throat and hauled me out of the car.

"You're going to make me wish I'd shot you, aren't you?" my attacker barked in my face as he slammed the door.

"I didn't think she was going to fight like that," the other one exclaimed.

"This one's a fucking hellcat." My attacker clenched his grip tighter. "Lucky she's not going to be our problem for much longer."

I gasped and wheezed, stumbling to the side as he wrenched me by my throat. *"Please,"* I croaked as they dragged me through the open gates and through the door of the hangar.

46

Lazarus

The world seemed to bow and scrape for Haelstrom Hale. He moved in like a plague, spilling out of the conference room to infect the rest of the building, demanding to be taken to the island's control room and to speak with the guard behind the monitors.

And all the while, I hated and seethed, rolling those words around in my head. *Make no mistake, boy, when this is over, she won't belong to you.* Freddy and Logan stood at my back as Hale left with Kat's dad at his back. It was easy to see why the woman had hidden so many fucking secrets from me. Dark secrets. *Chilling secrets.*

They were a new breed, the filthy rich. A whole new fucking breed.

Mateo just stood there, watching as they slowly took over his building, and all the while, the smirking Damon Zakharov followed them around like a lovesick puppy. I watched as he strode past, tottering after them, his shit-eating grin stretching the corners of his swollen lips.

"Nice teeth," I muttered as he passed.

That grin faltered, but the cruel gleam in his eyes remained as he strode through the door. I followed with my gaze until we were the only ones left in the room. "I fucking hate him." The words echoed deep within my belly. "*I hate all of them.*"

Logan just cleared his throat carefully and answered, "They're her family."

"Not Hale," I spat. "No fucking way."

"Did you know about that?" Freddy muttered, taking a step into view.

I stared at the open door as remnants of the last week hit home. Had I known she was somehow *taken? She's Hale's, but he'll let you have her, at least until they're married...*Zakharov's words whispered from that pit of emptiness inside me. "Not from her, no."

"So she didn't tell you anything about that Hale?" he muttered, and scowled. "Makes perfect fucking sense then."

My senses piqued, forcing my focus to narrow in. "What makes sense?"

There was a battle in his eyes, then a shake of his head, before he turned away.

"What makes sense, *brother?*" I strode forward and grabbed his arm.

"Nothing." He tugged his arm free. "Forget I spoke."

But I couldn't forget. Not what he said or the way he was avoiding it now. The way he was avoiding *me*. I stepped in front of him, forcing his gaze to mine. *"Tell me, Freddy."*

Nothing else mattered in that moment.

Nothing mattered but unearthing what he had to say.

I wanted every secret of hers, *needed* them like I needed air to fucking breathe. I craved every quiet smile, every whisper of her fucking scent. I thirsted for any trace of her, no matter how little it was. Because without them...*without them*...she slipped away from me.

Freddy saw that hunger, saw how crazed I'd become in the wake of her abduction. He saw how that slithering thing inside me was rising to the surface, pushing me to the edge...*and that was never a good thing.*

He licked his lips and cast a nervous glance at Logan, who just nodded, urging him on.

Freddy was all I cared about in that moment, the *brother* and the torment he wrestled with, torment that made my fucking pulse stutter and my breath catch.

"I don't know for sure, okay?" he started, then dragged his fingers through his hair, shifting from one foot to the other like a jumpy motherfucker.

"Just fucking spit it out," I snapped, unable to stand the fucking tension.

"She denied it, laughed it off like I was imagining things," Freddy's voice deepened as he looked away. He couldn't meet my eyes...*Jesus.* "But I wasn't imagining things, not things like that. I saw the way she moved when she forgot I was there, saw the way her hand cupped her belly, saw the way her fingers traced the fluttering in her belly. It was the exact same way Connie did. She lied to me when I confronted her, but I know without a shadow of a doubt, she's pregnant."

Something hit me.

Something big.

Like sledgehammer big...

Maybe it was even fucking Mars, leaving complete annihilation behind.

My breath left me. Frozen, I couldn't move. Couldn't think... *couldn't function.*

You don't want to go back, do you? My own words resounded.

No, I don't. And I won't be, she whispered in my head.

Pregnant.

She was fucking pregnant.

Pieces slipped into place. Pieces I hadn't even known weren't already fucking aligned. But my world shifted now, creating a whole new landscape, and in the middle of that new world was her. *Pregnant her.* No wonder she'd fought the connection we shared, wrestled with our love.

Because make no mistake, that's what thundered through my veins...love.

Sharp, cutting talons curving deep into my chest kind of love. The kind of love that terrified me.

If I tried to remove it...*it'd tear out my entire heart.*

"What the fuck did you say?" the deep snarl came from the open doorway.

Hale took a step inside, his gaze fixed like a predator on Freddy. "*My* Katerina is pregnant?"

My jaw tightened as his chest rose with a sudden breath. *Katerina?* I was starting to hate that fucking name. It wasn't hers, not anywhere near hers. She was Kat, beautiful, *perfect* Kat.

I could see it in his eyes. He was already branding her. Piece by fucking piece, he was laying claim to what was mine. Because if Freddy was right...*if* the woman who had my beating fucking heart in her grasp was pregnant—then there was no way possible I was the father.

I wasn't the father.

I wasn't the one to fill her with what was mine.

Hale took a step closer, those venomous eyes finding mine. Pride echoed deep inside him. A claiming took place right in front of my eyes as the corners of his lips curled slightly as he said the words I dreaded. "Then congratulations are in order, it looks like I'm about to be a father."

All I could see was them.

Writhing.

Fucking.

Him filling her as she cried out his name.

All I saw was the blissful gleam that shone after we were done. A gleam she'd given *him*. Agony coursed through my chest as the blade buried deep. In an instant, the walls in the conference room closed in, the air was *suffocating*.

"I came to tell you I'll be taking command." Hale seemed to grow larger by the second, swelling and consuming, eating the space around us with his presence as he glanced toward Logan. "I understand you have men on the ground on the mainland and I want their details. You will report to me...and *only* to me. *Everything* involving Katerina is now mine."

The fucking bastard looked at me when he said it.

And I'd never wanted to murder someone so badly before.

I'd never wanted to shove a gun into his mouth and pull the trigger.

I'd never wanted to look into his eyes as his light faded away.

But I did for this man. I wanted that light gone...that flame that flickered behind those pitch black eyes snuffed out until there was nothing but the flesh behind. Then I wanted to take a sledgehammer to the bastard. I wanted to smash and pound until there was no trace of the man left. I wanted him ugly and misshapen...*so she never wanted him ever again.*

I turned away and strode toward the door, desperately holding back the need to run and keep on running. Logan's deep growl echoed behind me, saying words I didn't catch. I was already gone, my body canting forward, desperate to gain inch by inch away from that fucking *evil*.

"Laz," Freddy called behind me.

I barely registered the hand on my arm, barely felt *anything* at all as he stopped me.

"Laz, I'm sorry." There was desperation in his eyes, pain that scrunched the corners. I looked at him and, for the first time...I didn't know who he was. But I knew in an instant the fault didn't lie with him. *It was me.*

I didn't know who *I* was.

No words came to me as Freddy's chest rose hard and fell. He licked his lips. "Laz..."

"It's okay, Freddy," I said, and stepped away.

I walked, and kept on walking, striding out of the foyer and into the night.

And somewhere out there, Kat held all the fucking cards in the palm of her hand.

47

Kat

Wind sheered across the tarmac, scattering my hair as I stared at the open door of the cargo plane.

"Move." My abductor shoved me forward with a punch to my shoulder.

I stumbled forward with my hands bound in front and cut a panicked glance around me, searching for a way out of this. But there wasn't a way, no matter how much I wanted there to be. There was just the yawning mouth of the rumbling plane as the engines started and the blades spun.

My feet stopped moving. I turned and ran straight into the massive chest of my captor.

"No you fucking don't," he growled, grabbing me by the shoulders and turning me back around once more.

He pushed me, driving my body forward. To keep from stumbling, I stepped, my bare feet stinging as they slapped on the asphalt, until I climbed onto the cold steel stairs.

I winced, drew my arms together, and grasped the railing. The inside was a steel tomb, dark and cold. Terror found me as I stumbled inside, finding myself the focus as heads turned toward me.

"Sit," my captor ordered, and pointed to a spot on the floor of the plane.

But I couldn't move. I was frozen, staring at the row of women sitting. Women with their hands tied to a chain that ran down the middle of the plane. Women who stared at me with sadness and beaten expressions, their clothes dirty, their pain, haunting. I was just like them in that moment. No longer a name...no longer a charade. No longer a decimal point in my bank balance. I was just a barefooted woman wearing sweats and a leather jacket, bound like an animal, ready for market.

Like them.

"I said, *sit.*" His weight bore down on my shoulder, buckling my knees.

I crumpled, hitting the floor hard. Pain tore through my ass and into my back as my captor knelt and grasped the chain against the floor.

"Here."

I lifted my gaze, finding a younger male with a French accent. He glanced at me, then watched as my captor clasped the lock closed and rose. There was something kind in his eyes. Something not hard like the others. My abductor rose, glanced from me to the young guy, then muttered something in French.

Something that made the younger guy flinch, his cheeks burning as he answered back in French. My captor just glared at me once more, then turned and left, making his way out of the plane and was gone.

The door closed with a *bang*. Then the plane was moving forward with a jolt, leaving me to look at the other women, who just stared at me. "Where...where are they taking us?" I asked the nearest women.

She just scowled at me for a second. "Où est-ce qu'ils nous amènent," she muttered. She looked behind her, then settled on me once more. "Chez nous...en France."

En France...

"To France?" I whispered, and the woman nodded.

The plane surged faster, driving me to the side, until my belly lurched and that weightless feeling lifted me. We were climbing. The wheels lifting from the tarmac as we left Mauritius behind and with it, Lazarus.

I yanked on the chain, testing the lock, then pressed my spine against the cold steel wall. We climbed and climbed. There wasn't even a window, not that I'd see anything in the dark. But the hope...*Jesus,* the hope was palpable inside me. I closed my eyes and drew my knees together, curling my spine as the tears came.

I sobbed, shuddering and jerking, curling my body over to protect the only thing I had.

This life growing inside me.

Murmurs fought the roar of the engines. Warmth pressed against my side. I lifted my head, letting the tears fall, to find the woman next to me looking at me with sadness. She spoke to me, whispering words I couldn't understand.

I lowered my head, taking comfort in her. She pulled against the chains, reaching to grasp my hand. Through the deafening drone of the engine, a voice broke through. A woman rocked ahead of us, mumbling in Spanish, some of that I knew. But the words were jumbled...disjointed.

"Hey," I called, my voice husky.

"Shhh," the woman next to me urged, and shook her head. Her wide eyes were etched with fear, the kind of fear I took notice of.

I glanced at the muttering woman who rocked back and forth, her gaze fixed on the chain in front of us. Then I settled my head back on the woman next to me. It was small comfort and, apart from Anna, the only female comfort I'd ever had in my entire life. The thought filled me with sadness.

A sadness that weighed me down.

"Sleep," the woman murmured in my ear. "*Sleep now,* chère."

It was the only English she'd said, and while I wanted to stay awake and fight through every minute, I knew that I needed strength for what was coming, strength to fight for my life. So I took refuge in her bony shoulder and closed my eyes.

Sleep came hard and fast, sweeping me away into the murky gloom of my mind. The same kind of gloom that waited behind the drooping limbs and delicate leaves of the willows, and the same kind of darkness that had waited for me in that classroom, along with Damon. I fought that terror, fought it in my sleep just as I'd fought it in my life. When the plane bounced hard, I jarred from sleep with grainy, stinging eyes, to find the green-gray of the airplane floor.

The woman next to me didn't smile, just stared at me and slowly nodded.

It's time, her gaze said. It's time.

It was light...finally. It felt like I'd lived in darkness, like that was all that waited for me. I was no longer allowed in the light. No longer allowed to feel the warmth of the sun ever again. The plane dropped hard, bouncing before it evened out, the engines roaring, before we dropped once more.

Lower and lower. My pulse stuttered, my breaths turned faster and shallow. Fear was echoed in every woman's eyes—all except for one.

The woman mumbling in Spanish just stared at the chain around her wrists, stared and stared, unable to look anywhere else. A cry tore from me as we dropped again, moving lower and lower. I could almost hear the rush of the air under the plane as we dipped closer to the ground. The pitch of the engine changed, growing louder and louder, until the floor shuddered and a growl came where there'd been none before.

I grabbed her hand as the wheels touched down and skidded, clutching this stranger's hand like it was the last contact I'd ever feel again.

"No...no, no, no..." she whispered as we lurched forward, the brakes cutting in hard.

We slowed suddenly, until the roar in my head matched the roar of the engines, then the plane turned. It felt like forever as we rolled and rolled, then finally came to a stop and the engine quieted.

I stared at the others and the door up ahead that had to lead to the cockpit as it opened. The young guy from before ducked his head and stepped out, followed by another male. They never looked at us, just strode past. Sunlight poured in as the rear door opened.

Two more men came in, one carrying a semi-automatic weapon. They took one look at us, then stilled on me. Orders were barked in French. I glanced at the woman at my side, desperate to understand, as the men moved toward us. One bent and unlocked the chains around our wrists, then moved along the line while the guy with the weapon watched.

France...

We were in France.

But why?

Because it was close to Mauritius. It was the only thing that made sense.

"Move!"

I flinched at the roar, and waited. Some of the women hurried forward, cowering as they crawled on hands and knees. The guard with the gun scowled as he watched them, before he stopped at me. Time seemed to stand still as movement came all around me. Even my careful companion pushed up on her hands and knees, before ducking lower before she moved.

"Move, *rich bitch*," the man with the keys snarled before he bent, grabbed me by the arm, and hauled me to my feet, driving me toward the open door.

But I wasn't the last one to reach the opening. I heard the *whack* of a blow behind me and glanced over my shoulder, to find the steely stare of the muttering woman. I tried to get my feet to work properly and stepped out into the biting wind.

It was almost the same small, unmanned hangar as the one in Mauritius. The shed was larger, the fence newer. But there was no one around us to help. No one who would see me and know who I was. It was just the plane and us.

"Keep walking," a man barked on the asphalt.

I made my way down the stairs as the rest of the women wrapped their arms around their bodies and walked toward the looming shed.

A scream ripped through the air behind me before I caught movement.

The woman who spoke Spanish lunged, tearing across the tarmac in a desperate attempt to get free. One of the men took off after her as the glint of a gun shone in the corner of my eye.

The *crack* was deafening as the woman was thrown forward and hit the ground.

She didn't move...

Not a flinch.

Not a tremor.

Blood seeped from her body, spilling outwards.

They killed her...

They killed her.

"Keep walking." The captor with the gun stared at me.

I walked, tearing my gaze from the dead woman, and hurried to the others.

48

Lazarus

He took over her building, her apartment, and her goddamn existence, writing his own set of narratives. I couldn't stand it. Every time I turned around, Haelstrom fucking Hale was there, with his pristine fucking suits and his beady eyes.

Eyes I saw everywhere I turned.

"Laz," Logan murmured, drawing my attention from Hale.

I flinched jerked my gaze from the window of her apartment and the movement behind the glass. I hated that he was up there, hated how he could touch her things. Even Fin's Anna didn't like him, and she was the kind of person who liked *everyone*. The corner of my mouth twitched as I fixed on the brother at my side.

"Let's get back. Yeah?"

He waited for me to nod and follow, and I did, because I was desperate to do the unthinkable. I wanted to charge up there, shove my gun in his face and...*and...kill him*. Kill him because he stood in my way. Kill him because I saw it in every gleam of his fucking eyes. He'd taken a piece of her, carried it with him like it was wrapped in a handkerchief and tucked into his pocket.

I didn't know what he had of hers. I prayed it wasn't her heart. Because *that*, for me, was unthinkable. That was beyond anything I could fathom. I didn't want to live in a world where she didn't love me. I didn't want to live in a world where her entire existence wasn't narrowed down to the exact moment our worlds collided.

I swallowed a shudder, shoved my fists into my pockets and walked, following Logan as we headed back. Logan's phone made a *beep* and he lifted it instantly, pressing the button. "Benj."

Dad...

The sound of his name made my pulse react. I craned my head, listening to every word, every snatch of information. I thought he'd been silent, thought he didn't care. But I was wrong. He'd been calling in every man he could, banging on doors with the Mauritian police, even waking Jugnauth, the damn Prime Minister, and dragging him out of bed, in the hopes we could tread where others couldn't.

Others being Hale.

"I get it," Logan muttered, and gave a deep sigh. "Yeah, thanks, Benj, for trying. Yeah, he's here..." Logan glanced my way.

I shook my head. There was no way I wanted to talk to him. No way I wanted to hear that desperation in his voice, the one that said the unthinkable, *that she was gone...just like that.* Gone.

"Talk to him," Logan demanded, as he shoved the phone my way. "He's your father, Laz."

I jerked my gaze to his, fighting that bark of rage inside me. I *know* he's my goddamn father...

I stared at the cell, then took it. "I'm here." The hoarse voice sounded nothing like mine.

"How are you holding up?"

"Fueled by rage and desperation," I answered.

"Good. Sometimes that's all you have in your arsenal...but just know this, son, you can't live like that forever. Sooner or later, everything catches up with you."

I clenched my jaw, but still my lip curled.

He was wrong.

I could live forever like this.

Bloodthirsty. Immortal. *Violent.*

"You're scaring me, Laz," Dad murmured.

That fanged serpent inside slithered under my skin. I could feel her working her way to the surface, evolving me...*changing me.* "I'm scaring me, too."

The empty words were all I had to offer. I handed the phone back to Logan and strode ahead, making my way to my building, listening to Logan as he muttered a few words of comfort and hung up.

Bright lights in the foyer were blinding, making me squint and look away. I couldn't remember the last time I'd slept...the last time I'd wanted to sleep. Food was shoved into my hand, but I couldn't force myself to eat. The taste of coffee struck my lips. That's all I had now, the adrenaline...the rush.

I refused to function without her.

Refused to know what peace was.

Refused the idea of any type of existence where there was anything other than torment without her.

I swallowed hard and punched the button for the elevator, then stepped inside as the doors opened, and Logan followed. I stared at the shimmering steel walls. "He couldn't find a way to get us in, could he?"

"They don't like outsiders, especially outsiders who want a piece of their investigation."

I jerked my gaze to his, that fire burning inside me. "But they're *not* investigating."

He just nodded. "It's how they work."

I clenched my jaw. We'd gone to the Mauritian police and handed over everything we knew. We'd begged them to let us assist. But the moment they knew who Kat really was, they'd clammed up, refusing our calls, ignoring our pleas. I clenched my fists. Word was, Hale was all over them, whispering in their ears, forcing us out into the damn cold.

Then congratulations are in order, it looks like I'm about to be a father...

A father.

Jesus, Kat...why?

The elevator stopped and the doors opened as the word resounded in my head. I stepped out into a flurry of voices as Logan's phone *beeped* once more.

"What have you got?" His command was instant.

It was the same words I'd heard a hundred times, words that repeated in my head when I closed my eyes, fighting for snatches of sleep. For the first hundred times, I'd gotten my hopes up. But not now, after call after call of no word as Logan's team made their way through the many fucking islands.

"Where?"

My steps faltered as Finley lifted his gaze from the table that was our command center. Maps were spread across the table, markers of islands and the picture of the boat and details.

"A shoe?" Logan added. My heart leaped with the word. I spun, searching the brother's gaze as he just nodded. "Hold tight. Don't...don't give *anyone* this information. Not until we get there."

He hung up the phone and lifted his gaze to mine.

And I knew...I. Just. Knew...

We found her.

"Go," Fin whispered as Logan's phone rang once more.

"It's Hale." Logan scowled at the screen. "How the fuck does that bastard know?"

"I don't like him." Fin strode toward me. "Don't ask me what it is, but he makes my skin crawl." He took one look at the ringing phone in Logan's hand and met my gaze. "Go, find her. I'll hold him off for as long as I can. But Laz...don't come back here. Run and keep on running. A man like that...he won't let her go."

I swallowed hard, my thoughts frantic, colliding with my need. A nod and I turned, finding Logan's hard stare.

"Let's go find her," he growled.

It was all the words I needed.

⸻

I GRIPPED the side of the boat as we rose with the wave, then crashed back down. My teeth gnashed together with the impact. The salty spray stung my eyes. Still, I stared into those dark murky waters as the sun rose in the distance, casting vibrant red and yellow across my world.

"How much longer?" I jerked my gaze to Logan's as he sat behind the wheel.

He looked at the compass and the map, navigating with the boat's system, before he nodded toward the lightening horizon. "Should be coming up any minute."

We'd been driving for an hour, hitting every fucking wave at speed. And as Logan slowed, turning the boat hard, I realized how long I'd been almost holding my breath, how that humming tension inside me was actually a scream. And with one harsh exhale, I heard that shrill sound, the one that coiled and unleashed, striking harder and harder with wicked fangs.

Out of the shadows came a man striding toward an old dock, holding a semi-automatic across his chest, looking like the badass Logan was. It was his man, it had to be.

"Ice," Logan called to the mercenary as he throttled the engine down, then killed it with a twist of the key.

The speedboat coasted sideways before hitting the pylons with a *thud*. Logan tossed him the rope, but I was already climbing out, with Freddy at my back.

"Where is it?" I growled.

The guy glanced at me, then Logan as he bent and secured the boat with a yank. "This way." He motioned with his head.

I glanced at the land and all I saw was a curtain. A blanket of mammoth willows, obscuring anything else. But it was those willows he strode toward. Leaves brushed my shoulders and my head like the soft caress of a lover. But it just made me shiver, and sent goosebumps along my skin.

A small cabin appeared out of nowhere, decrepit and dark. The smell of wet wood assaulted me as I came closer, climbing rickety old steps.

"We tracked movement of two men as they came to the island about a month ago," Ice disclosed, hanging back.

"A month ago?" Logan repeated, and glanced my way.

Memories were scattered in my mind. One of them important, slipping through my fingers as I tried to grasp it. Then it was gone as I stepped into that old, dank cabin and looked down.

There it was...

One small, black slip-on shoe.

The same shoe she'd worn that morning, the one that matched the dress still crumpled in the corner of my bathroom on the island. I took a step closer, my heart punching like a fist against my ribs. I hurt there, hurt like I'd been beaten by a hundred different men, hurt more than I thought I could ever hurt as I crouched and picked it up.

"Tire marks out front said it was a new car, thick, heavy tread, four-wheel drive, at least. The guys are working on those in the area, seeing what information we can shake loose."

"It's them, isn't it?" I glanced at Logan. "The two men from the picture, they're the ones who took her."

He just nodded. My hand shook as I gripped her shoe.

Two men like that. What they'd do to a woman like Kat.

"If they've been here a month, scouting out the place, then they're professionals."

Professionals.

Men who knew it wasn't about her.

Men who were focused on the outcome.

And not a piece of pussy they could take at whim. I held onto that as headlights cut across the darkness outside and the earpiece of our guy crackled. "Looks like we've got company," Ice muttered.

Car doors slammed outside before the crunch of boots on the ground sounded. Against the shining headlights pouring into the doorway behind me, came Hale.

Savage rage made his dark eyes appear like midnight pools. He scanned the room, finding Freddy, Logan, Ice...then me. He said nothing as he lowered his gaze to the shoe in my hand. But there was a flare of his jaw muscles before he met my gaze. "When were you going to tell me about this?"

When was I going to tell him?

How about never...does that work for you, motherfucker? I fought the urge to smirk. "When I had something to tell."

He strode toward me and snatched the shoe from my hand.

I never wanted to beat a man into oblivion as much as I wanted to beat him for that shoe, that lone fucking shoe. The last trace of her I had. Until a thought hit me. How the fuck did he find out? "You had us tracked."

The slow smile was chilling. "At least now we know exactly where we stand."

He trusted me about as much as I trusted him.

A low hum stole his attention. He reached into his pocket and snatched a cell phone free in the blink of an eye. "Hale," he barked. Like his name wasn't an answer, but a weapon. One he wielded like a blade. "Are you sure? France. Yes, have it ready immediately. I'm on my way."

He ended the call and with a smugness that sparkled like stars in his eyes, he murmured, "She's on a cargo plane that headed to France in the early hours of this morning."

France? Why the fuck was she taken to France?

"Give up, son." Hale murmured, his voice soft and full of sympathy. "I'll take it from here."

Then he was gone, striding back through the doorway, his boots crunching on the dirt outside. It wasn't until the car door thudded and the four-wheel drive had pulled away, that I realized he'd taken her shoe with him.

Just like that, he came, took, and left.

"I'm going to fucking kill him." The words slipped free, hate-filled and hollow. "Hale is mine."

I strode out of the cabin and into the night as Logan talked into the two-way, making his way toward an old Jeep. It hit me then, how Hale and I were worlds apart. I had money, more money than I could spend in a lifetime. But he *was* money, just like Kat was money. Real money, the kind that sets you apart from everyone else. The kind of money where even the mere mention of your name opened doors.

The only thing the Rossi name opened...was a case full of guns.

We climbed onto the old four-wheel drive, with Ice behind the wheel. The engine started and the wheels spun. We were moving as Logan relayed the information. "Looks like a small hangar, an hour south of here."

Ice gunned the engine as we tore along the dirt road, kicking up plumes of dust in our wake.

The further we drove, the lighter it grew outside. Darkened hues turned to vibrant color and, by the time the sight of a tall fence surrounding the small steel warehouse rose in the distance, we knew we were in trouble.

Hale was already in the air. His private jet had been waiting thirty minutes west of here. He'd driven straight there, not even bothering to check out the warehouse surrounded by warning signs.

He'd get to her first. I just knew it.

This game of cat and mouse was making me feel unraveled. I was becoming someone else now.

Someone dangerous.

49

Kat

The blare of horns was so close, so close I could glance over my shoulder and see the steady flow of traffic. So close I could see others hunched behind their steering wheels, their gazes fixed on the road ahead. And yet they may as well have been a million miles away.

"Walk," my captor warned, pressing against my side as he drove his fingers into my arm, bruising me even more.

So close and yet futile.

The *crack* of the gunshot, and the sight of all that blood slowly spilling along the asphalt were the things that kept me from trying to run. I didn't have to look into my abductor's eyes to know they'd shoot me. They'd shoot me and they'd run. How many women were killed just like that in Paris? How many were nothing more than fleeting reports on the evening news? I knew in my heart, one wrong move and that'd be me. Not even my name could save me.

I'd been separated from the other women, pushed toward a dark blue van while the others were ordered toward a waiting truck. The woman who'd sat next to me looked over her shoulder and back at me. There was real fear in her eyes as she found mine, palpable, beast-like fear. But then I was torn away and hauled into the van before we sped away.

I sat in the van, legs crossed, hands still clasped in front of me, surrounded by three men in the back and two in the front, one of them the young guy from the plane. The plastic binds cut deep when I moved, leaving a trail of blood to slide down the meat of my palm and along my thumb. But even with all that... it could be worse.

I could be dead.

I reminded myself of that as I stumbled toward some derelict building. The place was dirty and forgotten, splattered with vibrant colors of graffiti. I knew we were somewhere in the projects outside Paris. Somewhere that two men crowding around a woman as they ushered her forward wasn't cause for intervention. I lifted my head as they pushed me toward a looming eight-foot brick fence and through a gate.

Hinges howled before it was locked behind me. The building was big, four stories. It looked like it was once an apartment building, no doubt marked for demolition. But that could've been years go. Now it was overrun with weeds and spray paint.

"Up," the male at my back commanded.

I climbed, steadied by his hand around my arm. My bare feet were numb from the cold, so much colder here than the island. The railings were rusted and, as I scanned the levels above, I found some parts where the steel barrier had fallen away completely, probably into the thick, weed-choked garden below.

It could've been lovely, could've been filled with families and young couples with happy dogs that adored the cobbled courtyard and green parks in the distance. But instead, it was filled with hell. Hell that waited for me as I was driven up to the first floor, then further. My thighs ached, my feet stung. The agony from my captor's fists radiated around to the small of my back.

I felt every stare as I walked. Movement came from the corner of my eye as three more men stood at the railing, watching me.

"Over there," the male at my back ordered, his English thick with his French accent.

I looked at the men waiting for me outside an open doorway. They were massive, dressed in combat gear, their gazes cold and unflinching, mercenaries to the core. They looked even bigger than Logan, more lethal, too.

I swallowed hard and stepped through the open door, coming into some old apartment barely furnished, with three wooden chairs and a small TV on a stand. I glimpsed a kitchen through the empty space that was meant for a family room, and further along the hall it looked like the open doors of two bedrooms. I sucked in a breath, listening to heavy footsteps following me inside. "What are you going to do with me now?"

There was no answer, just that weighted feeling of their stares, until the young guy from the plane stepped close. "Bathroom down the hall. Go," he gently shoved me forward.

I glanced at the others watching me and hurried forward. *Jesus... Jesus...Jesus...*I scanned the open doors, found a glimpse of ugly green tiles, and rushed to step inside the bathroom and close the door. Voices drifted in, words heavy in French were spoken in a rush. I leaned against the doorway and closed my eyes.

This was bad...*really bad.*

My mind raced, desperate to find a way out of this and as always, my thoughts drifted to Lazarus. My senses tilted. The room swayed. Desperation moved through me like a summer squall, fast, terrifying...*consuming.* Blue eyes pierced the void. My body thrummed with the ache for him, to feel his hands on my body and hear that husky growl in my ear. I'd never wanted another to hold me as much as I did now.

A sob wedged into the back of my throat, pulsing and aching, desperate to get out.

But the heavy thud of approaching footsteps wrenched me free. I stumbled backwards, scanned the room, and settled on the filthy toilet. The bowl was black, the seat shattered, the edges sharp. Revulsion moved through me as my bladder unleashed a pang of pain. My stomach clenched at the thought of using *that.* As the pang of pain turned into agony, I knew I had no choice.

"*Hey!*" A hard *thud* came on the other side of the door.

"Just a minute!" I snapped, and swallowed my revulsion, turning my back to the filthy sight and, with my bound hands, I pushed my pants low.

I hovered, thighs trembling, and focused on my body and not the man armed with a gun on the other side of the door. Fire ripped through me, the sting making me clench my teeth as a tiny dribble spilled free. There wasn't enough. Two days of a couple of bottles of water and a piece of fruit. My body was shutting down.

The toilet paper holder was empty, a filthy rag sat on the floor near a dripping sink. There was no way in *hell* that was going anywhere *near* my body. So I reached between my legs and swiped my hand along my crease, taking the moisture with me, then pulled up my pants before turning and stabbing the button.

The cistern let out a groan, a trickle of water dribbled into the bowl. I turned away and took a step toward the sink, hitting the faucet, and finding nothing. *Drip...drip...drip...*that was all I got. I lowered my head, my shoulders sagging as I held my hand under the dribble as tears came.

"Hey...now!" the mercenary barked.

Tears slipped free as I rubbed my hand with as much water as I could, and turned. I didn't care who saw me cry now, didn't care about holding back my tears, didn't care what the world saw. There were no paparazzi waiting for me on the other side of the door, just guns and greed.

I twisted and yanked the door open, finding cold scrutiny on the other side.

"Move," I snarled, and stepped forward, pushing past him as I went through the doorway.

He just grabbed my arm and shoved. Ache on top of ache. There was no end to the hurting as I was driven toward the wooden chairs.

"Sit," my captor barked, stabbing his finger toward a chair.

But I stopped before obeying and instead, I stared into that empty gaze. "I need water and I need food."

He just curled his body, moving close as he growled, "*Sit.*"

I swallowed hard. *No,* that voice inside me urged. *Fuck them.*

But it was that tremble deep in my belly that made me take a step backward, that life that was growing inside me, needing me to pick my battles. It was for that life that my knees buckled and I sank to the seat. They moved around me, talking amongst themselves. All except for one.

The young guy from the plane.

He just watched me with sad eyes.

That sent a tremor of hope soaring to the surface inside me.

And while the tide shifted as a number of the men walked out the door, their heavy steps, he remained behind, watching me.

"*Hey!*" one of the others barked, taking a step forward to swat the young guy across the back of the head.

He ducked, then jerked his gaze toward the older male, answering in French. But the bully just watched me with the kind of savagery that made me lower my gaze.

An icy breeze seemed to find its way into the apartment and slither along my skin. They moved away, leaving me alone in the middle of the room. I sat, shifting on the hard seat, as the door opened and closed and armed men came and went. I lost track of how many there were and how many times they came in to glare at me and snap orders in French to the young male. But I knew this had moved beyond a kidnapping and ransom... well beyond. And as the bright morning sun spilled in from the front window and softened to the dimmer afternoon, I knew time was running out for me.

"Here."

I lifted my head and found the soft brown eyes of my younger captor as he handed me a bottle of water and a sandwich wrapped in plastic. My stomach clenched at the sight and my mouth watered. But I just looked into his gaze, searching it for a flicker of compassion and whispered, "Why?"

"Why?" He glanced at the food in his hand. "Why a sandwich?"

"Why be nice to me?"

There was a moment of confusion before he glanced at the door and the rest of the room. We were alone, so he moved closer. "Because I don't like this at all."

Hope flared. But it was a desperate hope, a *hungry* hope. "Then let me go."

"You know I can't do that," he whispered, and glanced around the room once more. "They'd kill me."

"Boo-fucking-hoo," I growled, and shoved to stand. My knees trembled as the blood rushed to my feet. "I've been kidnapped and beaten. I've been forced into a boat, into a four-wheel drive, into a plane and a fucking van at gunpoint. I've been starved, had no water and *no fucking explanation as to what's going on,* and now you..." I glanced at his hand as rage continued to bubble up to the surface. "You hand me a fucking sandwich and think you're doing me a favor?"

"It's peanut butter," he answered meekly.

Rage lashed deep inside me, making me curl my lips and bare my teeth. "Let. Me. Go."

He winced, his mouth twisting as he glanced toward the doorway once more. "These men...these men are dangerous, trained. They'll shoot me, then you, before we got more than a step out of here."

"There has to be another way." I scanned the hallway. "A back door...*something.*"

He just shook his head. "It's locked and I don't have the key."

"Then get me a weapon," I whispered. "I'll take care of the rest myself."

He came close, so close the knuckles of his hand that gripped the sandwich brushed my belly. "I do that and you're dead for sure. All I know is, they're in negotiations with someone called Hale."

Hale...

Fear gripped me. But underneath that, beneath the dark, revolting terror, was a spark of hope. Hope I'd get out of here... hope he'd make sure I was safe, *even if I was negotiating one hell for another.* My breaths came faster now, tearing from my chest. One hell for another, that's what this was.

I saw it now. He'd roll up in his black limousine and the door would open. I'd be forced in there, taking a seat opposite him, in silence. I'd become aware of every breath from him, every glance, every sigh, every shift of his body against the plush leather seats. My life would end then.

End in the back of his car.

I'd become a shell. A body...*a currency.*

Forever.

"No." The word slipped free. I jerked my gaze to my captor. "I'd rather take my chances with a weapon."

Footsteps boomed outside the door. My captor jumped backwards, his panicked gaze shifting to the door as it opened and one of the mercenaries strode through.

"Food," the young captor barked, and shoved the sandwich into my hand, then the water. "Eat, *drink*."

I had no choice but to take the sandwich and stumble back to the seat, wincing as I sat once more. The mercenary glared at me as he came through the door. Orders were given in French, and a jerk of his head my way told me all I needed to know.

Hale was coming.

Like a fucking silent tornado, I wouldn't hear him coming, but he'd leave desolation in his wake.

My hands shook, clenching around the water.

That flutter in my belly grew stronger now, drawing my focus. That life urging me to consider the unthinkable. The only thought that had driven me to the kitchen on that first night, to consider taking my life. The one thought that chilled me to the bone.

What if I had a daughter?

My father. Hale. All the men that came for me would come for her.

That I couldn't allow.

That I wouldn't allow.

Heavy steps echoed, slipping away from me as the mercenary headed down the hall until the *thud* of the bathroom door echoed. The bottle of water slipped from my hand and hit the floor with a *bang*. I was already driving to my feet, already shifting my focus to the front door, already taking a step.

It didn't matter what waited outside that door for me.

It couldn't be any worse than my own private hell.

I crossed the floor in an instant, gripped the handle, and pulled.

"What the fuck are you doing?" the young captor hissed behind me.

But he was too late. The vibrant splash of color from the evening sky assaulted me. I squinted into the glare and took a step outside. A dark blur of movement came at the far end of the landing as one of the mercenaries stood guard, his gun at his side.

I jerked my gaze from him, finding the entrance to the stairs. My heart drove into the back of my throat as I took a step. Everything inside me was screaming *run...run...RUN*.

I lunged, driving my body through the air, until an arm wrapped around my chest, and a savage snarl echoed in my ear, *"Where the fuck do you think you're going?"*

50

Lazarus

The jet bounced and surged, piloted by Ice, who stabbed every button and fiddled with every damn control, muttering under his breath. The former SEAL could fly pretty much anything, only this wasn't his plane and the old jet had seen better days. But it was the only one we could find at a moment's notice...

Commandeer, anyway.

Where money didn't speak a gun in the face got the message across loud and clear.

The asshole in the hangar was lucky I was desperate enough to leave him alive.

And as we approached a private airstrip outside Paris, Logan's phone rang. He answered it with a bark as I sat across from him, gripping the armrest while the jet shuddered and shook, dipping lower in a steep descent.

I closed my eyes until Logan hung up the phone and spoke. "We got them...one of them, at least." Then I wrenched open my eyes, meeting his. "Where?"

"A hangar twenty minutes away. My men are bringing him to us."

I jerked my gaze toward the cockpit. "Logan..."

"Hold on, buddy," he said carefully. "We're going as fast as we can."

But it wasn't fast enough...

It wasn't anywhere near fast enough.

And this time when the plane dipped, I welcomed the panic, swallowing it down instead. I'd drop us from the sky if I thought I could save her and we wouldn't all die. So I focused on the thrumming in my head as we dipped lower and lower still.

Twenty minutes...

It may as well be a lifetime.

By the time the wheels touched down, I was clawing the buckle on my seatbelt. Logan was a heartbeat behind me as Ice swung the nose toward the small hangar used by former US military. I didn't ask anymore, didn't want to know. Whatever we needed, it happened. Only it wasn't fast enough.

My brother's phone rang again, only this time when he answered, it was with a curt, "Logan." Silence as the plane jerked and slowed. "I see...yeah, thanks."

I turned, meeting the wince in his gaze. "Hale's heading into the city, word is he's made contact with whoever has her."

Made contact...

"That means—" Logan started.

"I *know* what it means," I growled and stood, gripping the handle of the door and yanking. It meant Hale was about to ride in like a fucking knight in shining armor and take what was mine. And when he did...I'd never see her again.

The steel door shuddered and shook before flying open. I shoved the steel stairs forward as the plane jerked to a halt. Night waited for me. But it was a new night...fresh, cold, *biting*. The wind cut through my t-shirt, chilling me to my bones. The engines roared as I stepped out, scanning the larger hangar, finding a towering male with arms crossed over his chest waiting for us in the murky light that spilled from inside.

My hair scattered as I strode forward and reached out my hand. But it wasn't in greeting. Steel slapped my palm before I shoved the Glock into the waistband of my jeans and pulled out my shirt. I wanted no warmth, no kindness. I wanted not a second wasted. "Where is he?" I met his gaze.

He glanced to Logan, then answered. "Inside...but I gotta warn you..."

No, he didn't. I strode forward, leaving his warning behind. Every gaze bore down on me as I focused on the wide-open door of the hangar. The engine of the jet wound down, leaving my ears humming in the silence. The harsh yellow light barely reached the walls. Inside, I saw a single-engine plane, a four-wheeler ATV, and a black Range Rover with the rear door still open.

"Fuck you!"

The roar ripped through the space, drawing me to the guy strapped to the chair. He was big...bigger than Logan, not quite as big as the mountain outside. But his thick muscles bulged as he gripped the armrests with massive hands, hands that'd wrap easily around my throat. Veins popped out of his arms. This was a man who spent every waking minute he had in the gym, or training.

Highly skilled. A tough one to crack.

I stepped ahead, catching sight of the other beast of a male who'd captured him. He just smiled at the guy, calm, relaxed. These Special Forces were a breed unto themselves.

"And who the fuck are you?" the beefcake roared as he set his gaze on mine.

"The redhead." My voice was husky, strange and detached. "Where did they take her?"

"Back to my place." He grinned, eyes wide with rage. "Where I'm gonna fuck her."

A nerve twitched in the corner of my eye as I reached around and palmed the weapon. "I'm going to ask you one last time. Be very careful how you answer."

"Laz," Logan warned.

But I was past listening, past caring, past any savage boundary I'd ever had.

A serpent lived under my skin.

Black, *gleaming*. I felt the smoothness of its scales, and the flicker of its forked tongue. It scented him now, tasted his fear that tainted the air and as I took a step closer, I saw the flare of surprise in the asshole's eyes. "Where...did...they...take...her?"

His breath caught. Eyes widened. I drew the Glock out from behind me.

"G-Gare du Nord," he whispered.

"Where?" I murmured, lifting the gun.

"Breguet—"

Bang! I pulled the trigger, watching his head fly backwards. Blood splatter misted in the air as I turned to the towering former solider. "How long?"

"Twenty min—" he started, staring at the dead man.

"You've got ten." I strode toward the open doors of the four-wheel drive.

They said nothing as they climbed in around me. Not Logan, not Freddy nor Ice as he climbed into the passenger's seat, leaving our contact to slide into the driver's seat.

They watched me like I was a stranger. Maybe I was...I glanced out the window as the engine gunned and we shot forward. Lights twinkled in the distance. And even as they grew closer, I knew it wasn't fast enough.

We'd never make it.

Not in time to save her from those who'd abducted her.

Or Hale.

51

Kat

"*Let me go!*" I screamed, until the heavy hand clamped around my mouth.

I kicked and bucked, clawing like a wildcat, and tried to breathe. But the hold over my face smashed my lips against my teeth, smothering my nose.

My ribs couldn't move, lungs held tight. The howl for air was desperate inside me as the stairs blurred.

"*Enough!*" my captor roared, dragging me backwards.

No...NO! The glint of headlights in the distance drove me harder. Salvation was just a glimpse away. I opened my mouth until the edges of my lips burned, then *bit. My* teeth sank into soft flesh, carving deep, until the fetid, metallic tang of blood bloomed in my mouth.

The howl was instant. Deafening.

Movement came from the corner of my eye before my head cracked to the side. Agony detonated, ripping through my skull. Stars were all I saw. White, hot...*blinding*.

"You *fucking* bitch!" he roared, wrenching me around to face him.

Pitiless dark eyes met mine as his hand slipped from my mouth and grasped my neck. His fingers clenched tight, driving the *boom...boom...boom* of my pulse through my head. I slapped and fought, pushing through the blinding pain to lash out with my bare feet. But there was no stopping his wrath. There was no stopping his strength.

His fist came again, driving into my temple. *Crack!* I was dazed, stunned. My hands dropped from his arms. It was all he needed, all he cared about, and like a predator with his fangs deep into his prey, he dragged me to the door. Until that fire exploded inside me like an inferno.

My fingers twitched, my hands rose, gripping the doorframe as we passed. *"NO! LET ME GO!"*

His fist drove into my side. Pain lashed, finding that deep, already bruised agony, a remnant of previous fists and rage.

"I will *fucking kill you!*" my captor screamed into my face.

He spun, tearing my hold free, and slammed me backwards.

My head impacted with the wall with a *thud!* Then I was thrown. Air slapped my face, before I hit the wooden chair, knocking it over, and crashed to the ground. Pain exploded through my mouth as my face collided with the floor.

"I'll fucking kill you..."

Darkness came for me, striding across the space as the front door slammed shut. I twisted, lifting one hand toward him, and wrapped the other around my belly. But it was all too late as he wrenched his foot backwards and drove it through the air.

My knuckles crunched under the steel of his boot as agony exploded through my belly.

It was all I knew in that moment, all that consumed me.

The desperate need to protect made me curl my spine and hug my belly. But he didn't care as, incensed with barbaric hunger, he drove his boot in again...and again...*and again*. Darkness swam in my vision as something inside me went *crunch*. Black ate away at the edges of my world, leaving the glimpses of light to swim. Fresh agony moved through me, carving like a knife.

Until the blows ended.

And screams moved into my world.

52

Lazarus

We weren't going to make it...

Streetlights swept by in a blur.

Faces from the crowds melted into nothing.

And that serpent inside me coiled, lifting its head to stare at me with yellow eyes.

I gripped my gun until the patterned grip embedded into my flesh. And as the sparkling lights of Paris's seedy underbelly rose in the distance, Logan's phone rang once more.

"Yeah..." he answered. "*What?* What do you mean he's not moving? Okay...okay. Fuck, I'll let him know."

My brother's savage gaze met mine in the sideview mirror of the four-wheel drive as he ended the call. He watched me...*they all watched me.*

"Hale hasn't gone in." My gut clenched in hope. "He's waiting for reinforcements."

And that savagery in me hissed, baring its fangs.

"He's waiting for reinforcements?" I repeated as the sound of sirens echoed in the distance.

"Seems like he doesn't trust them, he's out front with his driver."

I clenched my hold around my rage and cut my gaze to the driver, who punched the accelerator even harder, driving me against the back of the seat. "Eight minutes," the enforcer announced, glancing at the GPS in front of him.

My hand was already on the handle as we braked, tires skidding, as we cut tight around a corner, mounting the curb hard, then hit bounced back against the asphalt. He was out front... and we were going in the back.

"Faster!" I roared.

Hale was waiting outside the building where Kat was being held captive...too precious to risk creasing his fucking suit. I wanted nothing more than to wear my goddamn ruin. *I craved the feel of blood...*

They were *all* my enemies this night.

All standing in my fucking way.

Unable to hold back a second longer, I yanked the handle as we cut around another corner. The door swung open and then thudded closed.

"Through that lane. *Stealth, yeah?"* Ice growled and jerked his gaze toward mine as he cut the engine, slamming us to a stop. *"Leash him!"* the mercenary growled to Logan as I yanked the handle and shoved the door wide. "Before he lets the entire fucking city know we're here."

I just smiled and lunged, driving my body through the darkness. There was no leashing me, not anymore. I was finally free. Free to become what I was created for. *Nothing more than Stidda scum.*

Savage.

Barbaric.

A brutal street thug.

And as I charged toward the darkened lane at the end of the street, the thunder of my boots mingled with my pulse. All I saw was her. Those sad fucking eyes that punctured my soul. That perfect goddamn mouth, lips that wrecked me.

Lazarus...

She whispered inside my head.

I lifted my gaze, fixed in the darkness as Logan met my stride. We were too loud, too slow...*too fucking everything.*

"There." Logan jerked his gaze toward a towering brick fence that surrounded the complex.

Movement came from my left, stepping out of the shadows. White eyes, dressed in black. The glint of steel shone in the moonlight.

Pfftt. Ice fired and charged as the guy fell. He jerked his gaze to mine, then lowered it to the gun in my hand, a gun without a silencer, and held his finger to his lips. *Shh...*

I got the fucking hint. I slipped my gun into the waistband of my jeans and stopped at the fence. Ice and Logan were up and over in an instant. Freddy stopped next to me as I ground my teeth, took a step backwards, then ran and lunged.

Air hit my face as I swung my feet, sliding over the top.

Pfftt.

Pfftt.

Shots came ahead of us. I couldn't fire my gun, not without drawing attention. But as one of the armed bastards stepped out, Ice heading one way around the compound and Logan the other, he was all mine. That venomous side of my nature struck.

I wrenched back my fist and drove it into the fucker's face. He was bigger than me, heavier too. But I had rage on my side. I was already wretched, already damned, and as I took him down to the ground, unleashing that serpent with bestial blows, I lost myself in the movement.

All I saw was Hale.

Crunch.

Crunch.

Crun—

"Laz," Freddy called my name as he sucked in hard breaths, staring at the mess under me.

Deja vu hit me like a truck. I was back here, back to the beast, back to the rage, and I didn't care. Instead, I welcomed it. The guy's head fell to the side. His face was smashed in, eyes bulging from the sockets as blood spilled along the concrete under me.

I shoved to a stand, my knuckles bloody, breaths hard. I just lunged, driving my body forward, as a scream cut through the night. A woman's scream. Piercing. *Like a knife through my fucking heart.*

It was Kat...

Stairs appeared in front of me. I lunged, grasped the railing, and climbed as two more men came from below. I jerked my gaze from them to Freddy as he lifted his gun and met my gaze. "Go...find her."

The *crack* of a gunshot rang out. Freddy ducked before unleashing a fury of return gunfire.

I leaped, driving my body higher and higher, climbing as that shattering cry ended, leaving an empty silence behind. They were hurting her...*terrorizing her.*

Crack!

Crack!

The night was filled with the bark of guns. I climbed to the first level and ran toward where the sound had come from, pulling my gun out.

Boom!

A window shattered just in front of me. I spun, lifting my gun, as shadows rushed toward me. They seemed to come out of nowhere, spilling from darkened doorways to step into my path. *Boom!* A shot hit the steel railing as I took aim and pulled the trigger.

Boom!

Boom.

Boom.

The gun buckled against the webbing of my hand as I charged forward, firing. I hit once, then wide, unleashing my rage as her cries came once more, only this time *above me.*

"Fuck!"

I roared and spun, finding one of those fuckers rushing me. He hit me like a fucking truck. Arms like steel cables wrapped around me and drove me against the wall. But I was already pulling the trigger and screaming into the fucker's face.

Boom! The sound was muffled between our bodies. *Boom!* Flashes of gunfire detonated around me as I pushed him backwards and he dropped. A cough from the asshole under me splattered blood across my cheek. All I heard was her cries as I lifted the gun and pulled the trigger. *Boom.*

I was shut down, cold...brutal. I fired until I couldn't feel the kick in my hand, then stopped pulling the trigger. I didn't know how many shots I had left...and I didn't care.

I stepped away and raced for the stairs, taking three at a time as the savage wet sounds of fists on flesh came from below me. Fights and battles raged all around me, and still that driving desperation was howling with through me as I stopped climbing and raced forward.

The taste of blood filled my mouth as I breathed in. The warm slick across my face turned cold as I ran forward. I knew I must look like an animal. One look at me and I'd terrify her. But one look from her, and that was all I needed.

I only wanted to know she was safe.

Wanted to know *I* was the one to protect her.

To avenge her.

To give her freedom.

A light was on inside an apartment up ahead, softly spilling through the window. A woman's moan came from inside, low, tortured, *filled with agony.*

That sound shattered something inside me.

The last fragile hold on the man I once was.

I was beyond that now, so far removed from anything that felt alive. I was cold now, cold, empty, *slithering*. I gripped the door handle and twisted, stepped inside the derelict apartment, and stopped.

She was strapped to a chair, bloody and beaten. Her face was a fucking mess, her long red hair spilled across her face as her head rolled. "Kat?" I whispered her name, but my voice was guttural and strange.

She blinked, then closed her eyes, unable to look at me.

They took her.

They hurt her.

They fucking beat her...

"D-don't fucking m-move."

I just stood there as some young punk stepped out of the kitchen, wielding a fucking knife. He took one look at her, and then fixed those wide eyes on me before muttering with a heavy French accent, "I...I didn't do this...*I didn't do this to her.*"

I screamed my rage, unable to stop myself any longer, and charged.

I hit him hard. Agony slashed across my side. I remembered the knife. But I didn't care and didn't hesitate, lifting my gun and smashed it into the fucker's face. He dodged the blow, throwing his head forward to smash into my face. Agony roared through me, intense and wretched. Stunned, he drove me backwards across the room until we tripped.

The gun flew out of my hand as we hit the floor. But I just grasped at the agony in my side, finding the blade plunged deep. The asshole looked down, his eyes widening in horror. I gripped the hilt and wrenched the knife free. It tore from me slick and smooth and, as I lifted the blade, the asshole above me screamed.

I plunged the knife deep, striking like my own set of fangs, and buried the blade into the side of his neck. Blood spurted, smacking me in the face. His eyes widened in shock. But he was done now...

"Laz?"

The sound of my name on her lips drew my gaze.

She stared at me, her brow creased down the middle as though she thought she was dreaming. Movement from deeper in the house drew her focus. She stiffened and paled as terror crossed her face. Her swollen, bloodied lips parted as a big bastard stepped out of the hallway and settled his savage gaze on me.

He looked at my gun lying on the floor, just out of my reach, and smiled.

Time moved slowly as he lifted the gun, and took aim.

"*Lazarus!*" she screamed.

All I heard was that scream.

And knew in my heart it was the last sound I'd hear...*forever.*

53

Kat

"*No!*" I screamed as the piece of shit that had beaten me took aim.

All I saw was Lazarus dying...all I saw was my life over. I shoved forward, stumbling with my hands tied to the back of the chair, as a shadow burst through the door of the apartment. Logan was a blur, sweeping his gun through the room and firing.

Bang...

A single shot was all it took.

Blood bloomed in the center of the bastard's forehead before he buckled. My knees went with him, sending me crashing to the floor.

"Kat?" Lazarus's voice was devoid of emotion.

Still, he called my name. And that was all I'd prayed for, just to hear him once more.

"Laz," Logan growled from the doorway. "We have to go."

Lazarus bent, grasped the blade embedded in the young guy's neck, and yanked it free. I blinked as the room spun. Agony was a fist in my belly. I tried to breathe through the pain as it clenched and clenched. I couldn't help but flinch as Lazarus took a step toward me with the knife in his hand.

He stopped for a second, then picked up his gun and hurried toward me. "Easy," he murmured. "I'm here now."

Tears slipped from my eyes as he sawed at my bonds. My arms screamed with agony as they burst free. I slipped, falling to the side, before he caught me. The knife clattered to the floor as he slipped one arm behind my back and slid the other under my knees, lifting me.

The smear of blood between my thighs was neon bright under the murky lights. I whimpered at the sight as Lazarus pulled me closer until he froze. Blood marred the gray sweatpants that were once his. He scowled, unable to understand, as agony rocked me.

"The baby," I whimpered.

He jerked his gaze to mine, darkness waiting there. Confusion. Pain...and it was all my fault. But then we were moving. I wound my arms around his neck and clung tight as we stepped through the doorway and out into the cold.

"This way," Logan directed.

Time slipped from me as darkness closed in. My teeth chattered, even though I wasn't cold. I wasn't anything. Just empty. Hollow and empty as Lazarus carried me down the stairs and hurried around the back.

"Give her to me," Logan commanded.

My hold tightened around his neck at the same time as his did around my waist.

"You want Hale to see her?" Logan warned.

I lifted my gaze to those blue eyes and then shifted to Logan before Lazarus handed me over. Careful hands held me. But there was no affection, nothing more than strength as Freddy stumbled forward from out of nowhere, bloody and exhausted. He glanced over his shoulder as the screech of tires came.

Hale...

Hale was here.

Lazarus was gone in an instant, lunging over the high fence.

"Hold on, Kat," Logan urged.

I closed my eyes and tightened my grip as Logan lunged, punching out with one arm while he gripped me with the other, and with a grunt, we landed on the other side. Relief swept through me and tears followed silently as Lazarus stepped close, taking me from the bodyguard.

An engine started and headlights came on instantly as a four-wheel drive shot forward and skidded to a stop in front us. Cramps tore through my belly, making me curl over and whimper. Lazarus slid me along the rear seat and slid in after me. Freddy came from the other side. I closed my eyes as the doors slammed and we peeled away.

"Kat," Lazarus called my name. "Kat, talk to me."

I wanted to.

But what could I say?

"She needs a damn hospital," Lazarus growled as he pulled me against him.

Sharp, searing agony made me cry out. I clutched my belly and tried to hold on, as I screamed until the darkness closed in.

"Hey..." Lazarus whispered, brushing my hair from my face, those blue eyes piercing in the night.

I thought he was a dream, a beautiful, *brutal* dream filled with vengeance and wrath.

But his voice was distant, fading even further as I closed my eyes.

Snatches of memories moved in. Lights flashed in my eyes, blinding for a second before they were gone. Pain slashed across my middle before a sting in my arm. A man murmured in my ear, offering words of encouragement. But I couldn't hold onto those words, I couldn't hear anything but the screams in my head.

Lazarus's screams moved in like a rush, threatening and roaring. He was a man possessed with hunger. A serpent desperate to strike. That's what I'd seen in his eyes when he charged into the apartment, his blue eyes spliced by black. I tried to find those blue eyes now. Desperation drove me to open mine. The *beep...beep...beep...*of a machine dragged me to the surface. And with it came the sight of that *bastard* as he stepped out of the darkness and took aim at Lazarus.

It played in slow motion. All I felt was the terror and my heart breaking.

He'd die trying to save me.

But without him...*I was dead anyway.*

"Hey there."

I blinked and turned my head, finding neon blue in the murky room. His face sharpened as he tried to smile, and winced instead. I tried to think, tried to focus, and looked at my hand in his. A needle stuck out of the back of my hand, clear liquid feeding into my vein. Heavy bedsheets covered my body, but they weren't hospital sheets, and the murky gloom of this room filled with boxes and equipment told me this was no hospital room.

But my body...*there was something about my body...*

"What happened?" I asked, the words a husky whisper.

Agony tore across his face. "It's okay," he whispered, his thumb gently skimming the back of my hand. "You're safe now. You're safe with me."

Safe...

Flashes of memories assaulted me. Darkness and danger. Lazarus's face filled with rage as he drove that knife into my captor. I closed my eyes once more. Blood...and death. And under it all...*Hale waited.*

My body clenched and my heart stuttered. The faint *beep... beep...beep* of the machine grew frantic.

"Hey...hey now," Lazarus grunted.

The bed shifted, dipping hard with his weight. I was in his arms once more, pulled against his hard chest, his hard, warm, *beautiful* chest.

"I'll die if I go back to him." The words tore free like they were somehow part of me...*part of me I wanted out.* I opened my eyes as Lazarus pulled away.

"I *will* die if you send me back to Hale." I insisted as I met his gaze. I wanted that *savage secret* inside me *out*. I wanted it ripped from my body like the sick, gnarled tumor it was.

"*I will die if you go back to him,*" Lazarus answered.

Just like that. Simple. No demands. Just a statement of fact. Hope trembled inside me as he brushed strands of hair from my face. I didn't care where I was, didn't care *who* I was, not when he was here.

And when he leaned down and brushed his lips across mine, tears slipped free.

There was no one else for me.

No one except for Lazarus, who bent to kiss me.

I'd thought I'd die in that filthy apartment, die from those blows to my stomach. My hand splayed onto my belly at the memory as Lazarus's kiss deepened, taking just a little more. My senses were divided between the low ache in my belly and the warmth of his mouth.

Giving...always giving.

And I was an empty well, desperate to be filled by him. *By all of him.* I lifted my hands and slid them around his neck. He broke the kiss and instead, tucked his head against mine, drawing us in until we sheltered in each other's breaths. "I'm so sorry, Kat" he whispered. "Sorry, I couldn't find you sooner. Sorry, you were taken at all."

We came for your boyfriend...but fuck, we'll just take you instead.

Those words swam to the surface as the slick trail of tears slipped free.

I understood now how loyalty worked. The kind of loyalty that protected with their life. The kind of loyalty that loved like no other. *Logan. Freddy.* Brothers, a family built on love.

And now me...

"I love you," I whispered. "Lazarus, I love you."

The earth stood still for me.

Tilted.

Trembling.

Waiting for him.

He pulled away and for a heartbeat, I was too terrified to look into his eyes, too scared at what I might find. What if his loyalty was different somehow, what if it wasn't *this?*

"You love me?" Confusion flared for a second as those black pupils expanded.

I swallowed the fear and nodded. "Yeah, I guess I do."

His smile was hard and fast, stretching wide, taking the focus from the haunted expression in his eyes. He gave a tiny bark of laughter. "That's good...*no, that's a fucking relief,*" he chuckled, and then in an instant, he froze, the laughter dying away. He was all serious now, *deadly serious.* "Because I love you. I love you so much it fucking scares me. I love you so much I'd fucking die without you."

The tears came harder as I smiled, carving a steady line down my cheeks to drip from the edge of my jaw.

He loved me.

Loved...me.

He cupped my cheek, tilting my face toward his, and kissed me hard and brutal. My lips throbbed, my jaw throbbed. Agony carved through me, lingering in my belly and my side. And I didn't care about any of that. I didn't care about the pain or the past. I didn't care about anything other than the future... chasing it a heartbeat at a time, as long as I had him.

There was a low clearing of a throat, drawing my focus away from us. and I realized suddenly that we weren't alone. "Now that we have that cleared up..."

The familiar growl was etched with happiness.

Lazarus pulled away to turn his head.

From the gloomy corner of the room rose Benjamin Rossi. He glanced at Lazarus, then fixed his gaze on mine. Then he smiled, a big smile. "Kat. So good to see you, honey."

I smiled at him as Lazarus took my hand. "Mr. Rossi."

"Benjamin." He laughed and shook his head. "I'm no Mr. Rossi, kid. Just Benj or Benjamin...*or*..." he let the last part trail off as he looked at Lazarus. "You want to tell her, or should I?"

Fear moved through me.

My hand dropped to my belly, fingers splayed, desperate to hold on.

"Hale is...making demands," Lazarus murmured.

I glanced at him as my breaths deepened. Cold moved into the edges of my world.

"He's doing a lot more than that," Benjamin added. "He's tearing the entire fucking Commission apart, working on

Dominic Salvatore, pitting him against us in an effort to find you."

I glanced around the room. The room that should be clinical and white, filled with the best doctors and medical staff. Instead, I was in some kind of bunker, a hidden bunker in a makeshift hospital.

"Don't worry," a voice came from the other side of the room. A guy dressed in combat fatigues strode forward, his kind brown eyes fixed on mine. "I'm Kirkland Greenhouse, specialist with the US Navy and a trained emergency doctor. Not quite what you need, but I'll do in a pinch." He glanced at Benjamin, then Lazarus, and nodded. "Given your...*circumstances*, we couldn't risk taking you to a hospital."

"Where am I?" I whispered.

"A safe house..." he answered. "Don't worry, I just moved you in here for privacy. Through those doors is a fully equipped, sterilized operating room. When you're strong enough, we need to talk about what happened to you."

I swallowed hard, driving down the thunder in my chest and followed his gaze to a set of double doors. It was a makeshift hospital. Hale going after Lazarus's family. It was all because of me...*all because of me...*

"You're not going back there, Kat," Lazarus stated. "Not now... not ever."

"No, you're not," Benjamin added as he took a step toward me, his dark eyes fixed on mine. I shifted under the focus, now knowing where Lazarus got the intensity from. "Not if you don't want to. So, if you don't want to, Kat, then we're going to need to make it so you don't."

Make it so I don't?

Lazarus slipped from the side of the bed, staring down at me as though somehow, I should understand what they were saying.

"Kat," he started, and with a trembling breath, finished. "Will you marry me?"

54

Kat

Two weeks later...

"NOT QUITE WHAT you had in mind, is it?" the familiar murmur came from behind me.

I turned, watching Anna step closer. She was beautiful, dressed in a pale pink dress that reached her knees and holding a small, simple bouquet of bloomed white roses and bohemian pampas grass.

She smiled, but it was a sad smile, one filled with torment and regret. But she didn't need to feel like that, not for me. A low ache spread through my side as I turned toward her. "No, it isn't. It's better."

Confusion flared in her eyes as I dropped my hand and smoothed down my dress. My fingers skimmed silk as they ran down the elegant, simple, floor-length gown. My knuckles were swollen and bruised. Acrylic nails hid the torn, swollen nail beds. Underneath this dress was a bruised and swollen, moody sky filled with purple and blue..

I hurt everywhere, even after the painkillers.

But in that moment, standing here in this small, ancient, private homestead off the coast of Normandy, I'd never felt better. I was no longer that woman who'd desperately gone to that island off Mauritius, searching for a way out of the madness. No longer that woman who'd dragged herself to the kitchen in the middle of the night to end her own life, to protect a dark, dangerous secret.

I was soon to be Kat Rossi, wife to a man who'd risked his life and the lives of his family to save me, daughter to a man who'd stood by his son's side, risking the wrath of the entire Mafia Commission to hide me away.

Soft violin music spilled through the tall, stone doorway that led to an expansive cobbled courtyard outside. Burnt amber hues of the setting sun splashed against the wall, enticing me to step closer and look at the beauty waiting for me. "You ready?" I murmured.

"If you are." Anna stepped close and pulled me into a gentle hug. "I love you. I'll always love you."

"I love you, too." I forced the words around the lump in my throat. "Now don't make me cry, I'll ruin my makeup...again."

We'd spent the last three hours doing and redoing the damn stuff. Each time, the tears would come and they wouldn't stop. I hadn't seen her until this morning, not daring to risk Hale tracking them to find me. But there was no way I was going through this without having her at my side. Anna Shaw was my family.

"Then let's do this," Anna murmured, squeezing me again, then let me go. "Let's get you married."

Married...

The word sent a shiver through me as the violin from outside grew louder. Anna smoothed her dress down once more, straightened her spine, and took a step toward the doorway. I tried to remember to breathe and took one last look at the woman who stared back at me from the large oval mirror, then followed.

I walked through that doorway to the cobblestone courtyard. knowing that, somewhere out there, the wolves were circling.

Hale and my father were relentless, hiring mercenary after mercenary to find us.

We'd spent the last two weeks in hiding, moving from town to town under the cover of darkness while my body healed. But really, we'd been racing headlong toward this moment. And as I stepped down the stairs to the small group waiting for me, I realized I'd spent longer than the last two weeks waiting for this moment.

I'd spent my entire life.

The tempo of the violin changed as a young woman stepped closer and lifted a microphone to her lips. She didn't smile at me, didn't say words of encouragement, just started singing her hauntingly beautiful song, *Lonely*. The small crowd parted in front of me as Logan turned, meeting my gaze, and smiled. He looked wonderful, dressed in a dark gray suit, standing tall and proud next to Freddy, in a black tux, as he grinned from ear to ear.

Anna stepped ahead, glancing at Finley, who hadn't given me a second glance. His gaze was on her, like a lion fixed on his kill. That intensity might've scared the Kat I was before. She might've seen all the makings of a monster in Finley's eyes. But I knew it for what it was now...because I saw the same in the arctic blue eyes of the man who stood straight ahead, waiting for me.

Lazarus Rossi wasn't dressed in a ten-thousand-dollar suit like Hale.

He didn't even wear a jacket. He wore black tuxedo pants and a white, open-collared shirt. His dirty blonde hair, washed and styled in soft waves, was pushed back from his face. But it was his eyes I watched, as they widened and his chest rose with a sudden breath, and stopped.

Fear punched through me as I stepped closer. *Breathe, Lazarus,* I urged inside my head. *Breathe.* But he didn't, just stood there, dumbstruck. A hard jab to his ribs from his father at his side expelled the air in a rush. I took a breath of relief, casting a smile toward Benjamin.

"Okay," the small old man murmured from the front of the group. He was dressed in a simple robe and carried a bible so old that it looked like it had been written by Jesus himself. "We are ready?" he asked, his voice heavy with a French accent.

Lazarus just looked at me, waiting for an answer as I stepped up to his side. "Yes," I answered for the two of us. "I think we are."

"You are fucking stunning," Lazarus murmured, earning another hard jab from his father.

"Language, Laz," Benj muttered, and jerked his gaze toward the priest waiting for us.

But I didn't care. I didn't even hear the sermon when the priest started to speak. Words floated through my mind, but they weren't laden with an accent. They were low and growling, savagely seductive. Lazarus told me all I needed to know in the arctic blaze of his focus.

"I do," I whispered when asked.

"I do," Lazarus repeated.

Never once shifting his gaze from mine.

"Then I pronounce you husband and wife," the priest declared. "You may now—"

Lazarus took a sudden step toward me, not bothering to kiss me, and instead, swept me off my feet and carried me away.

"Umm, *wait*," the old man called behind us.

But there would be no more waiting...we'd waited long enough.

"I think you can pretty well expect they'll kiss." Benjamin Rossi consoled the stuttering priest. "Amongst other things."

We left them all behind.

Family.

Friends who were family.

The world as we knew it.

I wrapped my arms around Lazarus's neck as he carried me around the huge stone farmhouse to the driveway at the front. "Well," I murmured. "I guess we should finish this."

"There's no finishing this, Kat," he growled, striding toward the waiting black Chrysler. "Not now...not ever. I'll spend the rest of my goddamn life making sure you know that."

The chauffeur opened the rear door as we came close. But before Lazarus could lift me inside, he stopped and slowly lowered my feet to the ground. I tried to smother the wince, holding my breath as a flare of agony moved through my belly.

But no matter how hard I tried to keep him from noticing, he did anyway.

Hate moved through his eyes.

The kind of hate that scared me.

Vengeful...and relentless.

But this moment wasn't meant for that. He pushed that part of his nature down, burying it under his love for me. And it was his love that shone through as he gently took my face in his hands and kissed me.

Kissed me like I was everything.

Kissed me like I was the world.

Kissed me like he never wanted to stop kissing me.

I lifted my arms, pulling him hard against me as the kiss deepened.

I'd never met a man like Lazarus, never felt this kind of shift inside me, and as he broke away, he smiled. "Are you sure?"

"Yes," I answered. "Yes, I'm sure."

I turned, ducked my head, and slipped inside. Lazarus climbed in after me, pulling me against his side. "Welcome to the rest of your life, Mrs. Rossi."

I turned as the door closed, then the driver's door opened, and I took his hand in mine. The car started and pulled away and I forgot the rest of the world. The driver took us down to a small sandstone house at the far rear of the compound and pulled up on the pebbled driveway outside the front door.

The deep amber setting sun was darkening to black as we stepped out of the car and headed inside, closing and locking the door behind us. Logan would be outside the house tonight, and in the streets surrounding this small, quiet village, a team of ruthless men loyal to us would be waiting and watching.

We were safe tonight.

Safe from Hale.

Secure in our love.

There was a large dining table waiting for us, set for two. The delicious smell of food wafted out to greet us, making my belly rumble with hunger.

"You should eat first," my husband said, glancing my way and leading me toward the table.

But it wasn't food I wanted...*not yet.*

I lifted my hand as he pulled out my chair.

"Kat," he warned.

I loved it when he said my name like that, etched deep with desperation and frustration in equal measure. When I moved against him, he trembled. I lowered my gaze to that hard chest underneath the thin cotton shirt, the chest that held a heart that belonged to me…just as mine belonged to him. "Make love to me, Lazarus," I whispered, shifting my body to perch on the edge of the expansive wooden dining table.

The two place settings looked ridiculous amidst the large empty space. It was a family table, one designed for tiny cups and cutlery designed for little hands. Just as this house had been made for a family, it was made to be bustling and alive.

"Make love to me and never stop," I urged, pinning my focus on him.

He stilled, searching my gaze, as the front of my dress fell between my legs. I parted them, waiting for that space to be filled by him.

With a savage sound, he surged forward, grasped the back of my neck with a forceful but gentle grip, and kissed me, hard. The table settings were swept aside, plates and glasses crashing to the floor. The zipper at the back of my dress was yanked with trembling fingers before it was torn. I clawed him, tearing at his shirt, as that hunger inside me was unleashed.

We were frenzied and desperate.

We were in love.

His teeth bumped against mine as he kissed me. But his hands…his hands were so fucking gentle as they peeled my dress from my body. He broke the kiss, looking down at the soft lace bustier, and froze.

I didn't follow his gaze. I knew exactly what he saw.

His fingers trembled as he barely brushed the bruise that swept across my breast. I swallowed hard, finding my body in his gaze.

Sadness. Anger. He didn't hold back, sliding the strap down until the top of my breast spilled free. He lowered his head, those soft, warm lips finding every ache.

"Never again," he whispered against my skin.

The warmth of his breath teased my nipple. I closed my eyes and dropped my head back as he took me into his mouth. My hand found the back of his head, my fingers gliding through those soft curls as he peeled the rest of my bustier lower and pushing my dress to my waist.

With gentle force, he pushed me backwards, lay me down on the table, and stared down at me like I was the most delicious thing he'd ever seen.

"Tell me when to stop, Kat," he murmured, sliding under to hook his fingers in the sides of my panties.

If he was waiting for that, then he'd be waiting forever. He dragged my panties low as I lifted my hips, tugged them free, and grasped my hips. My pulse raced as I kicked off my heels and lifted my bare feet to the edge of the table.

One strong yank and I slid against him, opening my legs to capture his body.

"I never want this night to end," he said. "Never want this to end."

He slid his hand between my thighs and gentle fingers brushed along my crease. I was already desperate for him, already trembling with anticipation. It felt like forever since I'd felt him, a lifetime of torture to get to this moment.

And as his fingers sank into me, his thumb finding that aching throb, it was worth it.

All of it.

"Mine," he claimed, and slowly sank to his knees. "All mine."

I reached between my legs as he licked my clit, sucking it into his mouth. My fingers brushed his hair as he moved deeper, sliding his arm under my ass to devour me. I gave myself to him, letting him take me with his tongue until my body trembled and that hunger turned to fire inside me. "Lazarus..."

He lifted his head, his perfect lips glistening with my desire.

There were no words needed. He just reached between us with one hand and unbuckled his belt. His straining cock pushed against his white boxers as he slid the zipper down low. Still dressed in his white shirt, he shoved his pants and underwear down and leaned his cock against my crease.

"Are you sure you're okay?" he asked.

He was scared, I knew that. But I just nodded, splaying my legs wider as he slipped against me. Our gazes connected, fear a beast between us, as he slowly thrust, pushing inside. I moaned with the feeling, clenching my ass as he slowly worked in deeper. "I love you," I moaned. "I love you so much."

He never said the words.

Just let his body tell me what I already knew. Slow careful thrusts turned harder and urgent. He was holding back. I didn't want that, but it was too soon, and we had forever. He pulled me against him, sliding his hands under my back to pull me from the table and hold me against his chest.

I wrapped my legs tighter around him, pressing him deep inside me as he cradled me against his body and walked to where the faint crackle of an open fire waited. His heavy steps turned soft on the plush carpet. He kicked off his shoes, striding to where a thick, white rug lay in front of the fire.

He lowered me, laying me back down. Warmth danced across my skin with the heat of the fire as Lazarus pushed his pants and boxers off, then pulled his shirt over his head, kneeling naked in front of me. I lifted my hips. His cock slid out of me, and I ached with the loss. Careful hands helped me slide my dress the rest of the way down my thighs, then free before I unhooked my bustier and slid it free, leaving me bare.

"Fuck, you're beautiful." He gripped his cock, guiding it against me, and with a slow thrust, he entered me again, growling, "So fucking beautiful."

I arched my back and let out a low moan.

He fucked me until I cried out. Fucked me until my body trembled with exhaustion. Fucked me until the fire began to die. Then he rose, stoked the fire, and left me curled up and sated, then carried back plates of cold food to feed me from his hand.

Roast duck with orange. Decadent chocolate and strawberries. Champagne filled with bubbles. We ate, smiled, and laughed, sucking remnants from each other's fingers, and finally we curled against each other, turning silent and calm, then finally I slept.

This time, there were no dreams waiting for me.

This time, there was just him.

55

Lazarus

Five months later...

I SLID my hand into Kat's as we stepped into the elevator that'd take us all the way to the top floor of the VanHalen Building. She was shaking and terrified as she turned to meet my gaze, seeking comfort. It had taken her three days to work up to this. Three days of careful discussions. Three days of getting her to put her trust in me. Trust that I'd protect her. And I would. I'd make it my life's fucking mission to make sure she was safe every second of every day.

And after today, she'd know that for sure.

We'd spent the last five months since tying the knot traveling, healing...fucking. Most of that time, we'd been on our own, secluded in cabins deep in the forests of Costa Rica and on luxury cruisers in the middle of the Caribbean, where I helped her heal day by day, then held her close night after night when the nightmares came.

And one day, three months ago while we lay in bed, naked and spent, she'd told me the truth of what her life had been like. A truth I'd been preparing myself for. But no one could be prepared for what she'd told me. No one could ever ready themselves for the kind of horror this woman had endured at the hands of her father and men like Haelstrom Hale.

But the past hadn't come in a rush. As though it wanted to inflict as much damage as possible, it had clawed and scratched, tearing out of her in jagged, bleeding fragments. Still, she'd gripped my hand and bore down, tearing that tumor free piece by piece. She'd expelled it from her body, spitting it bloody and writhing into her hands to give to me.

She'd been a baby when her mother died. A car accident she said, but I had my doubts. Men like Sebastian VanHalen were always looking to the future, and when a perfect bundle of feminine joy came to him, I bet the piece of fucking filth was practically foaming with excitement.

I stood there, day after day, and held her hand as she told me about the beginning, about how her father's friends had been careful with her...until Hale decided he wanted her. Then, she told me, he took her relentlessly, even when she fought and kicked and screamed. When she told me he'd drugged her and made her fuck other men, I'd shaken with rage. Memories of Damon Zakharov only trigged the kind of savagery that stuck with me, staining my world with a blood-red hue.

And when she finally told me about the baby, I knew what I needed to do.

My life had purpose then, beyond my love for her.

Purpose darker and different than being the first son of a Rossi. I glanced at her and smiled. The path lay in front of me, paved with blood, stained with brutality. I'd become more than the Stidda Prince everyone was frightened of. I'd become the kind of monster men like VanHalen never expected—one who didn't give a fuck about his money. And who didn't wait for protection. I'd plunge into the bowels of Hell and drag that sick fuck with me, kicking and screaming.

"I love you," she whispered, as though the words were a shield.

I gave her a smile, but it was a careful smile, not one filled with warmth and sunshine.

But honed with a sharpened edge and deep-seated fury.

My love was her shield.

My body hers to take what she needed.

My soul waiting to be used to piece hers together.

Movement shifted at my back. Logan, Freddy, and Neon stared straight ahead. They weren't happy about this. Walking into the lion's den was never a good thing, but this...this was important.

Still, my brothers refused to let me do this alone, and when neither could outthreaten, or outplay each other to stand at my side, they all came, cramming their bodies into the elevator behind us.

"Freddy, did you just touch my ass?" Neon whispered.

From the corner of my eye, Kat smiled and looked away. *Fucking idiots.*

They were all fun and games, until the doors opened. Then they became what I needed them to be. Predatory, formidable, *brutally loyal.* I gripped Kat's hand and stepped out. Movement came from the edges of my vision. Men in thousand-dollar suits and women all dressed the same in knee-length black dresses and stilettos fluttered around the place. Phones rang, voices murmured. The place was a beehive of frenzied activity, but I didn't pay any attention. Instead, I strode forward, scanning the open floor until I caught sight of the bastard's name on an office door.

"Wait," a guy snapped, shoving himself upright from behind his desk as we headed toward that door. "You can't just—"

He reached for the phone on the desk in front of him, until Logan stepped forward. "I don't think so," the former SEAL murmured and stared him down.

All heads turned toward us and eyes widened, glancing from Kat to me. But I didn't give a fuck about their prissy goddamn expressions. One of them even burst into tears. Jesus fucking Christ. I reached the door, turned the handle, and shoved the fucking thing wide.

The scumbag was reclining behind his desk, talking on the phone, when we burst in. But there was no widening of his eyes as he shifted his gaze from me to the men at my back. I faintly heard the thunder of footsteps and the call for *"SECURITY!"*

"Go ahead, call them," I urged. "I've always wanted to see someone fly from this high up."

"Mr. VanHalen!" some asshole called behind us.

I just narrowed my gaze on his. Those beady fucking eyes didn't flinch. He knew...he knew that I knew.

"It's okay, Alex," he said carefully, and shifted his gaze to Kat's. "It's my daughter."

Her hand went slack in mine. Not from relief, from revulsion. *His daughter?* I don't think so.

"Close the door," VanHalen called softly. "And leave."

The foul bastard had the gall to look at Logan, Freddy, and Neon before meeting my gaze.

"They stay," I declared. "I have no secrets from my brothers."

And I didn't. It was the reason why they were here, why none was going to back down when it came to facing this monster. I wanted to kill him here and now, walk into this office, put a gun to his head, and pull the trigger. I wanted to splatter his brains all over the tinted glass walls behind him.

But that wasn't the plan.

Kill one rat and the others scurried. We might find some, we might not.

But if we waited...if we bided our time...

He didn't shift his gaze from mine until the door closed, then he looked at Kat, his gaze moving from her face to her belly, then to her hand in mine. "I see you've come home, Katerina."

I laughed. "Home?" I lifted my hand, showing him the ring. "This is all the home she needs."

Hate flared in the motherfucker's gaze. "That means nothing. She's my daughter."

"See," I let her hand go and splayed out my hands on the edge of his desk before leaning down. "She's not your daughter anymore. I don't even know if she was yours to begin with. You weren't a father, just a disgusting piece of fucking shit that let other men use and abuse her."

There was a twitch at the corner of his mouth. He didn't like others knowing...didn't like it one bit.

"But all that has ended. She's mine now, and if you and any of your fucking pedophile buddies even *think* about coming near her, I'll paint this fucking city red with your blood."

His jaw clenched as he jerked his gaze to mine. "I paid five million dollars to those assholes who kidnapped her."

"Neon," I murmured without looking away. "Pay the man."

Sebastian VanHalen just laughed. "Don't be ridiculous, you don't have that kind of money."

"Five million, you said?" Neon muttered, punching the details into his phone before glancing toward VanHalen. "Account number."

"What?" Sebastian VanHalen muttered.

"Your account number," Neon said slowly, as if to someone too stupid to understand.

He thought he was calling our bluff, rattling off the digits of his personal account, until his cell phone gave a *ding*. Then he snatched it from the desk and stared at the details.

"Paid in full," Neon murmured.

I didn't give a fuck about men like VanHalen. I had nothing to prove. I was nothing more than a street thug to him, and that's exactly how I wanted it to be. He just didn't know that the Rossis owned *all* the streets. And now that a certain 'launderer' was part of our family, we were making our name along both the East and West coasts.

Drugs, gambling, prostitution.

We owned it all.

That made us dangerous...and filthy fucking rich.

"Kat's a Rossi now," I snarled. "She doesn't owe you a damned thing. You come near her...you come near what's mine, and you're going to find me waiting for you late at night, in the dark."

Kat folded her arms. He looked at her, but wouldn't meet her gaze.

He couldn't look away.

I knew *exactly* what he was thinking. The money didn't matter, neither did the threats. Sebastian VanHalen wouldn't stop coming after her. I saw that now. Maybe deep down, I'd always known it. Still, I'd needed to see it for myself. Now I had.

THE ELECTRIC GATES OPENED, allowing Logan to drive through. Freddy and Neon were at Dad's, less than five miles away. We'd purchased the property after some careful negotiations. Basically, the owners were terrified of us moving into their neighborhood and figured it was better to sell to me than to have the value of this eight-bedroom cedarwood and black-tinted glass mansion driven into the gutter.

It was a wise move.

Kat loved the place.

She loved the woods that surrounded us, loved the three massive Dobermans she'd rescued, and loved the fact that Logan lived in the garage set off from the property. And on the nights and days he was away, there was a steady stream of trained mercenaries to take his place. She was safe here, protected and secluded. I made sure of it. I expected her to retreat from me when Logan dropped us off at the front door and drove away.

I expected her to pull away into some of those moments of silence that plagued her, but she didn't. I stepped into the house and closed the door behind us. Then she pounced, grabbing me and pushing me back against the door.

A chuckle slipped out. "Kitten want to play?"

"Kitten wants to be fucked," she growled. "*Lazarus.*"

She knew saying my name like that turned me the fuck on. Stars glittered in her eyes as she smiled. I pushed off the door, picked her up, and carried her in my arms across the foyer and up the stairs. Paws padded on the tile floor as the three Dobermans Kat called her little Hell's Angels followed as we ascended.

I took her to the bedroom and laid her down on the bed. "Take your clothes off, Kat."

She smiled, then in a throaty tease, she commanded, "Take them off me, *Lazarus.*"

I growled, desperate. Urgent. I yanked the gun from the back of my jeans and placed it on the dresser, kicked off my boots, and tore at my clothes. Still, it wasn't fast enough. The shirt was gone, jeans, socks, and boxers followed. She knew I secretly loved undressing her, loved peeling the layers from her body, exposing her inch by delicious inch. I held out my hand and she took it, rising from the bed. "Turn around."

She did, letting me slide the zipper of her dress low until it slipped from her body and hit the floor.

Her bra was next. I slid my hands around, pushing it from her, and cupped her breasts. "I'm going to lick your cunt until you scream," I whispered in her ear, feeling her tremble. "I want your ass in my face and my cock in your mouth."

She let out a moan.

She liked that.

The woman was insatiable, frequently waiting for me when I came through the door, waking me at ungodly hours of the fucking night with her hand down my damn pants. She said she was happiest when I was riding her, when she was full of me. And fuck me if I didn't like the sound of that.

"You like that, baby? You like the idea of swallowing my cum when you orgasm?"

I rubbed her breasts, skimming my calloused fingers over her nipples.

"Yes," she moaned. "Fuck, yes."

I slid my hands lower, sliding over the growing swell of her belly.

The swell we'd almost lost. I tried to push away the memories of that night, but even now, with her hand reaching for the back of my head and her fingers entangled in my hair, they came to me.

Incensed with rage.

Consumed by terror, I'd landed on Kirkland's doorstep with her in my arms. He'd taken one look at her and ushered us inside and down to the basement of his house. She was so fragile in my arms, even now, big and round and getting bigger every day, she's made of fucking crystal.

There was so much blood and, even though Kirkland said it looked worse than it was, he'd still worked for hours, giving her drugs to stop her uterus from contracting and losing the baby.

The baby she'd risked her life to protect.

The baby that was mine.

I pushed down her panties and reached around, sliding my fingers along her crease. She moaned and lifted her foot to the edge of the bed. Hot and wet, she was ready for me, thrusting her hips to the tempo of my fingers.

"Fuck, yes, don't stop," she moaned.

My cock thickened at the command. "I have no fucking intention of stopping, Kat," I growled as she reached behind her and grasped my length. "That's going to be in that pretty fucking mouth of yours in a second. I'm going to come, and you're going to swallow every goddamn drop, aren't you?"

"Mhmm," she whimpered as I sank my fingers deep.

She was already clenching, already bucking against my touch. I slipped my fingers free and stepped around her, lying in the middle of the bed. "Come on, Princess, I want you riding my face."

I held out my hands, steadying her as she climbed on top of me. My gaze moved to her belly as she settled herself and guided my cock to her mouth. She was greedy, taking all of me. Warmth slid across the head, making me curse under my breath. She was slick and ready, her pussy ripe and so fucking beautiful.

I grasped her hips, pulled her backwards, and opened my mouth.

She rode me, sliding her cunt along my tongue in a desperate attempt for friction. I slid my fingers inside as she gripped my balls and shoved her head down, taking all of me.

"Fuck *me*," I groaned against her pussy.

She rubbed harder, faster, sliding her fist up and down as that hunger in me kicked. And against my belly, I felt something else kick. *Mine*, that bestial part of my nature hissed. *Mine...*

I was more than a son of a Rossi...

I was now a husband.

And soon to be a father.

Because, make no mistake, I'd fight for this child.

I'd kill for them, as well.

I was looking forward to it.

56

Kat

Six months later...

THE SUN WAS SETTING when I cracked open the rear door of the Explorer. I glanced at the driver, giving him a small smile before I climbed out and walked around the back of the vehicle, opening the other side. "Ready, Princess?"

Sophie just looked up at me with those big dark, doe eyes. Thick black hair hung in curls around her face. Hair that was so very different from mine, or her daddy's. I winced, hating that flare of panic I felt whenever I looked at her. I didn't know if I'd ever shake that torment as she looked at me with eyes that belonged to the man who fathered her. *Just a sperm donor, that's all,* I tried to remind myself. *He was just a black hole in my past I never wanted to think about.*

But it was hard...Haelstrom Hale's hold hovered over me like a blade hanging by a single thread. One I was just desperate enough to break. If I gave him even an opening, he'd to force his way into my daughter's life, just like he forced his way inside my body. My belly gave a flutter, reminding me of the real reason I was here. Only happiness waited for me...*no, only happiness waited for us.*

I unbuckled the car seat and pulled her out, holding her against my hip with one hand as the familiar sound of my husband's car sounded in the distance. The ten-foot steel gate opened slowly as I dropped my other hand to my pocket. Fingers skimmed the outline of the test in my pocket. Anyone else would wait, standing patiently as he walked through the door of our home. But that was sone thing about us, *were weren't like anyone else.*

Lazarus turned his head my way as the black Explorer pulled into the driveway of the warehouse, followed by a steel gray one driven by Logan. There was a scowl from Laz before he shoved open the passenger's door, even as the car still rolled. I surged forward, meeting his long strides with my own.

"What's wrong?" He tore his gaze from me to Bella, ruffling her curls as he made sure she was okay, then met my stare. "Baby?"

"Everything's fine," I answered, smiling.

The Explorer braked; the engine died. Freddy was out from the driver's side in a second. Logan was just as fast driving the gray vehicle, both glanced my way with concern. They stood there, watching us. I rarely came to the warehouse, pretending I didn't know what went on here. But this was a good enough reason not to care.

"Kat," he called, carefully.

I was panicking him, I knew that. I took a breath, recording every second of this moment in my head. "So, I haven't wanted to stress you out," I started, watching the concern grow in his eyes. "But I've been sick."

"Sick?" he asked quickly. "How sick?"

"Sick enough."

He just stared at me for a long second. "Do you need to go to a doctor, a specialist? Why the fuck didn't you tell me?"

Because I wanted to make sure...

I reached into my pocket and dragged the test free. For a moment he didn't register it, not until I said carefully. "Congratulations, daddy."

His focus was riveted to those two thin, blue lines. "What are you saying?"

"I'm saying that I'm pregnant."

He jerked his head up, the words finally registering. "You're pregnant?"

My smile grew wider. "Yes, Laz, I'm pregnant."

I swear the world shifted in his piercing blue stare. Then he turned his head, finding the two men who'd been by his side when he stormed that house where I'd been held captive. He beamed, punching his fist into the air. *"I'M GOING TO BE A DAD...AGAIN!"*

Logan was the first to start across the parking lot. His long strides growing faster until he reached us and clapped Laz hard on the back. "Congratulations!" Freddy was slower, concern darkened his stare, but he didn't reach for Lazarus, not first. He headed for me, wrapping me in a massive hug, holding me closer. If these were any other men, they'd be eating Laz's fist.

But these weren't just bodyguards...or friends. These men were family, *our family*.

"I'm so happy for you." Freddy deep voice resounded in my head.

Laz punched him playfully. Then it was on, hugs, slaps, shouts of happiness from all three of my big goofs; my heart ached at the sight.

"Right." Laz pulled me close, taking Sophie from my arms. "Do you need me to close up?"

"What?" Freddy cut him a glare. "No we don't fucking need you. Go, piss off...be with your goddamn family."

I just smiled and shook my head. Lazarus let out a deep chuckle and nodded slowly. "Fine, fix up the shipment on your own, then."

Logan roared laughing. It was obviously an inside joke. One I didn't want to be part of. He glanced toward my black Range Rover and motioned to the driver. Gareth climbed out and glanced at the others who suddenly went quiet. He was new, highly skilled, but still not one of us. The idea of that made me still. *One of us*...a Rossi.

"I'll drive them home," Laz instructed, his tone careful.

"As you wish, Mr. Rossi." My driver gave a careful nod, then glanced at the others.

We had a reputation, at least Lazarus did. The Stidda Mafia Prince who was young, hungry and dangerous. Freddy and Logan just stared at him, watching as he turned, strode back to my car and climbed in.

Laz brushed his hand along my cheek, drawing my attention back to him. "You ready?"

I gave a nod, handing over his daughter as she fussed. He was stunning as a dad, grabbing her and throwing her carefully into the air. She smiled at him, letting out a squeal of happiness. The kind reserved only for her dad.

We made our way to the black Explorer, and Laz loaded our daughter into the car seat he had in the back. It still made me smile that it was the sole reason they now took two cars everywhere they went. Four grown ass men, two cars, and a baby seat.

Laz leaned forward, kissed her head, and closed the door before moving to mine, opening it for me. Before I could slide in he stopped me with a hand on my arm, pulling me against him. "Have I told you how much I love you?"

"Not in the last few hours, no."

He smiled. "Then I guess I'll have to make up for it." He lowered his head. "As soon as I get you home."

My pulse sped as he kissed me. I wrapped my arms around his neck, sinking into the smell and the feel of him. That was the one thing I loved about him. He wasn't embarrassed to show me affection, even in front of some of the most ruthless hitmen I'd ever known.

He kissed me hard, taking my mouth and my breath, then broke away, jerking his head toward the open door with a smirk that foreshadowed a night of passion. My pulse thrummed as I climbed in, leaving him to close the door behind me. He walked around the front before climbing in and tossing the pregnancy test into the center console. I grabbed it. "I'll toss it into the bin when we get home."

He cut me a look as he started the engine, then glanced at the test. "Why?"

"Because it's got my pee on it, Laz."

He took it from my hand. "It's got you and our kid on it. So it stays with me."

I tugged on the seatbelt. So he was just going to drive around with a used pregnancy test in his car. That was Lazarus. He drove and I sat back, watching him. He reached for my hand as we made our way through the city and headed for our home, kissing my knuckles and placing my hand against his thigh. By the time we were home I was swept away by the tight smirk on his lips and the promise in his eyes.

He pulled up at our drive, waiting for the gate to roll away, then drove around to the back. Logan's Mustang sat gleaming parked outside the separate building at the rear of our house. The hitman was more than just family. He was our protector, and my comfort on the nights when Lazarus wasn't here. Because make no mistake, I might carry his baby...but this man, he had my heart.

He pulled up, parked, and climbed out before grabbing our daughter; then he reached for my hand. "We need to celebrate." He turned to Sophie. "How about that? A celebration with mom and dad?"

She giggled when he tickled her side. We went inside and he placed her down in her playpen with the monitors hooked up and visible. His belly let out a snarl when he straightened, looking down at her. He grabbed my hand and focused his attention on me.

"Now, how about we celebrate this?" His strong hand went around my neck, pulling me close.

He kissed me, taking my mouth hard, until I reached for him, that hunger burning inside. Hard breaths consumed him when he broke away and stared into my eyes. Then with a surge of strength he grabbed me around the waist and lifted me, carrying me from our daughter's room...and into ours.

"Pregnant," he murmured, laying me down gently. "With my child."

"Yes," I whispered as he dipped low, his hands sliding underneath my sundress. "We're going to make a beautiful child."

"A son," he murmured against my belly, as though willing it to be.

I laughed. "Or another daughter."

He lifted his head, those clear blue eyes glistening. "Another daughter. The Rossi girls...*I cannot fucking wait.*"

I laughed, until his fingers slipped under the elastic of my panties and dragged along my slit, finding my nub. Then laughter turned to a moan. He underdressed me slowly, tugging down my panties, and then dipped low. One shove of my leg aside and his mouth was on me.

I arched my back, my hands falling to the bedding beside me as he sucked my clit. "I can't wait for you to be big and round," he murmured, sliding his finger inside me. "I cannot wait to fuck you and feel my baby kick inside you. You know how horny you get. It's gonna be a full-time job taking care of your needs."

I unleashed a moan as he slipped inside, stroking me. "Oh God, are you up for that?"

"I'll give it my best fucking shot, Mrs. Rossi." He dipped, sliding down the end of the bed, his hand finding the back of my leg as he took my heels off one by one. "I'll give it a damn good shot."

He undressed me, sliding my dress up until I pulled my straps low. One tug at my zipper and I shrugged out of it. He rose, working the buttons of his black shirt, and I was mesmerised by the sight of him. Hard chest, powerful arms. There was something about Lazarus, a power that hummed beneath his skin.

A power that came through his eyes when he looked at me. He shoved his pants low and kicked off his boots before coming to me naked. I unhooked my bra, sliding it off, casting the rest of my clothes aside. My belly was still a little soft from Sophie, and he cupped that swell, kissing it. "Fuck you're beautiful," he murmured. "So goddamn beautiful."

And I was...to him.

I reached to him, pulling him up to kiss me. His hand cupped my breast as he moved between my thighs. "I should've known," he murmured, his hand sliding from my breast to between my legs. He stroked and teased, igniting that fire to burn even hotter. "Should've known by how the goddamn glow in your cheeks, and your damn insatiable need the last damn month."

I rose, reaching down to grasp his cock. Thick and firm. "Maybe it's you that makes me so damn insatiable?"

He smiled, pushing between my legs. I guided him inside me, biting my lip and easing back against the pillow. God, I loved watching him fuck. He looked down; his gaze fixed on the moment he pushed in...before he bit his lip.

"Jesus, Kat." He moaned, sliding all the way inside.

He fucked me this morning, rolling over to kiss the back of my neck. His hands running over my body. I knew what he needed...what he craved. "You did what you wanted, Laz. You put a baby inside me, so fuck me. Fuck me and take care of me and make me yours."

He unleashed a growl, driving his hips forward. "You are mine, Kat. *All fucking mine.*"

Need drove him, the need to protect and care for was stronger than anything else. It made him deadly...and an insatiable lover. He braced his hands on either side of me and lowered his head, taking my breast into his mouth. His body was a cage all around me as he bucked his hips, driving deep.

I was consumed by the feel of him. His cock. His mouth. I slid my hands along his back and inhaled deep, drawing in the scent of him. It wasn't just his body that stoked that climax inside me. It was him, *this.* Our love. I moaned as he licked.

"I love you," I whispered, my climax growing.

"I love you," he repeated, driving the words home with each powerful thrust. "My...fucking...wife."

My pulse raced, breath caught, trapped by the moan in the back of my throat until it tore free. He took his time, drawing me closer to the edge by pulling out, and sliding down, sucking my clit once more.

"Oh, God. Laz." I whimpered.

"Come for me, Kitten," he murmured, sliding his finger inside. "Let yourself go and come."

I did as he said, letting everything go, focusing on the feeling of his tongue and the stroke of his finger, before he rose, slamming home inside me and driving me to the brink.

"Mine," he growled out as I came apart.

I arched my back, clawed his shoulder, and shuddered. My orgasm barrelled into me, tearing from my head. My body pulsed, tightening around him. Laz stared down at me, his brow furrowed in a look of concentration, until he dropped his head and moaned, coming hard.

Warmth spilled as he trembled, then dropped his weight on top of me before rolling to the side. "Jesus, Kat." He moaned, sucking in a hard breath.

A smile crested my mouth right before my own belly unleashed a howl. He cracked one eye open and smiled. "Fuck then food, right?"

I rolled, sliding my hand along his arm. "Always."

He leaned down and kissed me before he rolled from the bed, yanked on a pair of cut-off sweats, and made his way out of the bedroom. I listened to his steps as they stopped outside our daughter's room before making his way to the kitchen.

He cooked for me, leaving me to roll out of bed, wrap my dressing gown around my body, and slowly make my way to the kitchen. The scent of searing salmon with steamed greens and a heated potato bake our chef baked for us permeated the air, making my belly snarl even louder.

We ate on the sofa, feet tucked up, a look of pure happiness.

"I want to be there for the first consultation," he murmured, stabbing a forkful of beans and shoving them into his mouth.

"Why?" I cut him a look. "Want to match the dates up, make sure the baby's yours?"

He just grinned. "Oh, I know the baby's mine, kitten." He leaned closer to whisper. "Because I have men watching you every second of the day, remember?"

My pulse raced with the words. How could I forget?

Possessive. Obsessive...my Stidda Mafia Prince. No one would dare compare.

I loaded the plates into the dishwasher as Laz made his way back into the bedroom. We fed, bathed and played with Sophie. She was a quiet baby, content and happy. By the time I put her down to sleep her eyes were almost closing.

And that tremble of fear came back, slipping through the cracks of my happiness, staining everything in its wake. "You won't know darkness," I whispered. "Not the kind that kills your soul. Not like I have. I'll make sure of it."

I meant every word. I'd keep her biological father out of our lives anyway I could...

He couldn't touch me, not anymore...

57

Kat

I cracked open my eyes to find Lazarus already awake and staring at me. He smiled, his head resting on his crooked arm. He licked his lips and murmured, "Hey."

My lips curled. My eyes barely cracked open. My first instinct was to look at the monitor, to check on Sophie, before I met his stare. "Hey yourself."

"She's fine, I've already been up and checked on her. You want me to cook you breakfast, or are you...you know, sick."

I let out a chuckle. I should've known he'd already been watching over her. "No, I'm not sick, Laz. I'm not sick. But I can't have breakfast either."

"Oh?" He rose up. "Why's that?"

"Monica and the girls want to throw me a pregnancy brunch."

He shoved upwards, concern flaring in his eyes. "Wait, you told Monica?"

I gave a shrug. "She called when I was doing the first test and it just kinda came out."

"First test, huh? Exactly how many tests were there?"

"Enough to make sure." I stilled a yawn. "I didn't want you to get excited over nothing."

"Kitten, there's never anything that's nothing when it comes to you. Do you want me to drive you into the city?"

"No." I shoved upwards, watching him as he climbed out of bed naked. "I know you're busy, besides that's why we have Gareth, right?" He stilled, he's back to me. But he said nothing, like he wasn't sure. "What? Do you not like him?"

"I don't have to like him, Kitten." He turned to me. "I just need him to do his job." He strode back to the bed, pulled me against him and captured the back of my neck in his hand. "But if you want me to, I'll blow off anything I have just to spend the day with you, even if it is in front of your stuck-up, snotty friends."

I stifled a smirk. He didn't like them, which was the complete opposite effect of him on them. They seem to adore him, gushing over how he came to my rescue. They knew a watered-down version of the events that happened at Cosa Nostra Island. If they knew the truth, maybe they wouldn't be so excited to flirt with someone like Lazarus, but then again, these women were always chasing the thrill. "It'll be boring. Stephanie will just gush over you and try and touch your thigh under the table again."

There was a twitch in the corner of his eye, that blue stare hardening. "She does that again, and I might just drive my steak knife through her palm."

I just let out a chuckle, that was Lazarus for you. Totally oblivious and pissed off with any other female attention. I leaned forward and kissed him, then pulled away. "Gareth will be fine. You go and deal with whatever you need to, and I'll call you as soon as I'm finished."

"Then we'll do something fun, maybe take a drive out to the cabin and meet up with Fin and Anna, how about that? Finley Salvatore was supposed to be his enemy. The son of a powerful family on the Commission, Fin was the exact opposite of his father. He just happened to be married to my best friend. He nodded and stepped away as Sophie let out a small cry. In an instant he was in dad mode, his gaze went to the monitor before he glanced my way, giving me a smile. "I'll grab her, you take a shower first."

He yanked on boxers and was out of our bedroom before I could even respond. I watched him as he walked into her bedroom on the monitor. His growly voice soft and playful as he neared her cot and picked her up. An ache thrummed in my chest. This was happiness...him, me, *us*.

I headed for the bathroom and took my time with my shower, knowing by the time I stepped out she would be fed and changed and waiting for me to pick out her outfit. I dried and dressed in jeans and a red cashmere top, drying my hair and scrunching it into curls before heading out, finding them in the kitchen.

Laz ate, biting into his toast as he carried her against his chest. I smiled, took her from him, and kissed his butter flavoured lips. His phone gave a *beep*, drawing his focus.

"Go," I urged. "Freddy will be pissy if he has to wait. I'll call you as soon as I can."

He gave me a smile and kissed me again. "The moment you walk out from those vipers, okay?"

I just nodded and watched him grab the other half of his toast before he headed for the bedroom. Twenty minutes and he was out the door, climbing into the passenger's seat of the Explorer, giving me a wave as they drove off. I danced with our daughter, heading to her room, and dressed her in pink.

The trip into the city was quiet. There was no music, no chatter. Gareth watched the rear-view mirror as we headed into the city. Once we pulled up outside the café, Maddison and Rayne and parked across the street, outside the park's entrance.

It was an exclusive café. Only the elite of the elite dined here, and I hadn't stepped foot inside the place in months. Not since the last time I caught up with Monica and the others. It wasn't a place that liked mothers with babies...until they heard my last name that was. Then they couldn't do enough to accommodate me.

Rossi...

The name was met with either fear or the kind of respect that bordered on a desperate hunger to know all the dark, dangerous things my husband did. The word *Mafia* had that effect on people. I tried to ignore it, pretending to smile, laugh and divert any attention away from Lazarus.

Still, I'd take the scrutiny of my name. I'd take the sneers and the jokes; anything was better than the name I previously carried. A name I wanted to scrub from my memory. VanHalen. The name was of opulence, money, and power to everyone else who didn't know the truth. But to me that name conjured terror and darkness. The kind of depravity that broke you. One that almost broke me. And it would have, if not for Lazarus.

I climbed out when we pulled up, wishing I was anywhere else except here. I shouldn't have let myself be talked into this. It'd been a moment of insanity and excitement that made me share my private moment with Monica when she called about Nieve's birthday party that's three months away. I didn't want to go to that, and I didn't want to go to this. But I was here, trying to be normal.

Still, excitement hovered on the horizon. The weekend with Fin and Anna would be vastly different to this. With them there was no pretense, and no lies and no secrets. They knew the real me, my name, my past and still none of that mattered. With them, I was just Kat.

Gareth hauled the stroller out of the rear of the Range Rover, then turned, giving me his back as he watched the traffic. Leaving me to load my bags of diapers, wipes, feeds, and a thousand other things I hauled around when we went out. Then, I opened the door, smiled at her happy face, and reached for her.

I had her loaded into the pram and strapped in in an instant. Gareth closed the doors, locked the car, and then we were moving crossing the street to the café. The waitress took one look at the pram, before curling her nose. "Sorry we're fully booked." She had the nerve to meet my gaze as she said the words.

"Kat!" The squeal came from the table near the window.

I turned back to the waitress. "That's fine, I can find my own way."

The waitresses' gaze widened, turning to Monica as she rushed over to me, grabbing me in a panicked embrace. "Oh my God, you should see Stewart Hamilton's new Maserati. I'm just *dying* to tell you about it." She gushed, never once looking at Sophie.

She pulled me from the waitress and towards a table where three of my former friends sat watching me. I called them *former* because they really didn't have any effect on my life. They were the people of my past. Ones I was desperate to cut away from, I just needed a reason.

"It's green. Can you imagine that?" Monica droned on.

I push the pram over, removing a chair and placing it against the wall to make room. I smiled at the others, took a seat, and pulled Sophie out of the pram. They looked at her with distaste, brows risen, arms folded across their body, as though having a child was nothing more than some viral disease they wanted no part of.

"It's hideous." Monica slumped into the seat across from me. She glanced at Sophie then, and for a second, I thought she might smile and ask about her. But all she did was scan the restaurant behind me and mutter. "So where is the nanny?"

"There is none," I answered, and gave a sigh, knowing what was about to come. This was the second time she decided to lecture me about my parenting. "I've explained this before."

"I just don't think that you can be a proper parent without at least some hired help. I mean how can you have time for your-self, time to be attentive to your husband. You and Lazarus are still together, right?"

There was hope sparkling in her eyes. Did she think that she had a chance with someone like Laz? If she knew how he really saw her, she'd never mention his name again. Still, she was shameless, leaning forward to touch the back of my hand. "It's okay, you're amongst friends. You can tell us."

I just chuckled and shook my head. "Did you forget the reason we're having brunch at all? Lazarus and I are expecting another baby. I'm pregnant, remember?"

Monica just glanced at Sophie. "Oh, that's right, I totally forgot."

I wanted to get up from the table then, grab my daughter and walk out. This was a waste of my time and a waste of my energy. I sighed, then glanced around finding the waiter hovering near. "Coffee, black, please."

He smiled, trying is best not to look at my daughter sitting on my lap. Christ, this place was pathetic. "Will that be all?"

"Katerina."

I stiffened with the voice, holding the waiter's gaze before slowly turning my head. Monica's cheeks grew red, and she looked away. From between the tables my father strode toward me, adjusting the buttons of his jacket, that chilling, emotionless gaze shifting from me to my daughter. Ice plunged through me as my hold tightened, pulling her against my chest.

"Mr. VanHalen," Monica mumbled, not once lifting her gaze.

She didn't need to, did she? Because she knew...

"What the fuck is this?" My voice was cold, and stony.

"Don't blame Monica," he murmured, stopping in front of me. "I was the one who asked her to contact you."

My heart thundered. Panic roared as I glanced toward the front of the café finding Gareth discreetly at a distance. But I didn't need him at a distance in this moment, I needed him here standing between me and the monster in front of me.

I rose, lifting Sophie back into the pram.

"Katarina," he murmured.

"Don't call me that," I snapped, then jerked to my glare to Monica. "And *you,* I can't believe you did this to me."

But the sick sonofabitch I shared blood with only cared about one thing—himself. "I wanted to see you and my grand-daughter."

A man like him didn't get to ask, not after what he'd done. "She's not your goddamn granddaughter, and *you* don't get to ask me a goddamn thing...unless you want to speak to my husband. I'm sure Laz will be only too happy to have a meeting with you."

I caught the flinch in his eyes, the silence that followed spoke volumes. The last time my husband saw my father he threatened to kill him if he so much as glanced my way. Then in a quiet, careful tone he said. "Halestom wants to see her, Kat. He has a right; he is her father after all."

My knees trembled. The room around me swayed.

I lifted my head, finding Gareth. He glanced at my father, concern flaring when he found the panic in my eyes. He moved in an instant, striding toward me.

"I'm leaving." I snapped.

"Wait." My father lifted his hand. "Let me go. I was the one who ruined this, I only wanted..."

I didn't care what he wanted. I only cared about getting out of here. My breaths raced, still I couldn't seem to catch them. *You're having a panic attack*...I needed Laz. I just needed Laz.

Tears pricked my eyes, blurring the pram as I clasped Sophie in and wrenched the pram around.

"Stop." My father lifted his hand and took a step backwards. "Don't ruin your morning on my account. I'm leaving."

Hard breaths consumed me. Monica looked up at him with needy eyes. Christ, she truly was pathetic. But if she thought my father was a substitute for her own daddy issues, then she was in for one hell of a shock. Unlike her absent father, mine just liked to whore his daughter out to all his sick, vile friends; even though I was a child.

Monica's cheeks blazed red as she waited for him to give her his attention. But he never gave her a second of his time, just glanced at my bodyguard and then strode away.

"Wow, that was kinda rude," Monica muttered as she glanced from my father to me.

I lunged, not giving a shit where I was, or who saw me, and grabbed her around the throat, unleashing the real me. "You pull another goddamn stunt like that and I'm going to show you a side of me you never want to see again."

Her eyes were wide, shining with fear...until they filled with tears.

"Ma'am." The waiter neared, horrified as he looked from Monica to me. "I'm afraid I'm going to have to ask you to leave."

"That's fine." I shoved Monica backwards, releasing my hold. "I was leaving anyway. Lose my fucking number." I glanced at the others. "All of you."

My hands were shaking as I wheeled my pram around to the exit.

"Everything okay?" Gareth glanced toward my friends.

My throat thickened, but I sure as hell wasn't about to cry in front of them. "Yes, just get me the hell out of here."

58

Kat

Tears blurred my steps as I pushed the pram, wielding it like a weapon as I rushed toward the front door. A waitress stepped in my way at the last second, coming out of nowhere. Her eyes widened when she saw me, then she stumbled backwards. The coffee cups rattled in her hands.

"I'm sorry," I offered, desperately trying to get out of the place without breaking down.

Gareth held the door open. He glanced around, watching those who walked past as I drove the pram through the door, then outside. "Home." I swallowed the ache in the back of my throat. "Please take me home."

He just nodded, then crossed the road, leaving me to walk close behind. I didn't want to look for the sleek, Rolls Royce my father used, but I did. My gaze moved to the tinted dark windows and the personalised plate as his car pulled away.

It's okay...it's okay.

I tried to control my racing heart, but my hands were shaking, and my knees were weak. It took everything not to crumble in the middle of the street. I wheeled the pram to the rear of the car and lunged, opening her door.

"Ms. Rossi!" Gareth called.

But I couldn't stop. I couldn't answer. My panic was screaming...*get out...get out...get out NOW!* I picked Sophie up out of the pram, knocking the baby bag over and upending the contents. Baby bottles fell and hit the asphalt, two of them rolling into oncoming traffic.

"Shit!" I screamed. Reflexes took over, and common sense took a back seat. I lunged, bending to grab the bottles as they rolled.

"Leave them!" Gareth barked, striding forward to snatch one from rolling into the path of a car.

Sophie let out a wail, the sound only kicked that panic in my head. I pressed her head against my chest, bouncing as I caught a blur of black in the corner of my eye. Confusion flared as he headed toward us. Tall and broad, wearing a dark hoody. I froze, mid-rock, that deep, terror clawing its way from my past as he pulled his hand from inside the pocket of his sweater and pulled out a gun.

Boom!

I flinched with the sound, unable to move as Gareth stumbled backwards, his hand moving to his jacket.

Boom!

Gareth jerked his gaze to me, hie eyes wide with fear. "Get in the car now!"

He unleashed a roar, driving upwards and charged toward the gunman. My pulse was booming, the sound deafening as I lunged, making for the driver's door and pressed Sophie against my chest. Until I realised...*the keys...the goddamn keys.*

BOOM! I stilled cold.

I stumbled backwards as the gunman rounded the rear of the four-wheel drive and stepped toward me. It's him...*him.* The maniac from the Island. He's back...and he's back for me. Terrified thoughts filled my head as I turned around and ran.

My steps were like thunder, my terror, real. I held Sophie against my chest and scanned the street for anyone who can help me and screamed, "Someone help!"

Cars tore past me. One swerved narrowly missing me as I stumbled into the street. He was a snarl of savagery behind me. His heavy steps and his rapid breath were all I could hear. I darted around a parked car and lunged, driving myself forward. There were people in the park, a female jogger, a man with two small kids. "Please somebody help me!" I cried.

Boom!

The gunshot rang out, making those who watched run for their lives. I wrenched my gaze over my shoulder as he descended, grabbing me around the neck before he yanked me backwards. "I don't think so."

I screamed and fought, holding my daughter with one hand as I went for this face with the other. Instinct collided with savagery. One born in that filthy room on the other side of the world.

Instead of trying to get away—I turned on him, knocking those black sunglasses off as I went for his eyes, until he shoved the gun in my face.

"*I will fucking kill you!*" he roared.

Crack!

He bucked in front of me, stumbled sideways, his eyes narrowing on the man behind me. Gareth stood there, his shirt a mess. Blood streaming down his forehead and in his eye as he glanced my way. "Kat...run."

I did, leaving him there, I stumbled backwards. The gunman let out a savage roar behind me but I was too busy running for my life. I kept Sophie close and hauled myself to the park's entrance, desperation roaring inside me.

Laz...

I shoved my hand into my pocket, fumbling for my phone. My hands shook, and I dropped the goddamn thing as I tore along the path and around the balustrade. Stifling a scream of frustration, stopped and snatched it from the ground and risked a glance behind me before I drove forward once more.

They were fighting in the distance. Gareth was slammed against the side of the car as the attacker wrestled him for the gun until it went off with a muffled *boom!*

I froze at the sight, my gaze fixed on the gunman as Gareth's knees buckled and he dropped to the ground. I didn't wait for what was to come. Instead, I charged forward, sliding across the screen before I found his number.

My breaths were heavy. Sophie's screams were shrill in my ears as Laz answered on the second ring. "Don't tell me, they didn't even care about the baby—"

"Laz!" I screamed his name. *"Laz please help me!"*

"Kat?" His tone went icy. That flicker of disappointment ripped away.

"There's a man with a gun. I think... I think Gareth is dead." My panicked words were nothing more than a roar. "It's him Laz...it's the man from the island."

"Where are you?"

The question made me freeze. I couldn't think, I couldn't figure out where exactly I was until the words came out of me in a rush. "The park across from Maddison and Rayne." I could hear the emptiness of my own voice echo back at me through the speaker of his phone.

His steps resounded, hard, fast, echoing in tandem as he screamed. "She's at the park. *Go! Go!*"

I scanned the trees, tearing away from the path and headed for the darkness. "He's got a gun, Laz...he's got a gun."

"Who the fuck is it?" Laz's words were quiet and controlled as the doors slammed shut and the engine roared to life. "Baby... baby who is it?"

I burst into tears. "I don't know."

"It's okay, are you listening to me? It's all going to be okay." I could hear the howl of tires as they left wherever they were and raced toward me. But they were still too far away. They were *still* too far away.

Loneliness swallowed me as I spun, searching for somewhere to hide. But it was useless. Sophie bucked and screamed, her voice carrying.

"It's okay, baby." I soothed, trying to press my hand over her mouth. "Shh...shh." I tried my best to muffle her screams as I raced out from under the cover of trees and headed toward a coffee van parked near the children's play area, but she was like a siren, drawing every gaze.

"Help me!" I screamed. "Please someone help me!"

"Don't." Laz's command filled my ear. "Now you need to listen to me, Kat." His words were careful, and controlled, pulling me away from the panic. "Can you see him, baby? Can you see the man with the gun?"

My fingers trembled, pressed against Sophie's mouth as I spun and searched the pathway behind me. There was nothing, no one. Just the sun and the trees, and a woman who rose from a bench with earphones in her ear. "No," I panted around the word. "No, I don't think so."

"Good," He murmured, trying his best to control his rage. "That's good. Keep running, baby. Do you her me? Keep running. Put as much distance as you can between you and the gunman. Don't stop. Don't stop for anyone. Just keep moving. We're on or wa—" he broke away. "How long?"

The savage growl of the Explorer's engine was deafening as Freddy barked. "Twenty minutes in this fucking traffic."

Twenty minutes...

Twenty minutes...

I wasn't going to make it.

The words killed me, filled me, but I didn't say the words. I kept running, doing exactly what Laz said as I tried to muffle Sophie's cries.

Crack!

I screamed with the gunshot, ducking my head as my fingers smothered her mouth.

Crack!

"LAZ! LAZ!"

I could hear him call my name through the speaker as the gunman unleashed a roar and grabbed me, throwing me forward and to the ground. The phone slipped from my hand and hit the asphalt as I stumbled. My knees buckled, sending me crashing to the ground. I threw my hand out, but it was useless.

Agony tore through my palm as my elbow buckled and I slammed into the ground. He was on top of me in an instant, wrenching me over until I lay on my back. But it wasn't my clothes or my rings he fought for...*it was my Sophie.*

"Let go!" he barked, those dark, soulless eyes were all I could see. I screamed, lashing out. I clawed his face as I kicked and bucked, screaming until my throat burned.

In the echo of my cell, Laz's rage bellowed. "I'll fucking kill you! I'll find you, and I'll fucking kill you!"

I fought for my baby's life as he grabbed her little arm and wrenched her from my hold.

"No! No!" I howled, kicking and thrashing, beating him off her with all that I had, until he lashed out, striking me with the end of his gun.

Agony was blinding, blurring the world in white. Still, I kept hold of her, my arms like a fortress around her body as I kicked and thrashed, howling and fighting.

Smack! The blow smashed my eye, knocking my head backwards.

"Stupid fucking bitch!" he barked.

Dazed, I felt my hold slipping...

No! No! I clawed for a hold, but it was too late. My daughter's face was bright red as unleashed blood-curdling screams. And in a second, she was gone, ripped from my arms. I shoved forward, scrambling as she stumbled backwards.

"Give her back! Give her back to ME!"

He stepped toward me, punching out his fist wrapped around the gun once more. The blow catching me in the cheek. But I didn't care about the agony. I didn't care about my pain. All I cared about my daughter.

"Laz!" I screamed his name as my attacker lashed out once more, this time the blow caught me on the side of my head

Sparks ignited behind my eyes, I stumbled, my knees buckling, sending me crashing to the ground. Something warm seeped into my eye as I shoved, fell...then shoved again...only this time the world around me spun, turning gray.

In the gloom I saw the face of my attacker as he stared at me, his face a mask of cold, savagery.

Blink...

I willed myself forward, desperation driving through me, even as the gray darkened.

"Stay the fuck down." My attacker's words were warped and strange. *"Stay the fuc—"*

I tried to hold on. Tried to push myself up. But I couldn't even keep my eyes open.

As my world narrowed, to a thin gray slit, I saw my daughter being carried away...in the arms of a stranger.

59

Kat

"Kat?"

I tried to open my eyes. Agony roared, making me whimper. Thunder filled my ears. *Boom...boom. BOOM.*

"Kat!"

Hands gripped me, forcing me to fight the agony. I cracked open my eyes, finding Laz as he ran, charging across some path toward me. For a second, I didn't understand. "Laz?" I whispered.

He descended like fury, skidding to stop beside me, he swiped the mess from my eyes and jerked his gaze around. "Find my goddamn daughter!"

Freddy's roar followed, barking orders. *Find my daughter...find my daughter.* The words meant nothing until fractured slices of my memory slid in, cutting me as they went. *A man...gunshots. Gareth falling...*then it all came rushing back to me and cold plunged through me, wrenching my eyes I open. "My daughter?"

Laz pulled me into his arms. "It's all going to be okay. You hear me? It's all going to be okay."

But I didn't want his comfort, I wanted my daughter. I shoved upwards, stumbling as I looked around. Memories of what happened blurred in my head. She was just here, right here in my arms. I lifted my shaking hands, the warmth of her was still there. Where is she?... Where is my daughter? I stumbled forward, a scream building in the back of my throat. I couldn't stop it, I couldn't do a damn thing other than let that sound out. With a sudden inhale, I unleashed a blood-curdling howl of agony.

Birds flooded from the trees, as terror and pain ripped through me. The few people that gathered witnessed the sound then looked away. But I couldn't stop myself, not anymore.

I stumbled forward, tearing around. She was here, I knew she was here.

"Kat..." Lazarus tried to pull me into his arms.

I shoved him away, still I was desperate to look into his eyes. "Where is she, Laz? *Where is our daughter?*"

Pain moved through his gaze; his brows creased as the thunder of footsteps drew my attention. From the other side of the park Freddy sprinted toward us. "A couple saw a man putting a baby into a car seat. Got a description, and I've got four of our best guys on it. We're gonna get her back to you, okay Kat?"

Freddy glanced at Lazarus, then slowly stepped forward and pulled me into a hug. His deep growl comforting. "I'm get her back, Kat. I want you to hear me, can you do that...can you hear me?"

There was nothing kind or soft about Freddy. Nothing tender. He was a savage and brutal, and right now that's exactly what I needed. I gave a slow nod and lifted my gaze. There were no tears, no weeping. Just unfathomable rage. I looked at my husband, knowing exactly *what...he...was...*

"Get her back to me," I snarled, my face throbbing and stinging. Never in my life had I ever felt this dangerous. "Get her back to me and never let this happen again."

Lazarus's blue eyes darkened to ice. I knew what I was doing. I was unleashing a monster. One who'd bled for me and would do again. But that wasn't what he was good at. Lazarus excelled at violence, he was bred to control and consume, with the right motivations, he'd bring anyone to his knees.

Including Haelstrom Hale.

Panic raced through my veins. My heart kicked in my chest. I stared into Lazarus's eyes knowing he thought the exact same thing. I tried to remember what the gunman looked like. "He was so ruthless, so intent. He didn't even try and go for my rings or my wallet. He wasn't interested in money, was he?"

Lazarus just held my gaze. "No."

The answer was cold and so clear. He knew this was calculated. He knew who this man's target was.

"Is it...*him.*" I couldn't even say his name. My body shook as I shook my head. "It's him, I just know it is."

Lazarus step closer, pulling me from Freddy's hold. "I don't know, but you can guarantee I'll find out."

I let my husband hold me, allowed him to be the strength that I needed. I lowered my head; it was filled with thoughts of all kinds of things. None of them any good. "If he hurts her, I'll kill him myself." My voice was quiet, but there was nothing dull about that need inside me.

In this moment I would've killed anybody just to get her back.

"Laz, Freddy," Logan called, making me lift my head from Laz's shoulder finding my husband's bodyguard striding along the path and heading toward us. "The cops are on their way, and we've got some footage from the camera above the restaurant. It confirms what we were told before, a man put a baby in a car seat, and it's Sophie."

Adrenaline burned through me. I took a step forward. "Are you sure?"

Logan just nodded. "Yeah, I'm sure."

It was her…

"Not the only thing," Logan said, glancing at Lazarus before he found me once more. "The car matches the description of your father's."

Ice plunges through me. *My father?* In my head the image of the tinted black windows rose inside me. "He was there, at the café. He told Monica to invite me there."

"He's the reason you left, isn't he?" Lazarus took a step closer, and I felt that tremor of fear of fear. "Kat."

I could only nod. "Yes, he wanted to see her."

"That sonofabitch," Laz muttered, fixing his gaze on me. "I need you to tell me exactly what he said."

I tried to recount the events that happened. My mind still trembling, unable to comprehend what was happening. By the time I finished, Laz clenched his jaw. "So, when the bastard couldn't talk you into letting him into your goddamn life, he decided to force his way in by taking our daughter."

The sun suddenly grew colder. I shivered, closing my eyes. "Lars, if he has her..."

I'd never seen a man rock backwards by words alone. But Laz did, his face paling. "That's not gonna happen. That's not gonna fucking happen, I'll kill him before he lays one hand on her. Find him, Logan. Whatever you have to do, understand me? Find him, and then finds this motherfucker who beat my goddamn wife."

My face throbbed; my head stung. The scent of my own blood was choking. But that was nothing compared to the desperation that consumed me. I took a step backwards, dropped my gaze, searching the ground. "My phone, someone help me find my phone."

Freddie sprang into action, striding off to search the grass and the asphalt, stopping to pick my cell from the ground instead of the screen. "It's cracked, but it's still working."

I was already stumbling toward him, lifting my hands to take the phone from his hands. My fingers shook as I pushed the buttons, finding a number I didn't think I'd ever call again, but here I was, desperate to hear my father's voice. "He'll answer, if he wants me back, then he'll answer."

"Speaker, Kitten," Laz demanded as the phone on the other end started to ring...and ring...and ring...

Until it went to voicemail. I looked to Laz. He just breathed hard, then muttered, "Try again, he'll answer."

But I wasn't sure anymore, hope was fading as I punched in his number and tried again. Then finally that stone, haunting tone filled my ear. "Katerina."

I didn't have to ask my father the question, I could hear my daughter screaming in the background. My hands shook with the sound, I tried to hold onto my cell as Lazarus stepped close, placing his hand on my shoulder. It was protective and comforting, but more than that, it was possessive.

"I gave you the option," my father said. "I told you I wanted to know my granddaughter... With or without her mother on the scene."

"So you just decide to pay someone to beat me and take her?" I couldn't stop the shrill sound of my rage cutting through.

"You were never meant to get hurt, for that I apologize."

I gripped the cell until that cracked screen broke. "I was never meant to get hurt? What did you think was going to happen when you ripped my child from me?"

But he didn't answer, leaving my daughter's screams to tear through the speaker and slam into me.

60

Kat

"Give her back to me," I demanded. "Give her back to me now."

"Now, Katerina. You're past the point of being able to give me demands. I gave you the opportunity to develop this relationship between us, but I see that is only false hope. I have a new opportunity now; one I fully intend to make right."

Ice plunged through me...

Make right.

Make right.

I closed my eyes as the sun dimmed. I couldn't feel the warmth anymore. "I'll come for her," I forced the words through clenched teeth. "Do you hear me? I'll come for her."

He gave a sigh, rumbling in my ear. "He can try to find her, but by the time you come anywhere close to us I'll have her out of the city, and the country. You'll spend your entire life searching and thinking about her, that I can promise."

My legs gave way with the threat, sending me crashing toward the ground. I would've collided with a cold, packed earth if Lazarus hadn't caught me. His hands were strong, his body warm, but still I shivered. "You can't do this," I whispered.

"Can and will." My father's voice grew husky as he murmured into the speaker of the phone. "I lost one child, so this is my opportunity to get it right, and I *will* get it right this time. That I can promise."

Get it right.

I knew only too well what that looked like.

Card games with his friends where they didn't play for houses or Bentley's...they played for night spent with me. My stomach clenched with the memory. No...*no*. I turned and met Lazarus's savage stare and whispered, "I'll come back."

My husband flinched as I gave my father the opportunity to have exactly what he wanted... Me.

"I'll come back. Do you hear me. I'll trade places."

"No," Lazarus hissed. His hands clenched tight around me. "No, Kat."

But I was already gripped by this way out. Even as that chill moved deeper inside me, I forced myself to straighten, and stepped away from Lazarus's arms. "This is what you want, right? Me..." There was silence on the other end of the line, and I knew this was the game all along. If he couldn't worm his way back into my life, then he'd force his way by holding my daughter ransom. "I'll come back to you. I'll come back."

"Without a fight?"

A tremor tore through me. I could almost hear the strained excitement in his tone. "Without a fight."

Lazarus' lips curled. "Over my dead body!" he screamed and lunged, snatching the phone from my hand. "You hear me? Over my dead fucking body!"

Tears sprang to my eyes as he jerked the phone away and stared at the cracked screen. I knew with one look that there was no one on the other end of the call. He was gone...of course he was. Because he got what he wanted.

I wrapped my arms around myself, feeling the flutter deep in my belly. That life grew inside me, demanding that I weigh up the risk of every step I took. Stress. Violence. Memories of what happened on that island resurfaced. I was back in that terror once more. Only this time it wasn't at the hands of a deranged killer. It was at the hands of my own father.

"No, Kat..." Lazarus strode toward me. "I'll put a bullet through his brain before I let him touch you again."

And he would...I was betting on it.

The faint wail of sirens stopped at the entrance to the park. I stood there, staring at him.

There was a twitch at the corner of Laz's mouth, his rage taking a backseat to the fact that the cops were about to swarm us. He strode forward, nodding at Logan, and set the protector into action before my husband grabbed my arm. "Let's go."

He drove me toward the opposite end of the park, leaving Logan to meet the cops, and Freddy to get our car. The police were involved now. All it needed was one mention of our name along with the mention of a murder and a child kidnapping and it'd be everywhere. We didn't need that...*we couldn't have that.*

Not now.

I moved by Lazarus's force alone as he led me away from the witnesses and out of the gate. The black Explorer pulled up fast. Lazarus had the rear door open in an instant and pushed me inside. My mind was numb as I reached for the baby seat beside me, then stopped. She didn't need securing, didn't need checking. Because she wasn't in there.

Car doors closed with a *thud* before we pulled away from the park and slipped into the traffic. Freddy drove fast, diving his attention between the cars in front of us and the rear-view mirror as he took the first side street he could. I wrapped my arms around myself, holding on as my mind replayed that moment the gunmen came up to me over and over again.

Crack!

I flinched with the sound in my head, staring into nothing. Laz's phone rang but he ignored it, instead focusing on getting me as far away from the police as possible. I clenched my fingers as that flutter in my belly turned into a stab of pain. I let out a moan and rocked forward. *No...no...*

"Kat?" Laz jerked his head around, his eye wide. "What is it? What's wrong?"

I gripped the back of the seat, my nails digging into the leather as the stabbing pain slowly subsided. "I'm okay...I'm okay." My breaths were heavy, my mind strained.

The four-wheel drive swayed as it too the corner hard.

"Doc Nelson," Freddy muttered, glancing Laz's way. "Call him."

"Do you need the doctor, baby?"

I lifted my gaze, finding fear in my husband's eyes. But the sudden pain faded, leaving me breathless. "No." I shook my head. "No, I'm okay."

Freddy glanced over his shoulder, then turned back, concentrating on the road. Panic moved through me. I focused on my breaths and trying hard not to break down as Freddy drove us back across the city and pulled into the entrance of the warehouse, stopping at the towering gate. The sensor flared, sending the gate rolling open.

We were through in a heartbeat, pulling around the rear and braking. Laz was out of the car in a heartbeat, yanking open my door and pulling me out. "What happened?" Concern raged in his eyes.

I shook my head. "I don't know." I pressed my hand against my belly.

That dangerous stare from Laz only grew harder. I knew he was thinking the same thing. If I lose this baby...

We'd never be the same again.

I stepped out of the open door, leaving Laz to shove it closed and take my hand. "I'll get her back, baby. Just don't fall apart on me. Can you do that? Can you hang on?" His gaze moved to my belly as we headed to the warehouse. "Can you just please let me take the burden of this."

The grating sound of steel cut through the air as the roller door lifted, then we were inside. The other men were waiting for us, standing there, guns strapped across their shoulders, armed to the teeth. "I want this fucker found," Freddie barked at them.

"Every cell reception, every correspondence, every second of this bastard's life I want ripped apart." He took a step toward Hercules, who towered over everyone else. "You find the man that took Sophie, and you bring him to me. Do you understand? I want him alive."

A shiver rippled through me at the words. But it was Laz who scared me. Laz who worked the buttons of his black shirt and reached for a T-shirt on the desk at the end of the warehouse. Crates filled the space at the end of warehouse. Ones I'd never seen before.

"Do you think this has something to do with Tobias?" Freddy muttered.

Laz tugged his shirt low.

Freddy took a step toward him. "One minute he's out of our lives, then the next his damn sister is taken by the Order. You know who runs that, don't you? Who *really* runs that?"

"I know," Laz muttered, and glanced my way. "If Hale is involved in this, then you can bet we're going to go to war. But until then...until we find out more, I'm focusing on one thing and one thing alone...getting my goddamn daughter back."

Halestrom Hale...

My father.

Lazarus strapped on his holster, securing it in place before he loaded it with guns.

I needed him like this.

I needed him desperate.

I needed him consumed with rage.

I lowered my hand to my belly.

He'll get her back. He'll get her back to me...and he'll tear the world apart doing it.

61

Kat

Lazarus stepped into his office when his cell phone rang. Commands were barked. I winced at the bite of my husband's tone, but no one else said anything. I waited for news from who was on the other end of the call...but by the dangerous glare on Laz's face, I could tell there was none. Hercules and the others left the warehouse, leaving Freddie to pace the floor with his gun in his hand.

I wrung my hands, unable to do a damn thing as my mind was filled with the worst-case scenario. Her screams still rang inside my head, until they were all I could hear. My father wouldn't hurt her, that I was sure of. He wanted to start over with a brand-new daughter. If my childhood was anything to go by, my father would his spend years grooming her to be exactly what he wanted.

But that was one thing I wouldn't allow. I lifted my gaze as Lazarus hung up the call, then made his way to me. "Hale is currently in England and has been for five days."

My pulse raced at the sound of his name. "So, what does that mean?"

"Nothing," Lazarus answered. "But it tells me that whatever your father has done, it was without that bastard's presence."

Without his presence, but was it also without his permission? Fear and hate coiled inside me when I thought about Halestrom. I couldn't think about him without remembering the nights he toyed with me, seduced me, took me into that room and didn't let me leave until he was done.

There was nothing romantic about his advances, nor was it sweet. It was a business transaction, cold, uncaring and like everything else Halestrom touched, it was for his benefit only. He wanted the daughter of a VanHalen, and he didn't care what he had to buy or manipulate to make it happen. The only thing he didn't count on was Lazarus Rossi.

"If he doesn't know, then maybe it's without his consent. After all," I whispered, but I couldn't say the words. *It is his daughter.*

Laz's jaw clenched, the muscles flaring before he turned away. I didn't need to say the words that resounded in my head. Lazarus already knew. I didn't like this any more than he did, but if there was a way to get my daughter back, then I didn't care who I had to call and talk to. Even if it was the devil himself.

"No." Laz shook his head. "We ask that bastard for nothing, you got that?" Those blue eyes were piercing when he turned to me. "I won't let him have a hold over you, Kat. Never again."

A tremor tore through me at the words, and as much as I hated it, I felt a sense of relief. To owe Halestrom anything was a sword hanging over your neck. In the event after the island, he became cold and distant. I was betting he knew the moment Lazarus and I were married, and he was already trying to work out a way to break us up. And something like this would be exactly how he'd go about it.

"I can't stand here and wait any longer, Laz," I whispered. "The wait is killing me."

I could see he was killing him as well. I lifted the cell, looked at him once more and hit the button, calling my father.

"Katerina," my father answered.

I hit the button to place him on speaker. But there were no shrill, familiar screams in the background. There was only silence. As much as I wanted to ask him where Sophie was, I didn't. If my father felt the slightest bit annoyed, he'd hang up once more, and we could lose her.

His threat still weighed heavy in my chest. One wrong move. One wrong word and my father would make it so that we never see our daughter again.

"Father," I murmured as I closed my eyes and tried to still the panic inside. This was his game now, and we had to play by his rules. Rules I was intimately familiar with. "I'm sorry about before."

There was silence on the other end of the line. But at least this time he didn't hang up. I didn't dare hope for much, only that he would listen. "I've had some time to think about what you asked for, and I realise that I was being inconsiderate to your feelings, and unreasonable." I look to Lazarus as he hangs onto that seething rage in his eyes. "If you're willing to try again, I'd really like us to make amends."

Lazarus glanced away and clenched his fists.

My father's answer was careful. "I'd like that very much."

It was the opening I was hoping for. One I intended to exploit at every opportunity. The deafening silence in the background was all I focused on. "I can come now if you like?"

"Hmmm... I mean, if you're not busy, I'd love to see you." His voice grew louder. "Contrary to what you believe, I actually miss you, Katerina."

That sickening shudder rippled through me.

"Katerina..." he urged. I knew what he wanted. The word stuck in the back of my throat. I swallowed and answered. "I miss you too, daddy."

"Then I'll see you soon," he answered carefully.

There was excitement in his voice, actual, vile, sickening excitement. I couldn't stop my hands from shaking as I lowered the phone and ended the call. Laz said nothing, just stared at me, then turned away.

Logan was there listening to everything. "This is good," he spoke to Laz, trying to calm him.

"The fuck it is," my husband snarled, white knuckles showing from his clenched fists.

"We can use this, Laz. All we need is to find this bastard and a way in and then he won't stand a chance."

Laz gave him his back. I felt the storm brewing, filling the air with the bitter stench of his rage.

Until with a rush Lazarus turned and lunged, grabbing Logan by the shirt and screaming. "Do you realise what I'm doing right now? The only fucking thing I promised to never do… using my goddamn wife as bait."

"I don't care." I stared at the concrete floor. "I don't care. We need to do whatever it takes to get her back."

62

Kat

Beep.

My cell vibrated. I looked down, finding a message.

Unknown Caller ID: *The car will be there within the hour to collect you. Don't bother having that thug you call a husband kill him. One wrong move, Katerina, and your daughter and I will be gone. This depends on you following my instructions carefully. Do you understand?*

Did I understand? I didn't have a choice. I had to follow his exact commands, or risk losing my daughter forever. Lazarus paced the warehouse as I typed out a response:

Me: *Yes, I understand.*

Laz glanced my way, watching as I replied. "The moment you get into that car you're going to be searched. They're going to throw everything at us, trying to get rid of the tail." He stepped closer, capturing my chin. "I'm going to need you to keep your head about this, kitten. Gonna need you to be careful."

"She needs a tracker." Logan turned and strode toward the end of the warehouse, disappearing into the gloom. He was gone for a while, and for a second I thought he'd left before he came striding back toward me, carrying a small plastic case in his hand.

"The office, Kat," he murmured.

I followed as he led the way, placing that small plastic case on the end of the desk.

"Close the door, Laz," he instructed, then pulled something tiny out from the foam insert.

The thud followed before my husband rounded the end of the desk. "This is gonna be too obvious," he muttered, glancing at Logan. "They'll scan her the moment she gets into the car."

"That's what we want." He pulled a tiny tracking device out from the case. "This one they're gonna find. We want them to find it."

He stepped closer, lifting his hand, and never once did he look away. "Open your blouse, Kat."

Laz scowled, but I didn't hesitate. I opened the buttons, leaving him to reach into his pocket and pull out a flick knife. One tiny slice in the lining of my bra and he slipped the tracker in before pressing down and leaving me to fix my strap.

"But it's this one they won't track." He lifted the tiny speck between two big fingers. "These ones I had made especially for this. I just wished I hadn't had a reason to use them."

He rounded the desk and yanked open the drawer, digging under the mess in the top drawer to pull out some wad of plastic. "I'm going to fix this on the inside. That way if they make you remove your underwear they won't even think about your ring."

He was right. They wouldn't. My father would think removing the gold from my fingers tacky, even if he did despise the man I married. I re-buttoned my top before sliding off my wedding ring. Logan grabbed it, his attention fixed on pressing the tracker against the putty and fixing it on the inside of the band.

"As long as you don't take this off, Kat, we'll be able to track you, no matter where they take you."

Laz let out a pent-up breath. "We need to get you ready. We'll have men right behind you, they'll be following you for as long as they can. But you need to be prepared for his driver to do everything he can to throw us off. Can you do that? Can you keep your head?"

"For you, and our daughter? Yeah, I can. Whatever it takes, right?"

He smiled and pulled me into his arms. That's my wife."

I read it myself as much as I could, adjusting my clothes and taking a drink of water, until there was a knock at the door. Logan walked around the desk and opened it.

"The car is at the front gate," one of the men said from outside the door.

I turned, sucked in a hard breath, and walked out of the office.

"Remember, keep your cool. We're gonna be right behind you," Logan urged behind me as I headed to the side door of the warehouse.

Laz opened the door and stopped, turning to me. "I'm going to be right behind you, okay?"

I swallowed and nodded, my pulse racing. "It's going to be okay." I wanted to believe that. "Whatever it takes to get her back."

"Whatever it takes." He leaned down and kissed me.

The sleek, black Audi was waiting at the gate. The driver standing outside the door, staring at Logan's men as they eyeballed him. I broke away from Laz and made my way slowly. My mind was racing, replaying my daughter's screams.

The gate opened as I neared. One glance over my shoulder and I left Laz behind, heading for the driver.

"Ms. VanHalen." He nodded, motioning me to lift my arms as I neared.

"Watch your fucking hands," Laz snapped as the driver neared.

But I had no choice but to comply, lifting my arms as I stopped at the passenger's door. The pat down was fast and useless, finding nothing. I was sure it was just a display of strength, one my father demanded. The driver opened the rear door and I slipped inside. There was a tense second after he closed the door and walked around to slip behind the wheel, when he met Lazarus's stare. I caught the movement of my husband's lips and didn't have to imagine what he'd be saying.

My stomach was hard and heavy when he climbed behind the wheel, started the engine and backed out of the driveway. I tried to slow my breaths and instead focused on where we drove. We headed not to the expensive residential Estates west of the city but to the city itself.

I wrung my fingers, fighting the need to look behind us to find the familiar dark Explorer. Towering buildings loomed in the distance as we headed for the Underground tunnel that would take us into the heart of the city. The driver accelerated hard, watching a rear-view mirror and a few minutes after we plunged into darkness, he hit the emergency lights and indicated pulling over hard.

"What are we doing?" Panic flared as I stared at the driver.

Cars flew passed us in a blur. I caught the hulking dark outline of the familiar four-wheel drive. Headlights blurred as the driver climbed out and then rounded at the front of the car to open my door. "Cell, Ms. VanHalen."

Anger burned with the name. The first time it was annoying, now it just pissed me off. "At least call me by my proper name," I snapped and handed it over.

But the moment I moved he grabbed me. Panic flared as I was spun and pushed against the side of the car. Headlights flared from the other motorists, watching this as they passed as the driver moved a device over my body until a piercing squeal came at the front of my bra.

"Off," he commanded. "Now, or I'll cut it off you."

I clenched my grip, tightening my wedding band against my finger. Then slowly turned. "In the car at least."

I jerked my gaze to him. His lips curled with a cruel snarl. For a second, I didn't think he was going to allow me the decency until with a jerk of his head he motioned me inside.

I climbed in, my hands shaking as I worked the strap of my bra under my sleeves then reached around and hooked it at the back. I tugged the black lace garment free, handing it over as he stood in the open door. His gaze lingered a little too long at my breasts. I clenched my jaw, biting down on all the things I wanted to say.

My father wanted to play games, then I'd play. The driver held my stare as I climbed out, motioning to a car that pulled into the emergency bay in front of us. Of course, there was a diversion. I ground my jaw and stepped out, leaving him behind, but the new driver was even less of a gentleman. Nodding toward the side of the car. "Hands up."

"We just did this," I snapped, but still I lifted my hands.

He pulled a wand out of his pocket, sweeping it over my arms and down my body. I tensed as he neared my breasts.

"Cell, Ms. VanHalen," the smarmy bastard muttered.

A nerve twitched in the corner of my eye as I handed it over. The back of my phone was open in an instant and my SIM card snapped in two before it was tossed to the ground. He reached out, handing me the cracked cell. I took one look at it and snarled. "Keep it." I yanked open the rear door myself and slipped inside.

We took off, pulling out hard into the flow of traffic and exiting the underground tunnel at the first sign. For half an hour we drove through the city, taking turn after turn until even I was lost.

Until finally we found ourselves on the other side and leaving the city center behind. I tried to find a bead on our location as residential houses replaced buildings. I didn't even have to try to search for Laz behind us; after all the driving, he'd be long gone. My only hope was the trackers embedded in my bra and behind my wedding ring.

We pulled into a quiet estate filled with the kinds of houses my father my would own. Expensive, distant, sitting back from the street. I couldn't stop the shudders as we slowed at a black gate. A guard stood inside the fence line, with a leash in his hand and a savage looking German Shepherd at his side.

He watched us, then the street as the car pulled up and the driver wound down his window, punching in the code into the code pad and waiting for the gate to open. A towering concrete structure rose in the distance as we drove forward. Black tinted windows reflected the sun. It didn't look like a house, but a bunker. A fort that looked impenetrable, locking him and my daughter inside forever. My stomach tightened at the thought. I tried to force the image of that back, but it clung to my mind.

Just him and her. I couldn't let that happen.

There were more guards patrolling the grounds closer to the house. The car pulled up outside, but this time I didn't wait for the driver, shoving the door open myself before climbing out. I searched the darkened windows, finding no movement inside.

"Ms. VanHalen," the driver called, motioning me forward.

I hadn't even heard him climb out. I followed, my heels crunching on the stones as I made my way inside. My heels clattered on the concrete Floor, the sound jarring. But I didn't care, all I was listening for was the sound of cries. "Sophie!" I called. "Sophie!"

I raced through the house, searching every room and headed for the hallway. But she was nowhere to be found. I shoved open the bedroom doors and search through each room, until I spun around, facing the drive. "Where the fuck is she?"

"Katerina." The stony tone of my father sound behind me.

I spun, coming face-to-face with him and from somewhere down below, the small cry of my daughter came. I charged forward, pushing him to the side in a desperate attempt to get to her.

63

Kat

I raced for the doorway behind him, shoved it open and stumbled down a set of stairs in the gloom. My ankle buckled, leaving me to fall. I threw out a hand, bracing it against the wall as I lunged forward, not caring about myself. All I cared about was getting to that sound.

"Sophie!" I screamed as I hit the bottom of the stairs and raced along the hallway.

And there she was, in the arms of a woman I've never seen before. Rage tore through me as I raced forward and snatched her out of the woman's arms. "Get the fuck away from my child."

"Katerina..." My father called behind me. "She's been well taken care of; Leslie has made sure she's unharmed."

"Unharmed?" I took a step toward him, pressing her against my chest. "You mean apart from being ripped from my arms and abducted by complete strangers?"

"I didn't want it to be this way." He took a step toward me, lifting his hand to brush her face. I tore her away from his touch, as revulsion rose inside me. "You're fucking lucky I don't kill you right here."

He never flinched with a threat, just stared at me. Then in a careful voice murmured. "I only wanted to have a relationship—"

I reacted by instinct, stepping forward, and lashing out. My palm hit his cheek, and my father's head flung to the side. "You fucking dare do that again, and I will kill you myself." My rage burned inside me.

He just lifted his hand, touching the sting on his face. "It seems like you've been spending far too much time with thugs and murderers, Katerina."

"They may be thugs and murderers to you, but to me they're family and far better than the one I had before. What, do we not want to talk about that, Daddy?"

His eyes glinted like stone. That's all he was, cold, hard, all the way to his core. There wasn't a hint of embarrassment as he answered. "I wanted to give us a chance to talk. This was the only way."

"No," I spat. "You wanted a chance to manipulate me again, and this was the only way you could get to me. You don't seem to realise how much I despise you."

"Despise, that's a strong word, Katerina." He took a step backward, looking around at the end living room that'd been built in the basement. "But we have more than enough time to work through this, together."

I took a step backward, then made for the door, until the guard standing behind my father moved in my way. He closed the door, locking it with a *thud.*

"What the hell is going on?" I looked at my father.

But he just held my gaze. "I told you, Katerina, I wanted a relationship with you and my granddaughter. This was the only way."

"So, what, you're just going to hold us prisoner?" I spat. Panic rose inside me, sending that sickening wave of desperation plunging to my stomach. My focus turned the ring on my finger, and the tracking device stuck against the inside of the band. "You can't do this."

"I can and have." My father smiled at my daughter and in that moment all the years came rushing back to me.

Pain flared in the back of my throat. I turned, and lunged, stepping around the guard until I yanked the door. "Open this now!"

"That's not going to happen," my father said carefully. "Now if you'll calm down, you'll see I'm not doing this to harm you. He's not good for you, Katerina. That thug you live with will only break your heart."

Tears threaten to fill my eyes. "Did you forget the reason why I was at that café this morning?"

"You were there because Monica invited you," he answered.

I spun, fixing on his stupid gaze. "I was there because they wanted to celebrate me being pregnant!"

His brow furrowed as he stared at me, stunned. There was a tiny shake of his head, as though he didn't want to hear those words.

"Oh, did Monica conveniently leave that fact out?" I took a step toward him as a *crack* sounded above. "She honestly didn't tell you, did she?"

"Tell me?"

The crack was followed with a *boom!* I knew the sound of gunshots when I heard it...and I also knew the sound of my husband's wrath. "Yes father, I'm pregnant with Lazarus' baby."

Boom!

The roar came from overhead. I took a step backward, distancing myself between whoever came through that door and the target for their rage. "You have no idea, do you," I answered, glancing at the man who manipulated and controlled and when he didn't get his own way—he forced. "You have no idea of the man I married. But you will...you will now."

Boom! The door in front of me shuddered. I pressed my hand against Sophie, shielding her as best I could as the door flew open, and chaos descended in a flurry of gunshots and roars.

64

Kat

"Get the fuck away from her!" Lazarus charged through the door; the gun raised in his hand. His gaze moved to me, and then to Sophie in my arms and that rage glinted in his ice-blue eyes.

"You," my father snapped, and motioned his guard forward. The mercenary lifted his gun, taking aim at my husband as Freddie and Logan thundered down the stairs two steps behind.

That was all it took. Freddie lifted his gun, taking aim, and pulled the trigger. *Crack.* The guard never had chance. His head snapped backward, and blood sprayed out.

I shielded her eyes, stumbling backwards until someone grabbed me from behind.

"Drop the gun," my father snapped. Cold steel pressed against my side. I stiffened and looked down to the gun pressed at my waist.

Freddie was savage, charging across the basement living room until Lazarus' eyes widened and he roared. "No!"

The gun stabbed, grinding against my ribs. I pulled away, turning to shield my daughter. If he pulled the tigger then I'd fall. I could hurt her...I could crush her.

"Stop." I shoved him away by my elbow, then turned, shoving Sophie toward Logan. "Take her...*take her now!*"

But the moment I lunged, driving her to safety, my father pounced. He grabbed her, yanking her against him so hard her little arm buckled, and she unleashed a blood-curdling scream.

I reacted instantly, not thinking about myself and lashed out, clawing his face. *Crack!* I sucked in a hard breath. The room was frozen in time, until my father roared. I lunged as Sophie fell. But Logan was there, driving forward faster than his big frame should move as my father shoved me toward the ground.

I hit the polished concrete floor and bounced. Agony ripped along my spine, unleashing a piercing cry.

Boom!

The gunshot rang out.

I looked up to see Laz with the muzzle aimed at my father. I sucked in a hard breath, watching the man who manipulated me my entire life stumble backward, and then fall. He hit the floor above me. Lazarus dropped to the ground next to me, pulling me into his arms.

"You're okay, Kat," he growled, holding me close. "You're okay."

I moaned with the pain, clutching my back, but still I tilted my head, finding the blood pooling under my father's head and shuddering.

"Easy," Lazarus murmured, sliding his hands carefully underneath me and lifting. Logan's soothing rumble echoed out as he held my daughter against his broad chest. His big hands still held a gun with one hand and my daughter in the other.

He looked dangerous...and loving all at once, lifting his head to Laz as my husband carried me in his arms. One look at my father's body and Logan muttered, "Let's get the fuck out of here."

Each step was agony. I gripped Laz's arms and cried out with the pain, replaying over and over in my head the second Sophie hurtled toward that shimmering hard ground. She would've fallen on her head. She could've broken her neck or died. The image of that filled me...followed by the pooling blood.

And even as agony carved through my body like a hot knife, I couldn't stop the shudder rippling from my chest. I was glad he was dead. Glad this was finally over.

Laz carried me through that house, and outside in the waiting Explorer, stepping around the dead bodies. The place was carnage. But that's what happens when you touch what belonged to Lazarus Rossi...

Prologue

Months later...

"MRS. ROSSI, have you heard anything I've said to you today?" The solicitor looked across the desk at me, his brow furrowed, his eyes intense. He'd been staring at me over the top of horn-rimmed glasses for the last three hours, repeating sections of my father's will over and over again like he was waiting for me to react.

"Yes, I'm quite sound of mind, George," I muttered, meeting his stare. "And I've heard everything you've told me here today."

"So, there's nothing that we've discussed that you want to talk about, or...contest?"

Contest, that's really what he wanted. He was even prepared for it. His secretary sat by his side. Neither of them had been taking notes the entire meeting and there was not a recording device in sight. "If I were your legal counsel, which I'm not, but if I was,

I'd be encouraging you to contest this, quite forcefully in fact. After all, there is quite a large sum of money at stake here."

Money... That's all that really ever come down to with my father. Money and power, I wasn't in need of either of those things, nor did I want them. "No." I shook my head. "I won't be contesting my father's will. If this is what he wanted, then so be it."

I rose from the seat, desperate to get out of here. Pale green walls made me feel nauseous, even more than I have been this entire pregnancy, which was a lot. I swallowed the urge to retch and looked away from the foul colour that made up one of the most prestigious solicitor's offices in the city.

"Fifty billion dollars is a lot to walk away from." The mutter came from behind me as George Huntley rose. Fifty billion was a nice cut for him if I did decide to contest it.

I lowered my hand to the swell of my belly, feeling that life inside me kick. I could do a lot with fifty billion, start my own women's shelter, hire a specialised group of mercenaries to track down and rescue trafficked women. I could do more with that money in a lifetime than maybe ten people could with the same amount. After all, I had the expertise at my fingers.

But I didn't touch a cent of that money. It wasn't the fact that I couldn't, I didn't want to. I strode out of the solicitor's office and made my way slowly out into the hallway. My gait was awkward, waddling more this time than I had when I was pregnant with Sophie.

The specialist diagnosed a fracture in my spine in the days after the attack. The pain radiated down my vertebrae and into my thighs, making it difficult in the months following the attack to take care of Sophie. But Lazarus had been there every second. He was the one who woke up with her in the middle of the night, and he was the one who took her on walks around the gardens, staying close to the house.

He was also the one who held me when I woke from nightmares screaming. Nightmares that hadn't plagued me before. Not even after my abduction from the island. But they did now. I couldn't stay away from her, sleeping on her floor, watching her every second of the day till Lazarus picked me up and carry me to bed. That was why I couldn't take his money, not one goddamn dollar. What is the payment for the horrible things he'd done to me—to us?

I wanted him to be buried with that money, but I knew that was never going to happen. I pressed the button for the elevator and stepped in when the doors opened, making my way down to the foyer where Lazarus was waiting for me.

He stood with his back against the wall, arms crossed over his chest, watching everybody who came and went until he saw me. He dropped his arms, striding forward until he pulled me against his chest. "You okay?"

Tears slipped down my cheeks as I nodded. "More than okay, perfect in fact."

He swiped a tear away. "You sure, Kitten? Doesn't look like that."

"It is, I mean I am." I forced a smile even as the tears flowed in steady streams to linger at the edge of my jaw before they fell. "He didn't leave me a cent. Not one fucking cent."

Lazarus' lips curled with a flare of anger until he froze. The he got it...he truly got it. "Good," he answered. "Fuck his money, you don't need it."

No, I didn't. Lazarus had more money than I could ever use in my lifetime. And it didn't come with abuse.

I let that happiness sink in, let it grow inside me warm and comforting until I turned my head, catching movement on the corner of my eye, and then stiffened.

Haelstrom Hale strode through the automatic doors in the prestigious solicitor's firm. Two men trailed behind him, one of them wearing a clerical collar, the other one a snarl. Both were wearing the stitched insignia H inside the O for Hale Order. A whimper tore from my throat as Hale turned his head and met my gaze. I hadn't seen him in over a year and here he was the demon of my past...and the father of my child.

Lazarus stared are Hale shifted his gaze, looking from me to my husband and then looked away as though we were no one. But I knew we weren't no one...not to him.

"Let's go." Laz took my hand as they stepped into the elevator.

I knew where my father's money was going now, and I knew the types of things it would be used for. Dark things...debased things. Things that would give me nightmares for the rest of my life. I reached out, grabbed hold of my husband's hand, and prayed.

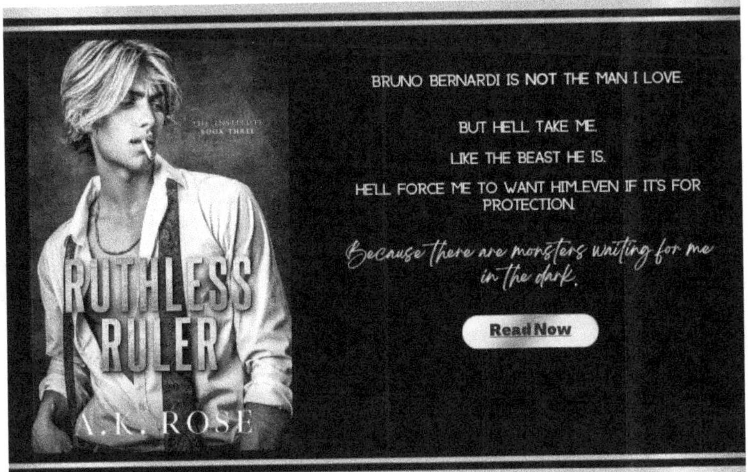

"You hate me. You hate me so fucking much. You don't wear your virginity as a shield...you wield it as a weapon. You use it to drive you harder, to make you more savage." He lowered his gaze to the open collar of my shirt and lifted his other hand, his finger working the top button until it opened, displaying my breasts against the lacy black push-up bra.

"You're not pure, Evan. No matter what that empty ache between your legs says. You're just as fucking sick and as twisted as the rest of us. You just haven't enjoyed the pleasure that comes with this fucking life." He lifted his gaze from my breasts to my eyes. "I'm going to enjoy teaching you that...*as your husband.*"

Keep reading The Institute here

Connect With Me

THANK YOU FOR READING!

Would you be willing to leave a review? I would be very grateful for one positive review. Your support is what allow us indie authors to do what we love. And the feedback would help us with our next book.

CLICK HERE TO REVIEW

Join My Facebook Group For Exclusive Sneak Peeks And Exclusive Giveaways